PRAISE FOR *BETTY*

An *Observer* Book of the Year

'This book will break your heart open, in the best way'
Good Housekeeping

'Despite the beauty of the landscape and the poetry of the language, this is not an easy read. It is worth the journey . . . At one stage, I put the novel aside but *Betty* kept calling me back. I wanted to know what happened. I'm glad I did. Once I had finished the book, I wanted to start again simply so that I could savour some of the language and the Cherokee wisdom. (I also wanted to give Betty a hug and tell her it would be OK.) This is a book that will stay with you'
Irish Independent

'A brilliant, expansive exploration of family and grief. An innovative coming-of-age story filled with magic in language and plot, it is beautiful and devastating. McDaniel continues to be someone to watch'
Daisy Johnson, *Observer*

'Breathtaking'
Vogue

'A brutal and moving story . . . With its troubling subject matter, emotional punch and the backdrop of racism in mid-century America, *Betty* has echoes of Alice Walker's *The Color Purple*'
Irish Times

'There's a good chance you haven't read a family saga like *Betty* . . . Their story is simultaneously extraordinary (they are subjected to unthinkable racism, financial hardships, and untimely deaths) and run-of-the-mill (at the heart, they are a family like any other). Each day in their life is supplanted with the mysticism and interconnectedness of their father's traditions, offering a light at the end of a very dark plot tunnel'
Entertainment Weekly

'The book is rich with the texture of everyday living. It's these details that sing *Betty* to life and bring readers fully into the Appalachian landscape and the social milieu of Breathed'
Los Angeles Times

BETTY

Tiffany McDaniel

WEIDENFELD & NICOLSON

First published in the United States by Alfred A. Knopf,
a division of Penguin Random House LLC, New York

First published in Great Britain in 2020 by Weidenfeld & Nicolson
This paperback edition published in 2021 by Weidenfeld & Nicolson
an imprint of The Orion Publishing Group Ltd
Carmelite House, 50 Victoria Embankment
London EC4Y 0DZ

An Hachette UK Company

5 7 9 10 8 6

A CIP catalogue record for this book is
available from the British Library.

ISBN (Paperback) 978 1 4746 1754 3
ISBN (eBook) 978 1 4746 1755 0

Printed in Great Britain by Clays Ltd, Elcograf S.p.A.

www.weidenfeldandnicolson.co.uk
www.orionbooks.co.uk

MY BROKEN HOME

You give me a wall,
And I'll give you a hole.
You give me a window,
And I'll give you a break.
You give me water,
And I'll give you blood.

—BETTY

Author's Note

This novel takes place in the foothills of the Ohio Appalachians in southern Ohio. Ohio Appalachia is a place where families are raised and individuals step into their own light. Southern Ohio has its own beautiful traditions, culture, history, and rich southern drawl and dialect. I have been honored to call this region my home. I hope, after reading this novel, that you love this part of Ohio as much as I do.

I further hope that you enjoy your time with this story, which is inspired by generations of my family. In particular, it is inspired by the strength of my mother and the women who have come before me. In the face of adversity, they rose to their own power. It has been an honor for me to tell such a story.

BETTY

Prologue

I thank my God upon every remembrance of you.

—PHILIPPIANS 1:3

I'm still a child, only as tall as my father's shotgun. Dad's asking me to bring it with me as I go out to where he is resting on the hood of the car. He lifts the shotgun out of my hands and lays it across his lap. When I sit next to him, I can feel the summer heat coming off his skin like he's just another tin roof on a hot day.

I don't mind that the tomato seeds, left over from his afternoon lunch in the garden, drop off his chin and land on my arm. The tiny seeds cling to my flesh and rise above it like Braille on a page.

"My heart is made of glass," he says as he starts to roll a cigarette. "My heart is made of glass and if I ever lose you, Betty, my heart will break into more hurt than eternity would have time to heal."

I reach into his pouch of tobacco and rub the dry leaves, feeling each as if it were its own animal, alive and moving from fingertip to fingertip.

"What's a glass heart like, Dad?" I ask because I feel like the answer will be greater than I can ever imagine.

"A hollow piece of glass shaped like a heart." His voice seems to soar above the hills around us.

"Is the glass red, Dad?"

"It's as red as the dress you're wearin' right now, Betty."

"But how is a piece of glass inside you?"

"It's hangin' in there from a sweet little string. Within the glass is the bird God caught all the way up in heaven."

"Why'd He put a bird in there?" I ask.

"So a little piece of heaven would always be in our hearts. Safest place for a piece of heaven, I reckon."

"What type of bird, Dad?"

"Well, Little Indian," he says, striking the match against the sand-paper ribbon on his wide-brimmed hat to light his cigarette, "I think she'd be a glitterin' bird and her whole body would shine like little fires of light, the way Dorothy's ruby slippers did in that movie."

"What movie?"

"*The Wizard of Oz*. Remember Toto?" He barks, ending with a long howl.

"The little black dog?"

"That's right." He lays my head against his chest. "Do you hear that? *Thumpity, thump.* Do you know what that sound is? *Thumpity, thump, thump.*"

"It's the beatin' of your heart."

"It's the noise of the little bird flappin' her wings."

"The bird?" I hold my hand over my own chest. "What happens to the bird, Dad?"

"You mean when we die?" He squints at me as if my face has become the sun.

"Yes, when we die, Dad."

"Well, the glass heart opens, like a locket, and the bird flies out to lead us to heaven so we don't get lost. It's very easy to get lost on the way to a place you've never been before."

I keep my ear against his chest, listening to the steady beating.

"Dad?" I ask. "Does everyone have glass hearts?"

"Nope." He takes a drag on his cigarette. "Just me and you, Little Indian. Just me and you."

He tells me to lean back and cover my ears. With the cigarette hanging in the corner of his mouth, he raises the shotgun and fires.

Part One

I Am

1909–1961

I

There shall be weeping and gnashing of teeth.

—MATTHEW 8:12

A girl comes of age against the knife. She must learn to bear its blade. To be cut. To bleed. To scar over and still, somehow, be beautiful and with good enough knees to take the sponge to the kitchen floor every Saturday. You're either lost or you're found. These truths can argue one another for an infinity. And what is infinity but a tangled swear. A cracked circle. A space of fuchsia sky. If we bring it down to earth, infinity is a series of rolling hills. A countryside in Ohio where all the tall-grass snakes know how angels lose their wings.

I remember the fierce love and devotion as much as I remember the violence. When I close my eyes, I see the lime-green clover that grew around our barn in the spring while wild dogs drove away our patience and our tenderness. Times will never be the same, so we give time another beautiful name until it's easier to carry as we go on remembering where it is we've come from. Where I came from was a family of eight children. More than one of us would die in the prizewinning years of youth. Some blamed God for taking too few. Others accused the devil of leaving too many. Between God and devil, our family tree grew with rotten roots, broken branches, and fungus on the leaves.

"It grows bitter and gnarled," Dad would say of the large pin oak in our backyard, "because it doubts the light."

My father was born April 7, 1909, in a Kentucky sorghum field downwind from a slaughterhouse. Because of this, the air smelled of blood and death. I imagine they all looked at him as if he were something born of these two things.

"My boy will need to be dunked in the river," his mother said over his tiny reaching fingers.

My father descended from the Cherokee through both his maternal and paternal lines. When I was a child, I thought to be Cherokee meant to be tethered to the moon, like a sliver of light unraveling from it.

"Tsa-la-gi. A-nv-da-di-s-di."

Following our bloodline back through the generations, we belonged to the Aniwodi clan. Members of this Cherokee clan were responsible for making a special red paint used in sacred ceremonies and at wartime.

"Our clan was the clan of creators," my father would say to me. "Teachers, too. They spoke of life and death, of the sacred fire that lights it all. Our people are keepers of this knowledge. Remember this, Betty. Remember you, too, know how to make red paint and speak of sacred fires."

The Aniwodi clan was also known for its healers and medicine men, those who were said to have "painted" their medicine on the sick or ill. My father, in his own way, would continue this.

"Your daddy's a medicine man," they would tease me in school while flapping feathers in my face. They thought it would make me love my father less, but I only loved him more.

"Tsa-la-gi. A-nv-da-di-s-di."

Throughout my childhood, Dad spoke of our ancestors, making sure we did not forget them.

"Our land used to be this much," he would say, holding his hands out to either side of him as he spoke of the eastern territory that had once belonged to the Cherokee before they were forcibly removed to Oklahoma.

Our Cherokee ancestors who managed to avoid going to this alien land called Oklahoma did so by hiding in the wilderness. But they were told if they wanted to stay, they would have to embrace the way of the white settlers. The higher powers had made it the law of the land that the Cherokee must be "civilized" or be taken from their home. They had little choice but to speak the English of the white man and convert to his religion. They were told Jesus had died for them, too.

Before Christianity, the Cherokee celebrated being a matriarchal and matrilineal society. Women were the head of the household, but Christianity positioned men at the top. In this conversion, Cherokee women were taken from the land they had once owned and worked. They were given aprons and placed inside the kitchen, where they were told they belonged. The Cherokee men, who had always been hunters, were told to now farm the land. The traditional Cherokee way of life was uprooted, along with the gender roles that had allowed women to have a presence equal to that of men.

Between the spinning wheel and the plow, there were Cherokee who fought to preserve their culture, but traditions became diluted. My father did his best to keep the water out of our blood by honoring the wisdom that had been passed down to him, like how to make a spoon from a squash leaf and stem or how to know when it's time to plant corn.

"When the wild gooseberry bush has exploded in leaf," he would say, "because the wild gooseberry is the first to open her eyes from her winter nap and say, 'The earth is warm enough.' Nature speaks to us. We just have to remember how to listen."

My father's soul was from another time. A time when the land was peopled by tribes who heard the earth and respected it. His own respect filled up inside him until he was the greatest man I ever knew. I loved him for this and more, like how he planted violets but never remembered they were purple. I loved him for getting his hair cut like a lopsided hat every Fourth of July and I loved him for holding a light on our coughs when we were sick.

"Can you see the germs?" he'd ask, shining the light beam on the air between us. "They're all playin' violin. Your cough is their song."

Through his stories, I waltzed across the sun without burning my feet.

My father was meant to be a father. And, despite the troubles between him and my mother, he was meant to be a husband, too. My parents met in a cemetery in Joyjug, Ohio, on a day given to the clouds. Dad wasn't wearing a shirt. It was in his hand and fashioned into a sack. Inside it were mushrooms that looked like pieces of a smoker's lung. As he scanned the area for more, he saw her. She was sitting on a quilt. You could tell the quilt had been handmade by a girl still learning. The stitches spaced unevenly. The crookedly cut sheets of fabric in two different shades of cream. In the center of the quilt was a large appliquéd tree made out of scraps of mismatched calico. She was seated on this tree and was eating an apple while facing the headstone of an unknown Civil War soldier.

What a peculiar girl, Dad thought, *to be sitting in a cemetery chomping an apple with all that death beneath her.*

"Excuse me, miss. You seen any of these around?" He held his shirt sack open. She briefly looked in at the mushrooms before glancing up at his face and shaking her head.

"You ever had one of these mushrooms, miss?" he asked. "Fried with butter? Mighty delicious."

She said nothing, so he went on to say she was a girl of many words.

"I bet you're the guardian of a lost language," he said. "That soldier one of your people?" He motioned toward the grave.

"How can he be?" she finally spoke. "No one even knows who he is." She flicked her hand in the direction of the headstone. "THE UNKNOWN SOLDIER. You can read, can't you?" She asked harsher than she meant to.

For a moment, he thought he might leave her be, but part of him existed there better with her so he sat on the grass outside the edge of the quilt. Leaning back, he looked up at the sky and remarked how it looked like rain. He then picked up one of the mushrooms and twirled it between his long fingers.

"They're ugly things, ain't they?" She frowned.

"They're beautiful," Dad said, insulted on the mushroom's behalf. "They call 'em the trumpet of death. It's why they grow so well in graveyards."

He held the small end of the mushroom to his mouth and made the noise of a trumpet.

"Toot-toot-ta-doo." He smiled. "They're more than beautiful. They're a good dose of nature's medicine. Good for all sorts of ailments. Maybe one day I'll fry ya some. Maybe I'll even grow ya an acre all your own."

"I don't want no mushrooms." She made a face. "I'd like lemons, though. A whole grove of 'em."

"You like lemons, do ya?" he asked.

She nodded.

"I like how yellow they are," she said. "How can you not be happy with all that yellow?"

She met his eyes but quickly looked away. For her sake, he turned to the mushroom in his hand. As he studied it, rubbing his fingers over its crinkled flesh, she slowly moved her eyes back to him. He was a tall, sharp-boned man who reminded her of the walking-stick insects that would climb the pane of her bedroom window every summer. His muddy pants were too big for him and were held up by a scuffed leather belt cinched around his thin waist.

He had no chest hair, which surprised her. She was used to seeing the curly coarse hairs on her father's barrel chest and the way they felt like tiny wires in her hands when she grabbed hold of them. She forced the image of her father out of her mind and continued to consider the man in front of her. His thick, black hair was cut short on the sides but left long on the top, where it flopped up as high as her hand, then down in waves.

Pappy would not approve, she said to herself.

She knew the man must have come from a household run by women. It was the way he had sat outside the quilt, rather than sitting on it. She could see both his mother and his grandmother. He held them there in his brown eyes. She trusted this about him. That he should hold women so close.

Something she could not ignore was his skin color.

Not negro dark, she thought in those 1930s, *but not white either, and that is just as dangerous.*

She lowered her stare to his bare feet. They were the feet of a man who traveled the woods and washed in the river.

"He's probably in love with a tree," she said under her breath.

When she raised her eyes, she found him staring at her. She turned back to her apple, which had only a few bites left.

"Excuse the dirt, miss," he said, dusting it from his pants. "But when you're the gravedigger, you can't help but get a little dirty. It ain't bad workin' here. Though it's bad for the folks I'm diggin' the holes for."

He saw her begin to smile from behind her apple, but she caught herself. He wondered what she thought of him. He was twenty-nine. She was eighteen. Her shoulder-length hair hung bagged in a white crocheted snood. The color and texture of her hair reminded him of pale wisps of corn silk in the light of the sun. Her skin was peachy against her mint-green dress while her small waist was girded tightly by a dingy white belt, matching her soiled crocheted wrist gloves. She was a girl of little means up close, but from afar she could look like she was more.

That's what the gloves are for, he thought. *To pretend she's a lady and not another muted beauty expected to rust her way out of creation like some broken-down tractor in a field.*

The apple was nearly at its core, but a patch of red skin was still visible around its stem. When she took a bite, the juice escaped out of the corners of her mouth. As he watched the wind blow the loose strays of hair above her small ears, he felt a gentle rain falling on his bare shoulders. He was surprised he could still feel something so soft and light. Hardness had not yet gotten the better of him. He looked up at the darkening sky.

"You don't get clouds like that unless they aim to prove they got a storm in 'em," he said. "We can either sit here and become part of the flood or seek to save ourselves best we can."

She stood and dropped what was left of the apple to the ground.

He noticed her feet. She was barefoot. If she and he were the same in anything, it was the way they walked the earth. He was about to say something he thought would interest her, but the rain fell harder. It beat on the two of them while the sky brightened with lightning. The storm was laying claim to my parents in ways not even they could have understood.

"We'll get some cover under that shagbark hickory," Dad said.

Keeping a grip on his shirt of mushrooms, Dad grabbed the quilt up off the ground to hold over her head. She allowed him to lead her to the tree.

"It won't last long," he said as they found relief beneath the dense canopy of the hickory's branches.

He shook the raindrops off the quilt before touching the shaggy bark of the tree.

"The Cherokee would boil this," he told her. "Sometimes for ailments, but sometimes for food. It's sweet, this bark. If you bubble it in milk, you've got a drink that'll—"

Before he could finish, she laid her lips upon his in the softest kiss he had ever known. She reached up under her dress to pull down her fraying panties. He stared at her and wondered, but he was a man, after all, so he set the mushrooms off to the side. When he spread the quilt on the ground, he did so slowly in case she wanted to change her mind.

Once she lay on the quilt, he lay down, too. In the fields around them, the ears of corn shot up like rocket ships while they smelled of each other and did not fall in love. But you don't need love for something to grow. In a few months' time, she could no longer hide what was developing inside her. Her father—the man I would come to call Grandpappy Lark—noticed her growing belly and struck her several times in the face until her nose bled and she saw small stars in front of her eyes. She cried out for her mother, who stood by but did nothing more than watch.

"You're a whore," her father told her as he removed his heavy leather belt from his pants. "What grows in your belly is sin. I should let the devil eat you alive. This is for your own good. Remember that."

He hit her across her midsection with the belt's metal buckle. She dropped to the floor, doing her best to cradle her stomach.

"Don't die, don't die, don't die," she whispered to the child inside her as her father beat her until he was satisfied.

"God's work has been done here," he said, slipping his belt back into the loops of his pants. "Now, what's for dinner?"

Later that night, she laid her hand upon her belly and felt certain that life continued. The next morning, she walked to find her mushroom man. It was the summer of 1938 and every expecting woman was expected to have a husband.

When she got to the cemetery, she scanned the open expanse before finding a man digging a grave with his back to her.

There he is, she thought to herself as she walked in between the rows of stones.

"Excuse me, sir?"

The man turned and was not him.

"I'm sorry." She looked away. "I thought you were someone I'm lookin' for. He also works here diggin' graves."

"What's his name?" the man asked, not stopping his work.

"I don't know, but I can tell you he's tall and thin. Black hair, dark brown eyes—"

"Dark skin, too?" He stabbed the shovel into the dirt. "I know who you're talkin' 'bout. Last I heard he got hired at the clothespin factory out on the edge of town."

She walked to the clothespin factory, where she stood outside the gates. At noon, when the horn blew, the men emerged from the building with their lunches. She strained to find him in the crowd of blue shirts and even darker blue pants. For a moment, she thought he was not there. Then she saw him. Unlike the other men, he had no lunch tin. He rolled and lit a cigarette, feeding on its smoke as his eyes moved across the treetops.

What is he looking at? she wondered as she, too, looked at the leaves blowing in the wind.

When she lowered her eyes, he was staring at her.

Is that the girl? he asked himself. He couldn't be sure. It had been some time since. Besides that, there were now bruises disguising her features. Her swollen eyes certainly didn't help. Then he saw the way her hair blew like corn silk over her ears and he knew she was the girl from the rain. The girl who had quickly put her panties on after.

He noticed how she rested her hand ever so gently on her stomach, which was not as flat as he had remembered. He exhaled enough smoke to hide his face as he walked back into the factory. The smell of wood, the grating sound of the saw, the fine dust filling the air like constellations of stars all did nothing but take him back to that moment in the cemetery. He thought of the rain and how it had dropped in between the tree branches and splashed against her pupils, the water puddling at the sides of her eyes to run down her cheeks.

When the factory's final horn blew hours later, he walked outside ahead of the other men. He found she had not left. She was sitting on the ground outside the factory's iron gates. She looked weary, as if she'd just marched a million funerals, the sole pallbearer at every one. She stood as he approached her.

"I have to speak with you." Her voice shook as she dusted dirt off the back of her skirt.

"Mine?" He motioned toward her stomach before starting to roll a fresh cigarette.

"Yes." She made sure to answer quickly.

He chased a bird across the sky with his eyes, then turned back to her and said, "It ain't the worst I've done in my life. You got a match by any chance?"

"I don't smoke."

He finished rolling the cigarette only to slide it behind his ear.

"I got work until five every day," he said. "But I get an hour for lunch. We'll go over to the courthouse. It's the best I can do. That okay?"

"Yes." She dug her bare toe into the ground between them.

He began to silently count her bruises.

"Who gave 'em to ya?" he asked.

"My pappy."

"How long the devil been livin' in your daddy's heart?"

"All my life," she said.

"Well, a man who beats a woman leaves me with little more than anger. The type of anger I can taste in the back of my throat. And boy is it a bad taste." He spit on the ground. "Pardon my action, but I can't keep that sort of thing to myself. My momma always said a man who strikes a woman has a crooked walk and a man with a crooked walk leaves behind a crooked footprint. You know what lives in a crooked footprint? Ain't nothin' but things that set fire to the eyes of God. Now I ain't a man of many talents, but I know how to spend my anger. Seein' how he is your daddy, I won't kill him if you don't want me to. I'll yield to your wishes, sure enough. But you're soon to be my wife and I wouldn't be worth a damn as a husband if I didn't raise my hand to the man who raised his to you."

"What would you do to him if you didn't kill him?" she asked, her swollen eyes brightening.

"You know your soul is right here?" He gently touched the bridge of her nose. It felt more intimate than anything they'd done before.

"That really where my soul is?" she asked. "In my nose?"

"Mmm-hmm. It's where everyone's soul is. When God told us to inhale our soul through our nostrils, it stayed right where it first entered."

"So what would you do?" she asked again, more impatient than before.

"I'd cut his soul out," he said. "That's worse than death in my opinion. Without a soul, who are you?"

She smiled. "What's your name, sir?"

"My name?" He dropped his hand from her face. "Landon Carpenter."

"I'm Alka Lark."

"Pleased to know you, Alka."

"Pleased to know you, Landon."

They each said the other's name once more beneath their breath as they walked to his old truck.

"I ain't used to takin' ladies on drives," he said, moving the dandelion roots off the seat for her to have a place to sit. "That's thyme you smell, by the way."

Tiny rocks embedded in the backs of her thighs when she sat. He closed the door after her. She carefully watched him walk around to get in on the driver's side. When he started the engine, she felt certain there was no going back.

"Whatcha thinkin' about?" he asked, seeing her eyes fill with the moment.

"It's just that . . ." She looked at her belly. "I'm not sure what kind of momma I'll be or what kind of baby I'll be gettin'."

"What kind of baby?" He chuckled. "Well, I'm not a very smart man, but I do know it'll be a boy or a girl. And they'll call me daddy and you momma. That's the kind of baby it'll be."

He pulled the truck out onto the road.

"There are poorer things to be called than momma, I reckon," she said before raising up in her seat in order to see over the herbs drying on the dash and give him directions to what had been her home.

When they arrived at the small white house, Grandpappy Lark was on the porch swing. Mamaw Lark was serving him a glass of milk. Mom walked so quickly past them both, she was nearly running, ignoring their questions of who the man with her was and why he thought he could just walk up on their porch.

Mom could hear the anger in Grandpappy Lark's voice growing as she raced into her bedroom. She started throwing what clothing she could grab on top of the quilt on her bed.

"What am I forgettin'?" She looked around the room.

She walked to the open window, but instead of focusing her eyes outside on her father—who was on his back in the yard, repeatedly being punched in the face by Dad—she looked at the short cotton curtains framing the window. The curtains were yellow and had little white flowers printed on them. She wondered if she needed such prettiness to dress up the place she was going, wherever that might be.

"Yes," she answered herself.

She yanked the curtains until the rod broke. She listened to her father scream outside as she removed the curtains and tossed them to the pile of clothes.

"That should do it," she said, pulling the edges of the quilt together and slinging it like a bag over her shoulder. On her way out of her room, she made sure to grab her pair of cameo earrings from off the dresser.

"I wouldn't forget you," she said to the girl etched into each earring just before she put them on.

Feeling as if the earrings meant there was more than one of *her*, she stepped out into the yard, less afraid. She walked past Mamaw Lark, who was still screaming. By that time, Dad had Grandpappy Lark by the hair and was pressing and twisting his face into the ground. When he let Grandpappy Lark up to breathe, Mom saw that her father had three teeth less than he did when the day had started.

"Only one thing left to do," Dad said to Mom as he got his pocket-knife out.

He put the wiggling Grandpappy Lark in a chokehold, then laid the blade against his nose.

"No." Mom held up her hand.

Dad looked at her, then back down at the knife.

"Sorry, Alka," he said. "But I told ya I was gonna cut his soul out, and that's what I'm gonna do."

Dad didn't hesitate pressing the blade into Grandpappy Lark's skin, causing a stream of blood to emerge alongside the metal. Grandpappy Lark cried out in pain as Dad cut the blade in deeper. More blood gushed and ran down Grandpappy Lark's cheek. Mamaw Lark disappeared up onto the porch, where she hid whimpering behind a post.

"You've done enough," Mom tried to tell Dad.

"Still ain't got the soul out of him just yet," Dad said, slicing the blade against the bone deeper until a flap of Grandpappy Lark's skin peeled up.

Dad removed the knife so he could look into the cut he'd made.

"Hot jumpin' coal," Dad told Grandpappy Lark, "you ain't got no soul. There ain't nothin' of God in ya. You're already hollowed out and damned, old man."

Having no fight left in him, Grandpappy Lark let his cheek rest on the dirt as Dad stood. He took the quilt bag off Mom's shoulder as he told her, "We best leave before you start to feel sorry for the old bastard."

"You don't have to worry about that."

Removing half of a chocolate bar from out of her dress pocket, she walked to her father. He rolled over onto his back and stared up at her. She laid the chocolate bar half on his chest.

Only when she heard the squeak of Dad's truck door opening behind her did she spit on her father and leave.

Mom thought the ride would be silent, but Dad asked her if she minded the smell of gas. At the time, he was renting a small room off the back of a filling station. The room had one window, upon which Mom hung her curtains. They laid the quilt on the bed, uniting hers with his old one beneath.

"I'll try to be a good husband," he told her. "A good man."

"That would be nice," she said, rubbing her stomach. "That would be awfully nice."

When I think of my family now, I think of a big ol' sorghum field, like the one my father was born in. Dry brown dirt, wet green leaves. A mad sweetness there in the hard canes. That's my family. Milk and honey and all that old-time bullshit.

2

A good tree cannot bring forth evil fruit,
neither *can* a corrupt tree bring forth good fruit.

—MATTHEW 7:18

When the first snow of each new winter came, my mother would go into the parlor. It had the furniture our father had built in it, but when I remember her there, I see the space nearly empty. There are only the boards of the wooden floor scratched from when we had dragged furniture across or ran too hard or played with knives. I see the cotton curtains on each of the windows and I see the old wooden rocking chair the color of molasses. My mother sits in this chair after opening all the windows. She's wearing her prettiest housedress. A pale pink one with clusters of tiny cream and bright blue flowers. I'm certain the flowers count out to any odd number. She's barefoot. Her toes curl as she rests her right foot on top of her left.

Depending on which way the wind is blowing, the snow comes in. At first the flurries melt before they land. Then they pile lightly like dust, bringing their cold in. I can see my mother's breath and the way her skin prickles. This is winter to me. My mother sitting in a spring dress in the middle of the parlor while the snow comes in. Dad running in and closing the windows in between wrapping a blanket around her. The snow left to melt into little puddles on the wooden floor of the house on Shady Lane in Breathed, Ohio. This is winter to me. This is marriage.

Houses are built in the beginning by the father and the mother.

Some houses have roofs that never leak. Some are built of brick, stone, or wood. Some have chimneys, porches, a cellar and an attic, all built by the hands of the parents. Hands of flesh, bone, and blood. But other things, too. My father's hands were soil. My mother's were rain. No wonder they could not hold one another without causing enough mud for two. And yet out of that mud, they built us a house that became a home.

The eldest of us was born in 1939 on a day defined by the brownest of tones like a sepia photograph. This blue-eyed son was named Leland. From the moment he was born, they knew how little the child looked like his father and how much he looked like his mother.

"He's got her blonde hair."

"Her paleness."

"Her cupid's bow."

With their new son, Mom and Dad decided to settle in Breathed, Ohio. It was the town Dad had grown up in after his family's move from Kentucky. He thought it would be a nice place to raise his own family. Never far from the river, Dad carried his infant son and briskly dunked him into the water as he would for each of us when we were born.

"So my children can be as strong as the river," he said.

Five years after Leland came Fraya, in 1944. Leland loved his little sister, but his love was like a bag on a vacuum, swelling with filth.

"God gave Leland to us to be our older brother," Fraya once said. "I can't think God was wrong."

When I remember Fraya, I conjure the blur of a thousand swinging lights. Particles that glint and glare before disappearing back to the black and to the buzzing I realize is the sound of bees.

"Sweet as honey," Fraya would say.

As she grew each passing year, Dad would hold up her arms.

"You're my measurement," he told her. "You'll measure how far apart everything grows in the garden and how far apart the fence posts will set."

"Why am I your measurement?" Fraya always asked, even though she knew what he was going to say.

"Because you're important." He would stretch her hands out to either side of her. "You're my centimeter, inch, and foot. The distance between your hands is the distance that measures everything between the sun and the moon. Only a woman can measure such things."

"Why?" Fraya asked to remind herself.

"Because you're powerful."

In 1945, Fraya became an older sister when Yarrow was born. After Dad plunged Yarrow into the river, he caught a crawdad. He lightly scratched the crawdad's claw against Yarrow's palm.

"So you will always have a strong grip," Dad told Yarrow.

From that time on, Yarrow grabbed everything. Marbles. Pebbles. Beads from out of Dad's pocket. Yarrow would grip onto these things so tightly, Dad called him Crawdad Boy. I never got the chance to call him this myself. When he was two years old, the boy who picked everything up lay with his hands open to the sky beneath the buckeye tree in the yard. A nut was lodged in his throat. Perhaps he thought the nut, with its shiny brown exterior, was a piece of hard candy.

After he was covered with dirt sown with yarrow seeds, Mom and Dad packed up Leland and Fraya. They not only left Breathed, they left Ohio and all her skinned houses and bloodshot glory, as Dad would say. They couldn't bear to live in a state whose symbol was the buckeye tree.

Once they left, they moved from place to place. Mom seemed to get pregnant in one state, just to have the child in another. In 1948, she nearly died delivering Waconda on the bank of the Solomon River in Kansas. Dad reckoned the baby weighed fourteen pounds when she was born. The afterbirth came before Waconda. Dad tried to stuff it back in, or at least that's how the story goes.

The baby was named after the Waconda Spring, which once existed with the river and was visited by Indians of the Great Plains who believed the spring had sacred powers. Spirit Water. That's what her name translated to.

Our Spirit Water lived for ten days and cried for each of them. Dad said it was because the shadow of a falcon flying overhead had fallen on Waconda, giving her the falcon's cry. Dad tried to release the cry by rubbing Waconda's throat with an earthworm. Come night, Mom would rock Waconda, hoping to nurse her to sleep. Nothing seemed to help.

The day in question, Waconda was crying in her cradle. Dad was in the kitchen using cotton balls to pat black tea on his poison ivy to dry it up.

"Waconda, please be peaceful," he said. "All this cryin' is gonna give you a watery soul."

Mom was in the bedroom using a cotton ball to apply witch hazel to her face.

"Won't the child ever shut up?" Mom asked her reflection in the mirror.

Nine-year-old Leland and four-year-old Fraya were on the living room floor, making sheep out of more cotton balls.

"Waconda." They both shouted, covering their ears.

Then, it was quiet. In the silence, Waconda was found with a cotton ball stuffed into her mouth.

Three years later, in 1951, another daughter came into the family. She was named Flossie and was born on a staircase in California, the edges of the steps driving into Mom's back as she gripped a baluster with one hand, the other pressed flat against the wall. Not more than a minute after Flossie was born, Dad took a dry bean and rubbed it across her lips so she would be protected against the birds flying overhead and their shadows. He also pressed a pinecone into her forehead to wish her a long life, at least longer than Waconda's or Yarrow's.

Flossie was Mom's easiest delivery.

"The girl came right out."

Flossie always was eager to make her grand entrance.

"Ain't no doubt I was born to be special, too," Flossie later said. "Most babies are born in some silly bed or the back of a stupid car. But me, I was born on a staircase. Like the one Gloria Swanson walked down in *Sunset Boulevard*," Flossie would say as she did her Swanson impression.

Despite it not being true, Flossie would claim she shared a birthday with Carole Lombard. Sometimes it was Lillian Gish, Irene Dunne, or Olivia de Havilland. In Flossie's mind, she was only ever a song and dance away from fame. In my mind, she was the girl born on a staircase who then became a woman torn between taking a step up into the light or a step down into the dark.

"Come with me," she'd say, "if you want, Betty."

Betty. Little ol' me. I was born in 1954 in a dry claw-foot bathtub in Arkansas. When Mom went into labor on the toilet, the closest place she had to lay in was the tub. In the face of Flossie's jealousy, I was named after Bette Davis.

Dad said he had met the actress at a dance when they were both young enough to not have dancing partners yet.

"She made me so nervous," he said, "my belly filled up with butterflies. I could feel 'em flutterin' from one side of me to the other. It was like I had inhaled a wind that never settled. To calm myself, I drank the glass of milk Bette handed me. With her knowledge or without it, the milk was ill with whatever ills milk.

"Most of the butterflies managed to move out of the way, but there was one butterfly that got splashed by the milk. To have a nauseous butterfly in one's stomach is not a good idea." Dad rubbed his belly in remembrance. "To get rid of the butterflies, I left Bette Davis to the moon and took a walk through the woods. Without Ms. Davis, I wasn't nervous no more, so all the butterflies flew out except for the one sickened by the milk. This butterfly had a fever high enough to make me feel I had lit a candle in my stomach.

"I knew I had to do somethin' so I caught a small black spider and swallowed it whole. The spider did what I wanted it to do, which was spin itself a web between my rib bones. The butterfly got caught in that web and my belly was ever so happy. The spider is still inside me. My tummy is its home now. Some days I feel like I got more web than anything else in me, but I'll tell you this, I haven't had a bellyache since because all the bad I eat, the spider catches. I wonder if God shouldn't have given us all spiders in our stomachs."

Instead of having the same spelling as Bette Davis, my name was spelled with a *y* rather than an *e* because Dad said a *y* reminded him of a slingshot and of a snake with its mouth open.

It was the *y* in my name—along with the crown of black waves I came into this world with—that Dad said attracted the rattler into my cradle.

Hiss, hiss, speak, girl, speak.

A snake that slithers into a cradle is up to no good, at least that's what Dad said. The rattlesnake bit him when he removed it from under my blanket. After sucking the venom from his veins, Dad cut the snake's head off. He buried the head in a hole as deep as his arm. He said a prayer over the rest of the body to appease the snake's ghost, before cutting the tail off and making me a baby toy out of it.

Shake, shake, rattle, rattle, speak, speak.

My father's hair was black. His skin was brown like the beautiful mud-bottom rivers he swam in. Shadows lived in the angles of his cheeks. His eyes were the color of the powder he made out of walnut hulls. He gave these features to me. The earth stamped on my soul. On my skin. On my hair. On my eyes. He gave these things to me.

"Because you're Cherokee," Dad said to me when I was four and old enough to ask why folks called me dark.

"They'll call you worse, Betty," he said.

"But what is cherry key?" I asked.

"Cherokee. Repeat after me. Cher-o-kee." He made his lips open funny when he said the *o* so I giggled.

"Cherry key," I said again, repeating it until I got it right. "But what is it?"

"Cherokee is you," he said, putting me on his lap.

From out of his pocket, he pulled a small piece of deerskin.

"It looks like a dog's back." I petted the side that had fur.

"It does, don't it?" he asked before turning the skin over to point out the strange lettering written on the smooth side. The ink was blue and blurring on the edges, as if water was taking the writing away.

"This is what it looks like to write Cherokee, Betty," he said. "My momma was given this skin by her mother. Momma called it her breath because whenever she felt she was out of it, she would look at her mother's deerskin and at her mother's words and get her breath back. Momma would be able to breathe again."

He inhaled until his chest filled. When he let the breath go, he blew the small hairs around my crown.

"I can't read it." I ran my tiny fingers over the fading words. "They're written funny. What do they say?"

"They say don't forget who you are."

"Did your mother forget who she was?" I asked. "Is that why she needed to be reminded?"

"There used to be a time when people like us wouldn't be able to say we were Cherokee," he said. "We would have to say we were Black Dutch."

"What's that?"

"A dark-skinned European."

"Why couldn't we say we were cherry key? I mean Cher-o-kee."

"Because it had to be hidden."

"But, why?"

"Cherokees were bein' moved off their land and onto reservations. If our people said they were Black Dutch, they were allowed to stay because someone of European roots could own land. But you can only lie to yourself for so long before it wears ya down. My daddy and momma had to say they were Black Dutch so often, it made Momma lose her breath. She had to remind herself who she truly was."

I looked up at him.

"Who am I?" I asked.

"You're you, Betty," he said.

"How can I be sure?"

"Because of who you come from. You come from great warriors." He laid his hand against my chest. "You come from great chiefs who led nations to both war and peace."

Then he would say "Tsa-la-gi," while holding my hands and writing the word in the air with his.

I would sometimes dream of these ancestors. Of them taking my hands in theirs and rubbing our palms together until our skin peeled back like tree bark and I could speak like them in the old way. I would wake up, hold my palm to my ear, and try to hear their voices. I waited for these voices to beat me alive.

Two years after I was born, I became an older sister. My little brother Trustin was born in Florida in 1956. When Dad was dunking him in the river, a bass swam by and struck Trustin's backside. Dad said it would make his son a good swimmer. When Trustin got old enough, he would dive into the water. He loved the splash and the way the water spotted the rocks on the bank.

"It's like a paintin'," he said, always finding images in the splash marks. "The kind of paintin' that goes away when it dries. It reminds us nothin' lasts forever."

A year later, in 1957, Mom delivered another son they decided to name Lint. They said he was Mom's midlife crisis baby.

"It's why he has nothin' but rocks in his head and on his mind," Flossie would later say. "Mom's crisis seeped into him."

Trying to understand Lint was like trying to find your way out of dark woods. All we knew was that he became easily upset. If he ate too much or spoke too loudly, he worried we would send him away. He grew increasingly concerned Mom and Dad would not stay together. By the time he was eight, he was standing at the ironing board until his clothes were pressed enough for him to believe there were no wrinkles between Mom and Dad.

After Lint, Mom counted the stretched scars on her belly and said there were to be no more children.

With that, Dad took the placenta from Lint's birth and buried it six feet deep. He covered it with stones to ensure Lint would be the last.

My father used to say that when a child is born, their very first breath is sent on the wind to become a plant or insect, a creature of feathers, fur, or scales. He would say that this human and this life are bound together as a reflection of one another.

"There are folks always reachin' for the sky, too large for our world, like giant sequoias," he said, stretching his arms up over his head as we sat at his feet in wonder. "Some people are as beautiful and soft as peonies, others as hard as a mountain. You'll come across those who are so unforgettable, they'll leave a rash on your memory as poison ivy does your skin."

He playfully scratched our arms until we laughed.

"Like spiders," he said, "there are folks who can't stop spinnin' webs in life, either through the work of their tongues or through the work of their hands." He bent his fingers like spider legs before making a buzzing sound with his tongue against his teeth. "*Bzzzzz.* But too many are as bothersome as pesky attic flies. *Bzzzzz.*" He flew his finger through the air.

"*Bzzzzz.*" We moved our fingers with his.

"You'll need to watch out for those who spread gossip as easily as dandelions spread their seed," he said. "But really keep an eye on the ones who live on decay, like the fungus that grows on hurt or weak trees."

"What are we like, Dad?" I asked.

"Well, us Carpenters are like berries. Rich, juicy berries that grow deep in the woods. Berries that—"

"Give sorrow to all who wander by," Mom's voice overtook Dad's, "curious with taste."

3

Awake, O north wind; and come, thou south;
blow upon my garden.

—SONG OF SOLOMON 4:16

Ozark, Arkansas. A place of deep green wilderness on the edge of mountains. It is where I was born and where we returned to after Lint came into the world. We lived in a small house Dad had partially built on a concrete foundation. The walls were not yet up, so the insulation showed while tarp hung from the unfinished roof. In between building the house, Dad sold moonshine and worked underground like a mole along with the other coal miners.

The only one of us kids not living at home was Leland. He was twenty by then and had already been gone two years after enlisting in the army at eighteen. He was currently stationed in Korea. He would write letters to Mom and Dad. Leland never wrote about anything related to the army or the reasons he was stationed in any particular place. He would write about things that made it seem like he was on a trip.

I did some fishing the other day, he wrote. *I used a Korean fishing pole. It's called a gyeonji. Caught a fish that looked like one of the bass back home.*

In his own letters, Dad would update Leland on where we were.

In Arkansas now, Dad wrote in his sideways cursive. *Lots of blue sage and coneflowers. I don't see much of it. Underground, there is only rock and crust. That's what I get for being a miner.*

The mines were not near to our house, so Dad would take the train and stay in a tent outside to save on expense. Days would go by before we'd hear from him again.

The afternoon he called, I was on my belly on the plywood floor. Scattered around me were crayons Dad had molded out of beeswax and tinted with things like coffee or blackberries. When the phone started to ring, I picked up the red crayon and continued writing.

"Jesus Crimson. Get the goddamn phone, Betty." Mom's voice came from the kitchen.

I grabbed the receiver.

"I was writin'," I said to whoever was on the line before I even said hello. "You've interrupted me."

"Betty?"

"Oh, hi, Dad. I'm writin' a story about a cat. The cat has a tail made of violets. I've made the violets red because you never remember they're purple. It's the tail that eats the mice, not the cat itself. Ain't that somethin'? I've never seen a cat's tail eat mice. It's always the mouth, but I don't see why it can't be the tail that eats the mice as long as the tail has teeth."

When I stopped to take a breath, Dad took the opportunity to ask where Mom was.

"She's in the kitchen with Lint," I said.

"Go get her. I need her to come pick me up from the mines." His voice was unusually tight, like wound-up wire.

"Why ain'tcha ridin' the train back?" I asked.

"It's not runnin' until late tonight. Now go get your momma. They're about to let the mine monster out. You don't want the monster to eat your dear ol' dad, do ya?"

I hollered to Mom that Dad was on the phone. Once I heard her coming, I slipped the red crayon into my pocket and ran outside.

Trustin and Flossie were in the backyard using sticks as guns to shoot one another, while Fraya sat on the grass chewing on a dandelion.

Pretending I would turn to stone if any of them saw me, I snuck out to our Rambler station wagon parked in the yard. I made sure to slap the raccoon tail hanging from the car's antenna like I did every time for luck.

Quietly, I climbed up on the bumper and crawled through the open tailgate window. I hid beneath some blankets and waited. I didn't make a sound as Mom came out of the house, letting the screen door slam after her. She had her tatty frame purse open under her arm and was using her free hands to undo a bobby pin to hold the blondest side of her hair back.

"Fraya?" Mom's voice was a harsh shout.

Fraya quickly got up and ran around to the front. She stopped halfway up the porch steps, her bare feet overlapping.

"Yes, Mom?" Fraya asked.

"Watch Lint." Mom pulled her purse out from under her arm and snapped it shut. "He's in the kitchen. If he starts cryin', show 'im a rock. I have to go pick up your father. Jesus Crimson. If it's not one thing with him, it's another."

Fraya walked sideways up the steps, giving Mom room to pass.

"Now, I don't wanna come back and hear Lint callin' you Momma again," Mom told Fraya. "Understand me, girl?"

"He does it on his own." Fraya looked down. "I don't teach 'im to say it or nothin'."

"Don't you act all innocent with me. I know what you been doin'. The way you cradle 'im and call 'im baby. You best straighten up and start actin' like a damn sister. Y'hear me, girl? You're fifteen now and I still gotta keep after you like you was four."

Fraya kept her eyes down as she nodded and walked up the rest of the stairs.

"I might as well count this day ruined," Mom said as she got into the car.

She tossed her purse to the dash and rubbed her hands before putting the key into the ignition. After three tries, the engine started. Mom took a sharp turn in the yard to pull out onto the dirt road.

"The man don't think I got anything else to do," she spoke aloud to herself, gripping the steering wheel with one hand, only to slap it with her other. "Never mind the wash and the dishes and the raisin' of his children. Naaaaw. I got all the time in the world to be on the road."

She turned on the radio. About midway through a song, she started to sing along. Hers was a voice that if you heard it you would say, "Gee, I bet she's a swell mother."

As we got closer to the mines, I covered my ears from the noise of the trucks rolling past. Mom turned off the radio and slowed the car as she made the turn into the office lot. I planned to pop out and surprise Dad, but when I peeked from beneath the blankets to look out the window, I was frightened by what I saw approaching.

"The mine monster," I whispered to myself.

His skin was black from coal dust. He was limping, dragging his right leg behind him. I knew he was in pain from the way he leaned forward, his arm resting against his stomach as if his ribs were done in. His bottom lip was cut open and there was a deep gash above his left brow. Though the injuries were fresh, it was hard to believe the blood and hurt weren't things he'd always been.

I wondered why he was coming toward us, but as he got closer, I could see his eyes. I realized the bent man was not the mine monster. He was my father.

"What in the world?" Mom put the car in neutral and engaged the emergency brake with a quick jerk.

She was about to open her door, but Dad waved for her to stay inside.

"C'mon, Landon." Her eyes darted around her, reminding me of a deer in an open field.

Dad cradled his stomach as he lurched forward. I could tell his ribs hurt. I had seen my father blackened by coal before, but this time, the color seemed to be layered. There were streaks on his left cheek where the layers had been smeared. I looked at his forehead. Someone had dragged a wet finger through the coal and written a word. I'd heard others call my father that word before. I mouthed it at the same time Mom said it aloud in a hushed whisper as she, too, stared at his forehead.

I sank my teeth into the blanket so I wouldn't scream.

How dare they do this to him, I thought. *Didn't they know who my dad was?*

He was a man who knew to plant a seed as deep as the second knuckle on your finger. And he knew never to stand corn so close.

"Makes for weaker stalks," he'd say. "The ears will be smaller. The kernels not as full."

Didn't they know this about him? That he was the wisest man in the whole damn county? Possibly the whole world?

I hid deeper beneath the blankets and listened to Dad groan as he lowered himself onto the front seat, keeping his right leg out.

"They smashed my knee like it was glass," he said as he lifted his leg into the car.

Mom was trying to get him to close his door faster.

"C'mon," she said. "Hurry up before they come to finish the job."

Once he was inside the car, she quickly put it in gear. She drove a stick better than most, but her nerves caused her to pop the clutch. The car lunged forward, pressing me up against the back of the seat as the engine stalled.

"Easy now, Alka. Easy." Dad tried to keep his voice from shaking. "We're okay. Start her up again."

"Oh, Jesus Crimson, lock your door." Her voice came out high-pitched as she turned the key, praying for the engine to start. When it did, she thanked God. She forced herself to lift her foot slowly from the clutch.

"Thatta girl." Dad looked out his window at the men staring at us. The men were black from the coal, too, but when they removed their goggles, I could see the white skin around their eyes.

"Let's leave this empty place," Dad said.

Mom drove fast, stirring up dust with our wheels. When she made the turn onto the main road, she took it so sharply, I thought we were going to flip over.

"Not so fast, Alka." Dad looked at the speedometer. "If we get stopped by the law, it'll only make things worse."

When she was going the legal limit, she looked over at him and asked what the hell had happened.

"I'd rather just go home and not talk about it," he said.

He saw coal dust on the car door. He became aware of how dirty he was. He leaned forward as if trying to save the seat.

"I wanna know what the hell happened," she said.

"Ain't nothin' new, Alka. Same old shit."

He told about how, from his first day at the mines, the other men would not call him Landon. They named him things like Tonto and Featherhead.

"Other names, too," he said, looking up toward his forehead.

He spoke more about how the men refused to ride in the shaft elevator with him.

"Get inside with ol' Landon Carpenter and you'll get yourself scalped."

He described how they hooted and slapped their mouths in an Indian war cry they had most likely seen in a western movie of studio tepees and scripted culture.

"You would think that down in the mines," he said, "where each man is blackened by the coal, that there would be no separation among us. That we would work together."

"You'll never be one of them." Mom kept her eyes on the road. "All they need is soap and water to be better than you."

"Is that what you think?" he asked.

"It's what the world thinks, Landon. Don't you understand? You can't wash it off."

"I don't want to," he said. "I just want to be able to work in peace and without fear."

Dad kept his face toward the window.

"They held me down until I couldn't move. One of 'em, the fella who laughed the most, spit on my cheek. He just spit on my cheek like I was nothin'. Then he used the spit to write on my forehead. Write what they all said was my true name."

Dad carefully touched the word written on his forehead as if it were something that was cut into his flesh. My heart whispered to my soul, and my soul whispered back, *Help him.* But I could not move. I was frightened by the story he was telling. By the way his voice got quieter as he spoke more of the men's laughter and of how their grips had tightened on his arms.

"You ever been pinned down before, Alka?" he asked. "Can't stop what somebody is doin' to ya? That ever happen to ya?"

Her jaw tightened as she drove in silence before pulling off to the side of the road. Dad put his hand on the door handle. He must have thought he was supposed to get out of the car.

"Stay put," Mom told him as she opened her purse.

She pulled out a clean white hankie. She spit on the end of it before dabbing it against his cheek. He jerked away.

"You'll ruin your pretty things," he said.

She pulled his face back to her and rubbed his cheek harder, wiping the coal and blood from his face. She looked up at the word on his forehead. Rolling down her window, she banged the handkerchief against the outside of the car. Much of the coal was ingrained, but the top layer of dust shook off. Then she wiped his forehead until the word was gone. Afterward, she stretched the handkerchief out before her. She frowned as if she could see the letters of the word on its fabric.

"I never much cared for this silly ol' thing anyways." She tossed it out the window before putting the car in gear and turning back onto the road.

I slid my hand into my pocket. Squeezing the red crayon, I pulled it out and used it to write on the metal bed of the tailgate. I wrote about my father slaying the cave monster with a thousand arrowheads pulsating from his forehead. I wrote until the crayon was so short, I had to hold it pinched between my two fingers, pressing it until I was able to write the happy ending I wanted to give him. Then I closed my eyes, knowing my birthplace was a bitter chapter in the story of my father.

For the next two years, we wandered across America. We learned history from the mouths of old-timers and foreign languages from the mouths of drunks. There was the hitchhiker we picked up in Colorado. She taught us science lessons on Newton and his apple. We met an ex-con at a diner in Arizona who taught us the laws of the world and the laws of prison. Most of all, we learned the names of states by looking at cars.

"I call Alaska," Fraya said.

"Idaho." Flossie spotted a red Ford. "I bet the trunk is full of potatoes."

Lint looked to see for himself.

"It's Texas." Trustin waved to the car. They did not wave back.

"There's home." Mom gestured to the Ohio license plate of a black Ford Thunderbird speeding past. "I wanna go home, Landon."

Part Two

King of Kings

1961–1963

4

Thy words were found, and I did eat them.

—JEREMIAH 15:16

It was 1961 and I was seven when Mom said she wanted to go home. Home was Ohio because that was where her roots were.

"Roots are the most important part of a plant," Dad would say. "It's through roots that a plant is fed and it's the roots that hold the plant in place when everything else gets washed away. Without roots, you're just flappin' in the wind."

Enough time had passed for our parents to forgive the Buckeye State.

We were piled in our fern-colored Rambler, which hauled a small flatbed trailer. The raccoon tail on the antenna flew back as Mom and Dad took turns driving. Come night, Mom was behind the wheel. I counted her yawns until Dad directed her to pull off into the woods, pointing toward a pair of gum trees.

Once Mom turned the engine off, Dad got out with a jar of moonshine as company. He was going to comb the forest floor for more plants even though we already had several herbs in bunches drying from various spots in the car like behind the seats and from the window frames.

After his foraging for the night, I knew Dad would make a bed on the hood of the car. Mom always got the front bench seat to herself. Trustin would fold down the tailgate and dangle his legs in between the trailer and the car while Fraya and Flossie lay on the backseat, their heads together, their bodies pointed in opposite directions, their feet protruding out of each of the back windows. Lint would lay on top of Fraya like a lap cat while she petted the top of his head. I was left to sleep on the backseat floorboard or sometimes the tailgate if Trustin decided to stretch out on the ground.

That night, the Rambler felt especially crowded, so I left in search of Dad.

Every tree I passed, I stopped long enough to write on its trunk with my finger. I thought if I wrote the trees something nice, they would be my map through the woods.

Dear great big oak, your bark is like my father's singing. Help me find my way. Dear beech, don't tell the oak, but your leaves make the best bookmarks. Help me find my way. Dear maple, you smell like the best poem. Help me find my way.

I was stepping from one tree to the next when my bare foot caught on a raised root. I fell and scuffed my knees. I sat on the ground and cried, not because I was hurt, but because I was lost.

"My, my." Dad clicked his tongue as he stood over me. "I'll be rich and famous for a find like you. They'll put me on the front page of every newspaper in the world with a headline that reads, LANDON CARPENTER FINDS MYSTERIOUS CREATURE IN WOODS. First, I gotta ask ya." He met my face with his. "Are you of God or the devil?"

"You're not funny, Dad, and you won't be on the covers of any newspapers," I said.

"Oh, no?" he asked.

"No." I frowned as hard as my little brows could. "I'm lost and now that you're here you're sure to be lost, too. You can't be on the cover of a newspaper when you're lost unless it's a story 'bout you bein' lost. In which case no one would write that story 'cause no one would care to read it."

I remembered back to the way the men had beat my father at the mines.

"You're not important," I said, as they must have. "You're Landon Carpenter."

He leaned back with a flick of anger.

"You're too little in the mouth for such mean talk," he said before taking a drink of his moonshine and stepping over to sit on a fallen tree trunk partially covered in brush and heavy moss.

I picked up a leaf and used it to wipe little spots of blood from my scuffed knees as I stood. Studying the woods around me, I decided I was not brave enough to test the darkness by myself so I sat beside my father. I stared at the jar in his hand. He had painted small black stars on the outside of the glass.

"Why you always paint stars on your moonshine jars?" I asked.

"Because the stars belong with the moon," he said before setting the jar on the ground by his feet.

He reached into his shirt pocket and pulled out his pouch of dried tobacco leaves. I watched him put a pinch onto a piece of rolling paper.

"Why don't you care we're lost, Dad?" I asked.

"You're the one lost, girl. I know exactly where I am."

He let me lick the edge of the rolling paper so he could wrap the tobacco. He then struck a match against the ribbon of sandpaper on his hat. As he lit the cigarette, I stared at the scar on his left palm. The way his skin curled and burled was as if his palm had almost melted away. He looked at the scar himself, studying it from all angles. When he started to frown, he turned away and took his hat off. He put it on me, then puffed on his cigarette.

"Ain'tcha scared we'll always be lost?" I asked. "I am. I'm scared."

When he exhaled, he blew toward the stars.

"Did you know that smoke is the mist of souls?" he asked. "That's what makes it so sacred and able to carry your fear up to the clouds, which is the home of the fear eaters."

"Fear eaters?"

"Good little creatures who will devour all that frightens you so you don't have to be afraid anymore."

He gave me the cigarette and told me to hold the smoke in my mouth before quickly releasing it. The best I could do was cough out the smoke. I went to inhale again, but Dad said to save my lungs.

"To run the fields with," he said, taking the cigarette back.

We watched the smoke drift away and disappear.

"I still feel lost," I said.

Dad looked at me before turning his eyes back out onto the darkness of the woods.

"You know," he said, "one time I come upon a devil-damn patch of woods. I'd gone out for some plant huntin', but fell asleep. When I woke, I lost my bearings."

"A bear ring?" I asked. "Ooo, how pretty. A bear give it to you? Does it have sparkly things on it? Lemme see it."

I started to dig through his pockets, but found only his loose ginseng beads. He laughed and held me back with his arm.

"Calm down now, Betty," he said, still laughing. "Not *bear ring*. My bearings. My knowledge of direction. I flattened the grass in front of me and I was lost. I flattened the grass behind me and I was lost still. By the time evenin' fell, I reckoned those woods would be my eternity."

"What'd you do, Dad?"

"I took some small rocks and spelled my name in the dirt so folks would know I had one. Then I laid down and looked up at the stars in the night sky. That was when I realized I knew right where I was."

"Where were you?"

"South of heaven."

"Where's that at?"

"Look up, Betty."

He gently guided my face to the sky with the back of his hand under my chin.

"Somewhere up there is heaven," he said. "And we're a little to the south of it. That's where south of heaven is. It's right here." He stomped the ground beneath us. "It doesn't matter where you are or where you're goin' because you'll always be south of heaven."

"I be south of heaven." In great wonder, I looked up at the sky.

"Ain't nowhere else to be," he said.

He pinched his cigarette out and shoved it inside his boot. He pretended to drop a stub down my shoe, but I was barefooted so he tickled my heel until I laughed.

"Ain't no bigger," he said of my foot, measuring it against his hand. "Won't never be so small ever again."

"I won't let it get any bigger, Dad."

"Oh, you won't, will you?" He chuckled as he set my foot back down. "We best get some rest. Got a long drive tomorrow. We'll see Ohio by the afternoon if we're lucky."

"Can I sleep on the hood with ya?"

"Don't you think you'll get cold?" he asked.

"I've got a scarf." I wrapped my long black hair around my neck. "See?"

"You sure you wouldn't wanna sleep in the Rambler?"

"I'd rather sleep on Mars, which by the way, I wrote a new story about. I wrote it on a napkin at the diner when we were passin' through Louisiana, but I forgot it."

"You forgot the story?" he asked.

"Oh, no." I shook my head. "I forgot the napkin. I remember the story. My best Martian story yet."

"You're always writin' 'bout Mars. I guess you got some Martian blood in ya."

"Hey, Martian blood is what my story is about."

"This I gotta hear." He stretched his legs out and crossed them at the ankles.

"Well, the Martians," I began, "they wanna invade earth."

"It seems Martians are always wantin' what's ours," he said.

"Just the way they're bent, I guess. To invade us, they send birds," I said, trying to make a bird shape with my hands. "The kind only found on Mars. The birds have wings identical to the checkerboard menus from the diner. Their bodies are like the diner's ketchup bottles and their heads are upside-down cups."

"Like the cups me and your momma drank our coffee from?" he asked, holding an imaginary coffee cup to his lips and slurping.

"Yep. And the birds' legs are long soda spoons, like what Trustin used when he ate his orange float. The ends of the spoons are bent and carry Martian blood. As the birds fly to earth, the blood falls out. Each drop of blood seeps into our earth like a seed. Before anybody knows it, they all got Martians growin' in their backyard."

"What do these Martians look like?"

"Instead of skin like you and me have, a Martian's skin is made of blue checkered tablecloths."

"I think the diner had those, too, didn't it?" he asked with a wide smile.

"Sure did." I nodded. "For fingers, the Martians have bendy straws." I bent my fingers toward his face. "Like the white straw with red stripes I drank my strawberry milkshake from. Remember that red flag blowin' outside the diner? Had that big blue X with white stars?"

"I remember it." His smile faded.

"That's what the Martians' hair is, only cut into strips for ease of brushin'. They've all got pickle eyebrows like the pin our waitress wore and their eyes are the same as the diner's ola . . . ola . . ."

"Olallieberry," Dad helped me with the word.

"*Olallieberry* pies," I said, "the juices from the berries runnin' down. *Rargh, rargh.*" I pawed at my cheeks until Dad laughed so hard he coughed.

"They got salt and pepper shaker antennas," I continued, "and shrunken-down dinner forks for teeth. It's their fork teeth that's gonna kill us because when them Martians get done growin', they'll break from their roots and smile at us. The shine from their metal teeth will make everyone crazy and we'll kill each other until only Martians remain."

Dad shimmied his shoulders as he said, "You got me so nervous I'm gonna be lookin' to the sky for ketchup bottle birds. What do you call this jewel of caution?"

" 'The Smilin' Martians,' " I sang out, sticking my tongue through the hole in my smile where I'd lost a baby tooth the previous week.

" 'The Smilin' Martians' might be my favorite story yet," Dad said.

We both turned to a thumping coming from the dark of the woods.

"What's that?" I pushed his hat up on my forehead in order to see better.

"Maybe it's one of your Martians," Dad said. "We best get to the Rambler before the ol' alien finds us and smiles."

He picked me up from off the tree and set my feet softly on the ground.

"Ain'tcha gonna get your jar of moonshine?" I asked.

"Naw," he said. "We'll let the Martian have it. That way he'll just fall right asleep and not be a bother the rest of the night."

I grabbed his hand as we walked through the woods. He limped with every step. Two years had passed since the mine incident, but it was still fresh in my mind. The color of Dad's blood. The way the coal dust had settled into the pained lines of his face. I thought of how he had said they'd smashed his knee like glass. I wondered if, like glass, sharp edges cut into him. He certainly walked as if they did. I decided to limp, too, so he wouldn't be alone. He looked at me, then tried not to limp so much himself.

"Can I sleep on the hood with ya, Dad?" I asked again. "It's too crowded in the Rambler. Mom is like a million people all in herself. When you think of it like that, you've got Fraya, Flossie, Trustin, Lint, Mom, and a million more people. You can't have a basket full of jars without the glasses bickerin' and clankin' against one another. You said that once. Remember?"

"I did, did I?"

"Hmm-mmm. Sure did, Dad. So can I sleep on the hood with ya?"

"You have to promise you won't get cold, Betty."

"I promise, promise, promise, promise, promise," I repeated until he held up his hand and laughed.

"I reckon there's room on the hood for a big Indian and a little one," he said.

I squeezed his hand as we limped together. When we passed the Rambler, Flossie stuck her tongue out at me. I returned the gesture.

Then she said goodnight, so I said it back. Both Flossie and I said goodnight to Fraya at the same time.

"Goodnight," Fraya said.

Dad lifted me up and set me feet first on the hood. I played with the raccoon tail tied to the antenna before putting the hat on top of it as Dad climbed up on the hood himself. He waved inside the car to Mom, but she was already asleep, stretched across the front seat with one leg perched on top of the steering wheel. Her snores sounded like animals scavenging for food with their snouts in the dirt.

"All right, Betty. Here's your hard bed." Dad patted the hood as he laid his upper body up against the windshield.

"Dad?" I asked as I sat beside him. "Did you like my Martian story? The truth."

"I really did."

Before I could say anything more, I heard a car door squeak open and softly close, followed by the padding of little feet against the twigs on the ground.

"No s-s-sleep." Lint came up on Dad's side of the hood.

Lint was rubbing his teary eyes with the backs of his fists. His little pockets bulged from rocks he had collected.

"Well, son, you're in luck because I got sleepin' dust in my pocket," Dad said as he pulled Lint up on the hood and put him in between us.

"You still afraid to go to sleep?" Dad asked him.

A couple of weeks prior, Lint had drawn a picture that showed a black scribble above his stick figure body. He was only four at the time, so his drawing had less meaning than when he explained it. He told Dad the black scribble was the night and that should he fall asleep, the night would steal his soul.

"My s-s-soul," Lint had said as he made the black scribble darker. "Night take it, Daddy. Take it to b-b-bury it. North. In the c-c-cold."

Remembering Lint's drawing, I looked out into the darkness around us as Dad promised Lint the night wouldn't steal his soul.

"I won't let it." Dad wrapped his arms around Lint.

"You can't s-s-stop it, Daddy."

"Your soul is right here." Dad gently laid his hand over the bridge of Lint's nose. "I'll keep my hand on it all night long while you sleep. Your soul will be here when you wake in the mornin'. I swear."

While Lint laid his head against Dad's chest, I curled up alone on the edge of the hood.

5

Gavest thou the goodly wings unto the peacocks?

—JOB 39:13

WELCOME TO BREATHED was painted in red on a splintery shred of barn wood nailed to an American sycamore. I would come to learn that between heaven and hell, Breathed was a piece of earth inside the throb, where lizards were crushed beneath wheels and the people spoke like thunder grinding on thunder. There, in southern Ohio, you woke to the barks of stray dogs while always aware of the shadows of larger wolves.

"How you say the town's name again?" Trustin asked. "Breathed?"

"Not like you breathed somethin' in." Dad looked through the rearview mirror at Trustin. "Say it like you're takin' a breath, then you say *ed*. Breath-ed."

All around, the hills stood like a great exclamation from man to the heavens. Known as the foothills of the Appalachians, the exposed sandstone formed ridges, cliffs, and gorges shaped and cut by glacier melting. Covered in a green mix of moss and lichen, the ancient sandstone was named after the things it resembled. There was the Devil's Tea Table, Lame Deer, and the Giant's Shadow. Names handed down to each new generation as if they were as valuable as heirloom jewels.

Passing through the hills and cutting across the land were not roads or streets but lanes, as the locals called them, as if to say the dirt-covered tracks were nothing more than widened paths. Main

Lane was where Saint Sammy's, Moogie's Toy Store, Fancy's Dress Shop, and other businesses were. From Main Lane branched residential lanes where every house had a family Bible and a good recipe for bread. Farther out, homesteads owned the acreage. In her most wholesome form, Breathed was a wife and mother who made sure to hang her flag banners on her porch rails every Fourth of July. At her darkest, she was the place you could bleed to death in without a single open wound.

Dad drove into Breathed slowly, like someone careful of where he steps. A white-haired man holding a yellow balloon soon came into view. He was standing by the edge of a wood line.

"Hey, old fella." Dad hollered out his open window as he waved at the man.

"Landon Carpenter?" The man waved back. "That really you?"

Dad's answer was a short honk of the car's horn as we continued past.

"That was ol' Cotton Whithers," Dad told us kids as we stared back at the man still waving with both arms.

"Hasn't stopped sendin' his letters, I see," Mom said as she watched the yellow balloon float up into the sky.

I turned my attention to the town around us. We had lived in wildernesses before. Trees as tall as the men were not. Meadows as lovely as the women were. Yet there was something different about Breathed. It seemed to inhale and exhale as if it was not a town that had been created by humankind, but a place born unto it. I wanted to write Breathed into a poem. I would rhyme the words if I must, but speak them like I was throwing stones into a river. That seemed the only way to represent a place where the dirt lanes looked like brown diamond snakes laid out, the scales reflecting the sunlight.

As Dad made a sharp turn, I looked up to see the lane sign.

"Shady Lane," I said the name aloud.

Towering trees lined both sides, their branches braiding like cold rivers. The lane dead-ended at the drive to our property, which was acres of woods and uncut field. In the overgrown drive, there was a red car. Standing up against it was Leland. He was on leave and Dad had written him about the new house, so Leland said he would meet us there. He was twenty-two then. His blonde hair was cut short and he was wearing his army service uniform.

Trustin squealed Leland's name when he got out of the car.

"Where'd you get that fancy new car from?" Dad asked as he stared at the shine of Leland's car.

"Oh, just borrowin' it from a friend," Leland said.

"You bring anything back from Japan for us?" Trustin asked.

Leland had written letters about having recently been stationed in Japan. He'd gotten us dreamy-eyed about the things he wrote. Women with white paint on their faces. Beautiful kimonos dragging the ground. Roofs which he said were called pagodas but were shaped like stacked squash blossoms.

"Heck, sure, I gotcha somethin'." Leland handed Trustin a paperweight with swirls of color inside it. For Lint, there was a round gray rock.

"I dug it up from Japanese soil myself," Leland told him.

"Look how round it is," Dad said to Lint. "It looks like a big old eye."

Lint smiled at the thought.

Flossie jumped up and down when Leland gave her a hand fan. She held it to her face and fluttered her lashes behind its illustrations of white butterflies and gilded leaves.

My present was a pink silk box. Inside was a pair of pajamas in the same silk. They had frog closures and knotted buttons. I was used to fabrics like denim, cotton, and flannel, but not silk. I'd never felt something so soft. I held it to my cheek while Flossie picked up a sleeve and held it to hers.

"It feels so cool," Flossie said, smiling.

"You know silk comes from a worm," Dad said.

"A worm?" Flossie pulled back. "Ugh."

Leland reached into the car and lifted out a jewelry box. It was the length of my whole arm. The top of it was shaped as a pagoda roof. On the shiny black lacquer were paintings of bonsai trees and lotus plants. Two front doors opened to a silk-lined interior that had little drawers and compartments surrounding a small female figurine who twirled to the music. Leland handed the box to Fraya, who awkwardly held it in her arms, quickly closing the doors so the music stopped.

"How come Fraya's gift is so big?" Flossie asked as she closed her fan.

Leland wiped his hands on his pants before getting two small bird figurines out of his glove compartment. The birds were made of red glass. He gave one to Mom and the other to Dad.

"It's real, real nice, son." Dad patted Leland's shoulder.

Leland stepped back and dug both his hands in his pockets as he nodded toward the house.

"I waited for y'all to get here," he said. "I ain't even peeped in the windas none."

Dad handed Mom his bird to hold with hers as he opened his arms out to the acreage.

"Can you believe it?" he asked. "All this land no one can tell us to get off of."

Each of us took our own path through the tall, patchy grass. There was an unattached garage where a raccoon darted. The house itself was large and heavily guarded by dark evergreen bushes. It appeared to belong to the earth more than it did to man. Entire walls exploded in ivy, and vines wrapped the surviving rails on the porch while pervading brush growing beneath the open bottom of the porch gave it a tilt to the right. There were mud dauber nests, hanging like hollowed-out rods, while darting lizards were not in want of hiding places.

"I'm gonna catch a hundred and keep 'em all in my room," Trustin said as he chased the reptiles.

The house was two stories, not including the attic. Its Victorian architecture had been distorted until it was nothing more than an old-fashioned dream tied down by the shadows of the pines that grew against its sides.

We walked up the rickety porch steps cautiously, as if they could collapse at any moment. Dad tested the strength of the porch posts by gripping each with both hands.

"She's steady," he said.

Mom was the last of us. Her heel had gotten stuck in the crack on the top step. She cursed as Dad tried to free her.

"The place is a trap," she said, putting her weight on his shoulder while she looked at the house. Its wooden boards had at one time been painted yellow, but that paint had peeled, exposing the naked wood, as eroded as the sandstone.

"What a dump," Mom said the very second Dad freed her shoe.

"It's worth its weight in acreage alone," he was quick to say. "Besides, ain't nothin' that can't be fixed."

"Along with everything else, huh?" Mom's tone was flat as she stared up at the sag in the porch's ceiling.

Walking toward the front door, we stepped around the tall prickly weeds growing through the spaces in the floor. The large picture window was not broken, but it was cracked and covered in dirt. There were areas on the glass that had been wiped by those locals too scared to chance the ghosts by going inside. They had instead pressed their faces against the window to see what lurked between rooms.

Dad started to fidget with the screen door, which was hanging on by only one hinge. The screen itself was cut, the loose side dangling. Suddenly, the door broke off its last rusty hinge, sending Dad barreling backward. He caught his footing before he fell all the way. He quickly set the door down as if he had meant to remove it all along.

"Would ya stop messin' around with everything?" Mom pushed past him. "Can't you tell this house is already in debt to the devil?"

She stopped at the wide front door. Three of its four panels were gone along with its knob and lock. She shook her head before pushing the door open the rest of the way.

Stepping into the house was like crossing the threshold into a tomb. Dry brown leaves were piled along the wood floor, which had originally been painted as a large clock face. A wide circling staircase centered the house. At one time, it had been grand. By then, the only things not stolen off it were the steps.

Branching from the staircase were two separate sitting rooms. Through the breaks in the walls, the outside crept in until real leaves grew against the printed ones on the wallpaper of old-time florals and vines. That wallpaper still comes back to me. Mint green, lilac, cream like a long spring. I imagined the woman who chose that wallpaper did so because she loved her house.

"The story about the Peacocks is true?" Fraya touched the bullet hole in the wall that separated the living room from the dining room. "I thought it was made up."

The Peacock family built the house in 1904. With their wealth, they spared no expense. In 1947, they decided to update their home to modern standards. Shortly after the renovation, all eight family members mysteriously disappeared. No bodies. No blood. Just eight bullet holes found in walls throughout the house.

Dad's childhood friend, Cinderblock John, got the Peacock property at auction. Cinderblock John owned various rental homes, but everyone told him he had bought a curse when he acquired the Peacocks' past. The property sat to become more ruinous with each passing year. Looters from out of town vandalized and stole what they could. They did not fear the curse as much as the townsfolk themselves did.

When Dad wrote Cinderblock John to let him know we were coming to Breathed, Cinderblock John swiftly wrote back:

> I have a house for you, but I'll tell ya, dear friend, it is
> cursed. Her owners vanished, ain't never to be seen again.
> All I can say with certainty is that I ain't seen no floating
> sheets. Ain't no door closed on its own. The bullet holes
> (there are eight of them) have never bled in my presence.
> If it's haunted, it ain't very good at it. I reckon it's cursed
> because everyone says it is. My reasons for giving you the
> house are selfish. I hope it'll be something that offers you
> enough of a home you can't bear to leave it. Consider me
> lonely all these years, dear friend.

Dad said there was no misfortune cast on the house and that the rumors were a small town's way of having something to talk about.

"Besides, what's a new curse to a family full of 'em," Mom had said.

Flossie twirled past as she pointed to where we could set a TV.

"To watch *American Bandstand*. Please let's get a TV." She tugged on Dad's shirt.

"We'll see," he said.

Lint walked past me and to a carved tiger standing against the front wall. The tiger was true to size, though it was missing its back left leg and its glass eyes had been removed.

Lint slid his thin fingers along the tiger's stripes. His fluffy brown hair fell into his deep brown eyes while he laid his head against the tiger's side as if listening for a heartbeat. Trustin snuck around to the other side and hid by the tiger's mouth, where he started growling. Frightened by the sounds, Lint fell back against the wall, trying to make himself smaller as he whimpered. Dad heard and came in, scooping Lint up while scolding Trustin.

"Geesh, I was only foolin'." Trustin stood up.

When Trustin saw me, he reached for his holster and removed his cap gun.

"I'll get me an Indian instead." He started chasing me.

"Leave me alone." I tried to outrun him.

"Can't." He shot his gun off in the air. "I got orders to run all savages off this land."

I hid behind Fraya.

"Don't let him get me." I tugged at her skirt.

Leland lunged into the room and yanked the gun out of Trustin's hand.

"You shouldn't chase your sister," Leland said, looking over the toy gun before holding it up in line with the bullet hole in the wall.

"Bang." His loud shout had caused Fraya to jump.

"The army give you a gun to shoot, Leland?" Trustin asked.

"Sure did." Leland handed the pistol back to Trustin.

"Bet it's not as good as mine," Trustin said before firing on an emerald-colored beetle crawling up the wall.

Fraya quickly grabbed my hand and together we walked into the kitchen. On the countertop were broken mixing bowls and no fewer than a dozen wooden rolling pins, piled as if firewood. In the bottom of the large wall-mounted sink, there was a cookbook. It was opened as though a woman had recently been there, thumbing through its pages.

"Betty." Fraya pointed at Flossie passing through the hall. "How 'bout we go see where she's headed? There might be treasures there."

Together we followed Flossie to the staircase. On the seventh step was a crudely carved heart. The random thought of a pocketknife.

"There's been lovers in our house," Flossie said as she stomped on the heart on her way up the steps.

All four bedrooms were on the second floor. I handed Fraya my box of pajamas so I could race Flossie to explore. The first bedroom was long enough to overlook both the front and back yards. Even though the door was missing, we knew the spacious room would be Mom and Dad's.

Across the hall was the only upstairs bathroom. It still had the cast-iron tub, which had been too heavy for anyone to steal. The toilet was there, too, but its tank lid was broken and the seat was off its hinges.

Flossie stuck her head into the smaller bedroom facing the back-yard and told Fraya it could be her room.

"Since you get a room to yourself, you don't need a real big one," Flossie said, flipping her hair.

"She gets a room to herself 'cause she's the oldest," I reminded Flossie.

"She's only seventeen. That barely makes her old enough to do anything important," Flossie said before deciding the room where Lint and Trustin would be was by Fraya's.

When Flossie stepped into the front bedroom, she clapped her hands and said, "Our room, Betty, shall be this one."

The room smelled damp. The water spots on the ceiling looked like young bruises, yellow and pale and green on the edges. There were spiderwebs, both new and old, while a tatty jump rope was coiled in a bowl like a snake. Scattered across the floor were rocks that had been thrown through the windows to break them.

"Gosh, you think there was nothin' better to do in this town than break windas," Fraya said as she came in and kicked at the rocks. "Lint will love seein' all of these."

The rocks were wrapped in pieces of paper that had been bound with rubber bands, now rotting. Names were written on the papers as if the house were a wishing well visited by those bidding to inflict the curse upon others.

In the middle of the room was a box smashed in on one side. I reached inside it and pulled out a tattered copy of Helen Hooven Santmyer's novel *Herbs and Apples,* along with an empty bottle of Blue Waltz perfume. Flossie snatched the heart-shaped bottle out of my hand.

"It's like being kissed by a prince." She clicked her tongue as she dabbed the bottle up her neck to her lips.

"What else is in there?" Fraya asked as she pointed toward the box.

I picked the box up and dumped it. A pale blue handkerchief floated out along with gold foil in the shapes of oak and maple leaves. There was a 1937 newspaper article detailing the disappearance of Amelia Earhart and several campaign buttons, including one for Alfred Landon's 1936 race. Under Landon's photograph was his slogan, LIFE, LIBERTY, AND LANDON.

"He's got the same name as Dad." I picked up the button and held it toward my sisters.

"Hmm" was the most Flossie said as she set the perfume bottle on the windowsill. "Oh, lookee." Her eye caught on the pair of bullet holes in between the two windows.

"Two holes means two people were shot in here." Mom's voice surrounded us.

We turned to see her looking in with sedated curiosity from the doorway.

"It could mean one person was shot twice," Fraya said. "And maybe they were missed shots. There's no bodies."

"They were murdered," Flossie said. "Probably not by a gun either. The murderer used an ax."

Flossie shrieked and lunged at me with her arms up. I pushed her back just as Leland poked his head into the room.

"You gonna be stayin' here?" Mom asked him.

"I'm jumpin' between a few places before I gotta go back to Uncle Sam." He leaned against the doorframe, digging the heels of his boots in and laying his chin on his chest.

"Well, I don't blame ya for not stayin' here," Mom said. "Ain't a house if you can see the ground through the floor and the sky through the ceilin'." She inhaled sharply before adding, "At least we know where the demons have been playin' this whole time."

She shook her head on her way out.

Leland took the opportunity to ease farther into the room and kick at the campaign buttons while Fraya leaned back against the bullet holes.

"You like your jewelry box, Fray?" Leland asked her. "You left it on the porch."

When Fraya didn't acknowledge him, his voice dropped deeper to ask, "You rather I gotcha pajamas?"

She hugged the box of my pajamas against her chest.

"I was only holdin' 'em for Betty," she said.

He turned to me and Flossie.

"You two beat it," he said.

"But it's our bedroom," I told him.

He nearly tore my arm off as he threw me out into the hall, pushing Flossie after me. He slammed the door before we could make it back in. I tried the knob, but he had his hand on the other side of it, so I hit the door with my small fists.

"It's not a big deal, Betty." Flossie hooked her arm through mine. "Let's see the rest of the house."

We walked across the hall. Instead of counting the dead beetles crunching beneath our steps like Flossie was, I thought about the last time we'd seen Leland. Dad had plotted a garden at a house we had been renting. In the garden were several rows of corn. Dad always told us that when an ear of corn was ripe, the silks would dry and the husk would darken.

"Some folks will open the husk to check the kernels," Dad would say. "Don't ever do that because if it's not ripe, you'll have to leave the ear on the stalk. But since you've opened the husk, the bugs will be able to get in and spoil the kernels."

Despite this, Leland opened ears of corn he knew were not ready.

"You're ruinin' the corn, son," Dad said to Leland.

When Leland didn't stop, him and Dad started to argue. I didn't know if Dad was the first to throw a punch, or if Leland was. All I did know is that the cornstalks were flattened by the time it was over and Dad had a shiner. Shortly after, Leland enlisted in the army.

"That's ninety-eight, ninety-nine, a hundred, a thousand beetles." Flossie kept counting the dead bugs.

The sliding noise down the hall caused her to stop. It was Dad pushing a mattress into his and Mom's room. Lint and Trustin were marching behind him like they were in a parade.

"Do you think, Betty, our brothers are perhaps the dumbest boys on the face of the earth?" Flossie asked.

Having heard her, Trustin stopped marching. He put his hand on his holster and said it was illegal for two girls to go around barefoot.

"Officer. Officer." He ran over to me and Flossie, firing his cap gun off in our faces.

"You're barefoot, too, idiot." My voice and Flossie's overlapped as we pushed him back.

"Hey, hey. No fightin' in our new home," Dad said, coming out into the hall with Lint on his heels.

Dad rubbed his hands as he looked around him with a smile.

"I feel like I can devour this whole house, I already love it so much," he said.

He looked toward the closed door at the end of the hall. The door had at one time been painted lavender. Remnants of the color clung like an adamant past. Its stained-glass panels had been broken, but shards of the colored glass lay on the floor as though they were gems. Dad, who was wearing his work boots, swept the sharp pieces over into the corner, making it safe for his barefooted children to walk behind him.

"I bet this door is the portal to the heavens," Dad said as he opened it.

We were met with crisscrossing lines of spiderwebs and a darkness that led up a narrow staircase.

"C-c-close door." Lint stepped back. "N-n-now."

"It's okay, son," Dad said. "There's nothin' to be afraid of. It's only an old staircase and an old attic. Nothin' more than wood and nails."

Not taking any chances, Lint ran to the other end of the hall, where he peeked at us from around the corner.

"We'll check it out first," Dad told him before turning back to the staircase.

"The rest of you watch your step," he said as he headed up first.

The steps creaked and groaned beneath our feet. I found myself searching for a rail to grip onto. I thought I heard something scratching. A cold draft prickled my skin as my heart beat so fast I could feel it in my fingertips. Flossie walked closer to me while Trustin kept his hand on his pistol as if ready to fire.

The farther up the stairs we got, the more a strange aroma saturated the air. The odor reminded me of the smell of a white bird feather I'd found one time laying in the moonlight.

"I bet the Peacocks' bodies are up here," Flossie said just before we got to the top.

But like the rest of the house, the attic was pretty well cleared out. What remained was a box of used combs and a jar of dirt labeled IMPORTANT.

"It stinks up here." Flossie held her nose as we separated to explore the large space.

"What's all this on the floor, Dad?" I asked as I turned my foot over to find what looked like little black worms embedded in my heel.

Dad picked up one of the black flecks.

"It's time we head back downstairs," he said.

A squeak from above caused us to look up. Dad quickly held his hand over Flossie's mouth before she could scream at the sight of hanging bats.

Dad whispered for me and Trustin to be quiet as we tiptoed back toward the steps. He waited until we were downstairs before he released Flossie.

"I can't live in a house with bats," she said.

"B-b-bats?" Lint cried from down the hall.

"They'll suck our blood when we're sleepin'." Flossie shuddered as if she could feel them crawling all over her.

"That's right, Dad," I added. "We'll all become vampires. We'll have to garden at night 'cause we won't be able to be in the sun no more."

"Bats won't harm us none." Dad softly closed the attic door. "They're good creatures."

"But we can't live with 'em." Flossie threw her arms up.

"I'll fly 'em out of the attic," Dad said. "Then make 'em a little house and put it on a pole in the field so even though they won't be livin' here, they'll still feel like they got a home with us Carpenters."

"How you gonna fly 'em out?" Trustin asked.

"I'll use blood stars." Dad deepened his voice.

"What's a blood star?" I asked, imagining the sky drenched in red.

"Stars full of the blood of our dead Cherokee elders," Dad said. "Their blood was so revered, it rose with their spirits and became red stars that then shined wisdom down on all the people."

"There's no such thing as blood stars," Flossie was quick to say.

"Oh, yes, there is, Flossie," Dad said. "Before blood stars, there were no seasons. One drop of blood for spring. Two for summer. Three for autumn and four for—"

"Silly Dad." Flossie walked ahead, using her pinkie to pretend to put on lipstick. "Let's go see the barn."

Flossie led the way while Dad picked Lint up, carrying him down the stairs as Trustin followed.

I stopped in front of my bedroom. The door was now open, but the room was empty. My pajamas were on the floor, having spilled out from the box, which had gotten broken as if stepped on.

In the next room, Mom was sitting on the mattress. As she rubbed her legs, I saw the familiar squares sandwiched between her nylons and her feet. At the time, I thought the squares were pieces of paper to keep her shoes from sliding.

"Where's Fraya and Leland?" I asked her.

"Leave me alone." She turned and began to crawl her way up the mattress. "I'm gonna take a nap before I have to make dinner."

"But where'd they go? Mom? Mmmommm?"

She raised up and looked at me, both her brows arched in their sharpest points as she said, "If you keep botherin' me, I'm gonna hang ya in a tree by that long Indian hair of yours and call for the crows to come peck your eyes out. You want that to happen, Pocahontas?"

I darted down the steps, nearly falling from the way the staircase curved. I caught up to Dad and the others. They were standing in the yard in front of the large barn. Its tall scarred sides met under a slate roof that had "1803" painted on it, each number as long as the roof itself.

"The date Ohio became a state," Dad told us.

We dropped our eyes to the faded handprints on the barn's boards. I imagined people dipping their hands in paint of every color, then throwing their whole bodies toward the barn, landing palms first. Some of the prints were smeared as if one night everyone started dancing and tried to get the barn to join in.

"The hands belong to the builders," Dad said, laying his own over the top of a yellow handprint. "Or they belong to someone who could not let go."

He smiled at the barn as if all of life's happiness could pivot on the ownership of one.

"I bet I find a pony inside," Trustin said as he and Flossie ran into the barn to explore.

Lint followed them, but kept stopping to pick up rocks.

"Dad?" I asked. "Do you know where Leland and Fraya went?"

"I saw 'em walkin' down the lane when we come out here. I reckon they're goin' into town to see how the folks grow."

He turned and looked over the acreage.

"Imagine the seasons here, Little Indian." He smiled. "The rest of this spring, you'll climb that tree there." He gestured to the large and crooked pin oak in the yard. "Then when summer arrives you'll spend all day eatin' tomatoes in the first vegetable garden, which will be over there." He pointed to a patch of long grass toward the side of the house. "In fall you'll sit on the back porch, watchin' the leaves go to ground. When winter comes, you'll tease the bare trees and say they all look like spiders on their backs."

He dug his heels into the ground, staring at the small stream of water running at the back of the property by a persimmon tree.

"There's no better place than right here at the end of Shady Lane," he said. "It's like God picked us up and tucked us in His pocket."

A crash of thunder echoed across the sky. Lint came running out of the barn toward Dad as I looked at the gray clouds gathering over the top of the tree line.

"Looks like smoke from fire," I said.

"Maybe that's all a storm is." Dad squinted toward the clouds. "We best get everything in before it really comes down."

Me and Lint followed Dad to the drive, where he flipped the mattress off the top of the car and onto his head. Lint mimicked Dad as they walked in step toward the porch.

I turned to the property beside ours. In the cut and neat yard was a young girl with a head full of short golden curls tied with a white ribbon. She had a big red ball in her arms. She bounced the rubber ball high over her head.

"I'm seven," I told her when I got close enough.

"I'm six," she said.

Her dress was an adorable blue and her socks had matching blue ruffles on them.

"I like your socks," I said.

She smiled. I looked behind me to see who she was smiling at. When I realized it was me, I beamed at her. She bounced the red ball toward me. I caught it and tossed it back to her. We passed it several more times. When she laughed, it sounded like a little bell.

"Throw higher," she said.

I threw as high as I could.

"You're my best friend," she said when she caught the ball.

"You're mine, too." I jumped up and down, clapping my hands.

"We'll play every day," she said as she bounced the ball back to me.

I caught it just as the freshly painted screen door on her stone house opened. A man, wearing blue pastel slacks, came out pointing at me.

"Give that ball back. Right this second," he said to me. "We don't steal things in this neighborhood."

"We're playin'," I said.

"We're playin', Daddy." The girl agreed.

"I ain't stealin' nothin'," I was sure to add.

"*Ain't* is a word for heathens," he said as he yanked his daughter behind him. "Now hand the ball over."

I threw the ball to him. I noticed he didn't have the hands of a poor man nor the invisibility of one neither. The face of his wristwatch reflected the sun in a blinding spot of light. His cold eyes appeared to do the same.

"Dear?" A woman's voice emerged as the screen door opened a second time. She seemed to float down into the yard and by her planted zinnias until she was standing behind the man. Looking over his broad shoulder, she asked him, "Where'd she come from?"

"Came from back there." I didn't mind answering her myself as I pointed to our house. "We're movin' in."

Her pearl earrings shook as she grabbed the man's forearm.

"A colored family?" She gasped. "When a colored moved into Mother's neighborhood, she said even the water started to taste different."

"Don't surprise me none," he said, before nodding to the ball. "She tried to steal this."

"We can't have the ball back now. Not after she's touched it." The woman scooped her little girl up. "The coloreds always have some sickness. Her germs are all over that ball."

"You're right." He quickly dropped it and got his crisp handkerchief out to wipe his hands on.

"Ruthis, you must be careful who you play with, darling." The mother cradled the girl's head against her shoulder as she carried her inside the house. "Dirty children will give you dirty things."

After his wife and child were safely inside the house, the man clapped at me.

"Get outta here. Go on. Get." He clapped louder, as if I walked on all fours and rubbed my belly in the dirt.

"I said get." He stomped his foot and took a big step toward me.

I ran back and stood in our driveway. He kept an eye on me as he walked up onto his porch. He fluffed the green striped pillows on the white wicker furniture before he went inside.

I made a quick decision to return to their yard and grab the red ball. I thought I heard their door open again, but I didn't stop running until I was safely in the tall weeds of our property. I bounced the ball up our driveway as I thought about the man and the way he had clapped his clean, white hands.

THE BREATHANIAN

Window Shatters in Dead of Night

Glass crunched underfoot as workers at Papa Juniper's Market began cleanup early this morning after discovering a large front window shot out. Several nearby residents came forward to give reports of having heard a gunshot in the vicinity around 1:30 in the morning.

When questioned on this act of vandalism, the sheriff commented, "We take intentional destruction very seriously here in Breathed."

Witness reports testify they saw a figure running from the market after the shot was heard. There has been no clear description of the suspect.

Local resident Grayson Elohim of Kettle Lane came to see the damage.

"It's a shame to see the window broken," he said. "It was good glass."

Blood was thought to have been found on the scene, but was later identified as being ketchup spilled from a broken bottle.

6

Hide me under the shadow of thy wings.

—PSALM 17:8

I remember the sweet smell of the earth and of the squash vines stretching out as long as my legs and arms as I lay in the garden. The prickly stems, the sound of dirt moving with the rocks. I stared into the squash's dark green leaves like I was staring into dark green eyes. The plant was still too small to bear any fruit. It had come up from Dad's seeds and it was late in the season by the time we'd moved into the house. Still, Dad reckoned we would have a crop before the first frost.

"My, my, there's a big squash," Dad's voice came, followed by a spray of cool water on my face. I opened my mouth, drinking the water from the hose in his hand.

"I envy you, Betty," he said. "You're free as a plant."

"You can be a plant, too, Dad," I said.

"All right. Let me try."

When he lay beside me, the sun washed over our faces.

"Do you like our garden, Betty?" he asked.

"I love it."

Gardening, in those early years, was always a family affair. In the garden, Dad would talk as much as he labored.

"To the Cherokee, the earth had a gender," he would tell us. "The mother. The *she*. The first she was Selu. She could make corn by patting her stomach and she could make beans by stroking her armpit.

But her magic was seen as witchcraft and she was murdered by wild boys. Her blood seeped into the soil. From it, everything grew. Even today, the blood of Selu is in our ground."

Though our grass would never be cut, the garden would be kept neat and trim by Dad, who mapped two vegetable plots separated by the eighty paces me and my sisters took. The first plot would be planted for three years, while the second would be left dormant.

"Ground has three good years in it," Dad told us. "First year will be a spectacular crop. The type you never forget. Second year will be a decent crop, but you'll only recall certain things about it. Third year will be a crop you don't remember at all. That's the ground sayin' it needs rest. So, you let that ground sleep for each of the years it gave you. Three years of gardening, three years of leavin' it alone."

He surrounded each plot with a grapevine fence made from the measurements of mine and my sisters' body parts.

"Where's my tape measure?" he would ask until one of us came up to him to offer our arm or the length of our finger.

He used soapberry bushes as fence gates. The bushes weren't for ornamental purpose, but rather they fed nitrogen naturally to the soil. Dad knew these things the way other men knew they could buy fertilizer already mixed in the store.

Dad was an encyclopedia of plants, especially the medicinal uses of them. Wherever we went, he always seemed to collect a small gathering of folks willing to pay him for teas, tonics, and other concoctions. Breathed was no different. Already he was helping an old man suffering from dropsy by brewing him a weak tea made from dogbane. Dad never claimed to have the cure. He only offered the botanic wisdom he said we were forgetting.

"Everything we need to live a life as long as we're allowed has been given to us in nature," he'd say. "That's not to claim if you eat this plant, you will never die, for the plant itself will one day die, and you are no more special than it. All we can do is try to heal the things that can be healed and ease the complaints of the things that cannot be. At the very least, we bring the earth inside us and restore the knowledge that even the smallest leaf has a soul."

It was important to our father that each of us learn how to garden ourselves, but Trustin wanted to draw the garden more than he wanted to be in it. Lint put all of his attention on collecting rocks. Flossie, meanwhile, kept stopping to sunbathe while reminding me that Mom had said for me to stay in the shade.

"You'll get too black." Flossie smiled, turning over on her back to tan her front.

Fraya was most interested in the garden's flowers. She liked the zinnias and peonies, but her favorite were the dandelions. Flossie always called them weeds, but Fraya never thought of them as anything less than roses. She would sit in the grass and eat the bright yellow blossoms until her tongue colored. She'd flash her yellow tongue from time to time as Dad spoke about what it was like to be Cherokee women in the past. These things he told me and my sisters because he said it was important we know how it used to be.

"In the old days, before the white man had yet to cast his shadow," he said, digging his spade into the earth, "it was the Cherokee women who gardened because women had the blood of Selu inside them. Blood is very powerful. After rain, after dust, it is blood that remains. Cherokee men didn't have the blood of Selu, so the land nor the crop belonged to them. It belonged only to the women."

"Then how come you garden now?" Flossie asked. "You ain't no woman, Dad."

"I garden because my momma and my grandmomma gave me permission. They taught me everything. I may not have their power of bein' a woman, but I have their wisdom. And that I can share with the three of you."

He grabbed a handful of soil. It was soft from him having burned dry twigs and saplings on top of it. He poured this loose dirt into my hands and those of my sisters.

"It isn't the sun that grows the crop," he said to us. "It's the energy comin' out of the three of you. Imagine what each of you can grow with the power you got inside you."

By a tree stump next to the garden, Dad built a stage of timber slabs raised on four wooden posts. The posts were about five feet high and set firmly in the ground. Dad cut steps into the stump, turning it into a ladder.

"A stage like this one was in my mother's garden," he said, "and the garden before hers, all the way back to the beginnin' of time. Women and girls would sit on a stage, and they would sing to keep the crows and insects away from the crop. As the women sang, their voices seeped into the ground, nourishin' the roots of the plants and makin' 'em stronger."

"Boys didn't talk and sing on the stage, too?" Fraya asked.

"No," Dad said. "They didn't have the power that the girls and women had."

Me and my sisters named the stage A Faraway Place, because even though it was in our yard, it seemed to be so far off in the distance, we were bound by no one and nothing. It was our world and if you would have heard the language we spoke there, it would have sounded like English to your ear, but we would swear it was something incomparable. In our language, we told stories that didn't end and songs were always of infinite choruses. We became one another until each of us was a storyteller, an actress, a singer-songwriter who measured the things around us until we felt as though we had mapped out the geometry from the life we had, to the life we felt certain we were destined for.

In many ways, A Faraway Place was our hopes and desires manifested into four corners of wood. I saw this in the way each one of my sisters would stand on the edge of the stage, the wind whipping their hair as they stood ever so still. They had never seemed so tall to me before as they each planted their feet at a distance that felt powerful to them. One hand would be bunching the fabric of their skirts, the other placed out in front of them, feeling the wind against their palms. The way they looked out from the stage, it was as though they'd been alive so long, they were already women.

Yet, we were still children there, too. We would run around the stage, never venturing beyond its edge as if the whole world was right there and it was large enough for the dreams of three girls. We pretended to be shot in the heart, only to rise from the dead. The sky turned upside down in an ocean we swam in, kicking our legs in the water as we kept one hand on the floating stage, the other free to splash in play or reach toward the whales swimming by. At night, when we felt the hard wood, it became the soft warm body of a bird large enough to break from the earth and fly us so high, there was no unhappiness to tell of. Flossie would run out onto a wing and say she was going to dive into the stars to become one. We shared one imagination then. One pure and beautiful thought. That we were important. And that anything was possible.

There would always be so much dancing at the end, we would fall asleep on the stage, only to wake the next morning at the very moment the sun rose. The pink and orange clouds performing, it seemed, just for us.

"That's a whole lot of sun," Fraya always said.

"Not enough," Flossie would reply.

I always fell somewhere in the middle when I said, "It's just right."

And so, it was *just right* on our faraway place.

"The curse cannot have us here." Flossie spoke in a particularly heavy southern drawl. "No, it cannot have us here."

But once we were off the stage and walking away from our world, reality was right there to greet us. The curse was part of that reality. Flossie seemed to embrace it as she often used the curse as material to hone her acting. She would rest her hand on her forehead and cry out, "The torment, our plague," before falling back as if she'd fainted.

I didn't want to believe there was a curse on us nor the house. Not after we had worked. We swept dust and debris out the door and into clouds that billowed down the porch steps. We scrubbed floors on our hands and knees and washed the walls until even the shadows were clean. I remember how the paneling shone after my mother had polished it. Later, the wood would swell in the heat, telling its own story.

Creak, creak.

Mom decided to hang the short yellow curtains from her childhood bedroom on the small window over the kitchen sink. She said it was a nice place for them as she stared at the white flowers printed on each panel. She then picked up her bucket and washed around the bullet holes. I expected to see blood on the rag afterward, but there was only plaster and splinters of wallpaper and wood.

During this time, my father worked on the house as well. He seemed like just another ordinary man with a hammer in hand. That is until he started telling stories to each nail he banged in. In between *once upon a time* and work, Dad cleared the bats out of the attic and reused leather from onetime belts as hinges for any door in need. He replaced the broken window glass and fixed the holes in the roof, walls, and floor, but the house would never look like it did in its heyday. Maybe if you looked at the house from a good angle, you could still see glimpses of what it had been. But seasons are hard for a home left all by itself. We did our best against the ruin. Despite its failings, I liked the house and I wondered if it liked us back. We had tried to fill it with nice things like the deerskin Dad hung to be the door for his and Mom's bedroom since it was without one. We laid our rag rugs on the floor throughout and moved in what furniture pieces we had. Any remaining tables, chairs, cabinets, or other fixtures still needed were items Dad would make over time in the tradition of his father.

We got some appliances from Cinderblock John, who, in addition to buying houses, bought the things that went with them. Dad paid Cinderblock John for the items by doing work on his rental properties. Soon, we had a monitor-top refrigerator and a chest freezer.

It wasn't long after that, Leland showed back up on our doorstep. He brought a cabinet television with him.

"How much you have to give for somethin' like this?" Dad asked.

"Just about free." Leland looked away and chewed the inside of his cheek. "You want it?"

"Oh, please, please, let's keep it." Flossie tugged on Dad's shirt.

"All right," Dad said before helping Leland carry the TV into the living room.

The picture was black and white, but Flossie squealed like it was a rainbow of color.

Leland stuck around after that. He'd sometimes sleep on the orange flowered sofa downstairs. When he didn't spend the night at the house, he would come home in the morning with his shirts half-buttoned and with an appetite that made it seem as though he could eat all the deer in the woods by himself. The army had only granted him a short leave, but he was out much longer. It was the first days of August when the military police showed up with their armbands on to take him back. They escorted him to their vehicle while our neighbors watched from their yards.

"Ain't a respectable one among 'em," their voices merged. "I hope they can learn somethin' of our town's morals."

Maybe they thought the best place we would learn those so-called morals was in their school. That year Fraya was going to be a junior in high school. Flossie was entering fifth grade. I hadn't been enrolled in school the previous year when I was six.

"I don't wanna leave Daddy," I had said.

Now in Breathed and seven years old, I'd be entering the first grade.

On the first day, I waited with my sisters for the bus. A shiny red car passed. Pressed against the back window was the face of the golden-haired girl from across the lane. I told Fraya and Flossie that the girl's name was Ruthis.

"Little Miss Ruthis." Flossie used the toes of her saddle shoe to kick the loose gravel.

"Betty, are you nervous?" Fraya asked, watching me pass one of Dad's ginseng beads back and forth in my hands.

"Why do I have to go to school?" I shrugged. "I know everything already."

"Betty." Flossie turned to me. "You know we can't hang around each other at school, right?"

"Flossie." Fraya elbowed her. "Stop it."

"I mean, at home it's fine, of course." Flossie ignored Fraya. "But at school, we can't be seen together."

"Why?" I asked.

"Isn't it obvious? I mean, look at you. You're not gonna be the coolest kid in class, Betty. I can't let you drag me down with you."

"I don't wanna be seen with you." I threw the bead at her.

"Good." She ground the bead into the dirt with her heel. "We're in agreement."

"I hate you," I told her. "I'm gonna smash a toad and tell God you did it."

"Shut up," she said. "You're just angry because you're not gonna make any friends."

"She doesn't mean it, Betty." Fraya reached out to me but I backed away.

"I'm gonna walk to school," I said. "Don't wanna be seen with ugly Flossie on the bus."

I took off running into the woods, while my sisters got on the bus. Instead of heading to school, I took the path back home.

When I got there, Dad was standing in front of the garage handing a jar of dark liquid to a woman I recognized from a few houses down. Up against Dad's leg was Lint. He had his thumb in his mouth and was listening to Dad tell the woman that what was in the jar was a decoction.

"It's different barks I boiled," he explained. "You ever hear of *Gleditsia triacanthos*? *Clethra acuminata?*"

The woman shook her head.

"It's honey locust and pepperbush," I said quietly to myself as I hunched below the bushes.

"It's honey locust and pepperbush," Dad told her. "It'll be good for your cough."

"How's it taste?" the woman asked.

"Don't matter how it tastes to you," Dad said. "It'll matter how it tastes to the serpent. That's why you got a cough. You got a serpent right there," he said, tapping her throat. "And to the serpent, that drink will taste mighty good. So good, in fact, the serpent will wanna slither right on out of you. If you feel that happenin', head to the river and let the vomit come. The water will weaken the anger of the cough and cool the heat of the serpent."

"I heard from others you might say somethin' strange like that," she said.

"I find a dose of storytelling helps with the remedy," he replied.

As the woman left, I snuck into the barn and climbed up to the loft. I took the notepad and pencil out of my skirt pocket and started to write. Seconds later, I heard Lint ask Dad why the handprints on the barn were moving.

"They're not, son," Dad said as their voices came into the barn.

"Are t-t-too," Lint said as he took a rock out of his pocket. He threw it toward the barn, striking it before running back to the house, where Trustin was drawing on the front porch.

"Betty?" Dad called up to me. "I know you're in here. I saw you crossin' the yard."

"No, you didn't," I said, scooting back. "I'm not here."

The loft ladder shifted under his weight as he started to climb it.

"Why ain'tcha in school?" he asked.

"I don't wanna go." I hissed like a cornered snake. "What if they make me breathe the last breath of a dyin' man."

"They ain't gonna do that, Betty."

"How you know?"

"Because I won't let 'em."

He was at the top of the ladder by then and was holding his hand out.

"C'mon, now," he said. "You can't hide in barn lofts, Little Indian. You'll never get educated. If you don't get educated, folks will have good reason to call you dumb as dishwater. You wanna be called dumb as dishwater?"

I shook my head.

"Then c'mon," he said. "I'll take ya there."

He talked about all the fun I was going to have at school as I climbed down the ladder.

"If it's so darn fun, how come you don't go?" I asked, jumping off the last rung to the ground.

"I went when I was a kid, but I had to stop at the third grade to work the fields and put food on the table. You know how lucky you are to be able to go to school? No one in our family has ever graduated. Fraya will be the first. Flossie will follow her. Then you and the boys. Don't turn your back on that opportunity, Little Indian." He wrapped his arm around me as we walked out of the barn. "You'll make so many friends."

"No I won't. They'll ask me why I look different. Folks always do."

"You tell 'em what we always tell 'em. You're—"

"Cherokee. I know." I looked down as we walked to the car. "I just don't wanna go."

"If you don't go," he said, "you won't be able to find the Fantastical Eye of Old."

"What Fantastical Eye of Old?" I asked.

"The one a Cherokee elder carved out a long time ago for children who had to go to school. This elder wanted to make an eye that had never been created before. One with five pupils and an iris that belongs to the river. Always movin', always a surprise beneath the surface. But only kids like you will be able to see it."

"Kids like me?" I asked.

"Cherokee," he said.

"What's so special about this eye anyway?"

"When you stare into it, you'll see everything you miss from home."

"Everything?" I looked up at him. "Even you?"

"Everything. Even me."

Imagining the eye, I skipped ahead of him and got into the Rambler. Dad would later swear I had a smile on my face the whole drive, but the closer we got to the school, the more nervous I became.

After my father parked by a stand of trees, I climbed out of the car, expecting him to drive off. Instead he got out with me.

"I can go by myself," I said.

"Oh, I know what you'll do," he replied. "You'll find another barn loft or a cave in the hills to hide out in."

"A cave." I muttered. "Now why didn't I think of that?"

Dad opened the door and we stepped inside the school. Unlike the beige brick exterior, it was all dark wood on the interior, causing the white porcelain light fixtures to stand out. The hallway was empty. Taped outside each closed door was a sign identifying the teacher and grade.

"Ah, here we are," Dad said, having found the First Grade sign.

He lightly knocked on the door but didn't give anyone inside the chance to open it before he did. The door was at the rear of the room. Everyone turned to stare at us. Some of the kids started laughing as they looked at my father. I studied him, trying to see what they might think was funny about him.

"May I help you?" the teacher asked.

"My little girl here is ready for her first day of class." Dad nudged me forward. "She's really excited, though she won't say it. She brushed her hair and everything."

The kids started to whisper amongst themselves.

"Look at all you youngins." Dad spoke to the class as he reached into his pocket, pulling out a peppermint.

He broke the candy with his fist against a desktop, each pound causing us to jump.

"A taste for each of ya," he told them, breaking the candy into enough pieces that he then passed around. Some of the bits were no more than shards.

"Class." The teacher clapped her hands. "Don't eat that candy."

"Just candy," Dad told her.

"I'm sure it is." She started collecting the pieces.

"I'm fine now, Dad." I tried to push him out of the room. "You can go."

"I'll find ya a good seat," he said, turning his hands into a telescope and looking out across the classroom. The class was small, yet he pretended he was searching a hundred acres.

"Dad." I tugged on his arm. "Right there is one."

I pointed toward the empty desk by the open windows. He lifted me up like he would Lint and carried me to the seat. I stared at the teacher the whole way. She was younger than I thought she'd be. I had imagined a gray bun, loafers with smashed heels, and a brooch at the collar of her blouse the way Flossie always described her teachers. But mine didn't look much older than Fraya. She wore heels and, instead of a brooch, had the collar of her polka-dot dress open.

"I can walk by myself, Dad." I wiggled out of his arms and immediately sat at the desk, trying to hide behind it. "All right, Dad. Go home now."

He told the teacher he'd like to speak to her. She touched the curl of strawberry blonde hair by her temple before joining my father in the hall.

The boy in the seat in front of me turned around to face me. He had stiff brown hair and close-set eyes.

"What's your name?" he asked.

"Betty."

He made a face.

"You talk funny," he said.

"You talk funnier," I told him.

"You look funny, too," he said. "So does your old man."

"You're the one who looks funny." I frowned. "And my dad ain't an old man. He's Dad."

The boy smacked his lips as he studied me.

"I've never seen one of you outside a picture," he said.

"There's lots of girls in the class." I pointed them out. "There. There. There—" My finger landed on Ruthis. She was staring at me.

"Heck, I know there's girls in the class." The boy turned all the way around to rest his arms on my desktop and face me. "I'm sayin' I've never seen a colored before."

"And I've never seen a butt for a face before but if you don't turn around right now, I'm gonna take my daddy's pocketknife and cut you up into tiny pieces to mail to your ugly momma in a heart-shaped box. She'll have to write letters to all the family tellin' 'em what became of you and she'll weep and weep until they have to put her down like a rabid dog."

"Child." The teacher's voice caused me to jump.

The boy giggled as he turned back around.

"Child," she said again, "we do not speak in such a way here."

I raised my eyes to see the scowl on her small face.

"What'd my daddy say to you?" I asked.

"You will address me as ma'am."

"Well, what'd my daddy say to you, *ma'am*?"

"He said that you're Betty Carpenter and you're sneaky."

"He wouldn't say that."

"Oh, yes he did." She picked up her yardstick from off her desk and smacked it against her palm. "He said you're sneaky and that I should keep an eye on you or else you'd sneak away." She ran two fingers through the air like they were legs. "You people are prone to bein' shifty, though, ain'tcha?"

She came over and swiped her finger on my bare arm. She looked at her finger as if expecting something to have come off.

"Why's her skin so dark, ma'am?" a girl at the far end of the class asked.

"Because she greases it," the teacher replied.

"I do not," I said.

"Yes, you do." The teacher stood over me. "You grease it and sit all day lazy in the sun, doin' nothin' but gettin' lazier and lazier and darker and darker."

"I don't grease my skin."

"You lie." She brought her yardstick down on the backs of my hands. I could feel the tears welling up in my eyes, but I would not let her see me cry.

"I'm gonna tell my daddy on you for hittin' me," I told her.

"If you do, I'll have your daddy dragged in here and he'll get beat, too."

"Will not."

"Oh, no? Test me, child, and see what happens."

She tapped the yardstick against her palm as she started explaining the difference between the jeans of twilled cotton denim and the roped genes of inheritance.

"Do you know what miscegenation is?" She pronounced the big word like it was a sin.

I shook my head.

"It means," she said, "that your father's genes and your mother's genes comin' together is unnatural. It's like stirrin' splinters in milk and sellin' it to the public. Would you wanna drink a jug of milk that had splinters in it, Betty?"

No, Mrs. Arrow.

"It'd be utterly unpleasant. Don't you agree, Betty?"

Yes, Mrs. Sword.

"And you must further agree, my little squaw, that you and your siblings are the splinters in our fresh, creamy, deliciously safe milk."

Yes, Mrs. Knife-in-my-gut.

I covered my face with my hands. When recess came, I was relieved to get outside and away from my classmates. While they swung on swings or spun on the merry-go-round, I walked out into the tall grass by the side of the building. It was the one place there at the school that reminded me of home.

"She is so weird."

I turned to the voice and saw a group of kids standing by the monkey bars. They were all staring at me. Ruthis was amongst them.

"Ain'tcha gonna swing on the bars?" one of the boys asked me. "They named after you. Monkey, monkey, monkey."

I looked at Ruthis, wondering if she remembered the red ball we'd once shared back and forth. I was about to ask her, but two girls started whispering in her ear.

"Do it," they said, nudging Ruthis forward.

"I can't." She turned around to them.

I knelt and said to the grass, "I don't wanna be friends with them anyways. I'd rather be friends with you." I ran my hands over the tall blades.

I was about to tell the grass how pretty it was when I saw an eye freshly carved into one of the trees by the spot Dad had parked the car earlier.

"The Fantastical Eye of Old." I ran to it.

The carving reminded me of the eyes Dad made for his wooden creatures, but I let myself believe that particular eye was not the work of his pocketknife. As I leaned in to stare into each of the eye's five pupils, I was shoved from behind. Falling, I reached out, but found no one to help me. My chest bounced against the ground. Even before I could lift my face, my skirt was flipped up while two kids held my arms.

"Stop," I said, screaming as my panties were pulled down to the backs of my knees.

"She ain't got one." I heard a voice.

The two holding my arms let me go. I quickly pulled up my panties and turned around to see it had been Ruthis who had pulled them down.

"She don't have one at all." Another voice came from behind her.

"Don't have what?" I quickly stood. My tears felt like fire on my cheeks.

"A tail." Ruthis looked away. "They dared me to do it."

"Why'd you think I had a tail?" I asked, gripping my skirt in case it was to happen again. "I ain't no cat or dog."

"People like you got tails," a boy said.

"Everyone says so," another one added.

"You stupids," I said. "I ain't got no tail."

The recess teacher blew her whistle and started calling everyone back inside. The group disbanded. Ruthis was the last to go, leaving me alone. I turned to look at the carved eye.

"You see what they did to me?" I screamed at it because I had to scream at something. "You didn't even do nothin'."

I picked up a rock and threw it, striking the eye in its five pupils. With nothing more to give, I walked back inside the school, keeping my hands on my skirt the whole way out of fear it would all happen again.

Even though not one of my classmates had seen a tail, by the time we got to our desks, everyone was whispering about what it had looked like.

"It had thick black hair and was as long as my thumb," one girl said.

I laid my head on top of my desk the rest of the school day. When the final bell rang, I ran past the buses. I saw Flossie talking to a group of girls who seemed to already be her best friends. Fraya was walking through the group of first graders. I knew she was searching for me.

I darted as quick as I could into the woods to get home. When I got there, Dad was building shelves against the back wall.

"You made me go to that horrible place," I said to him.

I ran back out, but he caught me in the yard and told me to calm down.

"I hate you." I banged my tiny fists against him.

"It's okay." He pulled me into him.

I buried my face into his shoulder and cried. "They said I have a tail. But I don't have a tail. I don't."

"Of course you don't, Little Indian."

He coaxed me to raise my face from his shoulder. He pinched the tears from my cheek like he was pinching off deer ticks.

"I was goin' in the woods to get me some ginseng," he said. "Wanna come along?"

I wiped my nose on his shirtsleeve before nodding.

"Let me get my bag." He stepped into the garage to grab his drawstring bag full of beads he had made out of twigs and branches.

"Ready?" he asked.

He held out his hand and together we walked into the woods. He pointed out trees as we passed.

"That one there is a blackhaw shrub, Betty. It's an Ohio native. The birds will eat the berries in the summer. And that's an eastern red cedar. Notice how the bark has been scratched. It means a buck has been by here, rubbin' its antlers. When you harvest bark—now remember this, Betty—you always peel it from where?"

"The side the sun hits," I said.

"That's right. And what roots should you always harvest?"

"The ones that path to the east."

"Very good."

"See? I know everything. I don't need to go back to school. Say I don't have to go back, Dad." I tugged on his hand. "Please."

"Ah, here we are." He broke away and walked ahead to the pawpaw trees, where the ginseng liked to grow.

Passing the immature plants at the bottom of the hill, Dad climbed up the steep side to the older plants, ready to be harvested.

"Help me find a ginseng that has three prongs," he said to me. "So we know this is not its first season."

I searched through the plants until I found three prongs. I made sure to count them aloud.

"That's right," Dad said. "You're a true ginseng hunter."

Despite the stiffening pain in his right leg, he lowered himself to his knees because this is what he felt was required of him. It was all part of his ritual in asking the ginseng its permission before he could dig it up. I dropped to my knees beside him as he closed his eyes and started silently moving his lips. I studied him as he did this. His brows were tightly drawn together, his concentration informing the way he bowed his head toward the earth rather than up to the sky. I wondered if I could ever speak to nature as deeply as he could.

Copying him, I closed my eyes and laid my hands on the ground. I didn't know what to say at first, so I let myself feel instead. The soft dirt pushing up between my fingers. The sun's warm light on my shoulders. The plants blowing in the wind and brushing against the sides of my legs. I became overcome by the feeling it was possible for my fingers to lengthen and turn into rivers and for my body to lay so still, it could become a mountain. My lips had started to move before I was even aware of it. I was asking the earth where it came from and telling it where I did. All of this circled back around to the ginseng, whose blessing I asked just before opening my eyes.

I found Dad staring at me with a smile.

"Let's begin, Betty," he said.

He first picked the red berries off the plant, dropping them into my hand. Using the screwdriver from his pocket, he dug around the roots until they were loosened, making sure to keep all the little hairs intact as he pulled the ginseng up. From out of his bag, he chose a bead. He squeezed it before dropping it into the hole.

"All right, Little Indian." He turned to me. "Put your seed in now."

Just as he had squeezed the bead, I gently did the same to the ginseng berries before dropping them into the hole. The berries would keep the ginseng population steady. The bead was Dad's payment for Mother Nature's blessing.

"We have thanked the earth," he said, filling in the hole.

On the walk back home with our harvest, Dad tore a small strip of bark off a tulip tree. We returned to the garage, which he had been converting into his plant workshop. He already had a counter space constructed and an additional shelving unit on the far wall. In the corner was a small wood fire cookstove he had put in and on which he would boil his harvests for a tea or a decoction that he would then store in one of the jars lining the countertop.

"I gotta get my tooth." He reached for the tin toward the back of the counter. Inside it was the tooth he had removed from the rattlesnake that had bit him as he was taking it out of my crib when I was an infant.

"The spirit of the rattlesnake is in this tooth," Dad said. "A spirit that almost killed me when the rattlesnake's fang pierced my flesh. That spirit is great power. *Hiss, hiss.*" He spoke like the rattlesnake.

I shook his gourd rattle while he filled a pot with river water out of the bucket on the floor.

"Always water from the river," he said. "Remember that, Betty."

He moved the rattler's tooth around in his mouth, hanging it out over his lip until I laughed. Then he carried the pot of water to the woodstove.

"To get as hot as the sun," he said.

As he put more logs in the stove to build the fire, I laid down the gourd rattle to pick up a pine branch. I dipped it into the water, dusting the droplets upon my forehead.

"Always water from the river," he said again as he ground ginseng root with his hammer. He dropped the root and leaves, along with the piece of tulip bark, into the water to boil, adding torn ginseng leaves to float on top.

From out of a tin can, he grabbed two dried pods from a honey locust tree. He released the pods into the boiling water. They would make the liquid sweeter. I figured he must be making the drink for someone who could not stomach a bitter taste. As he stirred the mixture, he continued his teaching.

"For chills, *Prunis virginiana* is good."

"Prune . . . knees . . ." I did my best repeating the name.

"Common name is the chokecherry."

"Good for chills," I said, to which he nodded.

"For fever," he added, "use *Castanea pumila*."

"Cat a . . ."

"*Castanea pumila*. Common name, dwarf chestnut."

He paused to look up at the spiderweb in the corner.

"You know you can use spiderweb to stop a wound from bleedin'?" he asked. "Remember all of this, Betty."

He stepped away from the boiling water to grab a tin of arrowheads. He chose one the color of the sandstone and dropped it into the pot.

"So the strength of the arrowhead will be given to the liquid," he said.

I listened to the arrowhead continuously clack against the bottom of the pan in the boiling water.

"I learn more from you, Dad," I said, "than I do from some stupid school."

He ladled the boiling mixture into a wooden cup and set it on the counter to cool.

"If you don't go to school, they win, Betty," he said. "They win like the war was just so damn easy all they had to do was push you down."

He removed the rattlesnake tooth out of his mouth and held it between us.

"It's like when I was bit by the rattlesnake," he said. "I thought I was beat, but what had bit me made me stronger. You're bein' bitten right now."

He took my hand in his and pricked my palm with the fang.

"Ow." I jerked back.

"You have to survive it, Betty."

"Can't." I rubbed my palm. "Ain't strong like you."

"You are strong. You just have to remind yourself." He picked up the wooden cup. "That's why I made ya this."

"It's only ginseng."

"And an arrowhead," he said. "That makes it the drink of a warrior."

He handed me the cup, still warm on the sides. I looked into the brown liquid and squinted my eyes from the steam.

"It'll burn my mouth," I said.

"It's cool enough."

Staring into the liquid, I watched it swirl before lifting the cup to my lips and slowly sipping the hot liquid. I drank until only the arrow-head and the piece of bark remained.

"You feel the spirit in ya?" Dad asked.

"I feel dirt in my teeth." I licked them as I set the cup down.

"But do you feel the spirit, Little Indian?"

"I don't know." I looked deep into his eyes. "How can I be sure?"

"I'll show you." He grabbed my hand and, mindful of his bad leg, started to jump. He laughed as if he had never before had so much fun. "If you just stand still, Betty, you'll miss somethin' extraordinary."

I jumped only a little at first, but my father's great big smile sent me higher and higher off the ground until we were jumping together like we could touch the sky.

"Do you feel it?" he asked. "Do you feel the spirit?"

"I feel somethin'," I said, feeling the thud of the landing.

"You've got to feel it all." He pulled me after him to run laps inside the garage.

"Do you feel it now?" He looked back at me.

"I feel more of it."

"You've got to feel it all," he said again as he broke us out of the garage. Still holding tight to my hand, he led us running into the field.

"Where we runnin' to?" I asked.

"To somethin' wonderful," he said.

Our feet beat in rhythm until we were moving so fast, I was certain I had lifted off the ground.

"I feel it," I said. "I feel it all."

And I did. Like something pouring into me, I saw colors streaking by. Blue, yellow, green. The sky, the sun, the grass. My school experience had put knots on my soul I was now able to run out to pasture. I felt a sudden affection for each thing around me, bucking back at the loneliness that had nearly overwhelmed me on the playground.

Ruthis and the others were somewhere else. I was certain I could hold the heaviest things in the world. Not stone or iron, but rather whorls and all the things that spiral and spin.

I was running so fast, I was passing Dad, and he was letting me, my hand slipping out of his. I circled the field before turning back to my father, who stood there with his arms open to me. I realized then that what we'd been running to was each other. I jumped up into his arms.

"My little warrior," he said, nuzzling his face into mine.

7

And the wild beasts of the islands shall cry
in their desolate houses, and the dragons
in *their* pleasant palaces.

—ISAIAH 13:22

Lint had the face of a child. He had the face of a child with the eyes of an old man. He had the face of a child with the eyes of an old man who was restless.

"September will soothe him," Dad said. "And all of Lint's fears will go before him like a fox runnin' off into the night."

Dad said this each new month as if the flip of the calendar's page was akin to opening a door. But when September arrived, slender enough to slip in between the tree branches, Lint came down with what Dad called the beetle shakes because of the way Lint shook like larvae.

"The boy is only four," Dad said. "Just a child. And children don't always believe they're seen unless they move. That's all he's doin'. Just movin' so we remember to see him. So we know that in this home, he is here with us."

As Lint continued to shake, Dad carried him outside to a fire he'd made in the field. By the fire's bright, orange flames, Dad warmed his hands. Then he laid them on Lint.

"I see ya, son," Dad said as he pressed his hands on Lint's chest. "I see you."

The shaking stopped first in Lint's right arm, then in his left.

"I see you."

It stopped in his legs before it stopped in his head.

"I see you."

When Lint was as still as the grass around them, Dad said, "Thatta boy. I see you."

Lint sat up and smiled. Perhaps Dad thought his son would be fine enough to move forward without ailment. That he would hold reason and that his laughter would say at least this much is true. But come Sunday, Lint had started to complain about animals inside of him.

"Under m-m-my skin," he said to Dad. "Movin' around. It itches and h-h-hurts. I feel deer antlers s-s-stickin', Daddy, stickin' in my back. A s-s-squirrel on my arm. A possum in my f-f-foot. Coyote st-st-standin' on my knee."

Wherever Lint would say there was an animal inside of him, Dad would blow on that part of Lint's body while mimicking the creature's call. When Lint told Dad there was a wolf in his elbow, Dad howled. When Lint said there was a tiger running up his back, Dad growled and bared his teeth. After Dad made the screeching sound of a hawk, Lint said that was the last animal.

Dad knew then that in loving Lint, there would be bridges to cross and they would not always be easy. In preparing for this, Dad said we were not to talk about our brother with outsiders.

"They'll only send him away," Dad told us when Lint was in the field foraging for rocks.

"Where would they send him?" I asked, unsure of who "they" were.

"To dwell in a house of scorpions," Dad said. "These scorpions will sting him until he forgets how to talk. More than that, they'll try to fix him, but all they'll really do is chase him out of this world."

Whenever Lint said he was sick with imaginary symptoms like sore eyelashes or spiders in his ears, Dad would treat him with remedies as if the illnesses were real.

"Promise you w-w-won't let the demons get me, Daddy."

Nights became increasingly difficult for Lint. He feared evil spirits were within five feet of him at any given time. Trustin oftentimes slept on the sofa downstairs because of Lint's chatter. Teas no longer helped ease his nerves, so Dad switched to coffee.

"Can't s-s-sleep," Lint said. "D-d-demons."

"You can't sleep," Dad told him, "because when you were born, I washed your eyes in water I had soaked a robin's feather in for three days. I wanted to make you an early riser, but I let the feather soak too long. Now you want to rise so early, you don't even lay down to begin with. There are no demons, son."

Still Lint cried out and reached for Dad.

"Daddy?" Lint asked. "Will you always b-b-be Daddy?"

"Of course," Dad answered with a nod.

"Will Mommy always be M-m-mommy?"

"Always."

"Don't wanna g-g-grow up. Don't wanna be a-a-alone." Lint clung tight to Dad. "I want to be with Mommy and Daddy f-f-forever."

We struggled to understand Lint. One minute he could be happy. The next, a shadow seemed to cross his face. Dad said it was something none of us could understand, but something we all needed to try to.

"It's not his fault if he cries or says things that are a little peculiar," Dad told us. "Dust enters into his ears and makes a great racket in his head. A racket we can't understand because we don't have to suffer it like he does. But he's still your baby brother. His feet still run to us. It's his mind that runs somewhere else. We have to be respectful of him. We have to understand that the things we do and say will affect him."

"Dad's right," Fraya said.

"We have to be a family for Lint," Dad continued. "I don't want any of you leavin' him by himself. He ain't gonna grow out of whatever it is that has ahold of him, if you don't spend time with him. If he's left alone, silence will feed his demons."

So we didn't leave Lint alone, but rather took him with us to places like the river.

"H-h-hell," he'd say, pointing toward the deep end. So he sat on the bank, splashing his small feet.

He enjoyed watching Trustin dive, so Trustin would climb up a tree, walk out onto a branch, and call to Lint, "Lookee at me, Lint. Lookee at me."

Lint always clapped as Trustin crowed like a rooster before narrowing his gaze on the water. Though Trustin was only five at the time, my brother was no more serious than when he was about to dive. The branch would slightly bounce under his weight as he propelled into the air. His legs perfectly together. His toes pointed as if he'd never been flat-footed in all his life. His body would be a straight line, directed by his arms and hands pressed together as if he were praying as he entered the water.

He would emerge on the bank where he'd shake his long black hair like a dog. The fray of his wet jean shorts clung to his thin thighs as he strutted along the bank, the sand pushing up between his toes.

"Man, that was a good dive." He'd congratulate himself. "Y'all see that?"

"Meh." Flossie would shrug. "I've seen better."

"It was good, Trustin," Fraya would be quick to say.

"Bigger splash," Lint always requested. "Make b-b-big splash, Trustin."

Trustin would climb the tree again, this time performing a cannonball. But even these were works of art. His arms carefully wrapping his legs as the sun appeared over the curvature of his spine. From the bank, Lint would clap and laugh each time the water splashed onto him.

Trustin would do this over and over again. Coming out of the river, his feet wet as he climbed the tree, each time saying, "This'll be my best dive yet. Wait and see."

"Yay." Lint would quack like a duck from the bank. "Big s-s-splash."

One particularly sunny afternoon, with Lint cheering him on, Trustin climbed higher than he ever had before. As he was about to crow like a rooster, his wet foot slipped.

His dives had been perfectly planned falls. But as he dropped through the air, the art of those dives was quickly replaced. His arms flailed as his legs kicked the air and his body contorted just before he hit the hard ground.

Me and my sisters hurriedly swam out of the water. Lint started praying on the bank for Trustin to be okay.

"Are you all right?" Fraya asked Trustin as she stood over him. She was out of breath. I wasn't sure if it was from the quick swim, or from the way Trustin was lying facedown.

"You dead?" Flossie nudged him with her toe.

"Stop that, Flossie." Fraya smacked her on the arm. "Trustin?" She turned back to him. "Can you hear us?"

He rolled over and stared up at the clouds floating above our heads.

"Just had the wind knocked out of ya, huh?" Fraya helped him sit up.

"Ain'tcha gonna say nothin'?" I asked him. "You get your voice knocked out of ya, too?"

He looked up at the tree he'd fallen from as if it was so very tall.

"Well," he said.

If we thought he would say anything more, we were mistaken as he stood and walked in the direction of home.

Funny thing was, Trustin hadn't screamed as he fell. When we told Dad later that night, he said it was a good thing we were around.

"A boy who falls that silently," Dad said, "needs someone around to scream for him."

8

They *are* all dumb dogs, they cannot bark;
sleeping, lying down, loving to slumber.

—ISAIAH 56:10

I lost whole afternoons to the hills, running into caves and kissing their cold walls. I splashed in the brown water of the ponds and swung on grapevines until I became dizzy enough to scatter like a light beam. Flossie, meanwhile, was kidnapping Corncob Diamondback.

Flossie loved movies. The drive-in and cinema were her favorite places on earth. As the movie played, she would copy her idols' gestures and facial expressions. She became obsessed with screen star magazines and their full-color photographs of actresses lounging on sofas at home.

"They all live in Hollywood, Betty," she said while flipping the pages of the magazines in my face. "I was born in California for a reason. I'm meant to live there. Not here in silly old Breathed. I need neon lights and white velvet."

Flossie thought if she kidnapped Corncob, she could buy a bus ticket with the ransom money. There was a reason she chose Corncob. He was the dog of Americus Diamondback. Flossie heard Americus had come from New York City in the 1930s. Every day he wore a three-piece suit with a Cottle watch in the pocket. He always had a cigar and wore a fedora garnished with the feathers of a golden pheasant. He carried *The New York Times* under his arm and read it daily on a bench in front of the barbershop.

Flossie knew Americus wore the same herringbone suit every day and that it was tattered and torn, but she didn't care. Nor did she care that he read the same *New York Times* from 1929 with the headline THE GREAT CRASH. His fedora had a rip in the side while the pheasant feathers had become broken quills. The single cigar was his only one. This was why he never lit it, though he would rest it between his lips as if he had. Americus was no richer than we were, but for a ten-year-old girl desperate to run away to her dream, it's easy to believe a man who used to be rich always would be.

It wasn't difficult for Flossie to capture Corncob. The dog was often in the fields, slowly searching for corncobs he would pick up and carry in his toothless mouth as he dug holes to hide them. Flossie wagged one of these corncobs until the dog came ambling toward her. She led him through the woods. It took her all afternoon. The animal had gotten as slow as all old things do. Flossie only rewarded him with the corncob once he was in the shed.

Throughout dinner that night, Flossie bounced in her chair. Dad asked her what she was smiling about. She crammed more succotash in her mouth and said, "Nothin'."

Later, after Mom and Dad had gone to sleep, I sat up in bed writing a poem about a girl shrunken to the size of a leaf.

She rides the acorn cap down the side of a hill, I wrote, *avoiding the wolves at the bottom—*

Flossie yanked my pencil out of my hand and tried to stick it up my nose.

"Get away." I slapped her off.

"C'mon. I wanna show you somethin'," she said.

"I'm writin'."

"Betty, what I have to show you is more important than one of your stupid stories."

"Leave me alone, Flossie." I growled like a dog at her.

"Fine." She growled back like a wolf. "I won't show you then."

She slid away with my pencil still in her hand. Stopping in front of our dresser mirror, she pulled her shirt up. When she placed my pencil on her bare chest, I asked her what she was doing.

"The pencil test," she said as if I was the stupid one for not knowing. "I read about it in a magazine at Papa Juniper's. You put the pencil beneath your boobies and if it stays there, then you're ready for a bra. But if it falls, you're still just a little girl who shouldn't wear anything more than flowers in her hair."

When she let go of the pencil, it fell and clinked against the floor.

"You're not gonna grow boobs tonight, stupid," I said.

She did the test a few more times before dropping the pencil for good. She stepped over it and pulled on my arm.

"C'mon, Betty. I wanna show you somethin' incredible."

"I'm not interested."

"It's alive." She widened her eyes.

"Alive?" I stood out of bed, wrapping the blanket around my shoulders. "You didn't tell me it was alive."

"I knew you'd wanna see it, Betty."

We peeked our heads out of our bedroom. Then we quietly slid our feet across the hall floor so as not to chance a creak of the wood.

"Don't you like bein' awake when everyone else is asleep?" Flossie spoke into my ear as we walked against the wall down the stairs.

Once outside, she tried to get under the blanket with me. I pushed her away and pulled the blanket tighter as she stomped ahead. She startled at the possum crossing her path.

"Funny how the night makes everything so spooky," she said as a gust of wind came and seemed to rattle the ground. In the distance, an owl hooted. Flossie walked even closer to me.

"You're scared," I said. "Scaredy-cat. *Meow, meow, meow.*"

"Shut up." She stopped and looked behind us. "Do you feel that?"

"Feel what?"

"Feels like someone is followin' us."

We heard a twig snap underfoot. Flossie breathed in deeply.

"You smell that?" she asked. "Smells like myrrh."

"Myrrh? What movie you see that in?" I asked.

"I really smell it."

"You know why it smells like myrrh, don't you?" I asked in my best ominous voice.

She shook her head.

"It smells like myrrh," I said, "because that's the odor one always smells when the man with the red belly is near."

"Why's he got a red belly?" she asked, darting her eyes from shadow to shadow.

"Because his belly is soaked with the blood of all the girls he's murdered and devoured in the middle of the night." I blew on the back of her neck. "You can always tell when the man with the red belly is gettin' closer 'cause the smell of myrrh gets stronger."

"Shut up, Betty," she spoke in a whisper.

"What's that movin'?" I pointed toward the darkness. "Oh my God. What is that, Flossie?"

"Stop it, Betty."

"I'm serious. There's somethin' out there. It's—it's—the man with the red belly!" I grabbed her.

She jumped and cried out. "Don't let him eat me."

When I laughed, it took her a few seconds to realize there was no real danger.

"I wasn't ever scared," she said, huffing as she walked ahead.

"You sure looked it." I skipped up by her.

"I was only perfectin' my fear face for all the horror pictures I'll be in one day."

Saying no more about it, she led me to the shed built onto the back of the barn. At one time, the shed had been constructed with an aviary. The screens were long gone, birds had not been there for years, and vines wrapped around the wood frame until it was partially collapsed. The shed had housed supplies for the aviary.

Flossie turned to me and laid her fingers against her lips before quietly unlatching and opening the door. A soft snore floated out from the darkness of the shed. Flossie pulled the string on the lightbulb. In the wash of bright light, my eyes first scanned the dusty shelves before dropping to the sleeping dog, his gray head resting on an empty birdseed bag. Before I could ask any questions, Flossie explained in detail how she'd trapped the dog and what her plans were.

"You're rotten," I told her. "Kidnappin' a dog just to get money."

"I'm not gonna hurt 'im or nothin'," she said. "Besides, maybe he likes the fame of bein' the kidnapped dog. We can be famous together."

She got down and wrapped her gangly arms around his neck, waking him. He did little more than yawn. While his mouth was open, she looked inside and said he only had one tooth.

"Must be a lucky tooth." She spoke to Corncob.

"He never barks or nothin'?" I asked.

"I think he's too old to remember how to," she said.

I laid beside Corncob and scratched beneath his chin. The corners of his mouth curled up as his back leg thumped the ground.

"I bet by tomorrow Americus will have a thousand posters up on every tree in Breathed," Flossie said. "How much you think he'll pay, Betty?"

"I'd say everything he has," I said as she nuzzled noses with Corncob.

"You really think so?" she asked.

"Sure." I nodded. "Dad says if you have a hard heart, an old dog will soften it. That's why they're so valuable."

"I wonder how you get a hard heart."

"Eat a lot of Lint's rocks, I guess," I said.

We giggled as we left the shed. Flossie talked more about how much money Americus was going to pay.

"Probably more money than I'll even need," she said, grinning ear to ear.

But Americus did not put up posters. What he did do was get a runt from one of the local hog farms to take Corncob's place. Flossie was so angry, she ran up and slapped the runt on the behind. Americus and Flossie locked eyes before she ran away.

"This is what we'll do," she said to me later that day after she'd sat on a tree stump and thought. "We'll take a photo of Corncob."

"We don't have a camera," I reminded her.

"Well, then Trustin can draw Corncob and that'll be just as good." Her voice rose in excitement. "Then we'll take the drawin' to Americus. Maybe he got the pig because he thinks Corncob is dead. We'll put a note with the drawin', askin' for fifteen dollars. No, wait. Twenty dollars ought to do it."

"Why you keep sayin' 'we'?" I crossed my arms. "I didn't kidnap him."

"I'll give you some of the money," she said.

Before I could answer, she threw in four marbles, a fireball, and the cracked turtle shell she'd recently found by the riverbank. That was a million dollars to a dirt road kid like me. We instantly spit on our palms and shook on the deal. When we went out to the shed to tell Corncob about the plan, we found him lying on his side. His mouth was open, resting in a puddle of foam.

"Have you been feedin' him?" I asked.

Flossie dropped to her knees by his side. "Yeah. I fed him biscuits and gravy just this mornin'."

"You leave him any water?"

She nodded to an old coffee can sitting under the shelves. Floating on top of the water was a small tin.

"Rat poison." I read the label to Flossie.

She quickly stood and looked into the murky water, then up at the shelves the water had been sitting under.

"The poison must have fallen off and opened in the water," she said. "When he got a drink, he drank poison." Her eyes widened. "He's dead, Betty."

"Dead?" I realized Corncob hadn't moved since we'd been there.

"Of all the things that could have fallen in the water, Betty. That box of buttons or those broken hat pins." She pointed these things out to me so I'd be sure to get her point. "Why the poison, dear sister? And why, after all these years? That rat poison belonged to the Peacocks. Hidin' on the shelf for decades. If Dad had found it, he'd have gotten rid of it. You know how he hates poisons. But it lay undiscovered, been here all these years, and just now happened to fall off the shelf. Why? I'll tell you why. It's the curse of the house."

She grabbed both sides of her face as though she was in a horror movie.

"Why'd you have to set the can beneath the shelves? It's your fault, Flossie."

"Is not. I didn't want the sun heatin' the water. It was nice and dark beneath the shelves. I wanted him to be able to get a cool drink."

She placed her hand over her heart.

"Oh, we'll have to bury the body so no one knows but us," she said.

"We have to tell Dad." I carried the can outside and dumped the water so nothing else could drink it.

"Please, Betty. If Dad knows, the boys will find out. The whole town will hear about it. I don't wanna be called a dog killer. Besides, if I go down, I'll say it was your idea to kidnap Corncob. An actress knows how to lie until everyone believes her. I was born on Carole Lombard's birthday. I know how to take on a role. C'mon, Betty. Please help me."

She wrapped her arms around mine and made her eyes large and teary.

"Fine." I gave in, stabbing my finger into her chest. "But you're diggin' the hole."

"Of course." She nodded. "I wouldn't have it any other way."

Together we lifted Corncob's body into the wheelbarrow.

"Wait." Flossie picked up the corncob she'd used to lure him. She placed it beside his body. "Everyone should be buried with somethin' they love."

We laid the shovel across the top of the wheelbarrow and pushed it together until we got to the railroad tracks.

"That way he can watch the trains comin' and goin'," Flossie said as she tried to hand the shovel to me.

I reminded her I wasn't digging the hole.

"But, Betty, I just painted my fingernails."

She held her nails up. She didn't have money for store-bought polish and she knew better than to use Mom's, so Flossie got the idea to melt our beeswax crayons. She used a cotton swab to apply the wax onto her nails. This left little strands of cotton sticking out of the wax after it dried, but you couldn't see such imperfections from far away.

"My nails are too pretty to ruin," she added.

"So are mine," I said, showing my bare fingernails crusted with dirt from digging for earthworms earlier.

Flossie rolled her eyes before reluctantly stabbing the shovel into the ground. The dirt was not soft, so she couldn't get the blade to dig deeper than a few inches.

"Please, Betty. Help me."

"I knew this was gonna happen," I said, grabbing the shovel's handle. Together we dug a hole wide enough for Corncob to be laid in it.

"I'm sorry, Corncob," Flossie said as we let his body slide down the side of the hole. "It wasn't supposed to happen like this. You weren't supposed to die."

She got the corncob out of the wheelbarrow and tossed it on top of Corncob's body.

"You think the old dog thought I poisoned him?" Flossie asked as we filled in the grave.

"You made him a bed and fed him biscuits and gravy. He wouldn't think a girl who does that would poison him," I said.

She raised her eyes to mine.

"Do you think it was painful when he died, Betty?"

I remembered the puddle of foamy saliva beneath his mouth. I quickly shook my head. That seemed to satisfy her.

"We should go now," I said before she could ask anything more.

When we got back to the barn, Dad was inside getting more nails to finish his work on cold frames he was building out of old windows.

"What you two doin'?" Dad asked as he stopped to stare at the shovel between us.

"A wild turkey got hit on Shady Lane," I said. "We took him into the woods to bury him like you always do when you see a dead animal."

"It ain't respectful to leave 'em to keep gettin' ran over," he said. "How'd you manage to lift such a heavy bird by yourselves?"

"We did it together," Flossie said before I could answer.

"Well, you two done right by the turkey. The earth will remember." Dad picked up a can of nails and turned to leave.

"What if there *is* a curse?" I asked, stopping my father in his tracks. "What if the dog—"

Flossie elbowed me.

"I mean the turkey." I avoided Dad's eyes. "What if the turkey dyin' is the first?"

"The first of what?" he asked.

"The first of all of us disappearin'. Like the Peacocks."

"Critters get hit in the road, Betty. It's not hocus-pocus."

While Dad hammered, me and Flossie headed out to A Faraway Place, where she had the broken turtle shell. Together, we lay back on the stage, staring up at the sky. We didn't say anything. We merely passed the shell back and forth, running our fingers down the crack until we closed our eyes.

9

In the midst of wolves.

—Matthew 10:16

Jack-o'-lanterns out on porches quick to greet me with a smile and triangle eyes. Grocery store candy rustling in bags while crisp leaves blow past the rake of the old man too weary to pile them. A single purple scarf carried by the wind down a dirt lane and a crow of no name flying overhead. This is October to me. A conquering circle of autumnal shadows, ghosts, and mothers.

That Halloween when Mom called me into her room to dress me in my costume, I walked in knowing exactly what I wanted.

"Cicadas," I told her. "I want to be a princess with a dress made of cicada shells. I want wings, too. Wings made of violets and—"

"And I want to be a queen with the vagina of a virgin," she said, "but that ain't gonna happen now, is it?" She applied a fresh layer of lipstick to her already red lips. "Anyways, princesses do not look like you, Betty. That mud-colored skin and stringy hair of yours. You ever seen a princess look like you?"

She laid down her lipstick and yanked me in front of her to face the dresser mirror.

"What do you see?" she asked, her reflection staring at my own.

What I saw in me was my father. The same black hair, the identical full brows. I had his strong jawline and nose. He would say the bones in our cheeks were the leg bones of the first deer. Our cheeks as close to the sky as the deer could leap. Then there was our brown skin. Something I would try to be rid of by making sacrifices to the river. They were sacrifices I thought the river would like. Cherry blossoms, tree bark, a pair of Mom's nylons. I even caught a cricket and threw her into the brown water. I thought the cricket would reach the edge, but she drowned before she got there. I hoped that sacrifice would be enough, so I jumped into the river and held my breath for as long as my lungs would allow. I believed that when I breached the surface, the water would have washed the color from me. The cricket drowned for no reason at all.

"Even if you were beautiful, Betty," Mom said, "you could not be a princess. A Carpenter cannot afford a crown or a throne."

She picked up an old robe that had been in the corner of Trustin and Lint's room when we moved in. After cleaning the house and throwing away most of the decrepit items, Mom kept the robe. It was the color of rust. The stains on it were like places where something once bled and broke away. In the front pocket was a mouse skeleton, partially preserved, the dehydrated skin clinging to all the tiny bones. The mouse was wrapped in yellowed paper with the words of Emily Dickinson written on it in shaky cursive, *Because I could not stop for death, he kindly stopped for me.* To remove the skeleton felt to be disturbing a grave, so we let the remains be.

"Aw, Mom, I don't wanna wear the robe," I said.

She yelled when she thought it took me too long to put my arms through the sleeves. Afterward, she placed a pillow against my stomach. While she closed and tightened the robe over the pillow, I asked her what I was supposed to be.

"A witch," she replied. "A she-monster. A female demon." She bared her teeth. "Also known as a hag, which is certainly somethin' a Carpenter girl can afford to be."

She oinked as she prodded my pillow belly with her finger.

"Nothin' more haggish than a girl who cannot control her appetite," she said before laughing as she grabbed a shoe box of dirty shoelaces from under the bed. She tied them into my hair, creating a series of tiny ponytails. From off a bedside table, she picked up a used match by the candle. She took my face in her free hand and dug her thumb-nail into my chin to keep my head steady while she used the match to draw on my forehead.

"I don't believe I've ever told you how my brother came to be in the ground," she said. "Brother was as beautiful as a sunset. If you would have asked me if he had any secrets, I would have said not one. Then came the day I heard sounds comin' from the attic."

Mom re-created the moans harshly like someone who's had too much to drink, yet that day I smelled nothing more than a peppermint candy on her breath.

"I followed the noise up to the attic," she said. "Of all the things I thought I'd find, I never thought I'd see my brother bent over a table, our neighbor boy behind him."

She pressed the match so hard into my skin, I flinched.

"At first," she continued, "I thought my brother might be gettin' attacked. Then I realized he was merely makin' love." She *tsk-tsked* with her tongue. "After I told Pappy what I saw, he forced Brother to eat the Bible, page by page, in order to swallow his sin. Brother fought back, but Pappy always was a strong man. Halfway through Adam and Eve's saga, Pappy had crammed so many pages into Brother's mouth, his cheeks were stretched full of 'em. Even after Brother choked to death, Pappy kept addin' pages until Brother's lips were forced open so wide, they started to tear at the corners."

She turned me to face the mirror. I stared at the reflection of the black eye she'd drawn in the middle of my forehead.

"All because of what I saw," she said, pressing her finger into the pupil of the eye.

She gave one of those deep chuckles that always made me think there wasn't anything more to do but run away from her. Before I could, she yanked me toward the closet. She handed me a pillowcase that had a border of embroidered June bugs.

"To hold your candy," she told me.

She studied me a moment longer, then drew with the match on my cheek. I tried to look in the mirror, but she stopped me.

"It's only a flower." She promised. "Now, get outta here."

The robe was long on my seven-year-old frame. Once I was outside, it dragged along the ground picking up dead leaves and other debris.

"I wish I was a princess," I chanted as I stepped out onto Shady Lane. It was crowded with candy hounds in all kinds of costumes. A whoopee cushion. A grandfather clock. A Chinese finger trap. Then again, maybe they were all just little monsters.

Gathered in the middle of the lane was a group of kids from my class. Ruthis was there. She stopped counting her lollipops when she saw me approaching. She snickered as she straightened the small tiara on her head. The gemstones were fake, but the tiara still made her a princess.

"Why you trick-or-treatin'?" she asked me. "I thought you only ate corn and cowboys."

She slapped her mouth as she did a whooping call. There are no small wars between girls. Everything is as epic as two wild birds sparring over the last worm.

"Oh my God, Ruthis, you're just so funny." I hooked a finger in each side of my mouth and pulled to make my lips wide as I crossed my eyes. "Look at me. I'm Ruthis. The world's *prettiest* girl. At least that's what the circus said."

"Kiss my ass, squaw," she said before spitting on the top of my bare foot. Her spit was colored red from candy.

I dropped my fingers from my mouth and stepped closer to her, tightening my hands into fists.

"Kiss your ass?" I asked loudly. "Ha. I wouldn't kiss your ass if it was dipped in chocolate God made Himself."

I'd heard Mom use that line once in an argument with Dad. I had been waiting for the chance to use it myself.

"Why you stringy-haired half-breed." Ruthis stepped closer to me. We were the same height, so the tips of our noses were touching.

She gritted her teeth as we kept our eyes locked. "I'm gonna—"

A boy dressed as his mother's rolling pin interrupted Ruthis. He was asking what was written on my cheek. Ruthis stepped back to see for herself. When she smiled, I realized my mother had not given me a flower after all.

"It says 'hag.'" Ruthis laughed the loudest of them all.

"She's a hag for Halloween?" someone asked.

"She's a hag all year." Ruthis snorted so hard she couldn't catch her breath.

The four Jubilee brothers came forth dressed as a barbershop quartet in their striped waistcoats, straw boater hats, and stick-on handlebar mustaches. They began snapping their fingers, a beat which got everyone around blowing into their candy whistles. The eldest Jubilee brother jiggled his hook-on bow tie and sang as his younger brothers provided the melody.

"Here in Breathed, there's a hag. Her name is Betty, she makes us gag. On her head, she should wear a bag. We would rather kiss a shitty rag than Betty, Breathed's famous hag of hags."

"Hag, hag, hag." Ruthis cackled.

"Shut up." I screamed over her laughter, and covered my ears with my hands.

When she didn't stop, I dropped my pillowcase and ripped the tiara off her head.

"Give it back." She latched on to one end of the tiara while I yanked on the other until the gemstones popped off.

"You dirty pig." She started to collect the stones. "I'm gonna tell my mother and father on you. They'll run you out of town. They say you're filthy. That you'll bring disease."

I bent the tiara until the thin metal snapped. I dropped the two halves to the ground in front of her.

"You don't deserve a crown, Ruthis," I said. "You're no princess. A real princess wouldn't say mean words to someone like you say to me."

Ruthis let the gemstones spill from her palm as she slowly stood. Narrowing her eyes at me, she straightened her pink princess dress as she tilted her chin.

"I don't need a crown to be better than you," she said with a smile. "Don't you get it? I'll always be better than you, Little Injun."

Ruthis led the chorus of laughter as I grabbed my pillowcase and ran back home. I huddled in front of the hubcap of the Rambler parked in the yard. I used my spit to wipe dirt off the chrome so I could see my reflection and the HAG Mom had written on my cheek.

"Why you cryin', Little Indian?" Dad stepped out of the garage.

"I'm not cryin'." I quickly wiped my tears away. "And stop callin' me Little Indian."

"What'd you write on your face there?" he asked.

He tried to touch my cheek, but I didn't let him.

"I didn't write it," I said.

"Who did?"

"Mom. She said she was drawin' a flower."

I slipped the pillowcase over the top of my head, hoping I could disappear into its white cotton and never be seen again.

"Then let's make it a flower," Dad said as he gently lifted the pillowcase off my head.

He was kneeling in front of me, despite his bad knee. He reached into his pocket and pulled out a match. He lit it only to blow it back out.

"It's not fair," I said as he used the blackened tip of the match to draw on my cheek. "Halloween is the chance to be someone else, but I'm still me."

"Who'd you wanna be?" he asked.

"Anybody but me, but I really wanted to be a princess of Breathed, with a dress made out of the shells of cicadas. But most of all I wanted a pair of wings made of violets."

"Ah, the reddest flower of 'em all."

"They're purple, Dad. You never remember violets are purple."

He laughed before saying, "You know, the Cherokee didn't have no princesses."

"It doesn't mean I don't wanna be one," I said.

He nodded. "When I was your age, I wanted to be someone else, too."

"Who'd you wanna be, Dad?"

"Someone important. You know why I call you Little Indian?" He stopped drawing and looked into my eyes. "So that you know you're already someone important."

He turned me toward the hubcap. In my reflection I saw that HAG was now the black heart of Dad's crudely drawn flower.

"Let's go get your wings, my princess," he said before scooping me up in his arms. He carried me to the silver maple in our front yard, where he set me on my feet.

After some searching through the fallen leaves, he picked up two. One was a blistering vermillion with golden veins. The other was a murky burgundy with curling terra-cotta colored ends.

"What you gonna do, Dad?" I asked as he stood behind me with the leaves.

"I'm gonna give you your wings, Little Indian. I'm sorry they ain't gonna be wings made out of no red violets, but if you ask me, leaves of a silver maple are the best damn wings to have."

He used tape to stick the leaves by their stems to the back of the robe.

"They ain't the wings of a princess," I said, twisting my head around as far as it'd go to see the leaves. "They're the wings of someone who can't afford feathers."

"Betty, you have to remember that other girls only get to be a princess for Halloween," he said. "Even then, these girls can only pretend to be a princess. But you're a real princess every day of your life. You come from a Cherokee king."

"Who?" I asked.

"Me. I'm a king. Didn't you know that about ol' Landon Carpenter?" I shook my head.

"I'm the mighty king of the garden," he said. "And that makes you a Cherokee princess. No one can take that away from you because it's in your blood."

He pulled up the sleeves of the robe and tapped the veins on the undersides of my wrists.

"In your blood," he said again.

"In my blood," I said, looking down at my veins as if I could see inside them. "But I thought you said Cherokee didn't have princesses."

"Don't mean you can't be one." He smiled.

As I stepped down Shady Lane, I tried to believe I was a real princess. I took each step as if my wings were real. The wind blew through my hair and the sun shone on my face until I felt as though I really did matter.

"I am a princess. I matter. I am important."

Then I saw Ruthis still laughing, and I realized the sun that shines on me would always have a cloud. Perhaps Flossie was right. Maybe we were cursed to the stations in our lives and could hope for no better. I wished then for Halloween to be over. For autumn to be gone. For the winter to come and freeze Ruthis' laugh until February, when I would be eight and perhaps old enough to become who I wanted to be.

I felt a hand gently grabbing my own. I looked down and saw Trustin. Mom had costumed him by setting a cardboard box on top of his head.

"I'll walk with ya if it'll make ya stop cryin'." He peeked out at me from under the box's flap.

"I'm not cryin'," I said, wiping my eyes. "What are you supposed to be?"

"A box." He grinned with pride at his costume. "Mom said boxes are the best thing to be 'cause everyone needs one at least once in their damn life."

He looked me up and down, then asked, "What are you, Betty?"

"I'm a—"

"Wait," he said. "I know what you are, Betty. You're an angel. Look at your wings."

THE BREATHANIAN

Same Gun Used in Mysterious Peacock Disappearances

It has now been confirmed that the gun used to shatter the front window of Papa Juniper's Market is of the same model shotgun on record as being fired into the walls of the former Peacock house amid their disappearance.

The news has created a profound stir in the entire community. The very mention of the Peacocks and their enigmatic vanishing causes a visible shudder through residents here. It can be said that the mother is scarce who does not caution her child away from what had been the Peacock residence, which is now that of the Carpenters.

"I remember when the Peacocks disappeared," local resident Fedelia Spicer commented. "It feels like the original poison is still present. Like it never went away. There's always been something sinister about the Peacocks going missing. Now, it feels like the same

snake has its mouth open once more."

With concern growing in the community, Sheriff Sands released a statement.

"With the facts as they are now, we can't separate the recent shooting from the Peacocks' disappearance."

With fear now permeating the air, many residents have taken up arms to protect themselves.

"I don't want to disappear the way the Peacocks did," said a resident of Red Possum Lane who wished to remain anonymous. The resident went on to give a theory of who they think the shooter may be.

"I can't trust someone whose face blends into the night," they said. "It's how I was raised to think and I still think the same. When there's no separation in the races, we have violence like this."

10

Fall into the mouth of the eater.

—Nahum 3:12

After that Halloween, I folded the robe and hid it in a corner of the attic. When I turned eight in February, I blew out my candles with the wish that the robe would turn into a princess dress more beautiful than Ruthis'. I ran up to the attic to see, but the robe had not changed. Grabbing a sleeve, I dragged the robe behind me as I walked out of the house. Stomping into the woods, I chose a path that had the most leaf litter. It clung to the fabric until it looked as though I was dragging nothing more than a fallen branch. When I felt I had walked long enough, I spit on the robe, cursed it, then buried it in an unmarked grave.

"You shouldn't have wasted your wish on that nasty robe, Betty," Flossie said. "You should have wished for a bra for me."

Ever since she turned eleven, a bra seemed to be on Flossie's mind more than anything else. She still failed the pencil test, but begged Mom for a training bra anyway.

"Oh, c'mon, Mom." Flossie held her hands together. "I'll die if I don't get one."

"You don't have no boobs for a bra," Mom told her.

"I've been prayin' for them, too," Flossie replied.

"Stop prayin' for an extra pound of flesh before you're ready to carry it," Mom said.

Flossie's prayer was finally answered in a package on her bed. She immediately tore it open.

"It's beautiful," she said, smiling so wide at the bra in her hands, I thought she was going to eat it.

"Happy now?" Mom stood in the doorway behind us.

"I love it." Flossie took off her shirt and put on the bra. She touched the small cream bow in between the cups, which were too big.

"I'll grow into 'em," she said before I could say anything.

Mom shook her head and went downstairs.

"I'm gonna show Fraya." Flossie darted across the hall into Fraya's room.

Fraya was sitting on her bed with her diary. I could see musical notes she had scribbled on the page. She was trying to match her voice to each.

"Lookee, Fraya." Flossie whirled in the room for her. "Ain't it beautiful?"

"You can't walk around in a bra, Flossie," Fraya said. "Your brothers will see you."

"So?" Flossie pulled at the straps, showing her first hint of discomfort.

"Never let your brothers see you half-dressed," Fraya said. "It's a sin. You'll make God scratch His own eyes out until He's blind for all eternity."

"There's no brothers around," Flossie said.

Fraya pointed at Lint's feet sticking out from under her bed. I bent down to see Lint placing a rock on the floor.

"Lint don't count," Flossie said, catching her image in the dresser mirror. She smiled at her reflection before leaning in to kiss it.

From that winter into spring, the bra became Flossie's prop. When she reenacted scenes from movies, she would take off the bra and use it to slap her imaginary male lead's face. Once warmer weather arrived in March, she would lay on A Faraway Place and sunbathe in the bra and a pair of shorts. Every time Fraya told Flossie it was inappropriate, Flossie would roll her eyes and say, "The bra is just like a bathin' suit top. Geesh, Fraya. You'd think you were a hundred years old."

Later that day, while Flossie was sunning herself, I sat on the stage, writing a story about the way Fraya had walked into the woods, carrying a small piece of paper in her hand.

The girl went off, I wrote. *No one knowing where to or why. She simply walked into the woods, disappearing behind the trees until I could no longer see her or the blue skirt of her dress.*

As I turned over on the stage to lie on my belly, my shorts were yanked down. I looked back to see my sister's grinning face.

"What are you doin'?" I pulled up my shorts.

"I wanted to see if you have a tail," Flossie said.

"You know I don't. Besides if I had one, you would, too. We're sisters, Flossie."

"We don't look it though." She held the strands of her light brown hair, twirling them around. "They say your dad's black."

"He's your dad, too, stupid."

"I don't know," she said. "My green eyes might be from a man who has movie star skin and a vault full of emeralds."

She put her shirt on before hopping off the stage. She said she was going into town to meet up with some girls at the movie house. She didn't ask me if I wanted to go. She never did when she was with her friends.

Once she was gone, I went inside the house to get one of the biscuits Mom had made earlier. On the kitchen counter was a pile of lemon pulp, but none of the skins. I found only an empty pitcher in the refrigerator.

"Mom? Where's the lemonade?" I called throughout the house.

Only the floorboards creaking above answered me. Grabbing one of the biscuits, I walked up the stairs. I found Mom sitting ever so straight on the edge of her bed. Her feet and legs were pressed tightly together. The lemon skins missing from downstairs were fastened with safety pins over the images of the lemons printed on her baby blue dress. On her head was the same bright yellow cellophane we would use to wrap our spring baskets each year. The cellophane was over her head, neatly tied at the front of her neck like the little scarf she'd wear into town when she wanted to look particularly fine.

I could see her face through the transparent wrapping. Her makeup was clownish. The bright red lipstick. The thick mascara. Two circles of blush on her cheeks like moons against the white face powder. All of it given a tint as if inside the cellophane there was a separate light, one that turned my mother yellow. I wasn't taken aback by seeing her with cellophane on her head. I was used to her filling up the tub and saying she'd rather drown than live. Her unplugging a lamp and wrapping its cord around her neck saying it was the last of her. Dad told us she didn't mean any of it. We thought he was right because she never carried through. The tub would be drained, the lamp would be plugged back in, and she would go on with whatever it was she had been doing before the incident took place.

I ate the last of the biscuit while I watched her breath steam the inside of the cellophane.

"I don't know how you're breathin' in there," I said, stepping closer.

I thought she didn't hear me, so I said it louder, but she still didn't answer.

"Well, Dad will be angry if I just leave ya like this," I said.

I untied the knot at her neck and took the cellophane off her head. The whole time, her eyes were fixed on the wall in front of her as if there was a thread between it and her.

As I turned to leave, I heard her voice but couldn't make out what she had said.

"What'd you say, Mom?" I asked.

"It was so beautiful in that yellow world."

I waited for her to say more, but she sat there as still as anyone I'd ever seen.

Out in the hall, I held the cellophane to my eyes. Everything was colored yellow from the wood floor to Trustin's charcoal drawings Dad had hung on the wall. The longer I stared through the color, I found these things dropping away until I stood in a field of tall yellow grass, gently bending from a breeze. It was as though it was a sweet and tender dream my mother had passed to me.

"It's so beautiful in this yellow world," I said just before Mom's scream pierced my ears.

I ran back into her room. I saw the blood first. Then I saw her on the floor, a sharp kitchen knife off to her side.

"Mom, what'd you do?"

Her wrists were cut. She trembled, curling herself into a ball. For all the ways she wanted away from life, she was absolutely terrified of what that meant. What was death to a woman like her? Maybe at that moment, so close to it, she worried death would be her over and over again. Her coiling up into herself until she could taste her own breasts and choke on her own thighs.

I slipped on the blood, falling forward into a puddle of it. I dropped the cellophane and grabbed her arms. Her hands seemed flimsy, like a ragdoll's. I held her wrists against my chest. I could feel her warm blood soaking through my shirt as her eyes rolled back and her head fell off to the side.

"What happened to the yellow?" she asked.

I picked up the cellophane and laid it over her eyes so her world could be beautiful again.

"I'll be back," I said as I got up. I thought she should know I wasn't simply running away.

Earlier, Dad had taken Trustin and Lint to the river to fish. I ran through brush in the woods, trampling twigs and pinecones. All I could think about was the color of my mother's blood. It reminded me of the beets she'd sent me out that morning to pick. She had given me a large yellow bowl and told me to fill it up with the first of the spring crop. Before I got to the garden, she yelled for me to come back.

"But I ain't got the beets yet," I told her.

"Come back," she said again.

I returned, showing her the empty bowl, to which she slapped me across the face.

"I told you to fill it up," she said.

"I was tryin', Mom. You called me back."

With a flick of her hand, she sent me on my way again. Once more, she called for me.

"Come back, Betty."

By the time I turned around, she was gone. I filled the bowl with beets until they spilled over the edges.

"Come back." I darted through the woods.

When I got to the river, I smelled smoke. I followed it upstream, where I found Dad. He was throwing fish meat into the flames of a small fire.

"We offer part of the fish to the fire," he was telling my brothers, who were faced in my direction and staring at me. "The fire will calm the anger of the dead animal's spirit. If you do not calm the spirit, it will seek revenge and take a new shape from the spilled blood."

"Like her?" Trustin pointed at me.

Dad turned and jumped at the sight of me.

"Where you hurt at, Betty?" He felt his hands up and down my arms, frantically searching for the wound.

"Not my blood," I said, pointing back. "Mom's."

Dad pushed past me as he yelled for us to throw dirt on the fire. We quickly scooped up handfuls, extinguishing the flames.

"Hurry up," I told my brothers. "We have to help Dad save our family."

The three of us ran as fast as we could.

"W-w-wait for me," Lint said. Trustin fell back to grab Lint's hand and yank him faster. I left both of them behind to try to catch up to Dad.

"Alka? I'm comin'." He continued to holler her name through the woods as if she could hear him.

Once we made it to the house, he took the steps on the staircase three at a time.

He found Mom unconscious on the floor of their bedroom. Dad slid in the blood and fell on his front side, crawling the rest of the way to her. My brothers stopped just behind me. Lint started shaking and crying, so Trustin pulled him back out into the hallway.

"It's okay, Lint," I could hear Trustin saying. "Why don't you show me what new rocks you have in your pockets?"

I watched Dad lay his hands over Mom's cuts. The blood oozed out between his fingers.

"Stop squeezin' her skin like that, Dad," I told him. "You're squeezin' more blood out."

That was what I thought. That his hands were squeezing her like she was a sponge.

"Call Doc Lad, Betty," he said.

Instead of going to the phone, I dragged Mom's stool across the floor to the back right corner of the room, where a large spiderweb stretched.

"What you doin', Betty?" Dad asked. "Call Doc."

"I'm gettin' the spider's web. Remember?" I climbed the stool and reached toward the corner, but I was several feet away from it. "You said you can use webbing to stop a wound from bleedin'."

"Dammit, Betty. Call Doc Lad. Now." He yanked the bedsheet off and wrapped it around Mom's wrists.

I jumped off the stool and darted past my brothers in the hall. I could hear Lint whimpering as I ran downstairs. I grabbed the pad of paper off the table by the phone. I searched through the names and numbers written in my mother's cursive. When I found Doc Lad's name, I put my finger in the rotary dial, counting the excruciating seconds for the dial to spin all the way around.

"My mom's cut herself," I said as soon as Doc Lad said hello. "There's red everywhere. Dad's got the sheet off the bed around her wrists, so she's gonna be awful angry when she's able again. Angry at him for ruinin' the good bedsheet."

"That Landon Carpenter's voice I hear in the background?" Doc Lad asked.

"Yeah, that's my dad," I said. "He's yellin' that you best bring somethin' to save her 'cause he don't think he can."

"This all happenin' on Shady Lane?"

"Yes."

"I'm on my way."

While waiting for Doc Lad, Dad told me and my brothers to go outside.

"You shouldn't be seein' this," he said.

Lint didn't stop running until he was out of the house and in the yard, where he moved his hands against the grass blades. Trustin spent the entire time drawing swirls with his finger on his arms as if he was making symbols with which to ward off evil spirits, or at the very least, keep the moment from settling into his soul.

I ran out into the drive, where I waved with both arms even though Doc Lad was not yet in sight. It wasn't long before I did see the front of a car. I jumped and waved bigger. He was driving so fast, rocks spit out from the back tires as he took the turn into our drive.

"She's upstairs, she's upstairs." I continued shouting as Doc Lad got out of the car with his black bag. He ran toward the house. I ran in step with him. "She's upstairs, she's upstairs," I kept saying.

I stopped at the foot of the porch steps as if it was a threshold I could not cross, while Doc Lad disappeared into the house.

"Be careful, there's a knife m-m-monster in there," Lint said after him.

My brothers closed in on either side of me as the three of us stared at the house, waiting.

"I wonder what they're doin' up there?" I asked at the very moment we heard footsteps booming down the stairs.

The screen door flew open and Dad came out of the house, carrying Mom. Doc Lad got ahead of them in order to open the rear door on his car. I stared at Mom as they passed. Her eyes were closed and her legs swung lifelessly.

"Where you goin'?" Trustin asked them.

At first, it appeared they were all leaving. Doc Lad got in the driver's seat while Dad carefully laid Mom on the backseat. But after Dad closed the door, he backed from the car.

"Doc Lad didn't give us no s-s-suckers," Lint said. "He always g-g-gives us suckers. Is he mad at us because of the b-b-blood?"

Trustin wrapped his arm around Lint as we watched Doc Lad drive away with our mother.

Once the car was out of sight, Dad turned to face the three of us. All we could do was stare at Mom's blood on him.

"Is she dead?" Trustin asked.

"No." Dad quickly stepped over to us, pulling us each into him. "She's not dead. All you have to remember about this day is that your mom was picklin' beets. The juice got all over her wrists. That's what the red is, kiddos. Just beet juice. She's gonna be fine."

Later that evening, me and my brothers would talk about the way our father's voice had cracked on the word "fine."

Dad didn't go to bed that night. He started cleaning the house instead. Husbands always do that. They think as long as the house is clean and the work done, their wives will be happy as if all the joy of life centers on a washed floor. In the days following, Dad finished several furniture pieces that had been works-in-progress and arranged them in the house until the rooms looked like a country sampler. He built a small dressing table for Mom all while he told us we were not to excite our mother when she returned. If the dishes were dirty, we were to wash them. If there was mud on the floor, we were to mop it up straightaway. We were to be silent children who stayed out of our mother's hair, as if that would be enough.

"When's Mommy c-c-comin' back?" Lint asked.

Dad never had an answer so he relied on saying, "Soon, son. Soon."

While Mom was away, Fraya dropped out of school. Dad was so disappointed, he painted the top step of the front porch black.

"Because a step has died here," he told Fraya.

"Steps don't die, Dad," she said.

"It died, Fraya, because you stopped walkin' up it to a better life."

"They're just porch steps, Dad. They get us in and out of the house is all."

"You know when folks have called me stupid," he said, "don't you know I've felt it? All because I'm a full-grown man with a third-grade education. It's a bitter place at the bottom of the steps, Fraya, and I should know. I've spent my whole life down here, only able to stare up to the top. You know what's there at the top?"

"What's there?" Fraya asked.

"It's a good look at the world," he said. "You're able to see all of it. From there, you get to decide which part of this great big world God made just for you. But by droppin' out of school, Fraya, you'll never climb to a better life at the top of the stairs. You were gonna be the first person in our family to be able to say you were educated. You didn't have to leave school. This isn't what your mom would want for you. You can still go back. I can paint the step white again. Resurrect it. Steps don't have to die forever."

"It's important I take on more responsibilities here around the house," Fraya said. "Mom is in need of help, don't you think, Dad?" She looked over at the black step. "I reckon that step ain't never been alive for me in the first place anyhow."

Fraya fell effortlessly into the role laid vacant in Mom's absence. She wore Mom's aprons and would pass through the house with a cloth in her hand as if she was a newly minted soldier in the war against dust. Dad did most of the cooking, but there was something about Fraya in the kitchen that made it seem as though she had done all the work. The way she ladled the hot soup in our bowls. The way she delivered the bread, warm from the oven, to the table. Through it all, she tended to Lint as if she had more mothering instinct inside her than she would ever need.

"I think you don't want Mom to come back at all," Flossie said to Fraya one day as the three of us stood in the kitchen. "I think you just wanna be everyone's mother."

Fraya took off Mom's apron and picked up the knife Mom had used to slice her wrists. She stepped outside through the screen door. I started to follow her but Flossie grabbed my arm.

"Are you crazy?" Flossie said. "She's gonna kill us with that knife. Our blood is probably gonna be her sacrifice to some god in exchange for a golden apron."

"Don't be stupid," I replied. "It's Fraya. She ain't gonna hurt us."

I ran out the door to catch up to her. Flossie hesitated, but soon joined. When we got to A Faraway Place, Fraya was already sitting cross-legged on the stage.

"What took you two so long?" she asked.

"Flossie thinks you're gonna stab us," I told Fraya as I sat beside her.

"It's only natural to think such a thing when girls are carryin' around knives," Flossie said as she flopped down.

"You think I'm gonna kill ya, huh?" Fraya asked Flossie before stabbing the knife into the stage.

Flossie jumped. Fraya looked at her before cutting a long slit in the wood, followed by another and another.

"They're cuts to match the ones in Mom's wrists," she told us. "If we carve out the wounds here on the stage, they'll heal faster on Mom."

Me and Flossie watched Fraya cut deeper into the wood with the knife before Flossie said, "I wonder why Mom did it anyway."

"Obsessed with sadness," Fraya said, shrugging.

"Is that what Mom is?" Flossie asked. "Obsessed with sadness?"

"It's what Leland said all women are." Fraya looked up at us. "But he's usually wrong about everything."

Fraya laid the knife off to the side.

"Now that we've put the cuts here, they won't have no choice but to heal."

Flossie didn't mock Fraya like I thought she might. Not even when Fraya told us to lay our hands with hers on top of the cuts. Flossie did so without hesitating. When me and Flossie noticed Fraya's fingers were trembling, we thought it was part of the power, so we trembled our fingers, too.

"I want Mom to come back." Fraya spoke directly to Flossie. "Just because I'm helpin' around the house don't mean I'm tryin' to take her place. Isn't she more than housework? Than the food on the table? Me doin' those things ain't bein' Mom because bein' her is somethin' only she can do."

Fraya started to sing. Me and Flossie joined in on the chorus.

"Momma, come home, we love you so. The house is cold without you, the flowers won't grow. We miss you dearly, we send you a kiss. Momma, come home, we love you so."

I sang loud enough to be off-note. The lyrics me and Flossie didn't know we made up, overlapping each other's voices.

After that night, we continued to visit A Faraway Place and sing over the cuts because, like Mom, we needed to heal, too. We thought our efforts had worked because when Mom came home, we didn't see the wounds on her wrists. They were behind bright white bandages.

"They're healed," Fraya told me and Flossie. "The cuts are far away. The bandages are only to keep out the sunlight so the scars don't shine and reopen. We have to make sure Mom never tries to hurt herself again. We'll continue to sing over the cuts on the stage every day. It's our responsibility as daughters."

We hoped that by our power, Mom's bandages would be removed. But they were still on when Leland appeared on our doorstep saying he'd gotten kicked out of the military.

"They tried to say I took things that weren't mine," Leland said. "They didn't have no proof, though. Best they could do was to give me the boot. Thought I could stay here for a bit."

He made the attic his bedroom, not doing much more than sticking bugs in his chewed gum on the walls.

With us all together, Dad decided a family picnic could lift the shadow that seemed to be cast over everything. He chirpily led the way through the woods behind our house. He held Mom's limp hand and swung the basket with his other as we followed.

On the way, Lint collected so many rocks, he ran out of room in his pockets so he started to drop rocks in mine, Fraya's, and Dad's pockets. He put some in Flossie's, too, but she took them out and dropped them when he wasn't looking.

Dad had a nice spot for our picnic. He spread out a white cotton blanket. He put food on Mom's plate, but the most of anything I saw her eat was a piece of biscuit.

"That's nice, Trustin," Fraya said when she saw the drawing he was working on. It was a still life of the picnic itself. To add color to the drawing, he pulled up grass blades and rubbed them on the paper until it was stained green.

"Do I look all r-r-right for a picnic?" Lint asked no one in particular as he rolled a rock over his shirt.

Flossie nudged me every time Mom moved.

"How much you wanna bet she tries to hang herself from one of these trees?" she whispered in my ear. "Or you think she'll stab a fork in her throat?"

I turned to see Leland offer a piece of Dad's jewel pie to Fraya.

"Want some jewels?" he asked her.

When cut, the pie exposed multicolored gelatin cubes suspended in pink gelatin. The dessert was Fraya's favorite. She always ate around the cubes, then lined them up on her plate.

"What beautiful jewels," she would say before popping them into her mouth, swallowing them whole as if her body was a vault guarding sapphires, emeralds, and rubies.

She never turned down a slice of that pie, yet when Leland offered it to her, she said she was full. He stared at the slice for some seconds, before eating it himself.

I felt a sudden jab in my side. Flossie's elbow was pressing into me. She nodded toward Mom, who was picking up the jar of pickled beets.

Mom turned the jar, reading the label that noted the date of the batch. Without warning, she poured the beets and their juice out onto the blanket. I had never before been aware of the way white cotton can stain, so sudden and beautiful.

Dad lifted Mom up and said we were all going to take a walk. He held tight to her hand as we got farther under the canopy of trees.

"Look up," he said.

When we raised our eyes, we saw lemons.

"Oh, my." Mom smiled. "You gave me my beautiful yellow world."

There were lemons dangling from maples, oaks, and sycamores, elms, walnuts, and pines. Trees that had never in their life borne such yellow fruit. This color stood out against them and was so grand, it was hard not to think the lemons were some sort of jewelry. It was like a dream. I wanted to savor it. I traced the edges of the lemons with my eyes. The yellow, so bright against the blue of the sky. In many ways they were like small orbs broken from the sun. They seemed to emit their own light.

Surely there are not so many, I said to myself, yet it felt as though my father had called all the trees in the woods to him and left his word on each one of them.

I reached my hand up toward one of the lemons. I thought of picking it, then worried the whole of them would come crashing as if they were all connected to the same stem, the same dream, the same pleasant moment I did not want to end.

"But why are they here?" Fraya asked.

"Because a long time ago," Dad said, "a girl once told me how nice it'd be to have a grove of lemons all to herself." He smiled at Mom. "I gotcha your lemon grove," he told her.

I didn't know what money Dad had bought all those lemons with. Nor did I know how he managed to hang them without great complaint about his rotten knee. But knowing such things would only have ruined the dream. None of those details mattered to Mom, either, as she pressed up against his side until I could no longer see her wrists.

Behind the lemons, a red balloon floated up into the sky.

"Ol' Cotton never misses a letter." Dad said what we were all thinking.

In 1935, Cotton's wife, Vickory, was beaten and hanged in a honey locust tree on the edge of Breathed. Vickory had been impaled on the honey locust's thorns, her arms forced out as if it was just another Sunday night crucifixion. By the time we were taking our walk beneath the lemons, it had been decades since they'd hanged her. Ever since then, Cotton had written her at least one letter every day. He would roll the letter up and put it inside a balloon he would fill with helium and release.

One time I found a balloon deflated on the ground. Cotton had written the letter inside as if Vickory had never been murdered. About the children they never had. About the life they never got to live:

My Hickory, Vickory tree,
Today our youngest stood in front of the preacher under
Papaw's magnolia. Our boy is marrying a wonderful gal, don't you
think? You certainly embarrassed him by crying so. You made my

handkerchief so wet I thought it was gonna come undone. Simply come undone. You baked our boy's favorite for their wedding cake. Your heart-stopping honey lemon cake with raspberry frosting, so sweet to our tongues. We had quite a time keeping the bees away though, didn't we?

My feet are furious at you for all that dancing you put them through, but I must say my heart is not. Why you still choose to dance with me after all these years, I will never know. I'm fearful, not of death, but of heaven. Why, you ask? Because I know you'll never ask me to dance there. No. You'll be waltzing with Hypatia and Sappho, the poets and philosophers, and God. All your favorites. I'll be in a quiet temper in the corner. I'll be in hell while I'm in heaven. But for now, I have you. I have you, for now. Tonight, we'll make love and share the same dream. Come tomorrow we'll sleep late and take a drive on the edge of Breathed. Will you be there? Please, be there. I may go mad.

A kiss on your heart from mine,
Your piece of Cotton

With racial slurs carved into Vickory's flesh, there wasn't much doubt about why she'd been killed. Cotton had been born and raised in Breathed and was as white as that which he was named after. Maybe those were the reasons they didn't hang him in that tree, too. Or maybe it was because you don't get the same thrill hanging a man as you do a woman.

"If she would've lived, he wouldn't have written her a single letter," Mom said, already gone from Dad's side a little more than she was before. "We think they were so in love 'cause she died in the midst of it, but if she would have lived they would either be divorced or unhappily married. They most certainly wouldn't be in love."

I think it was at that very moment all the lemons dropped from the trees at once and we looked to be strangers of no importance to one another at all.

II

And the stars of heaven fell unto the earth.

—REVELATION 6:13

That May of 1962, Flossie found a book about witchcraft that had been left in the house. The book was titled *The Dictionary of Souls*. On the inside cover, there was a hand-drawn illustration of a witch dragging a bag marked "souls." According to the directions written in black ink on the bag, if you wanted to find out if someone was a witch, you wrote their name on a slip of paper that you then put into a hot pan. If the paper did not burn it meant that person was a witch. Me and Flossie decided to give it a try. We headed into the kitchen, where Trustin was sitting at the table. He had loose paper and was sketching the way the flour, sugar, and tea canisters were lined up on the counter. Just when I would think he was a serious artist, he'd swipe his charcoaled fingers above his lip, giving himself a black mustache.

"*Bup, bup, bup.*" Trustin pretended the mustache had turned him into an old man as he spoke with a deep drawl. "Back in my day, God wasn't no more than four years old." He said the thing Dad would say when he was feeling ancient.

Both me and Flossie rolled our eyes at our brother as we set a cast-iron skillet on the stovetop. Trustin let us tear strips from his blank paper in order to write all the names we wanted to test. It wasn't a surprise that some burned slowly.

"Your turn now," Flossie said to Trustin as she dropped his name into the skillet. "Hey, Betty, remember when Dad told us about those wild boys who murdered that woman 'cause they thought she was a witch? Corn came from her blood after they killed her. If either of you is a witch, I'll kill you and see what comes from your blood."

Trustin stopped drawing to look at his slip of paper. It blackened into the pan.

"Might be nice to be a witch," he said. "I could turn you two into a couple of ugly toads. Oh, wait. You already are." He made a witch cackle until we pushed him back.

He continued to smile as he grabbed his art, leaving me and Flossie alone in the kitchen.

"Time for your name, Betty," she said.

Flossie laid the slip of paper in the middle of the skillet. She prodded it a few times with the spatula, then eyed me when the paper did nothing.

"Well, *Bell, Book and Candle,* you're a witch, Betty," Flossie said.

"I can't be a witch. I'm only eight. The pan's not hot enough."

"It was hot enough to burn everyone else's name, witch." Flossie dropped the spatula so she could hold her fingers up in a cross at me. "I'm gonna tell Dad you're a broom hag."

"No you won't," I said, shoving her hard.

She bumped against the countertop.

"You stinkin' shrew." She shoved me even harder. Before we knew it, we were entangled in one of our famous Carpenter sister brawls. We ended up on the floor, rolling across it and hoping to scratch each other's eyes out. As I was biting her arm, and she was trying to pinch off my nipples, Fraya came rushing in.

"You're gonna burn down the whole house." She used a pot holder to shove the smoking pan back. When she looked into it, she asked, "What is this you two burned?"

I knocked Flossie off and quickly stood to look into the pan. The piece of paper with my name on it was a black crisp.

"I told you I ain't no witch," I said to Flossie.

The strap of her bra had fallen. She pulled it up, then checked her hair. I had yanked it out of its ponytail. Her broken rubber band was on the floor along with a few strands of her light brown hair.

Flossie glared at me as she got a new rubber band from the drawer and tied her hair into an even higher ponytail. We both had bite marks and scratches up and down our arms. It was a known fact that the one with the most scrapes lost. We silently counted each other's badges of battle. Unable to determine a clear winner, neither of us said anything more. Instead, we both went to the window to see what Fraya had turned to look at.

"Dad's makin' his moonshine." She smiled at us. "Let's take a jar."

"Hell, yeah." Flossie perked up.

Seeing Flossie's excitement, Fraya added, "As long as we remember liquor is the devil melted."

"How we gonna get a jar?" Flossie asked, ignoring Fraya's warning.

"One of ya will have to get Dad's attention." Fraya looked at me. "Betty, it should be you."

"Why me?" I asked.

"'Cause you're his favorite," Fraya said.

"She is not." Flossie folded her arms while Fraya shooed me out through the screen door and onto the back porch.

"Keep his attention," Fraya said to me. "Flossie and I will sneak into the barn while you do."

I headed toward Dad, who was dumping his fermented brew of sugar, corn, and yeast into his homemade still. He had at one time sold moonshine when we were in Arkansas. Folks would stop by our house to buy some. One day the sheriff showed up, saying he'd heard Dad had been dealing in the illegal liquor business. Dad told the sheriff it was nothing more than tall tales and that he was welcome to search the property if he liked. So the sheriff, along with his deputy, walked around our yard, which was covered in large rocks Dad had placed in rows.

"What's with all the rocks?" the sheriff asked Dad.

"Oh." Dad rolled back on his heels with a grin. "I'm a rock farmer."

Dad had dug holes in the yard, placed the jars in them, then covered the holes with rocks, hiding the moonshine. The sheriff and his deputy had been walking on top of the moonshine that whole time and didn't even know it. Dad eventually stopped selling the liquor. He did, however, continue to make small batches for his own use.

Dad always made the moonshine with a look on his face like he was *makin' somethin' real special,* or so Mom always said. I saw this very look as I stepped to the barn and watched him take a spoonful of the brew. He held a lighter to the underside of the metal, smiling at the clean blue flame coming off the mixture.

"Woo-wee. That'll turn ya honest," he said, stepping over to his makeshift table, which was a piece of board supported by cinder blocks. The tails of two squirrels he had skinned earlier were left on top of the board. Dad always used every part of an animal. He even ate the squirrel brains. He'd boil the skulls in tomato juice, where they would toss in the rolling red bubbles. When Dad cracked the skulls open with his hammer, he did so delicately, peeling back the pieces of bone until he could pull the brain out whole and pop it in his mouth.

"Mmm-mmm. Don't I feel smarter." He'd chew and chew.

I approached the table where the squirrels' tails were. Dad would later prepare the hair to become bristles of paintbrushes for Trustin.

"Can we save one of the tails to put on the antenna with the raccoon's?" I asked Dad as I leaned against the table.

He raised his eyes and saw the scratches on me.

"You and Flossie been fightin' like rabid dogs again, I see," he said. "One of these days you two are gonna plain devour one another. Only the serpents will be happy then."

He came around the table.

"You get taller from yesterday?" He had his hand up and was using it to gauge my height.

"I don't think so." I looked at my legs to see for myself.

"That's the thing with kids," he said. "One day you're all small enough, I could lose ya down the bathtub drain. The next minute, I have to remember you were ever so small."

I stepped away from the table to sit in the yard far enough from the barn for my sisters to slip into it unnoticed.

"You got a story today?" I asked him.

"Don't I always? And it's a real good one," he said as he slowly sat beside me.

He had to angle his right leg to accommodate his knee while Flossie and Fraya made a quick dash to sneak in through the barn's side door.

"You ever hear of the Restless Star Catchers, Little Indian?" Dad asked.

Before I could answer, there was the sound of glass breaking in the barn. Dad started to get up, but I grabbed his arm.

"Tell me about the Restless Star Catchers," I said. "Who are they?"

"You didn't hear that noise?" he asked.

"I didn't hear nothin'." I imagined all the things Fraya and Flossie could have broken in the barn. "What's a Restless Star Catcher?"

He looked one last time toward the barn.

"Must have been hearin' things," he said, relaxing back. "Now, where was I?"

"You were about to tell me about the Restless Star Catchers."

"Oh, yes." He nodded as if ready to discuss something quite serious. "The Restless Star Catchers. They're restless 'cause they can never stop flyin'."

"Why can't they?" I asked.

"Because they have to catch stars, which have a habit of fallin'. In fact, one fell right here to our patch of Shady Lane last night."

I looked past Dad to see Fraya and Flossie had managed to make it out of the barn with a jar of moonshine. From the wood line, Flossie waved for me to hurry and follow them. Her ponytail bounced as she stepped back and disappeared after Fraya among the trees. Dad turned to see what I was looking at, but he saw only the blowing leaves.

"Where did the star fall, Dad?" I asked.

"Oh, well, right here by the barn," he said, pointing the spot out.

"I'd show the star to ya, but I had to give it to the Restless Star Catcher. You sure you never seen one, Betty?"

I nodded.

"Then you're really missin' somethin' special," he said. "They're beautiful black lions the size of our Rambler."

"That big?"

"That big," he said. "I could barely believe it myself. At first, I thought I might have been dreamin', so I walked around his giant paws and reached out to touch his thick, cold fur. I could smell the billions of years he had lived. It smelled like the earth after a heavy rain. When I looked into the lion's eyes, I saw no pupils or irises. His eyes were compasses. The arrows contantly spinnin', tracking the location of several things at once."

Dad touched his chin as if stroking a beard as he said, "His mane was the most spectacular part of him. The way it swirled and moved like dust, but not regular dust. This was the stuff of the universe. Little silver sparkles that constantly spun and was so alive, I started cryin'."

"But why, Dad?"

"Because it was so beautiful. I think the lion wondered why I was cryin', too, for he just looked at me a moment. Then he spoke and it was deep and gentle."

"What'd he say?"

"That he had come for the star. He picked it up with his large paw, then laid it on his back, where the star was absorbed into his fur, disappearin' into the black. I thought he would leave as quickly as he had appeared. Instead his mane started to lift and divide itself. One half went out to the right, the other to the left. I thought his mane was large before, but it started growing even larger, lengthening into feathers that were simply the sparkling spirals of the dust. His mane had become his wings.

"'Are you gonna fly away now?' I asked the great lion.

"'I can fly you to the moon to see a very special tree,' he replied.

"Well, hell, I wasn't gonna miss the chance. I climbed up on his great big back and held on tight as he kicked off the ground. His wings made out of his mane left trails of light as we soared. I looked down at the world I was leavin', before turnin' my eyes onto the space I was enterin'. When the moon came into view, it was spectacular, Little Indian. He flew us into one of its deep craters, where a massive tree grew. The tree had blood-red bark with golden hieroglyphics. Hangin' from the branches were purple bells of glass in which stars ripened. The lion told me I was the first human to see the tree and to pick of its fruit.

" 'But you may only pick what is unripe,' he told me, 'for no star can live on earth, but what is meant to be a star most certainly can.' "

Dad reached into his shirt pocket and pulled out a cratered rock.

"This here is the unripe star I picked," he said, passing the rock to me.

When he pulled up his pant leg, he showed me a purple discoloration on his right kneecap.

"I banged my bad knee on that big ol' tree trunk as I was climbin' it and got this here bruise." He laid his hand on his knee. "When folks ask why I limp, now I can say I busted my knee climbin' the tree of stars."

I looked closer at the purpled discoloration. It was the same staining he had on his fingertips from the blackberry jam at breakfast.

"Ain't no star," I said, holding up the rock. "Just some river litter you got from Lint. And that ain't no bruise. It's just you playin' around with jam."

"I never thought you'd ever stop believin', Little Indian." His voice seemed crushed beneath the weight of the sadness setting his brow. He dropped his eyes as if the ground could have an answer.

"I believe you went to the moon, Dad," I said, but it was too late. He put his weight on his left leg and slowly stood.

"Naw," he said, "it's like what ya said. It's just a rock. Nothin' more. It is silly to think I could ever fly to the moon, huh? Not an old Mr. Nobody like me."

I had put another crack in an already broken man.

He dropped his shoulders as he turned to walk away. I wondered where his path might lead him, then Lint came running out of the house.

"It bit me." He held the back of his hand.

"What did?" Dad rushed to his son.

"A rattle-s-s-snake." Lint let Dad see his hand.

The wound was nothing more than two red lines Lint had drawn on his skin with a red marker.

"It hurts, Daddy. H-h-help me." Lint moaned in pain.

"Let's get ya all healed up," Dad said, reaching into his pocket and pulling out his sack of dry tobacco. He put some in his mouth and chewed on it for a few seconds.

"The tobacco will help draw out the poison," Dad said before putting his mouth to the two red marks.

As Dad pretended to suck the poison out, I squeezed the rock and stepped into the woods, looking for my sisters. Almost immediately, something jumped onto my back and sent me crashing facefirst to the ground, knocking the rock out of my hand.

"Gotcha." Flossie shouted in my ear as she pressed her weight into my back.

"You possum face," I said. "Get off."

Flossie laughed as she stood.

"You took forever," she said.

I saw Fraya standing against a tree. She was holding a jar of moonshine.

"I told her not to surprise ya, Betty." Fraya sighed. "But you know how Flossie is."

Flossie stuck her tongue out at Fraya.

"You guys see where the unripe star went?" I asked as I got up.

"Unripe star?" Fraya looked around.

"There it is," I said, spotting it at the edge of a blackberry thicket.

I headed toward it, but Flossie grabbed my arm.

"Are you turnin' into Lint now?" she asked. "It's only a stupid rock. C'mon. Fraya's gonna show us an eagle."

Fraya had already taken off running, the skirt of her lavender dress flying up like a playful spirit. She was leading us through the woods to a pine grove of ancient dark trunks and sharp needles that made me think of all those fairy tales of girls being eaten by wolves.

"The nest is up there." Fraya stopped and pointed toward a towering pine.

Each of us stared up at the large gathering of twigs built into the fork of two branches.

"Dad says the eagle flies higher than any other bird," Fraya said as she cradled the jar. "He says most folks think it's a vulture that flies the highest. But they're wrong. It's the eagle. Dad says it's why their heads are white. Eagles fly so high, the tops of their heads touch heaven and turn the feathers white in how holy that touch is."

The mother eagle screeched. She had returned and was circling above the treetop.

"Give me some of that, will ya?" Flossie yanked the jar of moonshine out of Fraya's hand and immediately took a drink. "Woo-wee," she said afterward, making a pained face.

Keeping her eyes on the eagle, Fraya got a pencil and a piece of paper out of her dress pocket.

"I come out here to write my prayers," she said as she tore the paper evenly into three pieces. "You two can write your prayers, too. Then the eagle will fly 'em up to God."

"Ain't no bird gonna give God nothin'." Flossie smacked her lips.

"She will." Fraya looked at the eagle as if they were old friends. "Dad says so. That means it's true."

Fraya looked ready to cry at the thought. I realized then that not only did Dad need us to believe his stories, we needed to believe them as well. To believe in unripe stars and eagles able to do extraordinary things. What it boiled down to was a frenzied hope that there was more to life than the reality around us. Only then could we claim a destiny we did not feel cursed to.

"I believe," I told Fraya, taking the pencil and a slip of paper from her.

I wish I was an eagle to fly Fraya's prayer to God, I wrote.

I handed Flossie the pencil. She rolled her eyes but yanked her slip of paper from Fraya anyways.

"I pray to be a star and live in Hollywood and be more famous than Elizabeth Taylor," Flossie said her prayer as she wrote it.

Fraya quietly took her turn and made sure to write her prayer with her back to us.

"Let me see." Flossie tried to peek at what Fraya wrote. "Don't be so secretive."

Fraya would not share a single word with us and swiftly folded the paper up.

"Now they have to go into the nest," she said as she collected mine and Flossie's prayers.

I tugged on Fraya's skirt once she started to climb the tree.

"What if the eagle mom comes back?" I asked her. "She'll claw your eyes out, Fraya."

"It's okay, Betty girl." Fraya smiled. "I do this all the time. She lets me."

I reluctantly released my sister. When she reached the nest, she carefully tucked our prayers amongst the eggs.

"The eagle's gettin' closer, Fraya." I gripped onto the tree trunk as if I could shake her down. "Come on."

She started to leave the nest just as the eagle released a cry.

"Watch out," both me and Flossie yelled as the eagle flew, talons first, toward Fraya.

Fraya had no choice but to let go of the tree and fall the rest of the way. She landed with a thud on her backside. Flossie started laughing so hard she was snorting like a pig as I helped Fraya stand up.

"I'm fine," Fraya said, looking up at the eagle now standing in her nest. "We can leave now. She'll deliver our prayers where they need to go."

Fraya took the jar from me and had a long drink. She scrunched her face and grabbed her throat as she remarked how fiery the 'shine was.

"This is gonna burn our insides up," she said.

"I don't mind." Flossie tried to grab the jar.

Keeping hold of it, Fraya ran out of the pine grove. Flossie was on her heels. I stayed behind to watch the eagle step through her nest and count her eggs.

"One, two, three," I counted with her.

Satisfied, the eagle took flight, unknowingly carrying one of our prayers with her. As she flew, the paper dropped. I waited for it to fall through the branches.

"I've got you," I said to the prayer, catching it just before it landed on the ground. As if it were a butterfly I was frightened would fly away, I slowly opened my hands, peeking in at the paper. Carefully reaching in, I unfolded the paper and immediately recognized Fraya's cursive.

I want to be free. Please set me free from him, I pray.

"Him?" I asked. "Who's him?"

I remembered back to a song Fraya had written. It was about a boy who had snakes for fingers.

Hissin' and slitherin' up and down my body like sin. It's as if he ain't eaten since the Garden of Eden.

I slipped the paper into my pocket before running to catch up to my sisters. They were outside the pine grove, fighting over the moonshine.

"Betty ain't even had any yet, have ya, Betty?" Fraya handed me the jar as Flossie tried to capture it herself.

I slapped Flossie back and took a quick drink.

"It feels like I swallowed the sun," I said in between coughing.

We laughed and shared the jar the rest of the day as we swam naked in the river and danced through the hills. Fraya, who was eighteen at the time, had drunk nearly half the jar herself. I could only stomach a sip here and there, most of which I spit back out. Flossie, eleven years old and determined, worked her way into longer sips. By the time we came upon the tractor in the field, it was dark and we were as drunk as three sisters can be without falling over. Fraya walked against the tractor, running her hand along its side as she said she didn't think the shooter was any of us.

"I think it's Betty." Flossie showed all her teeth while balancing the jar in her hands.

"Ha." Fraya slapped her knees. "Don't you think someone would notice an eight-year-old girl carrying a big ol' shotgun? Besides, why would Betty shoot a gun?"

"Maybe only 'cause she don't have a bow and arrow." Flossie stuck her arm up behind her head like a feather.

"You're Cherokee, too, stupid." I pinched her arm.

"But your problem is you actually look like one." She pinched me back.

"Ain't a girl shootin'," Fraya said. "It's some damn man who ain't got nothin' better to do." She laid her cheek against the tractor as if trying to inhale it. "Wolves are out this hour. They'll smell our breasts and want to see them. We best get home."

With the three of us putting our drunken heads together, we started in a direction we were sure was the right one. Along the way we passed a church. It was the only building between what appeared to be never-ending fields of corn. We pressed our faces against one of the church's windows. There was one lamp on inside, lighting up the image of Jesus on the cross.

"The place is empty." Flossie smiled. "Let's go in and turn all the crosses upside down. When the preacher gets here tomorrow mornin', he'll think all his sins have done caught up to him."

Me and my sisters giggled at the thought as we pushed the front doors open. At the time, the church was never locked. That would mean the preacher didn't trust his flock. How could they then trust him?

"Knock, knock, are ya home, God?" Flossie asked, marching up the aisle.

It was our first time stepping into the church. Dad believed God was in the woods more than He was ever in a building.

"Don't need to sit in a pew to get the word of creation," Dad would say. "All ya have to do is to walk the hills to know there's somethin' bigger. A tree preaches better than any man can."

The church was paneled from floor to ceiling in narrow oak boards. There were ruffled brown curtains on the windows and burgundy carpet on the floor. By the lectern was a wood table on top of which sat an unlit candle.

Fraya reached into her pocket and pulled out a cigarette and match. As she lit the cigarette, she kept her eyes on the candle.

"To keep the demons away," she said, holding the flame of the match to the candle's wick until it started burning.

"That little ol' candle ain't no angel to us," Flossie said. "It ain't gonna put out enough light to keep the shadows away, let alone no demons."

She walked closer to the flame but tripped on her own feet. Falling forward, she caught herself on her knees while the jar of moonshine flew from her hand and rolled across the carpet. The remaining moonshine spilled, soaking the fibers under the table.

"I was gonna drink that." Flossie cursed and walked the rest of the way to the first pew on her knees. She pulled herself up on the seat.

"Girls and women ain't allowed in the first pew," Fraya told her in a voice mocking the preacher's. "Don't you know that, Flossie dear?"

Fraya walked over to hand her cigarette to Flossie.

"The first pew is where I wanna sit," Flossie said.

"You gotta sit in the back with all the other females." Fraya deepened her voice even more as she sashayed back to the lectern. "And ain't no girl or woman alive should wear pants, Betty." She pointed at my overalls. "Don'tcha know that's a damn sin?" She caught herself on the lectern, draping herself over it. "I do believe, my dears, we have drunk too damn much."

"Daughters in the back row. Sons in the first," Flossie said, frowning. "Ain't we got mouths? Ain't we got hands? No one thinks we'll do much with 'em. I hate anyplace boys get to do anything they want. Hell to 'em. We got an eagle all to ourselves to fly our prayers up." She raised her arms. "We have the power of the eagle mother and—and—well, I—I kind of forget what I was sayin'."

"I know what you're sayin'." Fraya kicked the lectern. It fell over on its side. "They take everything from us, even when we say no."

She unbuttoned her dress and stepped out of it, leaving her slip on.

"I don't feel so good," I said just before vomiting on the nearest pew.

"Ain't you a gas." Flossie made a face at me as she stood. With the cigarette held in the corner of her mouth, she wobbled toward the wall where there was a wooden cross. She turned it upside down. Then, perhaps fearing for her soul, turned it right side up again.

"I have to go to the river," I announced loudly. "I'm gonna vomit again. I have to go to the river so it'll carry it away."

"No wonder a woman is mostly anger," Fraya said, staring at the dress in her hands. "There's no room for happiness. Not after they get done with us."

I felt my way up the rows to the first pew, where I laid my dizzy head down.

"Eve ate the apple," Fraya said as she picked up the candle. She took her time staring at the flame before a smile crossed her lips. "Well, good for Eve, because the first thing we learned from that tree of knowledge was how to start a big goddamn fire."

"Fraya, don't," I said.

"We have to prove we can burn things, too, Betty," she said. "If we don't, the beasts will rule the world."

Her eyes widened as the flame reflected and flickered in her pupils. She tilted the candle, causing the hot wax to spill out as fire and fabric made contact. The cotton became engulfed, the smoke curling up toward the ceiling.

"It's so bright." Flossie laughed, then covered her mouth as if she wasn't sure whether the fire was funny or scary.

Once the flames started to crawl up the fabric toward Fraya's hands, she let go. We held our breath as the candle and dress fell onto the moonshine-soaked carpet. In an explosion of light, the flames fed on the liquor, growing larger and more devastating.

Fraya grabbed the vase full of wildflowers off the sideboard.

"Go out, you stupid fire." She dumped the water from the vase onto the blaze. The wildflowers spilled out, burning on contact.

"You're not gonna get the fire out." Flossie threw the cigarette into the flickering orange flashes as she danced around them. "It's the curse. We're all cursed."

"You're not supposed to use water to put fire out, Fraya," I told her as she yanked me up from the pew by my arm. "You know you have to use soil."

"We gotta get outta here, Betty." She pulled me down the aisle, all the while yelling for Flossie to follow us. Flossie continued to dance as she took her ponytail out. Her long hair glided across her back as she swayed from side to side.

"Dammit, Flossie. I said come on," Fraya said again.

Flossie ran up behind us giggling. When the three of us were safely outside, Fraya let my arm go.

"What have I done?" she asked as the flames reached up to devour the white cross on top of the steeple.

Flossie cheered and clapped. I pushed her out of the way and ran toward the church. I got as close to the inferno as I could without becoming ash. Reaching into my pocket, I found Fraya's prayer and threw it into the flames.

"Betty, look out." Fraya screamed as fiery beams crashed beside me.

I was knocked to the ground, where I could feel the heat coming off the grass. I thought I might lay there and melt. Then I felt hands wrapping around each of my arms. My sisters were saving me.

As we escaped up the nearby hill, I kept falling, but my sisters kept lifting me up. We were all breathing so hard, I didn't know how there wasn't something that came from our exhales, like a great wind or a flash of lightning.

We collapsed once we got to the top of the hill, where we watched the blaze. We knew one of the nearby farmers would see the fire soon, and call the sheriff.

"Damn this night," Fraya said, picking up a small rock and throwing it off the side of the hill. When she figured the rock had made it to the bottom, she asked me why I was running toward the fire.

"You could have burned up, Betty," she said.

"I'll tell you why she did it," Flossie answered for me, "because she's drunk off her ass."

The three of us listened to the fire truck's horn in the distance. While my sisters kept their eyes on the flames, I kept mine on the smoke.

"Smoke is sacred," I said, believing if smoke could carry fear up to the clouds, then it could carry Fraya's prayer farther up, to heaven.

12

The hills melt, and the earth is burned.

—Nahum 1:5

Even after bathing that night and washing my hair, I could still smell smoke coming off my skin like it lived there now. I lay in bed with my damp head and listened to Fraya's Japanese music box play from down the hall in her room.

"Goodnight." Her voice floated to me and Flossie.

"Goodnight," Flossie replied.

The silence waited for me.

"Goodnight," I said before closing my eyes to see three sisters. The orange flames. The dark night. The white boards of the church blackening to ash.

The most Flossie said about the fire was to melt an orange crayon and paint her nails. She would leave marks on the wallpaper from where she dragged her fingernails along as she walked. More marks were on her pillow from how she slept with her hands tucked under. I'd started to catch her running her nails on empty spaces of paper, drawing little orange streaks I realized were an inferno.

Fraya wouldn't even admit we'd been out the night of the fire. Then one day, about a week after the incident, she grabbed my hand and led me out of the house. I thought she might be taking me back to the eagle for another prayer.

"We're goin' to Papa Juniper's," she said when I asked.

She bought us each a bottle of pop, along with a pail of crushed ice. She placed the bottles in the pail to keep the pop cold as we walked up into the hills and sat in a meadow of tall grass the same color as the green dress she was wearing. She took the bottles out of the pail, then reached her hand into the ice.

"I feel somethin', Betty," she said as she moved her hand toward the bottom. "There's somethin' in here."

She dumped the ice out onto the ground. We watched a small orange roll out.

"God is meltin'," Fraya said as we watched the ice go to liquid in the sun. "But the orange is still so very cold."

She picked up the orange and held it to her sweet, soft cheek.

My sisters had their own way to accept what we'd done. Mine was to go into my parents' bedroom, where my mother's nylons were. She had enough to make a soft pile in her drawer, her extra garter belt lying on top. She bought nylons that had the seam running down the back. A line that traveled up her leg like a snake too honest to coil.

The nylons would hold the shape of my mother's calves and feet. I would sometimes put the stockings on my arms, thinking I could still feel the warmth of her body from when she'd last worn them. Most of the time, I would drape her nylons across the seat of the vanity chair so they hung from the cushion. I'd then lay on my belly beneath the chair, the stockings dangling and grazing the floorboards as if they were her legs.

I would perch my face in my hands and knock my heels as I hummed, imagining my mother sitting in the chair above me and putting her makeup on. Despite my mother's moods, I wanted to be close to her, at least to be in her orbit during the feminine routines that were still baffling to me at that age. I found comfort being at the feet of the stockings while imagining my mother sitting in the chair above me, tweezing peach fuzz off her cheeks.

This was the sort of comfort I pined for in the heat of the fire. I pushed the deerskin hanging in my parents' bedroom doorway aside, and stepped into their room. Mom was downstairs rolling out dough for noodles. I tiptoed to her vanity and opened the top drawer, lowering my hand beneath the nylons. I liked to feel their thin fabric against my flesh. It was like dipping my hand into a sea my mother kept as her little secret.

I usually never reached so far back. Flossie had warned me Mom fed on serpent tongues and kept a sealed jar of them in a drawer.

"If you so much as touch the jar, you'll go mad like Mom," Flossie swore. "You'll start eatin' serpent tongues, too, until only the things with forked tongues will ever love you."

Flossie told me Mom moved the jar into a different drawer each night, which was why I tried to never feel blindly into a drawer. But that day, the nylons were so very soft. I closed my eyes and let my hand sink deeper. It wasn't long before my fingertips brushed against something.

Had I found a serpent tongue fallen out of the jar?

I wrapped my hand around what I felt. When I pulled it out, I discovered it was a stack of identical photographs inside of a stocking. The image was of a little girl in a dark dress with a big cream bow, which dropped from a sailor collar. The girl was thin, her arms hanging awkwardly at her sides. Her pale hair fell forward across her small shoulders and down into her even paler face. She was not smiling. Her gray eyes almost looked white in the photo, but I could still see the fear in them. She seemed to be the type of child who could startle at the sound of rain. It was then I noticed her two fingers were crossed as if she was making a prayer.

Standing beside the girl was a man who looked to be in his twenties. His arms were straight by his sides. I took the photo over to the sunlight. I wanted to see the man's face clearer. There was something familiar in it. The bold but hard stare. The white-blonde hair. I instantly despised his clenched jaw. Something about him reminded me of bitter herbs.

"Who are you?" I asked the man in the photo as if he would come alive to answer me. He was wearing high-waisted work pants, suspenders, and a button-down that I could see the undershirt sticking out of.

Like the girl, he wasn't smiling, though he was looking straight at the camera, almost daring it to preserve his image. In body, he was a man. But in spirit, I knew he'd be a wolf.

I carried the photo downstairs. Flossie was in the living room, dancing to *American Bandstand*. Lint sat on the sofa, coloring little red dots all over his skin.

"What's the red dots, Lint?" I asked.

"F-f-fairy bites," he said. "I got 'em in the woods."

"Ain't he s-s-stupid?" Flossie mocked him as she kept dancing around us.

"I am not s-s-stupid," he said to her. "It's true, Betty." He looked up at me. "They are fairy bites. Most folks think it's m-m-mosquitoes bitin' 'em, but go catch one and you'll see. You gotta l-l-look close enough and you'll see it's really a tiny fairy, her teeth sharp as k-k-knives."

"C'mon, Betty." Flossie pulled on my arm and tried to get me to dance with her. "You don't wanna hang around Lint. His stutter might be c-c-contagious."

Lint made a face at her as he colored a large red dot on his arm.

"I can't stay," I said, breaking free from Flossie and heading toward the hall.

I went into the kitchen, where Mom was cutting dough she'd just rolled.

My mother always cooked barefoot. She was forty-two at the time, but seemed younger when she was bare-legged. Just a girl, really, who would stand with one foot on top of the other when she concentrated, as she was then.

I tried to tell what type of mood she was in. After she cut the dough, she put the knife off to the side and used her hands to delicately separate the noodles. She was humming. When she started to sing aloud, I knew it was okay to step closer to her.

"Who's this little girl and man?" I asked in a particularly sweet voice as I held the photo up for her to see.

When she saw the photo, she immediately slapped me across the face. I inhaled the small cloud of flour expelled from her palm.

She turned back to the noodles and I saw how her pale hair fell into her face. I studied the little girl in the photo and saw how her pale hair did the same. The girl had seemed stuck in time, incapable of aging one day more than the moment the photo had captured her in. And yet, that little girl had grown up. She stood before me, unraveling noodles to dry.

I wondered if my mother and I had grown up together as two girls, each no older than the other, if we would've been friends. I knew she would have been so quiet, I would have had to do all the talking. I could have taken her to A Faraway Place. Maybe we would have shared secrets there. Covering our mouths and whispering softly.

Mom set the timer for the noodles to dry. Only once the ticking began did she speak.

"Pappy's thirty-two there," she said. "A young man, if ever I'd seen one."

She dusted flour off her hands. When she began to peel potatoes, she told me to put the photo back where I'd found it.

I backed up so I would be out of reach of another slap as I asked, "Why you have so many copies of the same photo?"

She inhaled sharply, but didn't have the anger I expected as she said, "You can only step on somethin' so long before it disappears beneath your heel."

When she started to cut the potatoes into chunks to be boiled, I carried the photo back upstairs.

Instead of returning to my parents' bedroom, I followed the humming I heard coming from down the hall. It led me to Fraya's bedroom, where I found Leland propped against her wooden headboard, his legs stretched out on her bed. He had his boots on. Their dirty soles were leaving mud on Fraya's blanket. He hadn't noticed me yet and was still humming. I recognized the song as being one of Fraya's. I watched him a few seconds longer as he ate pickled beets out of a jar.

"That ain't your bed," I told him. "It's Fraya's."

"*That ain't your bed.*" He'd repeated what I'd said, trying to make his voice sound like mine. "You need to stop bein' such a pest, Betty. Why don't you worry about your own damn bed."

I stared at Grandpappy Lark in the photo. His eyes were the same eyes looking back at me from Fraya's bed.

"Why you frownin' like that?" Leland asked.

When I didn't answer, he patted the bed.

"C'mere," he said. "Tell me your newest story, Betty girl. I promise not to ruin the endin'."

I ran into our parents' room. I couldn't move quick enough putting all of the photos into the stocking. When I was placing it back into the drawer, I discovered more photos in a different stocking. I knew they were photos my mother had already stepped on. I could tell from the way the images were faded until I could see nothing more than the outlines of the trees. I closed the drawer, feeling as though I had found the serpent tongues after all.

On my way out of the room, I looked out the window and saw Fraya sitting on A Faraway Place. I whispered her name as I ran outside to her. The closer I got to the stage, the louder her singing became.

"Demons and angels, they spell my name, in fire and halo it all feels the same." She sang the lyrics she'd written herself. *"I thought you'd open me like a song. Boy was I wrong, boy was I wronnnggg."*

I climbed up onto the stage and sat beside her.

"You sing like a honeycomb," I told her.

"I do?" She turned to me. "Hey, Betty, you got a fallen eyelash."

She pressed her fingertip against my cheek, picking up the fallen hair.

"Your fingers are stained red," I said.

"I was eatin' pickled beets." She held the eyelash in front of my mouth. "You get to request somethin' from the wishin' well."

I looked over her shoulder and saw Leland standing on the porch. He held his lighter to a cigarette. Just as the end of it lit orange, I closed my eyes and blew the lash off my sister's finger.

THE BREATHANIAN

Devil Blamed for Shootings

The preacher has suggested the shooter is none other than the devil. He says this revelation came to him when he was buying a shiny new shovel from the hardware store.

"I come in to get a shovel to dig the hole for the best dog I ever had," the preacher said, "when I see a monstrous face reflected in the shovel's blade. I looked behind me but no one was there."

The preacher believes that, due to the church fire and the contin-ued blasts of gunfire, our town is falling victim to sin.

"I've fought the devil no less than seventeen times," the preacher added. "I know when he's around. He likes to gnaw on hearts and rob you of your soul. I suspect the devil is shooting Breathed because he knows we're straying from our good Lord. I invite everyone to our evening prayer. We need to pray this devil away before evil blooms on all sides of us."

13

He that troubleth his own house
shall inherit the wind.

—Proverbs 11:29

Dad's traditional tobacco plants bloomed toward the middle of June. We would pinch the blossoms off with our thumbnails, squinting when we did because after a while the tobacco stung our eyes like cutting an onion would.

After harvesting, we spread the blossoms out in the sun so Dad could oil them with animal fat. The flowers would dry all day, after which Dad chopped them into fine pieces. Unlike the leaves of the tobacco plant, which Dad smoked in rolling paper, he would save the dried blossoms to use in the soapstone pipe that had been his mother's.

"Blossoms are so darn pretty, they deserve somethin' better than the leaves," he'd say, content with the pipe in his mouth and the smoke from the flowers filling his nostrils.

Trustin and Lint were still young enough to sit at Dad's feet and pretend a stick was a pipe. Flossie called them babies for doing so, but when no one was looking, me and her would put sticks in our mouths, too. Dad tousled our hair and said it was all fine and good to pretend to smoke, but that we should wait until we got more than half a century on us before we smoked a real pipe.

"Save your lungs to run the fields with," he'd say, looking out at the garden, ever watchful on its yield.

Summer was a busy time for him as he grew herbs and harvested wild plants for his growing list of customers. Not only did Dad make recipes for what was becoming a fine business, but he also had to do the same for Lint and his fake ailments. Just that morning, Lint had started clenching his hands, saying they were turning into talons. He held his fingers at such an awkward angle, they did look akin to the nails of a hawk. Dad got his spoon and filled it with a decoction that he held over Lint's head.

"Get out of my son, you predator of the sky," Dad said as he flew the spoon toward Lint's mouth in a motion mimicking a diving hawk. "Take your spirit and fly away from here. This body is not yours, Hawk. My boy's fingers are not your talons. Find them where last you lost them, but do not find them here."

Dad lowered the decoction to Lint's mouth so he could drink. Sip by sip, Lint's fingers uncurled and his hands relaxed. The boy was back and the hawk was nowhere in sight.

"Maybe you only tire yourself with that child," Mom had said to Dad, "so you can claim small triumphs. But it's a fool's errand, and you should know it."

Dad would not give up on his son. In some ways, maybe Lint was merely just another plant Dad hoped he could ripen out of harsh conditions and against any adversity. For a good father, it is an awful thing to believe otherwise.

During this time, Dad had been hired on as part of the crew rebuilding the church. Sometimes I would go and watch the progress. The frame being erected. The roof being laid one shingle at a time. Trustin came with me one time. He sat in the grass and dipped his squirrel-hair paintbrush into a jar of black paint.

"Do you think someone burned the church, Betty?" he asked.

"It was faulty wirin'," I said. "Everybody knows that."

That was what the investigation had concluded. The most damning piece of evidence would have been Fraya's dress and that had burned.

"Just faulty wiring," I said again.

He returned to his painting while I watched Dad and the other workers. By autumn, they finished the outside of the church and were completing the interior.

When school started that year, Ruthis had told everyone, "Betty probably walked by the church and started it on fire 'cause of how ugly she is."

The others laughed at how clever she was.

What made matters worse was that Thanksgiving was quickly approaching. The whooping calls increased, as did the bird feathers taped to my desk. On top of that, every year the second-grade class held an annual First Thanksgiving play. It was my turn to be in the cast.

"Raise your hand if you would like to be a Pilgrim," Mr. Chill, who was our teacher, asked.

"Don't even think about raisin' your hand, Betty," Ruthis said to me. Her red plaid headband matched her plaid jumper perfectly. "You're gonna be an Indian."

When Mr. Chill saw me, he clicked his tongue.

"You'll be an Indian." He wrote my name on his clipboard.

"Told ya." Ruthis flipped her golden hair.

"Joke's on you, Ruthis," I said. "I ain't got no desire to be some stinkin' Pilgrim."

Later that day, we were called to the auditorium for rehearsals, which were led by Mrs. Needle, the music teacher. She was a tall woman whose right leg was thinner than her left. She had gotten polio as a kid and had to wear a brace, which consisted of metal rods and leather straps with uncomfortable-looking buckles. Because of the size difference in her legs, her right hip always rose slightly like she was walking out of joint.

"Everybody listen up," she said, stepping in front of us. Her brace squeaked as she directed all of the Pilgrims to one side of the stage and all of the Native Americans to the other.

Ruthis giggled with her fellow Pilgrims as I stood with the black-haired kids. Mrs. Needle came and put a feathered headdress on my head.

"My ancestors were Cherokees," I told her.

"That's wonderful, dear." She rested the back of her finger against her lips as she considered the placement of the feathers.

"Cherokees don't wear no headdresses," I said.

"Yeah-huh," Ruthis called from across the stage. "All Indians do."

"I think they do, dear." Mrs. Needle handed the boy beside me a hatchet made out of cardboard. She told him to stand over by the tepee.

"We don't," I said. "And we never lived in no tepees, either." I nudged the fabric tepee with my toe.

"I'm almost certain all Indians did, dear," Mrs. Needle said. "They wouldn't know any better."

She told us to stand on the square of green felt she'd laid on the stage.

"It represents the land," she said.

Ruthis stepped on the square at the same time I did.

"Get off," I told her. "This isn't your land."

"It's mine now." She pulled the felt out from under my feet and started rolling it up to her side.

"Thief." I pushed her down.

The kids around us oohed as Ruthis got up and clenched her fists.

"Now, now, children." Mrs. Needle raised her voice as she came and stood between us. "There's no sense in actin' like savages."

Later that same day, Ruthis accused me of stealing her coin purse. It was yellow rubber and had a smiley face on it. I would watch her open and close it in class, wishing I had one like it. Ruthis had not been blind to this.

"Betty took it," she said.

That single accusation was enough for Mr. Chill to come to my desk, lift its lid, and look under it.

"I told you, Mr. Chill, I didn't take it," I said.

He ordered me to stand and empty my pockets. He found nothing more than my handwritten poems and a tiny leaf I'd picked up earlier that morning because I thought its autumn colors were pretty.

"Take off your shoes and dump them over," Mr. Chill told me.

I did what he said.

"Now shake your hair out," he said, as if I had the coin purse hidden there.

"All right, Betty, where is it?" he asked, frustrated to find I was not hiding it on my person.

"All I know is I didn't take it," I said.

He grabbed his ruler from off his desk.

"Hold out your hands, Betty," he said.

"No." I hid them behind me. "I didn't do anything wrong."

"Young lady, hold those thievin' hands of yours out," he said.

"No. I'm tellin' the truth."

He backed me against the wall. I slid down it while my classmates stood on their chairs to watch. Pulling my knees up, I buried my hands in my lap.

"I want my daddy." I didn't care how childish I sounded. "I wanna go home."

"That's enough out of you." Mr. Chill pulled me up by my arm and yanked me toward my desk.

He tried to get my hands onto the desktop, but I stuck them into the waistband of my skirt and wouldn't budge.

"If that's how you want to do it, then fine." He pushed my body forward against the desk and started striking my backside with the ruler.

"Stop, Mr. Chill. Please."

I cried for Dad, hoping he might hear me wherever he was.

"Say you took it," Mr. Chill said over my screams.

"But I didn't take it. I swear."

"Liar."

He struck me so hard, the desk shifted beneath me. I tried to raise my head and stare out above the pain, to imagine myself in A Faraway Place and the sweet escape of that, but each time the ruler landed, I was back in the classroom until I could bear no more.

"I took Ruthis' coin purse." I cried into the lid of the desk. "I took it. Now, please, stop."

But he didn't.

"This is what liars get." He hit me so hard, I bit my tongue. I tasted blood just as Ruthis' voice rang out.

"I found it," she said.

Everyone turned to see her sitting at her desk with its lid up. Under it was her yellow coin purse.

"I guess it was here all along," she said, looking at the ruler in Mr. Chill's hand.

Mr. Chill pushed his glasses back up on his nose.

"Well, then that's settled." He headed to the front of the classroom.

"Ain't you gonna punish her?" I asked. "Ruthis lied. She had it this whole time. She lied on purpose."

Ruthis faced forward, not saying anything. Her legs were crossed at the ankles and her foot was quickly tapping.

"Class, open your history books to page—"

"It's not fair," I said.

"If you don't sit, Miss Carpenter, I will send you to the principal's office." He glared at me over his eyeglasses. "And I assure you, the principal's ruler is much larger than mine."

I eased onto my seat, my backside throbbing. I thought the others would laugh and point, but they only opened their books and listened to Mr. Chill begin to tell us about the Civil War.

After school, I walked home slowly through the woods. I hoped Dad might have a salve to draw out the pain, but when I made it to the garage, Lint was already in there. He had crumbled a biscuit on top of his head. He was telling Dad it was demon dust.

I silently headed into the house and to the upstairs bathroom. Standing in front of the mirror, I lifted the bottom of my shirt and stared at the red welts on my skin.

"What happened to you, Betty?"

I immediately pulled my shirt down. Trustin was standing in the doorway.

"Are you okay?" he asked.

I pushed past him and escaped outside to A Faraway Place.

It was painful to sit on the hard stage, but I endured it as I took my notepad out of my pocket. I removed my poems and laid the pages in a circle around me.

"La, la, la, go away, hurt," I sang, *"bury yourself into the dirt."*

I squeezed my eyes shut, only to open them again. The world was still right there. As the wind blew my circle of poems away, I left and went back inside. In my bedroom, I discovered birds drawn on the wall around my white iron headboard. Trustin was across the hall, laying his charcoal stick down.

"Seein' birds fly always makes me smile," he said. "Thought they might you, too."

14

Wander in the wilderness
where there is no way.

—Psalm 107:40

They finished the church in time for that year's Christmas services. Dad told us that while he was helping to build the church's frame, he had carved our names into one of the boards behind the drywall.

"That way no one can accuse a Carpenter of never bein' in church," he said with a laugh.

But for me, Flossie, and Fraya, this made us feel as if our signature was left at the scene of the crime.

"It was only a joke," Dad said when he saw our faces. "Besides, who needs to be in a church. God's in each tree, and we got plenty of them around."

I began to dream our names were enough to start another fire. The new flames beginning in the carvings Dad had made until the church burned a second time.

I woke from this vision on Christmas morning. I looked over to see Flossie was still asleep. She had small dots of blood on her pillow. The night before, she had pierced her ears with Dad's bone needle.

I got out of bed to see crust had formed around the wires of the earrings, which were the cameos that had belonged to Mom. She had passed the earrings down to Fraya, who had passed them to Flossie when it was time. The cameos were beautiful. They were of a girl who had ruby eyes and was wearing a bonnet strewn with flowers.

I could tell from the frown on Flossie's face that she could wake any moment. I quickly headed downstairs and found Lint on the bottom step. Beside him was a bag of sugar and an empty bottle of milk. Leading from the front door to the bottom step was a trail of melted snow he'd tracked in from outside. In the metal bowl on his lap was snow, sugar, and milk. He was stirring the three ingredients, turning them into our famous Carpenter snow ice cream.

"W-w-want some, Betty?" he asked.

I looked at his bare feet. They were still so very small. When he curled his toes up, they almost didn't exist. Snow had melted into puddles around them.

"Did you go outside without your shoes on again?" I asked. "You'll get frostbit, Lint."

"Only s-s-stepped on the porch," he said. "Came back in real q-q-quick."

"Don't do it again. Okay?" I tousled his hair.

"Okay." He took a rock out of his pocket and dropped it into the sugar bag.

"Mom's gonna get after you for puttin' rocks in the sugar."

"I ain't put r-r-rocks in the sugar."

"What's those?" I pointed down at the rocks.

"Those are s-s-sugar spiders. They're sweet like the sugar, and they don't bite. They're my f-f-friends."

I tousled his hair and told him he was silly. I left him to follow the sounds into the kitchen, where I found Dad mixing punch in a glass bowl.

"I'm glad you're up, Betty," he said, setting the punch in the fridge. "Let's go outside and get your present while it's still nice and quiet."

We opened the back door, pulling our coats tighter around us. It was snowing and had been for days. Breathed was white. It was white and cold and as Dad's boots and my own sank into the deep snow with each step, Dad rubbed his hands together in a way that made me think he had never been so cold.

I ran ahead to our Christmas tree, which was a spruce in our yard. We never had a tree set up in the house because Dad said it wasn't right to rip a tree up by its roots only so it could then be decorated with tinsel and artificial angels.

"The best Christmas tree of all," he said, "is one that is left in the earth, allowed to live and grow and have its own life."

Beneath the tree, I searched through the gifts. Dad had wrapped each in newspaper and bound them in twine. I tore the newspaper off the package with my name on it and discovered a carved wooden box.

"It looks like three curves put together." I felt the smooth sides.

"They're rivers tied up," Dad said. "That's why I painted 'em blue and put hinges on the side so you can open those rivers up."

Inside the box were new notebooks, pencils, and a pen.

"I had a dream the other night," he said. "It was about you, Little Indian. You were on a stage."

"Like A Faraway Place's stage?" I asked.

"Naw. One with big bright lights and a velvet curtain. You were wearin' a blue dress." He slowly waved his hands out to either side as if framing the scene. "The stage lights were shinin' on you as you wrote a poem. When you read the poem aloud it sounded like rivers tied up. Blue things. Things of curve that reach all the way around to the sea."

He cupped his bare hands and blew his hot breath in them. His fingers were red, matching the red in the plaid of his coat.

"So much snow, Little Indian. What you think it'd be like to live inside a snowflake?"

"Cold," I said.

"Betty, if you wrote about me livin' in a snowflake, what would you say?"

"I'd say my daddy lives in a snowflake. He is cold. I only see him in winter. One time I tried to hold him, but he melted in my hand. My daddy lives in a snowflake. He is cold. I miss him in summer."

He looked at me as if there was something final in the air around us.

"I suppose it is a bad idea to want to live in a snowflake after all," he said. "I forgot meltin'. I forgot summer."

"Why would you wanna live in a snowflake anyways, Dad?"

"Snowflakes are so peaceful. I think just by livin' in one, you'd have to be as peaceful as they are."

His brows settled and for a moment I lost his eyes. Before I could ask him anything more, I heard the back screen door squeak open. My siblings were coming out on the porch. I saw that Fraya had Lint's shoes in her hand. She slipped them on his feet before he stepped out into the snow.

Leland was the first at the tree. He opened his gift, which was a new pocketknife. He had recently broken the blade of his old one. Fraya received what she had asked for. A brown diary that had a quilted cat on the cover.

"W-w-what's this?" Lint asked as he held up the horn-shaped rock he got for his gift.

"It's called a horn coral fossil," Dad told him. "You know what a fossil is, son?"

Lint shook his head.

"It's the remains of somethin' that lived a long time ago," Dad said. "That fossil in your hand is over three hundred million years old. It's from the time Ohio used to be beneath a sea."

"My gift is better," Trustin said, holding up a squirrel skull that had a paintbrush sticking out of each eyehole. Dad had made a few of the paintbrushes' bristles out of squirrel fur, but others were made out of pine needles.

"I can't wait." Flossie ripped into her gift. When she saw what it was, she was so happy, she couldn't even speak. It was the one thing she seemed to want the most at the time. Elvis Presley. Elvis was always on the magazine covers then. Dad matted one with thin cardboard so it would look like an actual photo sent to fans. He signed Elvis' name with a black marker.

"Is this really Elvis' autograph?" Flossie grinned ear to ear, her ponytail bouncing.

"Sure is." Dad laughed.

I never did tell Flossie she was kissing the handwriting of her father.

"Landon, you got a customer." Mom came up behind us as she pointed over at Persimma.

Persimma was an elderly neighbor from a few houses down. She had frizzy red hair and never missed the chance to wear a sequined sweater. She was holding money in her arthritic hand. She waved it toward Dad. He gestured back to her, then went into the garage.

A couple of minutes later, he came out with a brown-tinged decoction. Before he took it to Persimma, he stopped in front of me and asked, "What type of insect you reckon these roots look like?"

He held the jar up to the light and pointed out the blackberry roots inside. The little hairs on the roots fanned out like squirming feet.

"A centipede," I answered.

"That's right," he said. "And why do some roots look like insects?"

"Because it's a root that . . ." I tried to remember, word for word, what he had said. "A root that the earth, in her wisdom, has preserved."

"That's right, Little Indian. We can only reckon the earth has chosen this particular insect because of its energy. An energy that we must lay our hands upon and use as wisely as the earth has."

I walked by his side as he carried the decoction to Persimma.

"Same as before?" she asked. "'Cause I don't want no tomato roots or nothin'." She eyed him like she was a first-time customer. "You understandin' me?"

"I assure you, Persimma, it's the same." He handed her the jar.

"I heard you take feathers as payment. That true?" she asked. "I don't wanna be payin' top dollar—"

"I don't take no feathers," he said without the anger I would have had. "No beads either, nor deerskin. No matter what you heard."

She handed him the money. He put it in his pocket without counting it. She stood there, lingering and biting her lip.

"Somethin' else?" he asked.

She leaned over and whispered in his ear. I tried to hear what she was saying, but all I could hear was the way her jaw cracked.

"Constipated, are ya?" he asked loudly.

"Curse men like you, Landon Carpenter." She slapped him on the arm until she, too, grinned.

"You got anything to help me?" she asked.

He told her to wait there, then he grabbed my hand and we walked to the slippery elm growing at the back side of our garage.

"Always harvest bark from where?" he asked me.

"From the side of the tree the sun shines on," I said.

He told me to lay my forefinger on the trunk to measure a piece of bark. With his knife, he cut into the tree, harvesting a small square no longer than my finger. As we walked back toward Persimma, he showed me how to peel the outer bark away, revealing the cream-colored heartwood on the inside.

He told Persimma she would have to boil it in water and drink the tea from it.

"They call it slippery elm," he said to her, "'cause once it's wet, it's just about the slipperiest thing you'll ever hold."

"I ain't got no more money on me," she said.

"You can pay me next trip you make."

"All right, all right, moneyman." She turned and walked with high knees through the snow back to her house.

Dad took the money out of his pocket and counted it. He gave it to me to count, but I only pretended to. We nodded at one another like we were in business together.

"Constipated means she can't shit, right?" I asked him as we walked back to the house.

"Yep." He smiled.

"Is the bark gonna make her shit?" I asked.

His laugh was loud.

"Yes," he said, "it'll make her shit."

We stomped the snow off our boots as we walked up to the back porch, where Mom and Fraya were. Fraya was hugging her diary to her chest while Mom was staring off at the flurries.

I stood next to Fraya, elbowing her to get her attention.

"You know that tree bark over there will make ya shit?" I told her, but she didn't giggle like Flossie would have. I straightened my face and asked Dad what else the bark was good for so I could show Fraya I could be serious, too.

"Oh, it's good for sore throats and—"

"Hey, Dad, Flossie and Lint are eatin' the puddin'," Trustin said from inside the kitchen.

"Shut up, tattletale," Flossie could be heard saying.

"That's for dessert, kids." Dad flung open the screen door and went inside.

Mom turned to me and Fraya.

"You know what else that tree is good for?" she asked in a hushed voice. "It'll make ya lose a baby."

"Lose a baby?" I asked as the image of a woman walking her child through the woods came into my mind. I imagined the child's hand slipping out of the mother's before they both disappeared into separate sides of the dark.

"You can't use bark for somethin' like that," Fraya said.

"Can, too," Mom said to Fraya. "When I was comin' up, I knew a girl who had got in trouble. She decided her only option was to stick a piece of slippery elm bark inside herself. The problem was, she couldn't get it back out. It ended up gettin' all soured up in there. Not only did the baby die, but she died, too. Now I always wonder when I see someone comin' by for slippery elm, if it's 'cause they're constipated, or 'cause they're *constipated*."

She patted her stomach before going into the house.

"I don't get it." I turned to Fraya. "Why'd the baby die?"

"Never mind, Betty," she said. "You're too little to have heard such things."

I started to head inside, where it was warmer, but Fraya stepped out into the yard. Tilting her head back, she let the snow fall into her eyes.

"Yeah," she said after I asked her if she was coming inside.

By that afternoon, Fraya was scribbling away in her diary. Leland was sitting on the sofa, using his new pocketknife to clean his finger-nails. Trustin was painting with one of his pine needle brushes, all while Flossie danced and kissed Elvis' photo. It was a good day, ending with a good meal that sent us all to bed happy. Lint was perhaps the happiest as he placed the horn beneath his bed.

"It's n-n-not a horn at all," he said. "It's the f-f-fossil of a demon eater's tooth. And it's gonna eat all the demons that h-h-hide under my bed."

I was writing about Lint's fossil that night as I sat under my blanket with a flashlight, when I heard soft footsteps on the other side of the closed door. I peeked over at Flossie. She was still asleep.

At the sound of another creak, I rose out of bed. Once out in the hall, I saw no one. At Mom and Dad's room, I held back the deerskin curtain to see them in bed. Dad was snoring and had all of the covers on him. Mom was asleep on her stomach, her arm hanging off the bed and her slip hitched up to her thighs. A small puddle of drool wet the pillowcase. I held my hand over my mouth and giggled.

I tiptoed down the stairs, where I looked over the rail just in time to see the end of a blanket trailing the floor behind a figure moving toward the back of the house. Moments later, I heard the kitchen screen door open and close, making a gentle tap against the frame. I hurried downstairs and immediately noticed a pair of snow boots missing from the pile by the door.

I ran to a nearby window and saw the figure move toward the ga-rage, their boots leaving prints behind them in the snow. Whoever it was had the blanket on their head like a cloak, hiding their face.

As if sensing me, the figure abruptly turned. I ducked beneath the window. I waited a few seconds before daring to peek again.

The person was disappearing behind the garage.

"What are they doin'?" I asked the lamp beside me.

When they next emerged, they had something in their hand as they headed toward A Faraway Place.

"You're not allowed there," I whispered.

Still, the figure climbed the ladder as they held tight to whatever was in their hand. They pushed the snow over and sat on the stage. Only when the blanket fell back did I see her face.

"Fraya?"

Her breath billowed against the cold as she sang, pulling the blanket tighter around her.

THE BREATHANIAN

Man Gored by Deer, Blames Gunfire

A farmer who was gored on his property by a buck charging out of the woods blames the unknown shooter for the incident, saying, "The deer got spooked by all this gunfire. I just happened to be in its path. I could have been killed by its antlers."

The man's condition is stable.

The buck, which was apprehended on the west side of the farmer's property, was shot and killed by Sheriff Sands. A doe approached from out of the woods and stood watch over the buck's body until it was removed.

15

To play the whore in her father's house.

—DEUTERONOMY 22:21

I woke the next morning to the sound of a gun firing. I quickly buried my head beneath my blanket, fearing the gunman was standing over me.

"What's the matter with you?" Flossie asked.

I peeked out to see her standing at the dresser, brushing her hair.

"Who has the gun?" I asked.

"What gun?" She shrugged.

"Didn't you hear it, Flossie? Someone fired a gun in our room."

"Betty, I was standin' here the whole time. No gun went off. You had a dream."

She laid the brush on the dresser and left the room.

Despite her saying no gun had gone off, I was certain one had. To be on the safe side, I checked beneath my bed and in the closet. Finding the room empty, I lay back down and shivered, still hearing the gunshot and waiting for my sisters and brothers to finish up in the bathroom.

When I heard the last of them going downstairs, I got up. I loudly yawned as I stepped into the bathroom, not expecting to find Fraya hunched over.

"Oh, sorry, I thought it was empty," I said to her as I stepped back out in the hall.

Her knuckles were white from gripping the sides of the sink.

"You sick, Fraya?" I asked.

She quickly wiped sweat off her forehead before grabbing two barrettes from the shelf to clip the sides of her hair back.

"I'm fine," she said before swallowing hard and looking at herself in the mirror. When she saw the top of her dress was unbuttoned, she quickly fixed it. Her fingers trembled as she did.

"You sure you're not sick?" I asked.

"Nothin's wrong, Betty."

She gnashed her teeth as she smiled. When she patted my cheek, her palm was clammy.

"You don't look good at all," I told her. "I think you got the flu or somethin'."

"I told ya, Betty girl, I feel great," she said, struggling to walk steady. She used the wall as her support to make it out into the hall.

"Maybe you got sick when you went outside last night," I said.

She paused at the top of the stairs.

"It was freezin' last night," she said. "I didn't even allow my feet outta the blanket."

"But I saw you. At least, I thought I did. I must have dreamed it, like the gunfire."

"You must have, 'cause I was in bed."

She walked down the stairs. I said nothing about the color that had drained from her cheeks.

Inside the bathroom, I stepped in something wet. When I turned my foot over, I saw a drop of blood smeared on my heel. I saw another drop on the toilet seat. I noticed the cabinet door was slightly open and Mom's sanitary napkins were pulled out. I pushed the box back and closed the cabinet before using a tissue to wipe the blood off the seat.

When I got downstairs, Fraya slid her plate of pancakes in front of me as I sat beside her at the table.

"You can have my breakfast, Betty girl," she said. "I'm not hungry."

She picked up the small pitcher of Dad's syrup and started to pour it over my plate. The syrup was just sugar boiled in water, but I liked lots of it. Fraya's hand was shaking so badly, though, I thought she was going to drop the pitcher.

"That's enough," I said.

She set the syrup down and fidgeted in her seat. Before I could ask what was wrong, she vomited on the table. Everyone pushed back in their chairs.

"Eww, Fraya." Flossie spit her bite of food out.

"I'm sorry." Fraya wobblily stood from her chair. Dad caught her before she fell backward.

"How long you feel sick for?" he asked.

"Just come on this mornin'." She wiped her mouth. "I need to lie down."

She curled inward, holding her stomach.

"You're burnin' up, girl." Dad felt her forehead. "I'll give Doc Lad a call."

"No." Fraya gripped Dad's arm. "I'm already startin' to feel better. Besides, don't you have a tea or somethin' you can give me?"

"I don't treat emergencies."

"Ain't an emergency, Dad. It's only the flu or somethin'. I just need to rest. I don't want a doctor to come. I don't want all the fuss."

Dad helped her get upstairs to her bed. Mom quickly started moving the plates to the sink. She told the rest of us to gather up the tablecloth and take it outside to shake the vomit off so she could wash it.

"It'll have to go in the river," I said. "So the water can carry it away."

Mom slapped the back of my head as she passed.

"And make sure y'all stay away from Fraya," she added. "Whatever bug she has will pass through everyone and there'll be so much sickness in this house, we'll have to move."

Flossie refused to touch even a corner of the tablecloth.

"It stinks." She held her nose. "I'm gonna be sick myself."

It was Leland who grabbed the tablecloth and carried it outside. He let the vomit slide off on top of the snow while he looked up at Fraya's window.

We all thought she would be better by the afternoon, but she threw up the tea Dad made her. He decided to burn sage and wave the smoke around the room to help disinfect it. Afterward, he went out to the garage to cook up a wild ginger syrup to rub on Fraya's stomach. I stared in at her as I stood out in the hall. Mom wouldn't let me in the room because of the germs. She told me to go back downstairs, where Flossie and the boys were watching TV, but something about the way Fraya was sweating through the sheets caused me to stay and keep watch.

"Well," Mom said to me, "if you're gonna hang around, you might as well be useful. Go wet a washcloth under cold water and bring it back to me."

I quickly did what she asked. She laid the wet cloth on Fraya's forehead.

"I'm gonna have to call Doc Lad," she said to Fraya. "If we don't get a jump on this flu, it could turn serious real quick. I've seen it before."

"Don't call Doc." Fraya reached out to Mom. "He's just gonna poke around and make me sicker. It'll pass. Please, Momma."

Maybe it was the way Fraya had called her "Momma" that made Mom give in.

"All right." She picked up the empty glass from the side table. "Let me fill this up with more water."

As Mom turned to leave, her eyes caught on the navy blanket draped over Fraya. There, around Fraya's hips, the fabric was darker than the rest. Mom set the glass down, then touched the blanket in the dark spot. Her fingers came away red. Mom jerked the blanket off and revealed a pool of blood drenching Fraya's skirt.

"Jesus Crimson." Mom grabbed her mouth.

"There were drops of blood in the bathroom this morning," I said.

"Why didn't you say somethin' earlier?" Mom turned to me.

"I thought it was from you. I saw your napkins out of the box. I thought it was—"

"Go get your father." She pushed me forward. "Now."

I hurried down the steps so quickly, I nearly fell.

"What is it, Betty?" Leland stood up from the sofa.

"I need Dad," I said, running past.

"He's out in the garage," Flossie said.

I threw open the front screen door and jumped over the steps into the snow.

"Dad, it's Fraya," I said out of breath when I'd made it to the garage. He had been preparing the ginger rub. He dropped it as he darted out of the garage and into the house, me on his heels.

When we got upstairs to Fraya, Mom pointed to the blood and said it was no flu.

Dad immediately ran back downstairs. I could hear him on the phone.

"Doc? Landon Carpenter here. My daughter's bleedin' real bad. No. Not like Alka. It's comin' from . . . Just get over here real quick."

Flossie and the boys started up the stairs to see what the commotion was. Leland pushed everyone out of the way to be the first to step into Fraya's room.

"What's wrong with her?" he asked Mom.

She pushed him back out in the hall.

"Y'all need to stay out from under Doc Lad's feet when he gets here," she said before turning to Fraya, who had started to repeatedly apologize. Mom tried to get answers out of her, like when the bleeding had first started.

"I don't know," Fraya replied, her voice shaking. "I woke up and it was there. It was spotty at first. I used one of your napkins."

Dad rushed up the steps.

"Doc Lad will be here soon," he said, going over to hold Fraya's hand. "Everything is gonna be fine, Fraya. We're all here."

He turned to us kids and waved us into the room.

"Grab my hand," he said to me. "And Flossie you grab hers. Boys, get in line. We're gonna pass our strength to Fraya. She needs her family."

We formed a chain around Fraya's bed, Mom holding Lint's hand at the end.

"You're gonna be fine, Fraya," Dad told her. "Ain't that right, kids?"

He waited for us all to nod.

"You're gonna be fine, Fraya" he said again. "You're gonna get well and write your songs and sing and sit out on A Faraway Place.

Here is your song, Fraya. Here in this room. Even in the pain. Don't think the sunrise won't come again. I can see images of you dottin' the acreage." He turned his head to look out the window by the bed. "I see these images of you on into the future. There you are singin' and joinin' each decade of your life, until you stand in the back of the field, with your hair silver, and all the life you're meant to live. The future is writin' to you now, Fraya. It's writin' to you now to say you do not die here in this bed." He turned back to her. "Remember how powerful you are, my girl. You are so very powerful."

I'm not sure Fraya even noticed we were there. She could barely keep her eyes open.

"This is stupid," Leland said, breaking the chain to pace the room. "Where's that damn doctor?"

A couple of minutes later, we heard Doc Lad's tires crunching over the gravel outside.

"Up here," Dad called down the steps to him.

When Doc Lad got upstairs, he smiled at us kids. He was someone who you thought had always been old with his musty smell, messy beard, and bifocals. Regularly he would give us kids worm pills like they were candy.

"Doc Lad's here now," he told us. "Nothin' to worry about."

But when he saw Fraya and the blood, he seemed to brace himself.

"Best get them youngins out of here, Landon," he said to Dad with a quick gesture of the hand.

Dad chased us out into the hall.

"Wait downstairs," he said, closing the door on us.

"I'm not goin' anywhere," Flossie said.

We each laid an ear against the door, listening to the voices on the other side.

"Honey, you understandin' me all right?" Doc Lad asked Fraya. "Did you do anythin' to yourself?"

"Why's he askin' that?" Trustin asked.

Leland slapped him and told him to shut up.

"I said did you do anythin' to yourself, honey?" Doc Lad asked again.

"No," Fraya said loud enough for us to hear.

I stepped back from the door.

"What's the matter with you?" Flossie asked me.

I flew down the stairs. Not stopping until I got outside to the slippery elm, I immediately found the spot on the trunk Dad had cut out for Persimma. Beside it was a new square where additional bark had been removed.

I turned back, falling in the drifts of snow.

"I'm comin', Fraya," I said as I ran into the house, finally making it upstairs.

"Where the heck did you go?" Flossie asked.

"I know why Fraya is bleedin'," I said.

"Why?" Leland asked.

When I didn't answer straightaway, Leland grabbed me by the shoulders and shook me.

"Goddamn it, Betty. Why?"

"'Cause of the bark," I said. "The slippery elm bark."

"What are you talkin' about?" Leland shook me harder. "Make sense."

"Mom knows about it. She—"

Before I could finish, Leland threw open Fraya's door and pushed me into the room. He ordered me to repeat what I'd told him.

"The bark," I said.

"What bark, Betty?" Dad asked.

"Mom, you know." I turned to her. "It's like what you said that girl did."

I looked at Fraya, who was weakly shaking her head at me to stop, but I didn't.

"Fraya put the slippery elm bark inside herself," I said, "like the girl you talked about. The one who wanted to lose the baby."

Flossie inhaled sharply and grabbed her mouth.

"Jesus Crimson." Mom dropped back into the chair behind her.

"Fraya?" Doc Lad bent over her. "Did you put somethin' inside you? Now don't lie to me, honey."

Fraya licked her lips like she was thirsty, then said, "Yes."

"A piece of bark, was it?" Doc Lad asked.

"Yes."

"How could you be so stupid?" Mom asked her.

"I thought I had to do it," Fraya said.

"I won't know the damage until I conduct an examination," Doc Lad spoke to Mom and Dad. "When an infection sets in—"

Fraya tugged on Doc Lad's sleeve.

"What, honey?" Doc Lad turned to her.

"I lost it," she said. "I lost the bark inside me."

"Good God. It's still in ya?"

She nodded.

"Lord help us, we gotta get it out right now." Doc Lad reached into his black bag and pulled out what I thought looked like a pair of large pliers. "Get them kids outta here."

Mom stood up from the chair and pushed us all back out into the hall. I ducked beneath her arms to see Dad grab Fraya's hand as Doc Lad spread her legs. He looked to be preparing to dig inside her.

"What are they doin' to her?" I fought Mom so I could get to Fraya.

"Stop it, Betty." Mom struggled to keep me back.

"Make them stop doin' that to her." I cried. "They're gonna hurt her."

Mom managed to pick me up and hand me off to Leland, who wrapped his arms around me. He carried me out into the hall while Mom closed the door. He let me tire myself by banging his chest with my fists before I dropped to the floor and scooted back against the wall.

Time seemed to tick by slowly. When the door finally opened, Dad emerged carrying Fraya in his arms. Doc Lad was not far behind and was saying, "We'll take her to my office and get some penicillin in her. We'll hope we got her early enough before the infection spread to her blood."

Mom had stayed in the room. I watched as she stripped the bed of its sheets. Her eyes were red as she stared at the pool of blood on the sheet. In the center of it was the piece of bark. Wet and slippery.

She quickly folded the corner of the sheet up around it and carried it against her chest all the way outside.

She dropped to her knees and broke the cold earth with a nearby rock until she had a hole she could put the sheet in. But she didn't bury it deep enough, so a corner stuck out from the dirt, marking the spot like a grave.

16

Thou *art* my God from my mother's belly.

—PSALM 22:10

The first night without Fraya in the house, me and Flossie lay in our beds saying goodnight to one another. When I said goodnight to Fraya, only the silence answered. The second evening she was away, Dad started gardening, even though it was the dead of winter. He went out to the vegetable plot and laid dry branches down and in the same direction. Then he burned the branches to loosen the soil. Bundled up, I sat on A Faraway Place and watched him stand by the fire, its flames reflecting in his glazed eyes.

"Never put fire out with water," he said more to himself than to me. "Fire hates water and water hates fire. Only the earth itself can come between flame and liquid to ease their old war."

Deciding the fire had burned long enough, Dad threw dirt upon it. With the fire out and the soil loosened from winter's clutches, he started in with his antler rake. He had made the rake by tying the shed antler of a deer to a long stick to be used as the handle. Dad liked antler because he said slugs hated horn and in turn there would be fewer slugs in the soil.

"The first woman was given antlers on her head to branch her power out into the world," he said, digging the rake in deeper. "Slugs are frightened of that power because they are spineless creatures, and all spineless creatures are frightened of a woman's power."

His voice faded as he let the rake drop off to the side. He used his hands to bring dirt up into rows.

"Go get my corn seeds out of the garage, Betty."

"Can't plant the garden in winter," I said.

"Get my seeds, Betty." His voice rose, echoing off the side of the house.

I jumped off the stage, landing hard on the cold ground. I ran into the garage and retrieved the sack of corn. I cradled it against me as I carried it out to him. He already had a whole row of dirt ready. He took the sack from me and put a few of the corn seeds into his mouth to wet them. When the seeds were soaked, he dropped them into my bare hand because he always said a woman or a girl had to do the planting for the crop to be worth a damn.

"And we really need it to be worth a damn right now," he said. "Remember, Little Indian, plant as deep as your second knuckle."

"But, Dad, it's winter. It's not gonna grow."

"From the warmth of your hands, you will bring spring back for the seeds and for Fraya," he said.

I looked away from the tears welling in his eyes and dropped to my knees in front of the hill of dirt before me. Using my two fingers and thumb, I planted the seeds.

"You're my width, length, and depth," he said, dropping more of the seeds into my hand. "A woman was always responsible for the gardenin'."

"I know, Dad." My hands shivered as I pushed the seed into the soil.

"If a woman fell ill and was unable to tend her garden, then her garden would be planted by the other women," he said. "They would do it for her, allowin' the sick woman to rest and get better because when they planted her garden, they planted her chance to get back her strength. Don't you understand, Betty? We're plantin' it for Fraya. When the corn grows tall and strong, so will she."

I didn't say any more about it being too cold or that the seed would not germinate. I merely kept accepting the seeds from my father's mouth to drop them into the frozen earth until we had two rows of corn.

"That should do it," Dad said.

He went into the warm garage and grabbed a gallon-size bucket full of river water. Taking handfuls of the water, he tossed it out on top of the seeds. In his mind, winter didn't exist.

He sat the bucket down and piled the remaining branches, lighting them in a new fire. I kept watch as he went inside the house to get coal to keep the flames burning longer.

He returned with Flossie and the boys. Lint and Trustin helped Dad with the fire while Leland stared off into the darkness.

"What the hell have you and Dad been doing out here?" Flossie asked me.

"Gardenin'," I said, as if it was perfectly normal.

She clicked her tongue before saying, "I think Fraya's gonna die."

"Shut up," I said. "She is not."

Flossie looked at our father and brothers to see if they were listening. Satisfied they weren't, she whispered in my ear, "I heard Mom cryin'. And Dad's actin' all strange. Maybe Fraya's already dead and they just haven't told us yet."

"I told you to shut up." I flicked water from the bucket on her. She screamed like I'd thrown the whole river on top of her head.

"Stop that fightin' and screamin' by the garden," Dad said. "The dirt will drink your screams and your fury until the ground cries and spoils the crop we're tryin' to raise up. We can't have that negative energy, not when we're tryin' to give all the goodness we can to Fraya."

I returned to watering the seeds while Flossie helped. Trustin picked up one of the extra sticks and dragged it through the softened soil, drawing the fire. Lint had turned his back and was wiping his eyes. Leland, still looking off into the darkness, walked out into it and disappeared. Dad watched, then he turned to us as if afraid we might disappear into the dark, too. He stared at the bucket at my feet, before scooping some of the water out with his hands. Mixing it with the loose garden dirt, he formed mud, which he shaped into a good-size ball.

"I figure we got a whole hell of a lot of mud in our lives at the moment," Dad said to us. "Might as well make somethin' out of it."

He smacked the mud ball onto one of the coals burning along the outer edge of the fire, making sure to press the mud hard enough against the coal that it got trapped. When he threw the ball up into the air, the coal burned bright orange against the night, tumbling and turning as if a piece of fire was falling back to the earth.

"Wow," Lint said.

"How cool." Trustin smiled.

"It's a star." Flossie clapped.

We excitedly started mixing water with dirt until we had mud we could shape into a ball that we hit hard against the coal, picking pieces up. The night became lit with glowing orbs crisscrossing one another. I hoped that wherever Fraya was, she could see all of our stars from her window and know we had made them for her.

Later that night, after the fire died and the coals had stopped shining, me and Flossie sat on our bed, our hair washed and our fingernails scrubbed clean.

"I didn't know she even had a boyfriend," Flossie said, making a face.

"Who?" I asked.

"Who do you think, raccoon breath. I mean, Fraya never went out on dates. I've never even seen her talkin' to a boy before. Ya know, besides our brothers. But they're not boys. They're not human enough." She ran the comb through her hair before saying, "That whole time she was pregnant and we had no idea. She didn't look fat or nothin'."

I kept combing my hair silently. Flossie looked at me, narrowing her eyes.

"Did you know she was pregnant, Betty? You knew about the bark. Maybe you knew she was pregnant. Oh." Flossie grabbed her mouth, then let it go to say, "You know who the father is. Who is it, Betty? Tell me." She hopped off her bed and onto mine. "Pretty please."

"I don't know who it is. And besides, maybe she wasn't pregnant."

"Don't be a dumb dog. She put the bark inside her to kill the baby."

"To *lose* it."

"It's the same thing, bucket head. What other reason could you possibly have to stick a dirty piece of bark up inside you?"

"Maybe she was constipated."

Flossie started to laugh, but stopped.

"Gosh, I wonder if she got any splinters," she said. "I wonder if she's already dead."

"I told you to shut up about that."

I pushed her off my bed. After turning off my table lamp, I closed my eyes and waited for Flossie to get into her bed. After she said goodnight to me, I said it back. We ended up saying goodnight to Fraya at the same time, our voices overlapping. We listened to the silence after. Unable to stand it any longer, I turned the lamp back on.

"We should take a jar and put our goodnights in it," I told Flossie. "So Fraya will know we didn't forget her. We can give her our goodnights when she comes back."

"That's silly," Flossie said. A few seconds later, she asked, "How would we do it?"

I tore a strip of paper out of my notebook and halved it, giving Flossie hers. We each wrote "Goodnight, Fraya." Then I got a jar and dropped the goodnights inside it, shaking them every so often to keep them alive.

We added goodnights for as long as Fraya was away. I hoped that by doing so, I could keep the fear that she might already be dead out of my mind. It was still the only thing I thought every time I saw my parents' faces.

In spite of Dad's hope that we could garden Fraya back to health, the ground was too cold to grow anything more than frost. So I took a few pine needles and bunched them together before sticking them into the rows over top of the seeds as if the green needles were the first signs of corn growing. I thought it must have helped, because a few days after that, Fraya came home.

"For you," I said to Fraya as I presented her with the jar of goodnights.

She reached inside and pulled one of the slips of paper out.

"So you know we said goodnight to you," I told her. "Even though you were away."

I wanted to say more, but Mom had warned me and the others not to talk about the bark with Fraya. We were to behave as if nothing had happened. Mom and Dad even flipped Fraya's mattress so the bloodstain would be hidden. Then Mom put new yellow sheets on the bed.

Aside from cleaning Fraya's room, Dad baked a cake for her homecoming. He put candles on it like it was Fraya's birthday. She awkwardly blew them out while the rest of us stood around her. Leland was the only one not home. He had gotten a job driving a truck cross-country. He said he would be gone for a few months, if not longer. Flossie said it was because he was looking for the boy who had gotten Fraya in trouble.

"It's the brother's responsibility to kill any boy who hurts his sister," Flossie said, looking directly at Lint and Trustin. "One day, you two will kill for me and Betty."

"I'll k-k-kill for you, Flossie." Lint didn't hesitate. "You, too, B-b-betty."

"I don't wanna kill no one," Trustin said.

"Too bad," Flossie told him. "It's what you'll have to do."

I thought of Leland in his truck, scouring the earth for the boy who, as Flossie put it, had hurt his sister. I was still thinking of this as I lay in bed unable to sleep that first night Fraya was home. I tossed and turned, trying to close my eyes, when I heard a soft padding coming from out in the hall. I got up and peeked out of my room. Fraya stood at the end of the hall by the steps.

She held her finger to her lips, then waved for me to follow her downstairs. She led the way out to the side porch, where the washing machine was. Searching through the dirty clothes in the hamper beside it, she asked, "Where is it? The sheet? The bark?"

"Mom buried it in the yard," I told her.

"Show me."

I took her out into the yard to the spot. She grabbed the corner of the sheet still sticking up and pulled on it until the cold ground broke away.

When the sheet was free, she hastily unfolded it, searching until she found the piece of bark. She cradled it in her arms as she went back inside the house. I silently followed her upstairs to her room.

"Get me a scrap of fabric out of my top drawer," she told me as she pointed to her dresser.

I opened the top drawer to find old dresses cut up for use as sewing projects.

"Choose the prettiest fabric," she said.

She continued to hold the bark in her arms and tenderly looked at it while I searched through the drawer. I ended up choosing a piece of pale pink fabric with dark pink blooms on it. When I handed it to her, she wrapped it around the bark so she could once again cradle it in her arms. She sat this way in the chair in the corner, rocking the bark and singing to it.

"Hush now, baby, don't say a word."

"Fraya?"

"Shh, Betty. Mustn't wake the baby."

17

Children, obey your parents in the Lord:
for this is right.

—EPHESIANS 6:1

Some little girls grow up with fathers who are decent, kind, and tenderly nested by their daughter's heart. Other little girls grow up with no father at all, thus ignorant of good men and the not so good ones. The unluckiest of all little girls grow up with fathers who know how to make storms out of sunshine and blue skies. My mother was one such unlucky little girl and suffered the childhood you run away from. Except if you have nowhere to run to.

My mother hailed from Joyjug, Ohio. She was a woman so lovely, mirrors grieved in absence of her. She was much more than her beauty. But no matter how many miles of fantastic wonders I saw inside my mother, she was already gone to me in a million different ways, even when I thought she was right in front of me. This was no more apparent than that February of 1963.

It had been one month since Fraya had returned home and I was going to be nine years old. Mom hollered me into her bedroom and told me my birthday gift was to be a true story she had never told before. She was dancing as jerky as a rattlesnake in a frypan, slipping across the floor in her nylons as Thurston Harris sang "Little Bitty Pretty One" from the radio. As she kicked up her feet, I saw a photograph beneath each of her heels.

"Little bitty pretty one, come on and talk-a to me," she sang as she

pulled me toward her and tried to get my arms to move as hers. *"Tell you a story, happened long time ago. Little bitty pretty one, I've been-a watchin' you grow."*

She had put on mascara heavier than usual and it had run down with the tears, making long black lines that reminded me of the previous summer, when the electric poles had been knocked down by a storm, their live wires twitching against the ground.

"You dance like shit," she told me once the song ended.

After she turned the radio off, she leaned back against the bedroom wall. She unfolded her arms, standing cruciform. The wallpaper behind her was something green, something purple, something I remember loving.

"My pappy," she said, "was a man who had his toes in God's river, but his heels in the devil's mud. I suppose that's why I've never much understood flat-footed garden men. What with their soft words and gentle bedside manner."

I couldn't tell you if Grandpappy Lark wore a hat to church or if Mamaw Lark really believed in God. I could tell you all about the cherry tree in their backyard though. When we went there, Dad never came and only my mother was allowed in her parents' house. Us kids favored the outside anyways, especially when the cherry tree was ripe.

We were allowed to stare up at the deep red fruit. We could lick our lips. We could even open our mouths and stand beneath a branch, waiting for a dangling cherry to drop. But we were never to pick any off the tree itself. Grandpappy's orders. Like scavenging animals, we were only allowed to eat cherries which had fallen. To make sure this was the case, Grandpappy would sit inside the house by an open window, holding the cotton curtain back with his flyswatter so he could keep an eye on us. To be so cruel to us must have given him great pleasure after the way our father had beat him in his own front yard. The cherry tree was Grandpappy Lark's way of beating Landon Carpenter back through his children, sending us home with bruises on the inside instead of on the out.

Grandpappy Lark had waited for revenge, and it came in the form of calling his daughter back to the house just so he could regain a measure of power. I suppose my mother returned to the monster so she could show him what the little girl he had hurt had grown up to be. A woman who was strong enough to remember everything.

I've never loved my grandpappy, and yet I have never been able to forget what he looked like. He was a short, fat man who always wore green suspenders to hold up his pants. He had a large white mole in the crease of his left nostril. I think he tried to hide it by stuffing that side of his mouth with chewing tobacco until his cheek bulged. The scar Dad had given him stood out on the bridge of his nose. It was this scar that connected the hateful look in each of his eyes. He had straight blonde hair, which had faded in age. He still wore it, as he always had, parted in the middle. His fair skin was at all times slightly burned no matter how much time he spent outdoors.

I thought his voice would sound like the hard part of a dead field, but it was soft. I imagined he could have sung a good lullaby if he were the type of man to know any. He never spoke to me, but he did say things about me.

"Don't go bringin' that half-breed with you when it's sick," he said to Mom on his porch when he saw me with a runny nose. "I'm an old man. You want me to catch somethin' and die? I know you're after my house. It's why you like bringin' all these beasts of yours. You're hopin' they make me sick with some savage disease. You're as nasty as your brother was." He frowned and smacked his lips. "A faggot and a whore. With children like that, who fears hell?"

Mamaw Lark always stood behind him. She never looked at us. It was as though she did her best to believe we did not even exist and were not her grandchildren. She was always in a housedress with an apron and was never without a dish towel in her hands, curling it about her large knuckles. Unlike Mom, Mamaw Lark would wear the same pair of flat black shoes that laced up. I thought it was so she could move quickly as she waited on her husband hand and foot.

I tried to imagine Mamaw Lark young, but her hair had whitened with age. She wore it in a tight bun. Her skin was so transparent, I could see her veins beneath. Sometimes I didn't even realize she was standing there unless she moved. She knew how to blend in with her little white house and its cross like a church.

"Where's your father at?" Mom asked as she slowly walked over to the dresser.

"He went to look at the roof on Mr. Deering's corncrib if it's not too icy," I said.

"Well, I hope your daddy don't fall off that roof. He's too poor to afford wings."

She turned on the fan sitting on the dresser top. Holding her hair up off the back of her pale neck, she looked at me.

"What did you say?" she asked above the fan's jagged humming.

"I didn't say nothin'."

"Don't you lie to me." She lunged toward me and grabbed my shoulders. "You're always lyin'."

She pulled up my shirtsleeve.

"Always sinnin' with the sun, too." She shouted over and over again in my face. "I told ya to stay out of it. It makes you black."

"It's winter, Mom. I ain't been in the sun."

"You're so goddamn black."

She yanked me over to her dresser, where she grabbed the puff and powder. She started harshly applying the white powder onto my skin until I was covered in it.

"Jesus Crimson." She pushed me back and threw the puff to the floor. "It's pointless."

She picked up the half-drunk whiskey bottle from off a shelf.

"It's time for your birthday gift," she said as she staggered toward the edge of the bed to sit.

She patted the spot beside her. Knowing I could not run away without my mother chasing me down and tearing my eyes out, I sat beside her.

"I was nine when God first turned his back on me," she said, keeping her eyes forward. "The age you've just become, little girl. Summer had brought so much rain to Joyjug, it felt like the flood was already there. 'Good thing we've swam before,' Pappy would say, practicing his stroke. Eventually the rain stopped and everything was left to drip and drop and mold. On the first dry day, I was in the backyard pluckin' one of our chickens for dinner. You ain't never had to take care of fixin' a chicken, so I'll tell ya the way to do it. First you gotta let the silly thing bleed out. To do that, you hang it by its feet and cut its neck."

She used her uneven pinkie nail as if it were a knife on my carotid.

"I always jarred the blood for Pappy," she said. "He'd drink it in the mornin' with biscuits and gravy."

She took a gulp of whiskey, her eyes glazing over until I thought I might have to lay her down to sleep.

"Once the chicken bleeds out," she continued, "you gotta put its body in boilin' water for a few minutes so the feathers are easier to pull. Then you hold the dead bird by its feet and start pluckin'."

She pretended to pluck feathers off the glass of the bottle as she held it up by its neck and said, *"Pluck, pluck, fuck."*

Stopping, she took another drink.

"While I was pluckin' the feathers," she said after, "Momma stood on the porch waitin' for Pappy to get home. She had a cool wet rag in her hand like she did every goddamn day. She would lay the rag on the back of his neck as he sat on the porch swing. Then she would get on her knees with a smile and take off his boots to massage his feet. I remember the time Momma forgot to smile. Pappy made her lick the mud off the bottom of his boots. I can still see her tongue fittin' in all the little grooves."

"She had to lick the mud off?" I asked.

I knew the moment I opened my mouth I had made a mistake. Still, I could not prepare myself for the hard slap my mother gave to the back of my head.

"She had to lick the mud off?" Mom mocked me before pouring more whiskey down her throat. I wondered how one woman could hold so much drink.

"It's hot as hell." She mumbled as she stood.

Carrying the bottle by its neck, she clumsily walked to a window. "Hot as hell," she said again.

It was February and cold, but what made my mother warm had

nothing to do with the weather. After she opened a window, she stuck her head out into the falling snow, the flakes landing in her hair like a dusting of flour. She slowly pulled back inside, facing me as she leaned against the sill.

"Once Momma took off Pappy's boots," Mom said, "he added more tobacco in his cheek before whispering in her ear. Afterward, he went inside the house while Momma came to me. Told me to lay the chicken in the grass. Said she'd finish it. She used her dishrag to dust the chicken feathers off my hands. Then she spit on the skirt of her apron and used it to clean the dirt from my face the way she did every Sunday before church. I even asked her, 'Are we goin' to church, Momma?' She didn't say nothin'. Just picked me up in her arms and patted my back like she would a baby as she carried me into hers and Pappy's bedroom.

"He was already in there takin' off his suspenders and undoin' the buttons of his shirt. She carried me to their bed and gently laid me down before she stepped over to the dresser to get her bottle of perfume. I'd helped her make that perfume from the roses that grew in our backyard. She bottled the scent in an old bitters bottle. I can still remember the label word for word. *Dr. Cherryweather's Bitters for a disagreeable stomach, a bellicose headache, for humors, biliousness, fever of the heart, and all complaints advocated by a poor condition of the blood.*"

I wanted Dad there more than I ever had. I hoped Mr. Deering's roof would be too slippery for Dad to climb and that he might come home, opening the door right that second and causing Mom to stop. Instead, there was only silence as Mom left the window and went to the dresser, where she picked up the whiskey bottle's cork stopper. She pushed it down into the bottle before tipping it so the remaining drink touched the underside of the cork.

"Momma put the perfume on my neck like this," Mom said as she dabbed the wet cork against my own neck. "Ain't it nice?" she asked. "Nice and cool." She had said "cool" in a way that made me think it was dangerous.

I watched her finish the last of the whiskey before throwing the empty bottle out the open window.

"You know what shortenin' is, don'tcha, Betty?" she asked. "Momma always kept a tin of it in her dresser drawer. Shortenin' ain't only for bakin'. It can be used for fuckin'. To allow the man to enter with ease. I should be thankful to Momma for takin' my underwear off and rubbin' the shortenin' between my legs. I know now she done it so I wouldn't get hurt so bad."

Mom made a pained face and seemed to hold her breath.

"Her rubbin' there was a peculiar feelin'," she said. "Frightened me so badly, I pissed. I thought Momma would kill me for ruinin' the clean sheets like that, but she didn't say nothin'. Just dabbed my legs and put a towel beneath me on the bed. She trimmed Pappy's fingernails before leavin'. 'Momma, where you goin'?' I cried out to her, but she only shut the door behind her. When I heard the front screen squeak, I knew she'd gone back outside to finish the chicken."

Not wanting to listen anymore, I stood and said, "I'm gonna go now."

Mom placed both her hands on my shoulders until she was lowering me back down to a seat.

"This is your birthday gift," she said. "You can't go until you get all of it."

She teetered back, wiping her eyes.

"With Momma gone, Pappy began to hum. When he took his pants off, it was the scariest thing I'd ever seen. I thought it looked like a growth. A wicked thing. Somethin' he should be sick by. He was so hard. Do you know what I mean?" She cupped her crotch the way I'd seen men do. "Do you know what I mean?" she asked again.

I nodded just so she would stop.

Her hand fell off to her side as she said, "I thought he was just climbin' up in the bed to take a nap beside me." She stared off into the distance. "He laid on top of me. I thought he was gonna keep me warm like a blanket until I fell asleep. He was so heavy, I couldn't breathe. I remember how sweat from his forehead had collected on the tips of his hair. I didn't want the sweat to drop in my eye, so I turned my face and felt it land on my temple."

She lightly brushed my temple.

"Then he started backin' up," she continued, "and I hoped he was gettin' off me, but he was only liftin' the skirt of my dress. It was my favorite dress. Momma made it for me. It was navy blue with a big cream bow that hung from a sailor collar."

Mom entwined her fingers and held her hands up against her chest.

"I didn't understand why he was touchin' me the way he was. I told him to stop. Why didn't he stop? I didn't scream because I didn't want to be a bad girl and get into trouble for makin' noise."

She went to stand in front of the fan once more. I thought about standing with her and raging together against everything, but I wasn't sure how to be that type of daughter to that type of mother. I looked toward the photographs beneath her feet as she moved her eyes around the room. She appeared tilted and lost as she paced, her hands dragging the wallpaper as if *searching, searching*. I thought the night would be too short for her to ever find what she wanted. I thought life would be even shorter. What she needed was a sudden infinity. Time as many bars of light she could find everything in.

"I need to get Dad," I said but didn't move as she began to dig her fingernails into the wallpaper, *digging, digging* like claws.

She's going to scream, I thought. *And it'll be something real. Something we have to chain up in the backyard and feed with bloody steaks.*

She laid her forehead against the wall and stood there until I thought it was where she'd always be. I said again that I should go and get Dad. Still I sat there unable to do that very thing.

As if suddenly aware I was still in the room, Mom left the wall and came to me. Her eyes looked washed in the rains and reddened in the fires.

"He brushed my hair with his hand like this." Her tone was soft as she moved her fingers through my loose strands, putting them behind my ears. "He forced me down like this." She raised her voice as she grabbed both my arms and pushed me back onto the middle of the bed. She climbed up herself until she was leaning over me as she said, "He undressed me like this."

She tried to pull off my pants, but I held on tight to them. She stopped and picked up the edges of the full skirt of her dress to straddle me.

"Juice from his chewin' tobacco fell on my cheek like this," she said, holding my face.

She moved her mouth around, collecting saliva before letting it slowly drop from her mouth and onto my cheek. I started slapping my cheek to get the spit off as she reached over and picked up the ruffled pillow shaped like a heart. She clutched it tight in her hands. I was aware of how deep under her I was.

"Mom, please stop," I said. "Please."

"I couldn't breathe, Betty. Just like this." She shoved the pillow on my face.

I tried to push the pillow off, but my mother had her weight on it.

"I wasn't prepared for the agonizing pain I would feel when he put himself inside my little body." Her voice was full of that same agony as she began to thrust herself on top of me. "I thought he was killin' me by rippin' me in two. I didn't even know such a pain was possible. I cried out, 'Momma. Momma, help me.' But she never came and he just kept diggin' into me. I knew then I wasn't loved. Oh, God, I can still hear the squeakin' of the bed."

Managing to turn my face beneath the pillow, I found a small air pocket and was able to get some breaths.

"All of him inside me, while God did nothin'," Mom said, thrusting harder. "No lightnin' bolts. No angels blarin' their trumpets to my rescue. Where was God when my daddy was on me? I was just a little girl. I was just a little girl," she said once more before rolling off me, taking the pillow with her.

She held the pillow against her heaving chest. I could do nothing more than lay there trembling.

As she got off the bed, she let the pillow drop to the floor. She stepped on it as she walked to the vanity. Digging in the bottom drawer, she pulled out a yellow handkerchief she had embroidered earwigs on. She used it to wipe her smudged mascara, but only smeared it more.

"After my pappy fucked me," she said as she wiped her cheeks harder, "he laid a half-eaten chocolate bar on my chest and left to have his meal. I could hear his fork hittin' and scrapin' against his plate as I lay there. Momma came in and told me we'd keep it all under the rose. 'It happens in every family,' Momma said. 'You'll get used to it.' Then she told me to get out of the bed so she could slip my dress back on me. She put a rag between my legs to catch the blood. She was wrong about gettin' used to it, though. You never get used to somethin' like that. I suppose she said it because it's easier to say than the truth, which is that the hurt stays with you as certain as the day is long. It's like bein' in a storm. The cold wind whippin' you about. The rain beatin' down hard. I try to find the child within me as if she still lives. I try to find her and pull her from the storm and ask her, 'What will you be when you grow up?' That way, I can pretend her future is not me. I can pretend the only reason her father sees her to bed, is to cover her up and wish her beautiful dreams. You know what the heaviest thing in the world is, Betty? It's a man on top of you when you don't want him to be."

Mom grabbed a tube of lipstick and snapped her fingers for me to get up and stand in front of her. She held my chin with her free hand as she said, "God hates us, Betty."

"The Carpenters?" I asked.

"Women." She dabbed the lipstick against my lips, using her pinkie to smooth it into the corners. "God made us from the rib of man. That has been our curse ever since. Because of it, men have the shovel and we have the land. It's right between our legs. There, they can bury all their sins. Bury 'em so deep, no one knows about 'em except for them and us."

With a delicate step back she looked at me, her eyes cutting where they landed.

"My, my, Betty girl." She smiled. "Red is not your color, darlin'. Now get outta here."

I darted out of her room and into mine. I fell down in the darkest corner I could find, where I quietly cried. When I raised my head, I saw sheets of paper and a pen on my desk. I grabbed them and escaped outside to A Faraway Place.

Sitting on the stage, I wrote everything Mom had said. I sometimes had to shut my eyes to keep from reading what I was writing and reliving it all over again, but I did not lay my pen down. I wrote as if it was flooding from my fingertips. All the cruelty, all the pain, I wrote it all in a story that was destroying me even as I created it.

I folded the pages against my chest. I tried to suffocate them as I went into the garage for an empty jar and a hand shovel.

Back at A Faraway Place, I crawled under the stage and broke the cold earth with the shovel. When I got the hole dug, I placed the story inside the jar as I repeated what my mother had said.

"Bury 'em so deep, no one knows about 'em except for them and us."

I twisted the lid on the jar as tight as I could. Then I buried the story alive, making sure it was deep enough, a wolf wouldn't smell blood on it and dig it up.

THE BREATHANIAN

Gunfire Reported Throughout the Night

Cinderblock John, who lives on county lane 3, reported seeing a bright light followed by gunfire near his house late last night. Sheriff Sands responded and found tracks in the snow leading from Cinderblock John's residence into the surrounding woods. Shell cases were recovered from the scene. Two trees on the property were found with bullet holes, but they were old and looked to be the result of a rifle. Cinderblock John said he saw several figures outside his window.

"They had elongated faces and silver bodies," he reported. "I went out to 'em and by God, they smelled like my momma's potato salad, but she's been in the grave thirty years."

Cinderblock John was later arrested for drunkenness as he attempted to steal the sheriff's car for what he said was "to race the sons of bitches in their ship." His heavy cinder block obstructed his effort. The sheriff says he will not charge Cinderblock John with attempted theft, but he did issue him a citation for being unruly.

If not for the second report made by an elderly pious lady, Cinderblock John's account of the nighttime shooting might have been written off as madness due to intoxication.

"The shots sounded like they were right inside my home," the churchgoing woman commented when questioned. "I was sitting up in bed reading the Bible and drinking tea. I live alone. I don't want no trouble. I don't know why anyone has to shoot by my house. I'm fearful now to go to the door when I hear a knock. What if I should open my door to the devil?"

Several more witnesses made reports throughout the night.

"It was as if the shooter was running all across town," one of them commented. "Unable to stay still, running from something or to something, I have no idea."

18

A woman shall compass a man.

—JEREMIAH 31:22

Sobered to my gender, I felt surrounded by the symmetry of the female form that shaped itself into a kitchen I dreamed my mother standing in. Her body naked, wearing only the sunlight. Her waist no wider than the water pouring out of the faucet while a swarm of children ate the flesh off her ankles as she stood at the stove boiling blood. Her throat was cracked like a porcelain vase. I could see the pink petals of a small flower protruding from the split at her collarbone. Written in small script around her nostrils were words reminding her to breathe. She had no lips. They were laying on the counter and were smiling under several layers of red lipstick. Dragging the children at her ankles, my mother walked across the kitchen and picked the lips up. She slapped them onto her face. When she moved her hand, the lips were still smiling while her fingers dissolved into gray swirls.

As I sat up in bed, still feeling the presence of the nightmare in the room, I wondered if my mother was awake on the other side of the wall, trying to time her sleep around the memories of her father. I looked over at Flossie's empty bed. I had written her a goodnight and left it on her pillow earlier in the evening. She was staying with a friend from school. It was best she was gone. With the secret so raw inside me, I didn't trust myself not to tell her, yet I knew Mom expected me to remain silent.

I understood why it was me my mother had chosen. Flossie would have exposed the past, if only so she wouldn't have to bear it alone, while Fraya would have turned even quieter and more inward under a revelation of that magnitude. Mom had to tell someone and she thought I was strong enough. Truth was, I had done with it what she had. Tried to bury it. Only I had buried the story in A Faraway Place, believing it was far enough away, I'd never think of it again. But thinking about it was all I was doing.

Get out of my head.

I soon realized there was enough space on the front porch to make a maze and trap myself there with my own thoughts.

Stay close, Betty, I said to myself. I could feel I was losing something of me while I choked on the smoke pouring out of our chimneys like a long shout against the cold sky.

Every time I looked at Mom, I saw her as a little girl, rubbing her tired eyes, unable to escape the violence being laid upon her. I had to get out and away from the house. I quickened my pace across the open and barren winter fields, shivering into the rapid beating of my heart. Those haunted hours became my fever. Spinning, I collapsed onto the ground, holding myself because there was no one else to do it.

I had my father's eyes, but now my mother's pain. I could feel this pain becoming a solid thing I feared would always be there. I wept thinking about how small her hands were as they tried to push him off and how tiny her body was beneath the enormity of his. I didn't know anything about sex at that age and I didn't have the word for rape, but I knew that what had happened to my mother was as awful as if she had been killed.

I couldn't understand how she'd endured it. I could understand even less how her heart had survived knowing her own mother was the one who carried her to the devil's bed. What do you do when the two people who are supposed to protect you the most are the monsters tearing you to pieces? No wonder Mom still hurt. She hadn't been loved enough.

I found myself holding our old family Bible. Opening it, I flipped past the dates of births, weddings, and deaths written in cursive on the interior flap. The tears that fell from my eyes dripped onto the thin paper as I kept turning. Seeing the name of God, I stopped at a page. One of my tears dropped on a single word, magnifying it.

"Faith," I said the word before closing the Bible.

"You s-s-see demons, too, Betty," Lint said to me later that day on the back porch.

"How can you tell?" I asked.

"I'm no f-f-fool." He started to pull on one ear, then the other. It was as though he wanted to yank them off.

"Why are you doin' that, Lint? Stop."

"I d-d-don't like my ears, Betty."

"Why not?"

"They're not in the r-r-right place for hearin' things."

"They're in the right place, Lint. Stop it."

"All right, Betty."

He reached into his pocket, pulling out a sack of Dad's chive seeds.

"What you doin'?" I asked.

"I've got l-l-lizards beneath my fingernails," he said.

I watched him take the tiny black seeds and push one beneath each of his fingernails.

"See the little b-b-black lizards?" He held his hand in my face, the teeny black seeds peeking out at me between his nail and skin.

I could not doubt his commitment. When he claimed to have pinkeye, he thawed a frozen strawberry and mashed it with graham cracker crumbs. He rubbed the mixture on his eyelid. When it was hay fever, he dripped corn syrup below his nostrils as if he had a runny nose and sucked on a hard candy to color his tongue and the back of his throat red. The most unusual display was when he claimed to have worms and taped white shoelaces to his belly.

"I can feel 'em squirmin' inside me," he had said.

For all of his faking, I don't remember Lint ever having so much as a cold. And yet, there he was coming down with lizards before my eyes.

"I think I have them beneath my fingernails, too," I said.

He took my hand in his. Carefully, he stuck a small black seed beneath each of my nails.

"Did you know r-r-rocks are the o-o-oldest things on earth?" he asked. "I've thought about it a long t-t-time, and I'm certain they m-m-must be. If you think about it, I b-b-bet the earth is one big rock."

When he finished with my other hand, he reached into his pocket and pulled out a clear rock.

"You s-s-see this?" he asked, pointing out a discoloration inside the rock that appeared to take on the shape of something mythical.

"It's a d-d-dragon," he said. "A dragon caught inside a rock."

"Who would have thought," I said, pointing out the dragon's tail so Lint would know I saw his dragon, too.

"You can find all k-k-kinds of things in rocks, Betty. They're more than just hard things. They're b-b-beautiful."

"Why don't we go and find some more?" I asked. "Maybe we'll find one that has a unicorn in it or a sphinx, like what they have in Egypt."

"Yeah." He excitedly sat up, before remembering he was supposed to be sick. "W-w-what about the lizards beneath our fingernails? We should be confined to bedrest."

"Wouldn't you rather look for rocks than stay in bed all day?" I asked. "We could find big ones and small ones. Blue ones and gray ones. Smooth ones and—"

"And ones with c-c-craters?" he asked.

"All the ones there is to find, we could find."

Lint led the way up one hill and across a meadow, where we walked through a grove of old apple trees, then past horses in pasture. The whole time, Lint spoke of sandstone and the way rock can be shaped.

"Sometimes I wonder if humans were f-f-first rocks that got r-r-rained on until we got faces," he said.

Each rock he picked up, he would examine, telling me why its color or shape was important.

"Oh, there's a g-g-good one," he said of the rock he'd just spotted. "Look how it shines in the sun. God must really l-l-love us. Look at all the r-r-rocks He gave. You don't give a world like this to someone you h-h-hate."

As he smiled at the rock, I looked at my fingernails.

"I ain't got lizards no more," I said. "You don't either." I pointed his out. "They must have dropped out while we were pickin' up rocks. Wherever the lizards landed, they'll grow beautiful green things. Ain't that nice?"

He quickly reached in his pocket for the bag of chive seeds.

"No," I said. "We don't need any more."

"But we're still s-s-sick."

"It was only pretend, Lint. Besides, we had fun today, didn't we? Pickin' up rocks and seein' all the ways they're wonderful."

He nodded.

"Why do you pretend anyways? To be bit by rattlesnakes? To have scarlet fever or an arm broken like a branch?"

"It really was broken like a b-b-branch."

"No, it wasn't, Lint. Why do you make up such things?"

He started whispering to the rock in his hand. Then he held it close to his ear as if the rock was talking back to him and he was listening to it. After a few moments of this, he nodded as if agreeing with the last thing the rock had whispered to him. When he looked at me, he lowered the rock.

"I p-p-pretend because maybe if Dad can h-h-heal me here," he said, touching his body, "then maybe he can heal m-m-me here." He touched his head.

"Don't you think if that was the way it worked, you wouldn't need to pretend anymore?"

"Maybe it t-t-takes a while," he said. "Maybe it's like rock. It has to be s-s-shaped."

"I don't think you should pretend anymore, Lint."

"It's n-n-not hurtin' anyone."

"Yes, it is. It's causin' cracks in Dad's heart. Did you know his heart is made of glass?"

Lint shook his head.

"It is," I said. "And there's a bird inside the glass. The bird is very delicate. Everything affects it."

"What you m-m-mean?"

"When Dad treats your fake symptoms, they become real. They float off you and into the air. But they have to go somewhere so when Dad breathes in, they go inside of him and make the bird in his glass heart as sick as you claim to be. When you pretended to have hay fever, the bird actually suffered it. When it was worms, it was the bird who got them. I can hear the glass of his heart crackin' each time he treats you. It's the bird beggin' for you to stop. Don't you want the bird in Dad's glass heart to be well?"

He nodded.

"Then you have to stop, Lint. If you don't, you'll crack Dad's heart so much, it'll break and all that glass will do him in."

"But if I d-d-don't . . . if Dad doesn't . . . I mean, what do I do with all these w-w-wars in my head?"

"I'll tell ya what," I said. "Anytime you feel like there's a war you gotta escape from, just let me know and we'll go hunt rocks together. We'll talk about their size, their colors, and all the ways they're beautiful and special. We'll talk about all of that until you feel like we've found some peace in the war. Arrows can't live forever, Lint. Bullets can't either. There is calm, even amidst the storms."

"You'd d-d-do that for me?" he asked.

"Heck, sure."

"What if it doesn't do any g-g-good?"

I wrapped my arm around him as I said, "You have to have a little *faith* that things will work out."

19

His lightnings enlightened the world:
the earth saw, and trembled.

—PSALM 97:4

The storms of spring 1963 seemed to get inside the house, climb the walls, and shake the candle flames. Relentless lightning lit up the sky in quick flashes and crooked wonder while black clouds deepened the night. That's a southern Ohio spring for you. Hard rain at midnight, wind until the electric cuts out, the river rising an inch at a time.

I was sitting on the floorboards of the back porch with Trustin, who was lying on his belly. I held a flashlight so he could see as he drew with his charcoal stick. I would sometimes imagine Trustin living like the artists in the photographs of the books he checked out from the library. I could see him grown up, as tall as our father, drippings of paint on concrete floors and heavy tarps covering all of his canvases to keep them out of the light. Charcoal fingerprints on everything white and enough drawings to preserve the beauty of his soul.

"You know when folks are hit by lightnin', their teeth will glow in the dark," he said. "I heard it from the old-timers outside the barbershop. They oughta know."

As Trustin drew the clouds, they billowed near, but they also seemed far, as if the storm stretched for miles. In the brightness of the white paper showing through behind his charcoal strokes you could see a country pressed upon by the sky and how a night could lose everything in an unbreakable rain. He was only seven then, but this was Trustin's gift. That he could draw a storm and make you feel the lightning in your bones.

"Why you think Mom did that with the chocolate?" he asked, looking up at me.

The day before, Mom had gone into Papa Juniper's to get groceries. Witnesses said Mom had stopped her cart in front of the chocolate bar display. She stood there for a good twenty minutes staring at the chocolate. One of the workers noticed and asked if he could help her with anything. There wasn't a question of *if* she had cried. There was a question of *how*. Some said her wailing was a long moan. Others said she cried quietly, the tears slipping down her cheeks while her shoulders shook. They all agreed on what happened next. They said she grabbed the chocolate bars and ripped their wrappers open. She ate half, discarding the other on the floor. She was like a starving wolf, they said, trying to devour the chocolate so quick she nearly choked. She scratched the store manager across the cheek when he tried to stop her. He'd always have a scar from it.

When Sheriff Sands got there, he found half-eaten candy bars scattered on the floor and my mother slowly pushing her cart down the aisle, sweetly checking off the remaining items on her list as if there hadn't been a scene and she didn't have chocolate smeared around her mouth. The sheriff ordered her to pay for each bar she destroyed. Dad worked it off by doing jobs for the market.

When Dad tried to find out from Mom why she'd done it, she said, "Because I was hungry."

"But why did you only eat half of each bar?" he asked her.

"Only half was mine." That was her answer and there was to be no more talk about it.

"Betty?" Trustin furrowed his small brow. "Why do you think she did it?"

"She already said why she did it."

"Yeah, but I don't think she did it just because she was hungry. I think it's because she's plannin' on runnin' away," he said, studying his drawing. "You ever hear of a paintin' called *Nighthawks*? I saw it in my library book. In the paintin' is a man sittin' at the counter of a restaurant. In the back of the man's suit is a shadow. I think I'd like to live there in the shadow of his dark blue suit. If one day I'm ever gone, you'll know I ran away to the back of that man's suit."

I studied my little brother as he colored the hills black.

"Trustin?"

"Yeah, Betty?"

"Would you draw me a whole bunch of storms? I'd like to send 'em to someone."

He blew charcoal dust off his paper.

"Sure, I'll draw you some storms, Betty."

A loud bang of thunder followed.

"It sounds like gunfire." He turned to look at both ends of the porch as if making certain we were alone. He leaned closer to me to whisper, "I know who the shooter is. It's Fraya. I saw her comin' outta the woods the other day. She had a shotgun in her hand."

"You really saw a shotgun?" I asked.

"I mean, it could have been a long stick. But before she come out of the woods, I heard the sound of a gun from the direction she come walkin' out from."

"The woods are big and sound echoes, Trust. You can't be sure where the sound came from. Besides, how can you believe Fraya could be the shooter? She ain't the type."

The look in Fraya's eyes as she lit her dress on fire in the church flashed in my mind.

"Flossie on the other hand," I said, "she's a girl born with a trigger finger."

"Sometimes it's the person we least expect, Betty."

He gathered his charcoal and paper and said he was going inside to get one of the spicy hermits Dad had made before the electric cut out.

Left alone, I took a small notepad and pen out of my pocket and wrote by flashlight.

Not long after, Dad came out onto the porch. He handed me a spicy hermit before sitting on the porch swing and looking out at the lightning.

"Lightnin' is the devil bangin' at heaven's door," he said. "Throwin' his whole body into it with so much force, he cracks the sky. But the devil only knocks on the door of heaven when it storms."

"Why?" I asked.

"So the rain will hide his tears as he bangs at his father's door, beggin' to be let back in."

I sat by Dad on the swing, eating my cookie and listening to the wind shake the house.

"Dad?" I dusted cookie crumbs off my hands. "Do you ever wanna leave the storm?"

"Don't worry, Little Indian. This weather can't last forever."

"I mean do you ever wanna run away? Trustin's gonna run away to the back of a man's suit. Mom will probably run away, too, though I don't know where to yet."

Dad sat quietly for as long as it took him to roll a cigarette and light it. Then he told about the time Mom realized she was pregnant with Leland.

"Your mom found me," he said. "I was a lost man, but, somehow, she still found me. I had neither a purpose nor a name before your momma. When I was growin' up folks called me Tomahawk Tom or Tepee Jack or Pow-wow Paul, every name but my own. No one ever even asked me my name until your momma did. Not only did she ask, but she tagged a 'sir' on the end of it. 'What's your name, *sir*?' I had never been called 'sir' before."

He exhaled a long stream of smoke.

"I started out life as nobody," he said, "but because your momma made me a father, I have a real chance to end my time on this earth as somebody worth rememberin'. Why the hell would I run away from that?"

"You are somebody worth rememberin', Dad," I said.

He wrapped his arm around me and pulled me against his side.

"Your feet touch now?" He leaned forward to see my toes resting against the porch boards. "Don't guess you need me to swing ya anymore," he said softly. "You can do it yourself now."

I lifted my legs until my feet weren't touching the floor.

"Nuh-uh," I said. "See." I swung my feet back and forth through the air. "I can't reach."

"Well, then." He smiled. "I guess I'm still needed after all."

He gently rocked us and looked out at the storm. Certain things about my father were beginning to chip away for me. When I had read the books I'd checked out over the years from the library, I used to think—like the stories I encountered—that my father had been born from the minds of writers. I believed the Great Creator had flown these writers on the backs of thunderbirds to the moon and told them to write me a father. Writers like Mary Shelley, who wrote my father to have a gothic understanding of the tenderness of all monsters.

It was Agatha Christie who created the mystery within my father and Edgar Allan Poe who gave darkness to him in ways that lifted him to the flight of the raven. William Shakespeare wrote my father a Romeo heart at the same time Susan Fenimore Cooper composed him to have sympathy toward nature and a longing for paradise to be regained.

Emily Dickinson shared her poet self so my father would know the most sacred text of mankind is in the way we do and do not rhyme, leaving John Steinbeck to gift my father a compass in his mind so he would always appreciate he was east of Eden and a little south of heaven. Not to be left out, Sophia Alice Callahan made sure there was a part of my father that would always remain a child of the forest, while Louisa May Alcott penned the loyalty and hope within his soul. It was Theodore Dreiser who was left the task of writing my father the destiny of being an American tragedy only after Shirley Jackson prepared my father for the horrors of that very thing.

As for my father's imagination, I believed God had stepped on Dad's mind. It was Steinbeck's fault, he having dropped my father's mind in the first place, which gave God the opportunity to step on it, leaving behind a small dent and the print of His foot. Who wouldn't have an imagination like my father's with God's footprint on their mind? More and more, though, this fantasy was fading and I was starting to see the flesh and bone of my father.

His right leg continued to pain him, causing his footsteps to become the shuffling of a tired man. He still lifted loads and dug holes, throwing his back into it, but this and more was beginning to wear on his body. All of his life, he'd had hard jobs. From the time he was a boy, he'd worked in the field or in the factory, but he'd been born into the world to do something more. Maybe that's why we had moved around so much when he was young enough to keep raging against turning a screw or punching a time clock.

Going from place to place meant money was not steady, especially in those early years. How worried my mother would look when all of her lipstick was gone from the tube and she could no longer scrape enough color out with her pinkie nail to cover half a lip.

"What a storm," my father said.

I slipped out from under his arm and returned to my notepad and pen. As the lightning crackled the sky and my father smoked, I turned to a fresh sheet of paper and wrote about the doughnuts.

I hadn't been more than four years old. Leland was already enlisted and Dad had gone on a job we wouldn't see money from until he came back. The rest of us kids were left with Mom. We weren't in Ohio then. We were in one of the states that had us only for a bit. It was winter and we'd eaten what food we had. Mom didn't have money to buy more. My siblings and I were so hungry that we sat on the kitchen floor as if a meal would appear in front of us. Flossie, seven, whined as she held her stomach. Trustin was too young at two to do anything more than rock back and forth. Fraya, who would have been fourteen at the time, sat with her legs crossed and played with her hair while one-year-old Lint sucked his thumb. Mom looked at us. Then she grabbed a big bowl.

"How about we have some doughnuts?" she asked.

We clapped our small hands and cheered while she got flour, sugar, and cinnamon. Our cabinets empty, her hands empty, the bowl empty as she stirred these invisible things.

"Four cups flour." She called out the ingredients. After she picked up the imaginary bag, she threw it up in the air as she laughed and said, "Look at all my flour-headed children."

She ruffled our hair until we imagined flour dusting off, then she pulled us up on our feet to help her with the other ingredients. You can imagine flour and eggs if you're hungry enough. You can see the brown specks of cinnamon in white sugar if you haven't eaten that day or the day before. We passed these empty bowls between us, wondering if we'd put in enough of something. Mom sang as she added buttermilk to the dry ingredients, making a dough she rolled out on the counter. She used a juice glass to cut circles. She told us to put a finger through the middle of each.

"Can't have a doughnut without a hole," she said as we laughed and poked our fingers through the air. She followed it up with a vat of oil that was so nonexistent a fly came and landed in the very place we imagined doughnuts were tossing and bubbling until they were golden enough to be removed and placed on a rack to cool.

"Look how pretty they are." Mom leaned over the emptiness on the counter. "How many of you want glazed? And how many want just sugar?"

"Me, me." We raised our hands.

"All right," she said. "We'll do some glazed and some with plain sugar."

She handed us the imaginary sugar bag and we passed it between us, dusting half the doughnuts with sugar while she took a bowl and stirred milk and powdered sugar. She went through the motion of drizzling the glaze on the remaining doughnuts until they shone. We ate these doughnuts that did not exist on the floor of the cold kitchen. What I remember so distinctly is how my mother ate not one herself.

"There's only ten left now," she would call out. "Only five now. Who wants 'em?"

"Me, me." We waved our hands in the air.

She let us have all the doughnuts as if they really did exist and she would not take one from out of her children's mouths.

"What's your story about?" Dad asked me just as thunder banged around us.

"It's not a story," I said.

"Oh?" He curiously looked toward the page. "What is it?"

"A memory of the time Mom made us doughnuts when you were gone."

"Oh, she did, did she?" He nodded. "Good mother there."

"Yes." I stared out at the lightning that was as close as it could get. "Good mother."

THE BREATHANIAN

War Veteran Disturbed by Gunfire

The granddaughter of a WWI veteran—who has been plagued by memory issues the last few years—has acknowledged her grandfather is suffering as a result of the gunfire that continues to increase throughout town.

"He hears the shots and thinks he's back in the war," the granddaughter said.

Dressed in his WWI uniform, the man has started marching and keeping guard. He has even put a barricade around his house.

When asked what the barricade was for, the man replied, "To keep the Germans out."

The granddaughter makes a heartfelt plea to the shooter to quit this "senseless" activity. "Please stop. The gunfire is in my papaw's hair, his eyes, his crying mind. Why must your misery become ours?"

A man who lives beside the veteran believes the shooter is female.

"It's like a woman to do something like this," the man commented. "When a man fires a gun, it's a distinct sound. You never question his motives."

When the man was asked what he thinks the motives are of the woman he believes to be at fault for the shooting, he said, "She probably just lost her lipstick."

20

We have a little sister, and she hath no breasts.

—Song of Solomon 8:8

Once the rain of that spring cleared, we began the growing season. The work always started with the weeding. Weeds that were too young to seed, we pulled out and threw to the wood line. The weeds that would spread were burned on the garden plot to loosen the soil for seeds.

"Always make the dirt into hills to plant corn in," Dad would tell us, "because hills will steady the stalks as they grow, the way Breathed's hills steady us." He'd wave at Breathed's hills.

Raising the dirt also shielded the corn's roots from the sun, which Dad said was important because a long time ago, corn had refused to be the sun's wife.

"Ever since," he said, "corn and sun have been enemies. Every chance the sun gets, he burns the corn's roots, trying to kill her."

Dad told these stories each new season as we dug our hands into the earth, making low hills for the beans because, unlike the corn, beans on high hills have weak vines, putting pressure on the roots following a rain.

"Remember all of this," Dad always said. "So one day, when you have your own gardens, you will never raise your bean hills so high."

Along with the corn and beans, there was zucchini, okra, peppers, and eggplants. Dad grew different melons, tomatoes, potatoes, and just about every leafed vegetable. There were berries, grapes, and all the sweet things you could think of. He grew so many varieties of plants that *The Breathanian* came out to take a picture of him standing in the garden.

THE GARDEN MAN OF BREATHED the headline read.

With such large gardens, hoeing was done daily and in the early morning hours. Each of us had a hoe of our own. Flossie would complain, saying no actress should have blisters on her hands. Fraya seemed to enjoy hoeing as she struck her blade into the dirt, a fierce determination on her face.

Some of the seeds, like the squash, were planted in late May. Dad had a pole we would hang seeds on to dry after blowing water onto them to sprout. We would then plant the squash in the sides of their hills because spring rain beat too hard on the hilltops, threatening to drown tender sprouts. The good thing about squash was that it grew quickly. Before we knew it, we began the blossom harvest.

"There are two types of blooms on a squash plant," Dad said as he pointed them out. "The female blossoms grow close to the roots and will bear fruit, but the blossoms that are male grow farther away on the stem and will bear nothing more than the color they are."

"How come male blossoms get no fruit?" I asked.

"Because they do not have the strength nor the power of the female flowers," Dad said.

Given the male blossoms would bear nothing, we picked them to eat as soon as they came on. If you waited too long, any rain would cause dirt to spray onto the soft petals, ruining them. Most of the blossoms we harvested to eat raw, piling the bright yellow flowers in our mouths and crushing the petals with our teeth. Some we dried on the tallest of the grass. We would do so by taking a single blossom and pinching off its calyx, before laying the blossom flat on the top of the grass.

"Now take a second blossom," Dad would instruct like it was our first time. "And tear it slightly on the side so it can be stacked on the first into a chain."

By midsummer it was a regular occurrence to see our grass tops covered. That July of 1963, Flossie and I had wandered out alone to make more blossom chains at the very back of the field.

As we stacked them, Flossie ate some, asking me, "Betty, how much weight you think I could lose if I only ate flowers?"

"You're not fat," I told her.

"Not yet. But I'm already twelve and every actress should know her best diet by the time she's thirteen." She looked up at the sun. "Let's go back to A Faraway Place. I've got some new screen magazines there to look at."

When we got to the garden, Dad was checking the tension of the string on the bean trellis.

"I brought the radio out," he said, pointing to the transistor radio lying on the stage.

Flossie grabbed it after she climbed up the ladder. Turning the radio on, she bopped her head at the same time she flipped through her magazines. I sat on the edge of the stage so I could dangle my legs and write.

The corn said to the sun, I do not love you. The sun said to the corn, I will destroy you.

While I wrote, I listened to the radio in the background. The announcer was saying the day was one of the hottest on record.

After the weather report, the station played Elvis' song "I Can't Help Falling in Love with You," which made Flossie squeal.

"Oh, Elvis, I can't wait to marry you," she said, scooting across the stage to sit beside me on the edge.

She swung her legs next to mine and asked if I thought Elvis read the letters she'd been sending him.

"You mean the letters you stuff in bottles and send out on the river?" I rolled my eyes. "Elvis ain't gonna get letters you send out to 'im on Breathed River, Flossie."

"Why the hell not?" She tugged her shirt down to show what little cleavage she had. "Breathed River runs into the Ohio River. The Ohio River eventually runs into the great Mississippi. The great Mississippi flows right by Graceland."

"You think Elvis is gonna be sittin' on the banks of the Mississippi waitin' to fish out bottles with letters inside written by a girl who can't even spell his last name?"

"I sure can. P, r, e, s, s, s—"

"Only one s, Flossie," Dad said, jerking his hips in his best Elvis impersonation. He twisted off a ripe okra and held it like a microphone as he mouthed the lyric about a river flowing to the sea.

"I told you." Flossie elbowed me. "Rivers even flow to the sea."

Dad continued to perform, getting into his Elvis impersonation by snarling his lip as he grabbed Flossie's hand. He took it to his mouth for a kiss. Flossie giggled until she just about giggled herself off the stage. Before Dad could grab my hand, I jumped down into the grass.

"I'm goin' fishin'," I said, slipping my notepad and pencil into my pocket.

I went into the garage and grabbed a cane fishing pole.

"C'mon, Flossie," I said. "I'll use you as bait."

We waved to Dad, who was still dancing and singing to himself, pretending to flip his collar up and point to a crowd.

"He really thinks he's Elvis." Flossie laughed. "Silly Dad. He could never be Elvis."

We laughed, running through the fields, only slowing down once we entered the woods.

Flossie wiped sweat off her forehead and said, "I doubt we'll catch any fish today. How 'bout we go into town and see what those Carnation boys are up to."

"Those Carnation boys are in high school, Flossie."

"I know." She smiled. When I just stared at her, she straightened her face and said, "I'm only sayin' we're not gonna catch anything so we might as well be entertained."

"The wind is comin' from the south," I said. "That means we're certain to catch somethin'. Even if it's only the scent of hell."

"Hold up. I gotta pee." She looked around for a good spot to squat.

I decided to do a little dryland fishing, which was what Dad used to do as a boy when the river went dry. He'd take his cane pole into the woods and bait it with a sweet birch leaf *'cause they're the sweetest,* or so he always said. A dryland fish, Dad swore, was all kinds of creatures wrapped up into one.

"Think of a fish," he'd say. "Then think of a squirrel. Now put those two things together and you got yourself one dryland fish out of a million others."

I picked up a fallen birch leaf and slid it on the hook. Without looking back, I cast the line behind me. When I jerked it forward, Flossie's bloodcurdling scream pierced the woods, causing the birds in the branches above to take flight in a great exodus.

I turned around to see why she had screamed. What I saw was her with her pants down. She was in a squat and there was blood on her butt cheek from the fish hook embedded in it.

"You did this on purpose," she said.

"It was an accident. I didn't know you were behind me."

"You wanted to hook me. You had this planned to do all day. *'C'mon, Flossie. I'll use you as bait.'*" She tried to imitate my voice but her rage was making it come out higher than it was. "That's exactly what you said to me, Betty."

"I didn't mean—"

"You've always been jealous of me. I'm prettier and I'm smarter and everyone loves me more. You just wait. When I get this hook out, I'm gonna stick it in your tongue."

"I don't suppose I'll help you get it out then." I dropped the fishing pole and slowly climbed up a nearby tree.

Flossie wrapped her arms around herself and stood moaning.

"Ow, it hurts. It hurts."

If fury wasn't going to get her anywhere, she'd try her dramatics.

"Oh, pity me." She laid her cheek against a tree. "The beautiful girl, caught on the hook of the ugly and jealous pig goat."

As she continued her soliloquy, I climbed higher, finding a branch I could straddle as though it were a horse. Even though I couldn't see the house anymore through the treetops, I whistled and held my hand above my eyes as if I were seeing something spectacular.

"What you whistling at, ya old slug butt?" Flossie asked as she looked in the direction I was.

"You ain't gonna believe this, Flossie." I swung my arms and legs as if my excitement was too much to contain. "A pink Cadillac just pulled up on Shady Lane."

"I don't believe you." She stepped forward, the fishing pole dragging behind her.

"Don't move, Flossie. You'll dig the hook in deeper."

"You don't see nothin'. We're too far away." She waited a second, before asking in a softer tone, "Where'd the Cadillac go?"

"To our house."

"I don't see nothin'." She struggled to find a break in the trees through which to see more clearly.

"Oh, Flossie, you are not gonna believe who is gettin' out of the Caddy. It's Elvis." I squealed his name like she would have. "The whole backseat of his Caddy is full of the bottles you sent him. They're stickin' out of the windas and everythin'. He's got your letters and now he's come to take you as his bride."

I fluttered my lashes at her and made kissy noises.

She gnashed her teeth while she pulled the bark off the tree like a rabid animal. Huffing and puffing, she said, "You rat hag. You think I need you? Flossie Carpenter don't need nobody. I'll get the hook out myself."

"Dad will need to snap the end off with pliers," I told her. "If you pull on it, the hook will tear your ass out. If you ask nicely, though, I'll get Dad for you. But you have to ask me nicely." I grinned.

She cursed a few more times before pushing her rage deep inside her. She squeezed her eyes until tears rolled down her cheeks.

"Pretty please, Betty." She spoke as though she were auditioning. "Won't you get our father lest I bleed out and—"

"All right, all right, Vivien Leigh." I got down from the tree.

She pulled up her panties so she could at least be partially covered.

When I got back to the garden, I excitedly ran up to Dad and told him I'd just caught a dryland fish.

"You did?" he asked as he dropped cucumbers into a basket.

"Yep." I nodded. "She's still on the hook in the woods, though. She was too big to drag all the way up here. I was hopin' you could go and get her off the hook for me."

"Well, what's this dryland fish look like?" He narrowed his eyes.

"She's the ugliest thing I ever have seen. She's got stringy hair and caterpillar eyebrows and she smells like piss." I held my nose. "I think the poor thing just got so scared."

"Uh-huh." He put his hands on his hips. "Where's Flossie, Betty?"

"I think she went into town to find some carnations," I said.

"Flossie don't even like carnations."

"She does when they're boys."

"All right, then." He started to make his way out of the garden. "Let's go see what ya caught."

"No." I shook my head. "I ain't goin' back there."

"Don't you wanna keep your catch?"

"Naw, I don't wanna eat a fish that's pissed herself. Throw her back in the woods. Let the wolves have a go at her."

With pliers in hand, Dad started through the woods. Once he was out of sight, I ran into the barn to hide out. I climbed up to the loft. Earlier that morning I had caught two bees in a jar. There were airholes in the lid, but one of the bees had still died. I opened the lid only wide enough to dump the body into my hand. Stretched across the loft's window was a spiderweb. I decided to hang the dead bee in it.

"You're pretty," I said to a spider watching me.

A squeak from below got my attention. I peeked over the edge of the loft and I saw Fraya. She had opened the door of the old truck Cinderblock John had parked a while back in our barn to store.

From the angle the truck was parked, I had a good view into the cab. I watched as Fraya slid onto the seat, her legs hanging out the open door. She had her diary. I read it once after she left it on her bed. There amidst the unreadable lettering was a sentence:

I caught a lightning bug. It hurt my palm to kill it. But I did anyways. I find it hard to remember to believe there is light in this world.

I still think about Fraya every day. Sometimes I think she's just hiding inside of me. If I could drop a long rope down my throat, maybe she'd climb out and eat pistachio pudding like she used to when she was still around to have dessert with. She was a wonderful girl. It's hard to say how many ways. Her light brown hair was still long then. Her gray eyes, like the edge of a storm. Her small body, a very little thing. You could fit all of her in the palm of your hand. Lose her the same way. It'd be so much easier if the bad things in our lives were kept in our skin that we could shed off like a snake. Then we could leave all the dried horrid things on the ground and step forward, free from them.

"No, ma'am," Fraya sang, "I ain't got no place to go. No, I ain't got no sense I know."

I thought that one day Fraya would be famous. She could sing just like Loretta Lynn. Fraya had even won a ribbon at the fair once for her singing. I wondered if she thought she could be famous, too.

I was about to climb down the ladder to tell her all about sticking Flossie with the fish hook, but the shadow of a figure stepping into the barn stopped me.

Leland.

He was home for a visit after having been gone months on the road. He had more hauls that would take him to California.

He stood in front of the truck as Fraya wrote in her diary. He seemed to like her not knowing he was there. He bit his lower lip and tilted his head to the side as if something was passing over his shoulder and he had to give it room.

He removed a cigarette from his pocket and lit it with his lighter, which was a naked woman with red rhinestone eyes.

"Why's her eyes red?" I once asked him.

"Because blood red is the color of all women's eyes," he had said.

The click of the lighter startled Fraya and caused her to stop singing and look up. As I watched Leland walk toward her, I found myself hiding back in the shadows.

"Don't give me another gash," he told Fraya as he pulled up his short sleeve, showing the fresh cut on the very top of his arm. "I'm out of bandages."

"Leland, not right now," she said, turning away from him. "I've just had a bath."

She quickly tried to close the door, but he caught it and held it open.

He squinted at something on the ground. I looked for myself but saw nothing.

"I had a dream about you last night," he told her. "You washed my socks and hung 'em on the clothesline to dry. Ain't that a strange dream to have, Fray?"

He always called her Fray. Like she was an unraveling thing.

"You ever dream of me, Fray?"

He offered her his cigarette. She took it with her head down.

"Fray?"

His voice was soft. Like the first beams of light in the morning.

She left the cigarette in her mouth for so long, she began to look older than her nineteen years.

"I once dreamed you had a million eyes and not one of 'em was lookin' at me," she said on an exhale of smoke. "I liked that dream."

He looked at her before taking the cigarette from her mouth, only to squash it beneath the heel of his boot. When he grabbed her neck, the most she did was gasp.

"Why'd you follow me in the woods the other day, Fray?"

"I wanted to see what you were doin'?"

"Are you gonna tell anyone what you saw?"

She didn't respond so he shook her, asking again if she was going to tell.

"Yes," she said. "You're sick. What you were doin' to my eagle—"

He threw her back on the seat. Her diary fell on the floor of the truck as she kicked his hands, which were quickly undoing his pants.

"I'll scream," she said. "If you don't leave right now, I swear to God, I will scream."

"No, you won't." He laughed.

Her tears seemed to boil against her cheeks as she narrowed her eyes at him until I thought her face would split between the brows.

"I hate you." She slapped him repeatedly. "I hate you."

"And I hate you."

He forced her right leg out to the side of him and her left to the other, pulling her closer as he lifted the layers of her full skirt. She fought back, so he hit her in the face before pressing his body down on top of hers. He grabbed a handful of her long hair and wrapped it around the driver's side window crank until she couldn't move her head.

"You have no idea how much I missed you on the road." He licked his lips as he pushed his jeans down the rest of the way to fall around his boots. And then he was *pushing, pushing* while the muscles at the backs of his legs quivered.

"Please," Fraya said, "stop."

Her head bobbed forward while the hair at her crown stretched from the window crank it was tied to.

"Betty did it on purpose, Dad. I know it." Flossie's voice drifted into the barn.

Leland stopped and laid his hand over Fraya's mouth.

"Don't you dare make a sound," he said to her in a whisper.

Flossie was speaking a mile a minute, her voice getting closer and closer.

"One day, you'll find me dead," Flossie said. "Betty's gonna kill me out of jealousy."

"It was only an accident, Flossie." Dad's voice trailed hers until they both ebbed into the distance.

I looked back at Leland and Fraya. Her eyes had never left his.

I opened my mouth and was about to yell for Dad to come back, but I remembered the story Mom had told me about the time she saw her brother in the attic. I knew my father was not like Grandpappy Lark. Yet, what if he did nothing to Leland but made Fraya eat the Bible, page by page? What if everyone would say it wasn't Leland's fault, but Fraya's?

I became frightened by the overwhelming possibility that Leland would not be the one punished, even though Fraya had done nothing wrong. This fear silenced me.

Waiting a second longer to make sure Flossie nor Dad was returning, Leland removed his hand from Fraya's mouth.

"I knew you wouldn't have the nerve to scream," he said with a
grin.

She closed her eyes and lay still as he continued what he had
started.

"No, ma'am, I ain't got no place to go," she softly sang, an expression
of pain warping her face.

I dug my fingernails into my scalp and backed against the wall.
I was too damn young. Only nine years old and I was floating over
the world, seeing fathers ruin their daughters. Brothers ruin their
sisters. I imagined that the story I'd buried in A Faraway Place of my
mother's rape was clawing itself up from its grave. Like the squeaking
of the bed from Mom's story, all I could hear was the squeaking of the
truck's seat. Needing to find a way to make it stop, I took my notepad
out of my pocket with the pencil. I wrote as quickly as I could.

The brother leaves the barn. He leaves the sister alone. It stops. It all sto—

I pressed the pencil so hard, the lead broke before I could finish. I
threw the pencil against the wall and watched it roll across the floor
to the jar with the one bee still alive. The bee was trying to understand why she was trapped. I quickly crawled over and picked up the
jar, removing its lid. Before the bee could fly away, I grabbed her and
squeezed until all I felt was her sting.

21

~

Hide them in the dust together;
and bind their faces in secret.

—Job 40:13

Fraya would make dandelion lotion. She'd spread it all over her body. The yellow on her skin, something I remember loving. I took this dandelion lotion and squeezed it out on top of my head. Yellow in my black hair. Yellow on my black eyebrows.

So this is being blonde, I thought as I stared in the mirror and did not like what I saw. It was the day after I had watched my brother rape my sister in the barn.

Dad was in the kitchen jarring plums. Whole, unsliced plums. Near to black plums. He always had a dreamy look in his eye when he jarred.

"My mother's favorite fruit to jar were plums," he said, keeping his eyes on his work. He pressed the plums firmly down into the jars, but not so hard that the skin broke. "Qua-nu-na-s-di." He carefully spoke the Cherokee word for plum. "Qua-nu-na-s-di," he sang it out a second time. "My mother taught me that," he said with pride. "One day, Betty, these plums will return to you when you are old. Then you, too, will jar them and say 'Qua-nu-na-s-di.'"

When I did not reply, he raised his eyes to me. The dreaminess left as he saw the yellow lotion dried into my strands.

"Why you have that on your hair?" he asked. "And why are your eyes so red? Have you been cryin'?"

"I'm blonde." I twirled for him like I thought Flossie might. "Don'tcha like it?"

"You want to be blonde, Little Indian?" His fingers were stained purple.

"Maybe then folks won't ask me if I grease my skin. Maybe then they won't call me a—"

"Don't say it, Betty."

With a plum still in his hand, he reached out and grabbed me by the shoulders. He gripped me so tight, the cooked fruit was squeezed between his palm and me. I watched its mushy insides spread out while the juice trickled, seeping into my sleeve as he shook me and demanded I never call myself what they did.

"Do you understand me?" He seemed out of breath as if there was a million miles he was trying to close between us.

"You don't have to break my bones over it," I said, shrugging out of his hands. I added a "Jesus Crimson" the way my mother would have.

"I want you to say you'll never call yourself what they call us." Dad once more grabbed me hard by the shoulders. The plum in his hand was no longer whole, but now a squashed thing he held between us.

"Okay. I won't. You're hurtin' me, Dad."

"Sorry." He released me. "I'm just—" He threw his arms up in the air. "Who would you be without that hair of yours? Your eyes, your skin. You wouldn't be my Little Indian."

"Holey moley, it's not a big deal. All right? I'll wash the dandelion lotion out."

I forced my tears to stay behind my eyelids.

"Besides," I added, "it's Fraya who should be angry. Not you."

"Why would she be angry?" he asked.

"Because all of her dandelion lotion is in my hair," I said with my guilt hovering in the back of my throat like a trapped fly. "She'll have to wait until next spring when there's enough blossoms to make more."

"Betty, why'd you go and use all her lotion like that?"

"Everyone does things to Fraya." I wiped my eyes with my fists. "Why the hell can't I?"

I grabbed an empty jar and ran out the back door to A Faraway Place. I crawled on my stomach and went under the stage. I got a pen and blank pieces of paper out of my pocket. A twig jabbed me in my chest as I wrote about Leland and what he'd done to Fraya in the barn. The bumpy ground beneath the paper caused my writing to waver and slant, but I thought it was only matching the way I was starting to see the world around me.

Putting a period at the last sentence, I dug a hole and placed the story into the jar. Speaking the Cherokee word for plum over the jar, I screwed the lid on tight before the word had a chance to escape. Then I buried Fraya's story beside our mother's.

When I climbed back out from under the stage, I stared at the barn. All the memories came flooding back. The way the hairs at Fraya's crown had stretched so taut. The way Leland grunted more at the end. I covered my ears, but the sounds were still there. I had to start moving out of fear if I stood still any longer, I'd shatter. I started running. Thin switches cut my legs as I ran through thorny thickets and briars of the woods. A bird screeched overhead. I ran faster and thought about the eagle. I knew then what Fraya's prayer had meant. The realization felt like an entity, panting and breathing down the back of my neck. How many prayers had she written, begging to be free from him?

Up ahead was a cliff. There, the light and branches began to shape themselves until, as if suspended from the sky, there was Fraya. She was ethereal and light, floating in a long dress that hid her feet. I ran faster to her as she reached out to me, a halo of light around her shoulders.

"Fraya."

I leapt off the cliff edge with my arms out, trying to grab my sister. She disappeared before I could. I was left to fall through the air, my body fusing to a splash before I sank beneath the water of the river just below the cliff.

The lotion washed away as I closed my eyes against the brown water, allowing it to carry me deeper and deeper. Only when my lungs felt like they were going to burst did I kick off the bottom to shoot back to the surface.

"Betty? That you?"

I turned around and found Leland fishing from the riverbank.

"Don't swim into my hook," he said.

He wasn't holding his fishing pole. It was next to him, propped against a rock as he lay back beside it. He didn't have a shirt on. He had the lean strong body that came with being twenty-four.

"I thought you were leavin'?" I asked him.

"What's with the tone, Betty baby? You know I'm here for a few days."

He looked out at the water, then up at the hot sun.

"I might get in for a dip myself," he said. "Ain't no fish today anyways."

He had his pants unbuckled before he stood.

"Don't get in," I told him. "I saw an old woman bathin' her black cat in the water up the bank there. The water is witchy today, Leland."

"Why the hell you swimmin' in it then?"

"I'm already a witch. Didn't Flossie tell ya? My name don't burn in a hot skillet."

I hoped that might make him too frightened to get into the water with me, but he still stripped down to his underwear and jumped into the water, causing a large splash. When he came up, he was right beside me. Ever since his trucking job, he'd started to smell like hot leather and siphoned metal. It was this odor I smelled even then in the river.

I started to swim away, but he grabbed my arm.

"Why you frownin' like that, Betty girl?" he asked. "Look just like a damn cabbage leaf."

He tossed me into the air.

"Stop, Leland." I kicked my legs out, hoping to hit him. "Don't touch me."

His grip was strong as he dunked me. I started to choke on the water.

"I'm sorry, Betty." He slapped me on the back. "Breathe. Just breathe." He whacked my back harder.

"I said don't touch me, Leland."

I wouldn't let myself cry in front of him, even though I could feel the tears wanting to come. I pushed him when he tried to get closer. He looked at me like he could steal all my teeth.

"Come on, Betty girl." He forcibly grabbed my hand underneath the water, jerking me toward the bank. "We don't spend enough time together."

He yanked me out of the water, throwing me onto the sandbank. When I tried to get away, he forced me to sit by his side.

"Now, we're gonna sit here, Betty. I said we're just gonna sit here together."

He wrapped his arms around my stomach, holding me against his wet chest. I managed to wiggle free, but he pulled me down by my ankles and was on top of me before I knew it, pinning my arms up over my head. His hot breath slipped into my mouth along with drops of water falling off his chin.

"What is the matter with you, Betty?"

He squeezed my wrists. His body was so heavy on me, I thought I was going to suffocate under the weight.

"Don't hurt me, Leland."

His eyes surprised me as they went soft on the edges.

"I only wanted you to sit with me for a bit," he said. "We don't know each other is all."

He sat back with his arms across his knees. His hands dangled softly. It was as if he was no meaner than a cold morning without socks. He spiraled no worse than the swirl of cinnamon he once gave me in my oatmeal. He did not coach the flies to damn the honey, he did not cripple ceilings over cradles, his soul was not a plunge into the deep barking dark. And yet, just the day before, I had watched him break my sister open.

I sat up beside him. The gritty sand of the bank had embedded in my wet clothes that clung to me until I felt naked. I noticed how Leland seemed to look at every inch of my body. I folded my arms across my chest. I could hear my heartbeat. I wondered if he could, too.

He turned to watch a bee fly from butterweed to butterweed.

"Fray's allergic to bees," he said. "I once saved her from one that came landin' on the back of her neck. She thought it was somethin' to smack. Like a fly or a mosquito. I stopped her just in time. If she would have struck the bee, its stinger would've pushed into her palm. You remember this now, Betty girl. I've saved the life of the girl allergic to bees."

He had said it almost boyishly as he stared into my eyes and I into his. I knew my memories of Leland would always be of the evil things he had done. But seeing him sitting there, I thought I should try to save a small sliver of goodness for my own sake. Like the way the sun shone on the wet strands of his blonde hair. Or the way his eyelid folded over his left eye as he squinted. What else could I save of a brother I had come to hate?

"Promise me something, Leland," I said. "Promise you'll never save me."

I got up and ran as fast as I could. I thought for a moment I heard his footsteps behind me, but I didn't dare look back.

I had every intention of screaming what Leland had done as soon as I threw open the screen door, but I found Fraya sitting at the table with Dad. They were jarring the rest of the plums.

"There you are, Betty girl," Fraya said. "You're all wet." She watched the water drip from me onto the floor.

"Fraya? You cut your hair?" I slowly stepped toward her.

"Do I look terrible?" She touched her hair. It was no more than a thumb's length all over.

"Naw," Dad was quick to say. "Just used to seein' ya with long hair. It's a shock is all. It looks real nice."

"Why'd you cut it, Fraya?" I asked.

"I wanted a change." Her eyes darted from Dad to me. "I thought it might be cooler for summer, too."

"I hate it." I picked up a jar of plums and threw it against the wall. Shards of glass settled into the floorboards.

"Betty," Dad said, "stop."

I threw jar after jar, the plums and their sweet liquid, spilling across the floor.

"Please, Betty." Fraya cried out, staring at the plums. "Stop."

Hearing her say "stop" reminded me of the way she had said it to Leland. I didn't want to keep going the way he had. I set the last jar down. With tears on my cheeks, I pushed past Fraya. I darted up the steps and into the upstairs bathroom.

I emptied out the wastebasket, but found only used tissue and cotton swabs. Hurrying down the hall to Fraya's bedroom, I quickly dumped her wastebasket out on the floor. Amidst the wadded-up tissue, I found her long beautiful hair. I got on my knees and gathered the light brown locks to my chest.

"Betty?" Fraya appeared in the doorway. "Are you okay?" She sat on her knees beside me. "It's not like I cut yours." She ran her fingers through my hair. "Why you care so much about mine?"

"Because your hair is you." I wiped my eyes. "And you just cut it off and threw it away."

"You're right," she said. "I shouldn't have thrown it away. We can put it outside in the woods so birds can collect it to build their nests with. C'mon, now. Isn't that a nice idea? Don't cry."

She pulled me against her. Before, I would have felt her long hair against my cheek. Now, it was only the cold cotton of her dress. I started to sing one of the songs we sang to the garden.

"La, la, la, la, peas of mine, la, la, won't you grow so fine. La, la, la, la."

"What you doin', Betty?" she asked.

"Singin' like we do to the plants," I said, "so your hair will grow long again."

"I don't want it to." She stiffened. "It kept gettin' wrapped around things."

The image of her hair tied around the truck's window crank flashed into my mind. I immediately dropped the clumps of hair and grabbed onto her.

"Thatta girl," she said. "I'm still me. I haven't thrown myself away. I'm right here."

"I'm sorry, Fraya."

"For what? My hair? Don't be." She looked at the puddle made from my dripping hair. "Were you swimmin' in the river, Betty?"

I nodded and sniffled against her chest.

"It's nice to swim in the river when it's so hot, ain't it?" She laid her hand on top of my head.

I nodded some more as I played with the buttons on her dress.

"I keep thinkin' you're still as small as a baby," she said as she tried to move me up on her lap, but I couldn't fit. "I have to remind myself you're growin' up."

"I don't mean to," I said before deciding to tell her I had seen Leland at the river. "He said he saved you." I looked up into her face. "From a bee."

She squinted as if trying to adjust to something far away.

"That's just a story he likes to tell," she said. "Boys are like that. Always tryin' to pretend they're savin' girls from somethin'. They never seem to realize, we can save ourselves."

22

Both low and high, rich and poor, together.

—Psalms 49:2

For a lost voice, gather small acorns, the bark of a dogwood, and some bitter apples. *Don't forget the cherry bark, Betty.* Boil this and drink it. Rub some on the throat, like Dad did mine. His hand pressing against my neck, saying, "We'll find your voice again, Betty."

But my voice wasn't lost. It was in my mind, circling the fire, preparing me to cut Leland's soul out of him.

"Feel better?" Dad asked, rubbing his hands up my throat. I only nodded. It was the end of that August. Leland was all the way in California. He'd left the day he walked back from the river.

I timed the weeks following the rape by watching Fraya's hair start to regrow. It would never be longer than her little finger. This was the way she tested it to make sure it would never be long enough to hold her down. By the time school started, I had gotten used to seeing her with short hair until the long-haired Fraya seemed like someone who'd walked out the front door, never to come back.

I hated that I had to start school after such a summer. Hated that I would have to face Ruthis and all her friends. I was entering the third grade. A new school year also meant a new teacher. Mrs. Hook. Before lunch, she called me up to her desk to drop my shame in my hand. Two green tokens. One for a carton of milk. The other for a tray of food. The tokens were part of the school program servicing the low-income families and fulfilling the school's obligation to provide a free lunch.

I quickly dropped the tokens into my pocket as Mrs. Hook wrote my name on the list. I walked back to my seat with my head down, passing Ruthis, who laughed and called me pathetic. I looked at the shiny quarters on her desk. There would never be tokens for Ruthis Ryewood. I wondered what it was like to be her.

When we lined up in the cafeteria, I waited for everyone to go ahead of me so I could be last. I took the tokens out of my pocket, smelling the mashed potatoes and gravy, which was one of my favorites.

"How come your dad don't work, Betty?" the boy in front of me turned around to ask. "If he worked, you wouldn't have to have those tokens. He must be really lazy."

"Her dad's a medicine man." Ruthis had overheard and didn't pass up the opportunity to say, "He only gets paid in beads. Maybe if lunch cost a bead, you'd be able to afford it, Betty."

I closed my hand around the tokens and hid them back in my pocket.

"What's the matter, Betty?" Ruthis smacked her lips. "Forget how to talk?"

"Maybe she just makes noises now," the girl next to her chimed in. *"Ooo, ooo, ah, ah."* She grunted as she scratched under her arms like a monkey.

The lunch teacher stood nearby. He looked me up and down before turning his back. Together he and another teacher spoke in whispers.

I slipped out of line and went into the bathroom, where I stayed in the stall, smelling the mashed potatoes I had wanted.

"Extra scoop of gravy please." I pretended to hold out a tray. "A roll, a chocolate milk, and a chocolate chip cookie. Might as well give me some of that ambrosia salad." I started requesting things not on the menu.

I sat the imaginary tray on my lap and began to go through the motions of eating. After the bell rang, I dropped my hands and returned to class. When the school day finally ended, I took the long way home.

Dad was sitting on the front porch, carving a turtle. Give my father a knife and a block of wood and he'd transform it into something beautiful. His work was throughout our house, from the bullfrogs resting on shelves to the bookends that were two sides of a covered bridge. He made magical creations from mermaids to little cubes, which he said held the fury of dragons. Many of his carvings were of the creatures we shared our world with, like the sparrows he made to hang in each window of the house.

"Sparrows are the eyes of a mother," he said when he hung them. "They'll keep watch over our home and beat their wings at the first sign of danger, and the first sign of frost."

There were grander carvings like the handkerchief tree, which was nearly as tall as Lint and was a tree that had the tattered shreads of an old paisley handkerchief hanging from its twisted and bent branches. Then there was his interpretation of the vessel Noah steered across the flood. Inside the ark were pairs of every animal Dad could think of.

Out of all of his creations, my favorites were the relief carvings he'd hang on our walls. He would slice a thick layer of wood from a stump. In the slice, he etched images. There was one of Shady Lane and another of the hills from a distance. They were so real-looking, you could hear crickets in the tall grass and the sound of a crow caw-ing overhead.

The relief carving hanging on my bedroom wall was of three girls going down Breathed River in a canoe. Each girl had a basket on her lap.

"They're the Three Sisters," Dad had said. "In different native tribes, the Three Sisters represent the three most important crops. Maize, beans, and squash. The crops grow together as sisters. The old-est is maize. She grows the tallest, supportin' the vines of her younger sisters. The middle sister is beans. She gives nitrogen and nutrition to the soil, which allows her sisters to grow resilient and strong. The youngest is squash. She is the protector of her sisters. She stretches her leaves to shade the ground and fight off weeds. It is squash's vines which tie the Three Sisters together in a bond that is the strongest of all. This was how I knew I'd have three daughters, even after Waconda died. Fraya's the corn. Flossie is the beans. And you, Betty, are squash. You must protect your sisters as squash protects the corn and beans."

Dad carved a small ear of corn for Fraya and a small pod of beans for Flossie. I was given a squash nesting in its leaf. He painted each carving. Bright yellow for Fraya's corn. Light green for Flossie's beans. Dark green for my leaf nestling an orange squash. He attached each charm to our own individual necklace of Cherokee corn beads, which he harvested from the garden.

Using more beads, Dad made him and Mom each a necklace. Their pendant was an apple he carved no bigger than the center of his palm. He painted the apple red, then cut it in half, splitting even the stem itself. Inside the apple halves he painted white flesh and black seeds.

"It's the apple you were eatin' the first time we met," Dad told Mom when he first showed her the necklaces. He was already wearing his, and was offering to put hers around her neck for her.

Once she felt the carving against her skin, she held it in her hand and said, "First it was half a chocolate bar. Now it's half an apple. How can a woman ever feel whole in this damn world?"

"Half a chocolate bar?" Dad asked.

Without answering, Mom stared at the apple as she quoted the Bible verse, "Comfort me with apples: for I am sick of love."

She wore the necklace every day. If ever the apple half happened to fall beneath her collar, she would lift it back out to rest against her chest for all to see.

My father was extraordinary with a piece of wood. I could spend hours watching him work. Ever since I'd broken the jars of plums, my father had picked up on his carving. I think it was a solace to him. To be able to hold wood and craft it so clearly it could not become something you did not will it to be. Maybe this is why I also found respite in watching him work. I knew he would never carve anything as awful as what Leland had done.

I sat in the rocker beside Dad's, watching him work on a turtle that was nearly the size of his lap. On the turtle's back were crisscrossing lines that ran to and from hills, mountains, and trees. As he carved out a valley, I held my foot up against the post in front of me. My foot used to be the length of the post's pedestal. But my toes had grown beyond the pedestal's edge. I lowered my foot and even tried to hide it under the rocker.

"See all of this?" Dad held up the turtle and pointed to the topography on the shell. "This is the map of heaven. It exists on the back of a turtle."

More than turtles and maps, I wished my father would whittle us enough money to buy ourselves a past, free from brutality. One where daughters do not have to fear their father in the bedroom. One where sisters do not have to fear the approach of their brothers. If only we could buy ourselves away from the Grandpappy Larks and Lelands of the world.

"Can I have some money?" I asked, my voice hoarse.

"First time you speak in weeks, and that's what you say?"

"Don't you ever wish you were rich, Dad? Your name would never be on a list for tokens and you could buy anything in the world."

"Anything?" He slowed his carving. "Don't know if I need that."

"Everybody needs that, Dad."

He blew wood dust off his knife before saying, "You know this here turtle sits like an island on a great and wondrous ocean."

"Dad, I'm tryin' to talk to you about somethin' important. Somethin' real."

He carved what he told me was a river on the turtle's back. Then he said, "It's gonna rain tonight, Little Indian. It'll rain hard and give the earth a good soakin'. When it does, I want you to meet me by the willa tree."

Knowing my father would say no more, I left him to his map of heaven and headed out to A Faraway Place to write.

Once upon a time, the girl was rich and she could buy herself all the happiness in the world.

I later woke to rain beating down on me. It was dark and my story had washed away. I left it in its puddle and jumped off the stage.

It felt as though I were walking against a flood as I trudged to the willow tree, which stood by the Shady Lane sign. Parting the tree's weeping branches, I stepped in under its canopy.

Suddenly, a hand gripped my shoulder. My whole body locked up. My first thought was that Leland had come back, followed me, and was now going to bury me, side by side, with the rain.

I slowly turned, shielding my eyes from a bright light.

"Sorry," Dad said.

He was wearing his old miner's hat. He turned the light so it would shine on the willow's trunk.

"What do you see, Little Indian, when you look at that ol' willa tree?"

"Bark and rain," I said, staring at the illuminated trunk.

"Don't you see the diamonds?" he asked.

"There are no diamonds, Dad."

"Look again. Don't you see that sparkle? Don't you see that shine?"

I watched the rain fall into the grooves and against the ridges of the bark. I saw how it reflected the light from Dad's hat.

"The world was very wet once," he said. "It rained day and night without end. Puddles turned into lakes. Lakes turned into rivers. Rivers became oceans. Oceans became a flood. The rain was the tears of a woman who would not stop cryin' over her dead children. Her tears poured from her until all the land was swallowed up. The only way to get around was by boats, but at night it was hard to see. This was a time before flashlights and lanterns. When torches could only light so far ahead. Boats wrecked. People drowned.

"The men blamed the trees. Said they were witches, purposely chokin' the glow from the moon with their net of branches. So the men, in their rage, began to heavy their hands with axes and saws, and the water splashed as the great mahoganies and hickories, pines and sycamores all fell. Anything with bark or branches was sent to the grave. The men said they were doin' it to make the waterways safer at night, but it was carnage. Old trees, young trees, they were cut down and left to rot in the water as if their lives didn't matter. The trees understood when man cut them down to use their timber to build homes out of or to turn their heartwood into paper for storytellers and poets to lay their pens upon. In doing so, the trees had given their life for a purpose. There was no purpose now, except to get them out of the way. So in order to protect themselves, the trees decided to wake their guardians. Every tree has one. A spirit inside it, hidden away, until it's needed."

Dad reached into his pocket and pulled out a small carving of a girl with wings. I knew he must have carved it that afternoon waiting for the rain. The girl's face was my own. I smiled up at my father for carving me with wings as he told about how the tree guardians flew to the men with the saws and the axes.

"The guardians begged the men to stop killin' the trees," he said. "But the men claimed the trees must be gotten rid of. Then the guardians saw the diamonds shinin' from barrels on the men's boats. The guardians said to the men, 'If you give us your diamonds, we can do somethin' about your boats crashin' into the trees.'

"'But our diamonds are what make us rich,' the men replied. 'We will be poor without them.'

"The guardians told the men they were foolish.

"'Your life is what makes you rich,' they insisted. 'The people you love and the people who love you back.'

"The men, knowin' the wisdom of the guardians, gave their diamonds to them. The guardians flew to each tree and placed the diamonds into the bark. The stones sparkled and shined like bright lights the people could use to find their way in the dark."

I watched the rain collect into a large puddle at the base of the willow.

"What happened to the flood?" I asked.

"After givin' the light," Dad said, "the guardians flew to the weepin' woman. They asked her to stop.

"'I will cry forever,' the woman said, 'so the world will always remember who I weep for.'

"The guardians told her they could make it so the world would never forget.

"'We will turn you into a tree,' they offered her. 'Your branches will hang low and drag on the ground. You'll grow seeds of white.

These seeds will blow over all the lands to seed more of you and your weepin'. You will forever mourn your children.

"This being what she wanted, the woman allowed them to change her into the tree we all know today as the weepin' willa."

I stepped close to the tree and saw each of our names carved into the bark.

"I cut 'em in there when we first moved here." Dad ran his fingers into the grooves of my name. "Anytime I start thinkin' I'm a man with no treasures, I come out here in the rain and I see my diamonds. You asked me if I wished I were rich, Betty, but I ain't a poor man. With all these diamonds, how can I be? You ain't poor either, Little Indian. It's the same thing the men on those boats came to learn. No matter if we can't find a single penny in our pockets, we got the wealth of the world between us."

He handed me the carved guardian.

"May she protect you against those who threaten to cut you down," he said.

"Can she protect anyone?" I looked up into his face.

"Anyone in the world who needs protection."

Not stopping to answer Dad's question of where I was off to in such a hurry, I ran home.

With the rain dripping off me and onto the floor, I walked into the house and up the stairs. I saw a light shining from Fraya's bedroom. As the youngest of the three sisters, I was squash. The one who was supposed to spread her leaves and guard her sisters. I now had something that could help me do that.

I quietly stood in Fraya's open doorway. She was leaning on a windowsill, staring up at the night sky.

"Fraya?"

"It's cold, Betty." She rubbed her arms. "Summer soon to be over, autumn here, winter there. The seasons come and go so quickly. Like a chainsaw in a field of sunflowers."

She turned and pointed to the bed, where a record lay.

"I made one of them recordin's in the coin-operated booth outside

Moogie's Toy Store," she said, looking at the record. "I don't know why I did. We ain't even got a record player. It's a silly song anyways."

I stepped into the room.

"I have somethin' for ya, Fraya," I said, opening my hand and revealing the guardian lying there.

"She'll protect you."

I didn't know I was crying until Fraya asked me why I was.

"Because I love you, Fraya." I wiped my tears.

"Well, gosh, I know that. Nothin' to cry over."

She took the angel from my hand. She stared at it a moment before sitting it on the table beside her. When she wrapped her soft arms around me, I nuzzled my face into her blouse and smelled her soft powder scent.

"Do you love me, Fraya?" I asked.

"Forever." She hugged me tighter. "Why is it you're always wet when I see you, Betty? From the river. From the rain—"

"Do you love Leland?"

She paused at the unexpectedness of my question.

"Sometimes he's like fallin' to the bottom of the stairs," she said. "But he's still my brother."

"Even though he hurts you?"

"He don't hurt me."

"I was in the barn the day he . . . I saw how he—"

"What do you know?" She jerked me to face her.

"I know he—"

Her slap stung and was something I felt from each of her fingers.

"You know what, Betty?" Her voice frightened me.

"I know he—"

Her hand struck my cheek with so much force, I didn't know she could ever be so very hard.

"You know what?" she asked again, her teeth clenched, her hand waiting to knock my head clean off.

"Nothin'." I rubbed the pain in my cheek. "I don't know anything."

"You don't know anything because nothin' has happened," she said, walking toward the far corner of the room. There, she buried her face. "Nothin' like that would ever happen to me. You disgust me, Betty. How could you think I would be part of somethin' like that? He's my brother." She turned to me. "You haven't told anyone, have you? Of course you have. You tell everything. Told on me about the bark."

"I had to. You were dyin'."

"So?"

"So I didn't want you to."

"It wasn't your choice, Betty." She wrung her hands. "Have you told anyone about what you think you saw in the barn?"

I shook my head.

"Well," she said, "if you ever do say anything about what you've made up in your head about Leland and me, I swear to God, Betty, I'll never forgive you."

"But, Fraya—"

"I'll kill myself, and it'll be all your fault, Betty. It'll be the same as if you killed me yourself. Would you be able to live with that?"

She reached into her dresser drawer, removing the piece of bark still wrapped in the handkerchief.

"Trust your big sister, Betty," she said, looking at the bark. "I know how all the ghosts have been made."

THE BREATHANIAN

Chickens Go Missing

Last night the sheriff's office was inundated with reports of gunfire. This morning, chickens were reported missing from a poultry farm. Upon arrival, the sheriff reported finding feathers loose on the ground. Some of the feathers looked as though they were from different species, such as from eagles or hawks.

"What was strange is that the feathers were arranged on the ground," the poultry farmer commented. When asked in what arrangement the feathers were constructed, the farmer said, "Hell, it looked like they were arranged to look like one of them headdresses. You know the kind you see Injuns wear on the westerns."

It is not yet known whether the missing chickens are related to the gunfire.

So far there has been no other property damage reported, though Mrs. Wilma Sweetface, 67, has made it known that her flowers have been trampled in front of her house. She believes the shooter is responsible, despite there being flower petals on the soles of her own shoes.

Part Three

Light of the World

1964–1966

23

~~~

Cursed *shalt* thou *be* when thou comest in,
and cursed *shalt* thou *be* when thou goest out.

—DEUTERONOMY 28:19

I would always remember 1964 as the year Fraya left. She waited until March, when daffodils were blooming by the well. As she packed to leave, I stood up against her doorframe.

"If you leave, Fraya, what will me and Flossie do? We won't be able to say goodnight to you."

She picked up the jar I had given her after she had come home from Doc Lad's. The goodnight slips were still inside it.

"Fill it with new goodnights," she said, handing me the jar. "I'll save my goodnights for you and Flossie. Then, when we see each other, we'll share the slips of paper and know each of us had remembered the other."

I smiled up at her.

"I'll m-m-miss you, Fraya," Lint said as he came running in.

"I won't be goin' far," she told him. "I'll visit you every day. When you come to the diner, I'll give you milkshakes."

He started to pull on his nose.

"As long as you stop pullin' on your nose and your ears and your hair." She gently took his hands in hers. "You're pullin' on all the good things. Don't you know that?"

She looked down at his feet.

"And as long as you keep your shoes on," she said. "You still got your soft baby feet. You need to protect 'em. Even Betty will wear shoes every now and then, but you never wanna wear 'em."

"I don't w-w-wanna lock my feet up like they did somethin' bad," he said.

"All right, c'mon, Lint." Mom was in the doorway. She had a rock in her hand. He ran up to her and gladly took it as they walked down the hall together. I could hear Mom telling him there were some pears in the kitchen.

I turned back to Fraya and watched her pack the rest of her stuff. The apartment she was moving into was over top of Dandelion Dimes, where she had gotten a job. Dandelion Dimes was a diner in town. Everything there was yellow, including Fraya's uniform, hat, and shoes. All of the waitresses had to wear diner-issued yellow socks, folded over with sheer ruffles, which bounced when they walked. Their womanly legs were made childlike in the way the ruffles seemed to make them appear no older than six-year-old girls.

Back when the diner had first been built, the founder had accepted dandelions as equal to one dime. It was a policy generations of the founder's family had continued after her death. You'd see dandelions in purses and wallets, being passed from the customers to the waitresses, and left as tips on the tables. There were even dandelions in the cash register as if they were as valuable as the dollar bills beside them.

Many of the dandelions, Fraya would carry up to her apartment to be turned into dandelion lotion. I missed being able to watch her make this lotion at home, the dandelion heads laid out on our kitchen counter to dry, some of them going to seed. These Fraya and I would secretly blow into the crevices of the kitchen before gathering all our wide-mouthed jars to infuse the remaining blossoms in oil. We'd set the jars in the windowsills to warm in the sun. The light would shine into the oil, as if every single summer ever had on this earth was right there between us.

There would be no more of these jars sitting in our windowsills after Fraya left. She started to make the lotion in her apartment. She had left home and taken her dandelions with her.

Trustin moved into her old bedroom. Flossie complained at first, but she knew Trustin needed space separate from Lint.

With Fraya now gone there was a noticeable absence. Mom tried to fill it by collecting Depression glass she bought for pennies at yard sales. She'd set the glass out in the rooms as if it meant a full house. She started doing other things, too, like making my bed and brushing my hair.

She'd sit on the top step of the back porch while I sat in between her legs, her bare feet on either side of me. For all of her clacking footsteps on the floors in her high heels, I remember my mother barefooted at times the ground seemed to be most dangerous. She was the type of woman to wear high heels on linoleum floor, but go barefoot for a walk across gravel.

While brushing my hair, my mother would either talk or not talk. It was absolute either way. When she didn't speak, the silence could be crushing. When she did talk, she spoke of things that hit me suddenly, like a punch to the gut.

"I went to the bus stop one day," she said, pulling the hairbrush through my hair. "It was some years ago. I had bought a one-way ticket to New Orleans. I don't know why New Orleans. Maybe it was the cheapest route for that day. I don't remember. What I do remember is that I took a brown bag keepin' a hard-boiled egg and a bruised apple. To get to my seat, I had to step over vomit in the aisle. Sawdust was everywhere."

"Sawdust?" I watched a small fly skim across her red-painted toenails.

"Jesus Crimson. They put sawdust on vomit so it don't move. You're ten years old now, Betty. You should know these things."

She laid the brush down and began to rake her fingers through my hair.

"As I was sittin' on the bus," she said, "waitin' for it to take off, I looked up and saw your daddy standin' at the front of the aisle. The bus was full. I was all the way in the back, so he hadn't seen me yet. The bus driver was askin' him for a ticket. Your daddy ignored him, so the driver started to push him off.

"'Get outta here.'" She dropped her voice low like the bus driver must have.

"Your daddy wasn't havin' none of that. Just as he was throwin' a punch, he saw me sittin' by the back window. The punch ended up knockin' the driver out. Your daddy stepped over him and lumbered toward me. He was barefoot and wearin' only his hat and a pair of underwear. I remember he was sweatin' so goddamn much, even though it was January."

She began to French-braid my hair, pulling it tight enough at the crown to make me wince.

"He handed me a buck," she said. "One lousy buck."

"'I'm sorry it's not more,' he said, 'but when I saw you come here, all I had to sell was my clothes. It won't get you far, but it'll get you farther from here.'

"Before he got off the bus he tossed me his Apache tear."

She dipped into her bra, pulling something out which her fist was closed around.

"Long ago," she said, "the Apaches were caught off guard in a surprise attack from the U.S. Cavalry. The tears of the Apache women turned to stone in their hands."

Mom opened her fingers, revealing a smooth black rock.

"Your daddy got this when we were passin' through Arizona," she said. "In your hand it looks like it's just another black rock. But the light changes it."

She held the dark rock in the light of the sun.

"Do you see, Betty?" she asked. "How you can see right through it? They say those who have a tear of the Apache will never weep again because the Apache women will cry for them."

She dropped the rock back into her bra and spit on her hands before rubbing them through the sides of my braid.

"After your daddy gave me the Apache tear," she continued, "he stood outside on the curb with his dirty hands and his messy hair.

" 'He really loves you,' the hag sittin' beside me said. 'Folks think it's when they beg you to stay, but it's when they let you go that you know they love you so goddamn much.'

"Do you think that's true, Betty? What the old hag said?"

"I reckon she wouldn't have said it if it don't mean nothin'," I quickly answered.

I waited for a crow in the woods to stop cawing before I asked her why she didn't leave.

"You were already on the bus," I said. "Why didn't you stay on it and go to New Orleans?"

She chewed the inside of her cheek before telling me to imagine a sheet up on a clothesline to dry.

"The sheet is put there against its will," she said. "No matter how hard it tries, it cannot free itself from the clothespins bindin' it. The sheet stays there for years. Over time, its fabric becomes battered and torn by the seasons. The flowers printed on it fade. Then a day comes that's so stormy, the sheet wonders if it'll survive.

"One day, though, the sheet got free from its clothespins. The sheet thought it could make it on its own. Then it saw its reflection in a puddle of rain from the storm. The fabric was no longer lovely and all the holes were lettin' the cold in. The sheet realized it was just another discarded thing by the side of the road. Somethin' no one could ever care about. But with the clothespins holdin' it to the line, the sheet could be high above the ground as if it were somethin' special. Although it would be anchored to the line and never completely free, at least three of its sides would be able to move in the manner of its choosin'.

"That was enough for the sheet so she allowed herself to be blown back to the line and hung up by his pins. The sheet only regrets her choice on good days when anything seems possible. Then comes the bad days when the sheet is glad to be held by the clothespins because who else in this damning world will hold her as tight as him? This sheet, this she—she—" Her voice dropped and she lowered her eyes with it. "Funny that 'she' should be in 'sheet,' ain't it? I reckon it's just another way to lay on a woman and get away with it."

She raised her eyes to mine and asked, "Betty, do you love me?"

Somewhere a chainsaw was revving up. But I was silent.

"You know, in some cultures, silence is taken as a yes," she said. "But in most, it's taken as the opposite. Oh, I'm not surprised you don't love me, Betty." She leaned her head against mine. "I'm not surprised because my momma told me I would not find love in this world and this world would not find love in me."

24

If we say that we have no sin,
we deceive ourselves.

—1 JOHN 1:8

Flossie had been staging plays all of that summer. At first, she thought of holding them on A Faraway Place. She decided she liked the willow tree better because she could stand under the tree's weeping branches and pretend she was emerging from a stage curtain.

In advance of a new show, she would cut small rectangles out of paper and write on them: ADMIT ONE TO THE GREATEST SHOW IN THIS UNIVERSE OR THE NEXT, STARRING FLOSSIE CARPENTER.

I helped her make these tickets as she memorized her lines from a book of Shakespeare's plays.

"All great actors start with Shakespeare," she had said when she staged her first play, which was *Hamlet*. She played the title role, as well as the supporting cast.

That weekend was to be *Romeo and Juliet*. I was sitting on the floor of our bedroom writing this on the backs of the makeshift tickets as Flossie lay on her bed, perfecting her dying Juliet. She had draped sheer scarves over the lampshades.

"To set the mood," she said as her shadow was cast on the wall in the dim light.

She had our hairbrush in her hand and was waving it about.

"O happy dagger." She used both hands to jab the handle of the brush toward her chest. She leaned into it, heaving over and rolling across the bed as she released a handful of cherry sours as if they were her blood. "Oh, pity me. For I am dyin' now." She attempted a British accent as she tossed herself around gurgling. Her eyes rolled back as the hairbrush fell out of her hand.

I giggled before noticing Trustin standing in our doorway.

"What's the matter with Flossie?" he asked.

"She's dead," I said.

Flossie slightly opened one eye. She quickly squeezed it shut as Trustin got closer.

"I can see ya breathin', Flossie," he said.

"Cannot." She thrust herself up on her feet and bounced on the bed as she announced, "I play dead as well as a corpse."

Trustin picked up a cherry sour and plopped it in his mouth. Flossie was still going on about how good she could play dead when Trustin grabbed his throat with one hand and pointed into his open mouth with the other.

"He's chokin'." I quickly stood, the tickets spilling from my lap.

Flossie jumped off the bed and slapped him on the back.

"Spit it out, stupid." She hit him harder.

I smacked him on the back, too, but he fell forward on the bed. He gurgled before going limp. His saliva, colored red by the cherry sour, ran out of the corner of his mouth.

"He's dead, Betty." Flossie drew in her breath.

"He's not dead," I said, trying to pull Trustin up.

"We'll have to wrap his body in a sheet to get him out of the house without anybody seein'." Her eyes were so wide, I thought they were going to pop out of her head. "We'll bury him by Corncob in the woods."

"Corncob?" Trustin sat up.

Me and Flossie screamed and jumped back.

"You jerk." Flossie pulled his hair.

"Ouch." He slapped her off. "What'd you two do to Corncob?"

"Exactly what we're gonna do to you, pinecone piss." Flossie lunged toward him, but he quickly got farther back on the bed. She climbed up after him until they both fell off and landed with a thud at the same time.

"You ain't gonna have to play dead no more." Flossie got up with her fists ready. "You're really gonna get buried this time."

"Help me, Betty." Trustin crawled under the bed.

"Leave 'im alone, Flossie." I tried to block her path.

Trustin shot out into the hall, sliding across it and into the wall. Flossie nearly had him, but I pulled her hair, giving him the chance to escape.

"You're supposed to be on my side." She pushed me before storming back into our room.

When I got in there, she was lying on her bed. She had the hair-brush in her hand and was reenacting the death scene once more. I sat on the floor and continued cutting out the tickets. We were great at picking up where we last left off.

Come Saturday, I stood with Flossie behind the curtain of branches at the willow while she rehearsed her lines. Over her shorts and tank top, she wore an outfit she'd sewn herself. It consisted of a long patch-work skirt made out of Mom's worn aprons. The upper part was fashioned out of an old fruit-printed tablecloth.

"I look all old-timey, don't you think?" she asked.

For the rest of her costume, Flossie had sewn two lace doilies together to make a glove for her left hand. She also had a cream lamp-shade. Trustin drew the faces of the play's major characters around the outside of the shade. When Flossie wasn't taking on the role of Romeo or Juliet, she would slip the lampshade over her head and play the remaining characters with their faces showing as her own. She deepened or raised her voice accordingly.

She was practicing this as Fraya stepped in under the branches to join us.

"This side of my face is Juliet." Flossie turned her right cheek toward Fraya and me.

Her right eye was heavy with mascara and she had been generous with the blush and lipstick. She had darkened her brow with eyeliner.

"This side is Romeo." She showed her unadorned eye. She had no blush on her left cheek and this half of her lips was bare. She'd also pulled her hair back with a clip.

"I hope I don't die today," Flossie said. "Like Juliet."

"Why would you say that?" Fraya asked.

"I haven't felt well since this mornin'. My stomach hurts."

"It's just nerves," Fraya told her.

I pulled back the tree branches slightly to see that Trustin, Lint, and Dad had arrived with a bowl of popcorn. Even though the show was free and Flossie had handed the tickets out, no one but us Carpenters were in attendance. That didn't matter to Flossie. She would perform as if she were in front of hundreds.

"I'm ready." She placed her hands together in front of her. "Open the curtain now, curtain people." She spoke with an air of aristocracy.

I exchanged a glance with Fraya before we pulled the willow's hanging branches back, allowing Flossie to emerge onto her stage. Dad immediately clapped while the boys continued to eat popcorn. Once Flossie was in her place, me and Fraya let the branches swing back together so we could take our seats on the grass.

"Two households, both alike in dignity, in fair Verona, where we lay our scene."

Flossie had memorized the opening without fault. It was the middle to later part of the play that would give her trouble. With the book open on his lap, Dad fed her lines when she faltered. Despite this, Flossie would oftentimes make up dialogue all her own.

"Oh, Romeo, you look like James Dean." She kissed her hand passionately. "Oh, your kisses, Romeo, they taste like a soda pop."

Lint and Trustin both booed as she continued to make out with her hand.

"That's enough, Flossie." Dad cleared his throat. He gave her the next line in the play as her cue.

Fraya couldn't stay the entire time. She had to go back to work. After she left, Lint had more and more difficulty sitting still. Then he noticed he had some wrinkles in his shorts, so he spent the rest of the time using a rock to iron them out. Trustin started to draw on paper he'd brought with him, capturing Flossie on the stage in charcoal. After he rubbed his finger on the paper to give the willow's branches more movement, he leaned over to whisper to me, "If she slits her throat, I'll applaud."

"Slits her throat?" I whispered.

"No." He shook his head. "I said if she *quits* this *goat*."

Perhaps I had heard him wrong, but only because Flossie had started to slide her fingers across her wrist. It made me think about what Fraya had said.

"I'll kill myself, and it'll be all your fault, Betty."

I lay back and listened to Flossie's voice float above me. A short while later, Trustin and Lint got up to leave. They had stayed as long as they had promised Dad they would. A monologue later, and Flossie was finally taking her bow. Dad stood and clapped before gathering dandelions to throw at Flossie's feet.

"Oh, what beautiful roses," she said as she collected the dandelions into a bouquet.

Dad told us we should take them to Dandelion Dimes and get a treat from Fraya, but Flossie said she wasn't hungry.

She walked ahead, carrying the bouquet back toward the house, but dropping blossoms along the way to clutch her stomach.

Me and Dad took our time getting back. He had a new letter from Leland.

"It came this mornin'," Dad said before silently reading.

"What's it say?" I asked.

"Says he ain't drivin' the truck no more. He got carpenter work in Alabama buildin' church pews. He's talkin' an awful lot about that church down there." He folded the letter. "Sounds like he might make a go in it."

"What you mean?"

"Sounds like minister talk if I ever heard it."

"Minister?" I stopped walking. "He can't be no minister."

"Well, it's not the vocation I would pursue." Dad stopped walking, too. "But if that's what the boy wants."

"I mean he can't be a minister. He ain't good enough."

"They teach ya everything you need to know," Dad said as if thinking of all the lessons himself. "He'll get good at it."

"I don't mean that, Dad. I mean his soul ain't good enough. God wouldn't want him."

"What do you mean, Betty?"

I wanted to tell my father, but I was afraid if I did, Fraya's blood would be all over my hands.

"Nothin'," I said. "Never mind."

I raced ahead, getting in the house before Dad. When I got upstairs, I found Flossie in bed.

"What's the matter with you?" I asked.

She rolled over and showed the back of her pale yellow shorts. There was a red spot. The sheet beneath her was spotted, too.

"What'd you sit in, Flossie?"

"I didn't sit in anything, manure face." She clutched her stomach even tighter.

It was then I realized the thing that Fraya had told us would happen to our bodies had happened to Flossie.

"I thought you'd be happy you started," I said.

"You ever been happy with a pain in your stomach, Betty?"

"But you wanted the bra and the—"

"I wanted those things for myself. This is forced upon us."

"Fraya said it don't hurt that bad."

"She only said that so we wouldn't be scared, Betty. Besides, I'm not Fraya. And this ain't her body. It's mine." Flossie glared at me. "And don't you tell anyone it's happened. I don't want 'em thinkin' they're gonna look at me any different."

"Fraya says it means you're a woman."

"Why we have to bleed to earn it?" Flossie slammed her fists on the mattress. "What happens when we get old and it stops? What then? We stop bein' a woman? Ain't the blood that defines us. It's our soul." She held her hand on the bridge of her nose, the exact place Dad always told us our souls were. "Souls don't have a monthly cycle. Souls just are." She curled up, holding her stomach. "Do somethin', Betty. It hurts."

I did what I thought Dad would have. I went outside to the garage.

I expected it to be empty, but I found Lint standing beneath the herbs hanging from the ceiling.

"What you doin'?" I asked him.

"I like to be out here while the p-p-plants are dryin'."

"I have to make a tea for Flossie." I started searching the shelves.

"What's w-w-wrong with her?"

"She's got a pain. Wanna help me make somethin' for her?"

Together we grabbed jars of chamomile, valerian root, and wild ginger. We dumped them into the hollow tree trunk by the garage. Using Dad's pestle, we ground the blossoms and roots, scraping them out with our hands and dumping them into a pot. We collected river water in the bucket and boiled the ground pieces until the liquid became a dark tea.

"This will h-h-help her," Lint said, pouring some into a wooden cup.

I carefully carried the tea inside. When I handed it to Flossie, I saw she had written, in black pen, *I hate you* over the bloodstain on the sheet.

She took a drink but spit it back out.

"It tastes like squirrel piss," she said. "I thought you were gonna do somethin' to help me, Betty?"

I stepped over to the radio and turned it on. It was playing a song I knew Flossie liked. As she held her stomach, I took the sheet beneath her off the corners of the bed, then pulled it from under her. Taking the pen she had used to write *I hate you*, I laid the sheet on the floor and turned the words into the swirling patterns of a dress that the blood stain became once I gave it sleeves and a skirt. Extending from the sleeves, I drew arms. Beneath the hemline, two legs. From the collar, I carefully made the neck and head of a girl with long hair that stuck out from her head in the five points of a star.

"Who is she?" Flossie asked.

"Our Cherokee great-great-great-great-grandmother when she was a girl," I said. "She dreamed of bein' a star, too."

I held the sheet up and started twirling with the drawn girl to the music.

"You know there's a Cherokee legend that says if you stop dancin', the world stops," I said. "I think the women in our family must have danced all the time. I think they danced when they were born. When they first saw the highest flyin' bird. When they ran the river the entire length to prove they could when everyone else said they couldn't. And I know they danced when they first bled. That's why a tea ain't gonna help you none, Flossie. You've got to dance, because it's what the women in our family have always done for the things in their life. It's why the world never stopped, because no matter what change or pain came to them, the women danced. They knew the world had to go on in order to see all the good things that came out of that change and pain. You don't want the world to end do you, Flossie? You'll never be a star then."

She watched me dance with the sheet, pulling it through the air like a ribbon twirling from the ends of my fingers. Without saying a word, she got up and took hold of the opposite edge until the sheet was stretched between us and the drawn girl was staring up at the ceiling. We spun and laughed. The room around us disappeared in our minds as we danced until we were in a clearing at night. The sky, starless. We lifted the sheet higher and higher, the drawn girl shooting up into the sky and breaking apart into a billion pieces of light.

25

Let the woman learn in silence.

—I TIMOTHY 2:11

When Mom's dad died a month later, I didn't mind. I was surprised, though, when Mom said we were going to his funeral. It was Mamaw Lark who had called to tell us he was dead. Mom picked up the phone, listened, and said, "Okay." Then she was in her room, laying out a black dress. *Okay*. She sat at the vanity and brushed her hair in slow strokes. *Okay*.

She picked up the one perfume she had. White Shoulders. She slipped off her blouse. Wearing only her bra, she sprayed the perfume on her own white shoulders. She spritzed pump after pump until the perfume ran down her arms and dripped to the floor from the crooks of her elbows. The whole room smelled like a summer of pale flowers. When the perfume was used up, she stared at the empty bottle and began to cry.

"Mom?" I took a step into her room, which suddenly felt no bigger than a crawlspace.

"It's all gone," she said, her fallen tears mixing with the perfume.

Instead of taking another step forward, I took a step back. I didn't know how to comfort a woman who used all of her one good perfume so she wouldn't have to face the aching truth that even though her father was now dead, what he had done to her would always live.

Grandpappy's funeral was the next day. Leland was driving in from

Alabama to attend and would meet us at the funeral home. Mom made sure Trustin and Lint tied their hair in low ponytails. They'd both been growing their hair out and it was now to their midback.

"And, Betty," she called from her bedroom down to me in mine, "make sure you wear a clean dress. No berry stains on it or earthworms in the pockets or—"

I stepped into her room wearing my best dress. The one with the pleats in the skirt and the scalloped collar. I did not dress to mourn, but to celebrate that an evil man was now gone from this world.

"Well, don't you look nice." She looked at me as if she just then realized I was no longer five years old.

She lowered her eyes to my chest.

"There's something you'll need," she said before stepping into her closet.

She came out with a wire hanger upon which hung a small camisole. It was cream-colored and had a little bow in the front like Flossie had on her training bra.

"You're not Flossie, I know," she said. "You won't get in a bra sooner than you need to. But this will be a first step."

She handed the camisole over. I took it with my head down and quickly returned to my room.

I closed my door and stood up against it, staring at what my mother had given me. The camisole was sheer. I could see the light on the other side of it. I ran my fingers across the lace on the top.

"You're stupid," I said to the camisole before throwing it on the bed.

I looked down at my chest. My dress was loose, but I could still see the outlines of two small points protruding. I pressed against my chest with both hands, but the two points remained, like two soft hills upon the landscape of my body.

I unbuttoned my dress and stepped out of it to put the camisole on. I didn't look in the mirror until I was fully dressed again. Only then did I carefully study my reflection, checking to make sure neither of the camisole's straps nor its lace were showing, as if the undergarment was a thing with tentacles I had to hide.

"For affliction of eyes," I spoke to my reflection, "take black gum bark and grind it."

I pressed my hands against one another.

"No, don't grind." I corrected myself. "Boil into a decoction. While still boiling, pour into eyes to burn everything away."

I laid my head back and held my hands up over my open eyes as if pouring liquid into them. Blinking a few times, I looked in the mirror to see nothing had changed with my reflection.

When I got downstairs, I wondered if anyone would notice I was wearing something different. Everyone just started heading out to the car, so I followed. As I passed the raccoon tail on the antenna, I wondered when I had stopped slapping it for luck.

Childish anyways, I said to myself as I twisted in the camisole and headed to the rear seat to sit by Fraya and Flossie.

On the drive, the three of us reached into our pockets and exchanged slips of paper with the goodnights we'd written on them. We passed them silently from hand to hand until we'd circulated them back into our pockets.

Once we got to the funeral home, we found Leland leaning up against his truck, waiting for us. Fraya merely slid her handbag into the crook of her arm and put her gloves on. It was hard to tell if Leland was watching. He was wearing sunglasses.

"Wait." Mom gave everyone a once-over to make sure we looked as respectable as possible. "All right," she said, only slightly satisfied. "We can go in."

The funeral home smelled of stale cigarettes. The low-pile carpeting was stained in places and looked to be about a century old. Mom signed our names in the guest book. Then, in a slow procession, we walked up the long room to stare at the wrinkled man in the cheap coffin. Few were in attendance. There was just some coughing old men, probably long-standing bar buddies of Grandpappy's who used to clap each other on the back and sing the same old songs they had sung when they were young enough to have better hearts, if ever they did. It was a short service, barely more than a reason for the men to put on their best pairs of jeans and their cleanest flannel shirts.

After Grandpappy's body was lowered into the ground at Joyjug's cemetery, we went to what had once been his house. I stood with my sisters and brothers in front of the screen door, unable to cross the threshold. We could hear Grandpappy's voice in our heads:

Don't you come into my home, you little shits. You stay outside with the rest of the indecent and hopeless animals.

"Don't just stand out there." Mamaw Lark's voice rose above his. "Unless you plan on paintin' the porch."

Every step we took inside, we anticipated Grandpappy's voice demanding we get out. Only when we checked around each corner and found he was really dead after all did we explore our surroundings.

I'm not sure how I expected the rooms to look. They were sparsely furnished. The most color was in a granny-square afghan draped on the back of a chair. There were three framed photos sharing a small table with a lamp. One photo was of a train engine. The smallest was of a large dog. The photo in the black frame between these two was of a young man, which Dad picked up.

"That's my husband as a youth," Mamaw Lark said.

"You're the spittin' image of your papaw, son." Dad held the photo up for Leland to see.

Leland briefly glanced at the photo, but was more interested in the way Fraya stood in front of the houseplant dying in the corner of the room.

Mom quickly took the photo from Dad and sat it back on the table on her way into the kitchen, where she could help her old mother make coffee. The two women did not speak to one another. If not for the shared gray eyes, no one would be able to tell they were mother and daughter. Not with the way they tried to be so separate from one another. I knew that at any given moment, whether fire, flood, or other disaster, they would not be able to count on one another. They would each let the other burn, drown, die in any number of horrible ways so as not to have to grab the other's hand and show even a flicker of love.

When they served the coffee in the living room, they did so with stiff jaws. Dad picked up a mug and blew on the hot liquid as he looked out a window at the clear blue sky.

"Sure is one hell of a nice day," he said.

"I wouldn't call it nice." Mamaw Lark looked at him in every damning way she could.

"I just mean to say the sunshine feels good." Dad quickly took a drink of his coffee.

Mom walked around the room as if she'd never once lived there. Her eye caught on the scattering of charcoal drawings on the sideboard. Trustin looked from me to the drawings. We both watched Mom as she carefully held the paper by its edges so as not to smear the charcoal or get any on her fingers. As if she herself could not name lightning and thunder, she asked her mother what the drawings were of.

"Storms." Mamaw Lark held the word a long time, then moved her mouth as if she had trouble swallowing. "We started gettin' 'em in the mail about a year or so ago in plain envelopes addressed to me and your dearly departed pappy. Lightnin', thunder, and plenty of rain. If you ask me, these storms is what killed your pappy. Feelin' the dread of such a storm comin' from someone out there in the world keeps a man from gettin' peace. Didn't your pappy deserve some peace? He was a mighty good man. You had no right to attack him the way you did, young man, when you took Alka away from us." She wagged her finger at Dad. "You nearly killed him. It's a wonder I even allow you in this house now, but I reckon death reduces old grudges."

"I didn't punish him without good reason." Dad looked out the window at the very spot in the yard he'd held Grandpappy Lark down. "A man who beats a woman the way he done, deserves a taste of hell."

With cherries on their minds, my siblings wandered into the kitchen. Trustin looked at me before following them. I heard the back screen door open and close. I decided to stay longer in the living room, watching Mom stare at the lightning bolts in the drawings. She knew who the artist of them was. The question she must have been asking herself was who had sent them. She knew Trustin would not be so deliberate. She raised her eyes to mine.

"That day was a long time ago." Mamaw spoke to Dad. "A bruise or a scar don't matter none now. I got some honeysuckle vines in the yard." She pointed out the window with her crooked finger. "They're yours if you want 'em. Alka tells me you like plants."

Mom's eyes darted to Dad. She seemed embarrassed it should be revealed she knew something about her husband after all. Next thing you knew, she'd start to say she loved him out loud. What a weakness that would have been to a woman like her, who displayed her thorns as wisely as any rose can.

While Mom was putting the storms back on the table, I took the opportunity to go outside and join my siblings. They were standing in the backyard beneath the old cherry tree. Trustin had stopped just short of it. I walked out beside him. We both looked up at the tree's branches. We'd come to realize that some things are never as big as we remember they are.

"You mad about where the storms ended up, Trustin?" I asked.

"You think the storms are what killed him?" He watched the leaves roll over in the wind.

"Would you care if they were?"

"Naw." He grabbed my hand and together we stepped in under the tree.

Leland, Fraya, Flossie, and Lint were each staring up at the fruit Grandpappy Lark had told us we were never to touch.

"Damn him to hell." Fraya reached up and plucked a cherry.

We watched as she turned it over in her hand, admiring the ripe curves and its earnest red hue. With childlike courage, she placed it in her mouth.

"What's it taste like, Fraya?" Flossie asked.

"Like something beautiful," Fraya said before grabbing more cherries by the handful and shoving them into her mouth until her cheeks ballooned.

As the juice dripped down her chin, I thought of how God exists in little ways we don't always see unless we happen to be looking at the very moment a sister dares the demons and reminds you that not all paradises have gone just yet.

Almost at once, we each began to pick our own cherries. Leland carried one over to the edge of the tree's shadow. Staring at the cherry, he seemed to be considering what to do with it. Deciding, he squeezed it between his fingers before throwing it to the ground.

The rest of us continued to eat what cherries we could reach. We laughed as we spit the pits out at one another, all while the sun shone through the branches. With a stem hanging between my lips, I looked back toward the little white house. I thought I saw Grandpappy Lark frowning in the window. But it was not Grandpappy Lark. It was our mother, and she was not frowning.

On the way back home, we shared the ride with the honeysuckle vines Dad had dug up. Long, thin vines that would bounce every time the tires rolled over loose gravel. The blooms filled the car with their light, crisp scent. I believed the little trumpet flowers were the origin of all music. Of the rhythms of things we feed on in the middle of the night when we're close enough to one another to feel the way sweat beads down the skin.

Leland drove behind us until he turned off on the road that would take him back to Alabama. He honked the horn and waved. Me and Fraya were the only ones who didn't wave back.

Once we got onto Main Lane, Dad dropped Fraya, Trustin, and Flossie off in town with enough pocket money to catch a movie. Lint didn't want to go because he didn't like sitting in the dark. I wasn't interested in seeing a movie because I wasn't in the mood to be annoyed by Flossie repeating the actors' lines in my ear, as she always did.

When the four of us got to the house, Dad and Lint carried the honeysuckle vines to the backyard to plant.

Meanwhile, Mom went to get the mail. As she was pulling it out of the box, a car drove up. I stayed on the front porch and watched a man hand her a folded paper through his open window. He spoke briefly to her before driving away.

Walking toward the house, Mom tucked the mail under her arm so she could unfold the paper the man had given her. She walked past me and into the house as she read. I followed her, all the way up the steps to her bedroom, where she laid her purse with the other mail on the bed. She went through these motions, never once taking her eyes from what she was reading.

"Who was that man?" I asked.

"The editor of our town's humble newspaper, *The Breathanian*," she said.

"*The Breathanian?* Did I win the poetry contest?" My eyes widened at the thought. "Is that why he was here? To tell you I'd won?"

"You write about gettin' fucked." She flicked the paper with my poem handwritten in cursive on it. "And you think a small-town newspaper is gonna give you somethin' for it? They want a sweet little rhyme about butterflies and birds. Imagine how many pretty sugar dishes would drop to the floor and break if this poem were to be opened at the breakfast table."

She began to read my poem aloud.

> *Fuchsia.*
> *Magenta.*
> *Rosy pink.*
> *These are the colors she is allowed to be.*
> *One day she will be ripped apart.*
> *These are the secrets we share.*
> *From mothers to daughters,*
> *from sister to sister.*
> *A high-flying eagle is not a sign of God.*
> *It is why our mothers and sisters cry.*
> *Later, maybe we will be happy.*
> *But today we put out flowers for who we once were.*
> *We are the girls who have just now realized*
> *we've been praying wrong this entire time*
> *you've been inside us.*

After her gentle delivery of the last line, Mom laid the poem on her dresser and opened her jar of lotion. She rubbed it on her bare elbows.

"My mother used to have figurines," Mom said as she lifted her chin as high as it would go as she added another layer of lotion to her neck and collarbone. "All of the female figurines you could take apart because they were boxes or bowls. They all held somethin'. In their skirts, in their bodies, they all held somethin'. None of the male figurines held anything. They were solid. You couldn't put anything in and you couldn't take anything out. I suppose if you think about it long enough, you'll see why this is like real life."

She placed the lid back onto the jar of lotion.

"There was one figurine in particular," she continued. "It was a woman lyin' on her back. Her stomach caved-in so she could hold anything for you. She was a bowl made of milk glass. So white and so pretty, I thought I'd die starin' at her."

I watched my mother as she slowly removed her earrings and placed them tenderly on the dresser top. She stared out the back windows and watched Dad plant the honeysuckle in the yard.

"My momma would pick our honeysuckle blooms," she said. "She put them in the bowl shaped like a woman. Some houses have peppermint candies in a dish or butter mints, but Momma always put honeysuckle blooms out like they were candy. In a way they were. We ain't ever had honeysuckle at the house here, so you don't know how to eat 'em, Betty."

She turned to me and used her hands to illustrate as she spoke.

"First you pick a bloom," she said. "You'll see a little string hangin' there where it used to be attached to the bush. We called it the honey string. You pull this string." She gently pulled her hands through the air. "At the end is a tiny drop of nectar. I'd sit by the bowl of honeysuckle blooms after my momma picked 'em and I'd pull those honey strings out and lick the nectar." Mom's soft laugh became a sigh as she turned back toward the window. "Momma took all those little yella honey strings I pulled out and she tied 'em up in a necklace. She called me her sweet little girl and giggled as I spun for her, the necklace spinnin' with me."

Mom dropped her hands to the Cherokee corn beads of the necklace Dad had made for her. She stared at the carving of the apple half.

"After what Pappy did to me, Momma never called me her sweet little girl again. And she never picked any more flowers for me to eat. The woman bowl was always empty after that. I hated that emptiness so I threw her against the wall. Momma didn't say nothin' about what I'd done. She just told me to go to Pappy, who was waitin' for me in the bed."

Mom laid her cheek on her shoulder. I thought she would speak no more, but she parted her lips to say, "Sometimes I think the universe is just a glow. The glow of a cigarette in the dark. All the stars, the planets, the galaxies, the infinite edges. It's all in the small glowin' tip of a cigarette in the hand of a man leanin' back against a wall, watchin' a girl walk by on her way home, knowin' she'll never get there."

26

Her young ones also suck up blood:
and where the slain *are,* there *is* she.

—Job 39:30

The morning seemed immortal in its calm mist. At last the rain had stopped. The sun hadn't been seen in Breathed since the week before, when we had buried Grandpappy Lark. That seemed a distant memory as I did my best to dodge rain puddles on my way to Papa Juniper's Market. Inside the store, I grabbed a basket and started filling it with items from Mom's list. After I'd finished, I went to the magazines.

Picking up one with a smiling woman on the cover, I flipped through its pages.

"Hey, buffalo hunter." Ruthis' voice came from behind me.

I didn't have to turn around to see she was with her friends. I could smell their perfumes mixing.

Ruthis jerked the magazine out of my hands to see the cover.

"Now isn't this sad," she said to the other girls, who giggled. "Betty thinks a magazine will tell her how to be pretty. Don't waste your money." She shoved the magazine against my chest. "There's nothin' that can help you. You'll always be ugly."

"Ruthis?" Her mother's high-pitched voice rang out. She was standing at the end of the aisle.

Ruthis answered her mother on command. The other girls fell in line behind her.

"I told you." Her mother scolded her as they left the aisle. "I don't want you hangin' 'round that Carpenter girl. She'll make your face break out."

I tore a page out of the magazine and quickly folded it down inside my pocket. Before I left the store, I remembered to add a can of tuna to my basket for the cat at the house. She'd started hanging around our back porch. She was fluffy with a gray body and white beard that matched her four white paws. I first saw her sitting in a tree in the backyard. She looked like a bird, so I named her Birdie. She arrived pregnant. Dad said she would have her kittens any day. I had blankets on my bedroom floor for when the time came.

In a hurry to get home to her, I quickly paid for the items in the basket.

At the house, I set the bag of groceries on the kitchen counter. Mom was at the sink washing squash to be boiled. A pot of boiling water was already on the stove. The large sunflower leaves Mom had lined the inside of the pot with hung out over the rim. After she washed the squash, she cut them into large chunks she then dropped into the boiling water. She folded the sunflower leaves over the top of the water like a lid for the squash to steam beneath.

Working around Mom, I opened the can of tuna and carried it upstairs to my room, where Birdie was asleep on my bed. She woke up to eat once I petted her. Remembering the magazine page, I took it out of my pocket. It was an advertisement of a blue-eyed woman selling grape juice. I cut the woman's eyes out.

Careful not to crease them, I crawled in under my bed. There on the floor was my magazine girl. I had been creating her over the past several weeks by choosing specific facial features from women in advertisements. I took the red lips from the model in the cigarette ad and the chin from the young mother endorsing her favorite brand of breakfast syrup. I decided I wanted the dark blonde eyebrows of the woman who was the face for corn dogs, while I selected the dainty nose and cheeks of the model selling the "world's best ice cream." I had pieced these facial features together with the creamy porcelain skin of the woman who was selling tomato soup.

"Hello," I said to the girl as I lay on my belly.

I created the girl beneath my bed because I didn't want Flossie to see her and laugh at me.

"Oh, silly Betty," I knew she would say. "You can't pray your way to pretty. Not a girl like you."

I ran my fingers down the magazine girl's long flowing blonde hair, which I'd cut from the model in the ad for boxed cake mix.

"I got your eyes today," I said to the girl. "Now, you'll be able to see."

I used tape to stick the blue eyes to the floor. The girl was now complete. I turned over and laid with the back of my head on top of her face, as if she was rising into me and I was falling back into her. I felt the floor until my fingers met the cool glass of a jar. Sliding it toward me, I rested it on my belly. There were air holes in the lid.

"So you can breathe," I told the praying mantis inside the jar. She tapped her hands against the glass.

Dad would say a praying mantis was the first prayer of the first human ever to live. Because the insect was prayer itself, there was power there.

With both my hands on the glass, I begged this power to make me as beautiful as I believed I wasn't.

"Make me look like the girl," I said. "Give me her blue eyes. Her blonde hair. Her peaches-and-cream skin."

I prayed with the mantis until I felt it was enough. With the jar, I slid out from under the bed and went to see myself in the mirror with the hope I would have turned into the magazine girl. I found I still looked like me.

"It didn't work," I told the mantis, who seemed to say, *Of course not, Betty.*

Sighing, I stared at my reflection. My skin had been darkened by the summer sun to a rich color not unlike our garden after a rain. I always thought it was a beautiful color, the garden after a rain. And yet, I wanted to be the bright-eyed child, too pale to live on barren land. At least that's what everyone but Dad seemed to be telling me I should want. To seek another face, one that would be pallid in the moonlight. But as I stared longer at my reflection, I asked myself what was so terribly wrong with the way I looked. After all, my ancestors had bundled magic on a thousand walks through Christ and millennias, denying the faintest suggestion that they were not beautiful enough. The black of my hair had been part of ancient ceremonies. My eyes were steeped in tradition, buoyed by the divinity of nature. Dad always said we came from great warriors. Did I not have this greatness in me? The power of a woman so ancient, but still young in her time. I imagined her as she was then. Her spirit fierce. Her bravery undeniable. How could I not be as powerful? Why could I not consider myself beautiful when I thought of her as the most beautiful one of all?

I left the mirror, cradling the jar against my chest.

"I'll set you free now," I told the mantis as I twisted the lid off the jar. She seemed happy to be released as she walked out my open window and hopped onto the roof.

I lay beside Birdie and ran her whiskers between my fingers.

"If you pull a cat's whiskers out, she'll either talk or go blind," Dad would say.

"I wonder what you would talk about," I asked her as I ran my fingers through her fur until I fell asleep.

It was still light outside when I woke. Birdie was no longer on my bed, nor was she in my room. I went out into the hall, following the sound of Dad's rocking chair into his and Mom's room. I found Mom in the chair barefoot and sitting on her left leg, using her right to rock her. She was still wearing her apron. She had pinned a yellow squash blossom to the apron's strap like a badge.

"It's ruined," she said, gesturing to the bed where Birdie lay. She had given birth on top of the quilt and was cleaning her kittens as they fed.

"Oh, look how cute you are," I said to the kittens.

"Have to wash the quilt before the stain sets," Mom said as she stood.

She walked to the bed, sliding her hands up the quilt to Birdie, who was purring.

"What are you doing?" I asked Mom as she lifted Birdie up. The kittens had no choice but to separate from their mother's nipples. "Where are you taking her?" I watched Mom carry Birdie across the room.

"Time to spread your wings, little Birdie." She tossed her out an open window.

If you would have asked me if there is a halt to the world after a woman throws a cat out of a window, I would have said of course there is a halt. At the very least, there should be a second in which to stop everything, but that second did not exist and I could stop nothing.

"Birdie?" I ran to the window. The first thing I saw was our wheelbarrow. There was also a pile of rocks on the ground for borders in the garden. What at first looked to be another gray rock, was Birdie's body. She was lying on her side. Blood streamed out of her ears and into the white fur on her chest.

It was either on the metal lip of the wheelbarrow or on the edge of one of the rocks that Birdie had hit her head, her skull cracking on impact in a force that jerked her neck back far enough to snap her spine. Her legs were still weak from having given birth. She hadn't been able to get her feet turned around in time. Flossie would have said it was the curse that had lined all those circumstances up so perfectly.

Out of all the windows, it was that one, I imagined her saying. *And out of all the days for the wheelbarrow to be there, it was that day. Of course it's the curse.*

I almost said it myself before Mom pushed me out of the way so she could see out the window, too. When her eyes settled on Birdie's body, she slowly closed the window, the blowing ends of the cotton curtains abruptly going still. She wrung her hands and turned back to the kittens.

"I hate you." I pounded my fists on her stomach. "You killed Birdie."

Mom smacked me away and started walking around the room as though she was suddenly lost and unsure of her surroundings. With a confused look on her face, she paced the bedside, before turning to the kittens.

"Momma is gonna be so angry I got blood on the sheets," she said. "A girl who's got a mess in her bed is a girl who's got a mess in her head." There was a bounce in her voice as she stripped the pillows of their cases in quick, jerky movements. "Get rid of the mess. Clean your bed. That's what Momma always said."

She smiled. It was like seeing the ads I had collected come to life. Her blonde hair glistening in the sunlight. Her pale skin, almost too colorless to exist.

"Shhh." She slowly laid her finger against her lips as she looked toward the doorway. "Pappy will be home soon. He'll be wantin' what he always wants."

She dropped the pillowcases and bent over the crying kittens on the bed. She started raking in the edges of the quilt until they were up around the kittens. She lifted the quilt like it was a bag that the crying kittens were inside of.

I shouted for Dad even though I knew he was in town on a job building new shelves at the library.

"Don't call Pappy in. Jesus Crimson." Mom looked terrified, as if she truly did expect Grandpappy Lark to appear in the doorway with all ten of his claws. "Don't you know what he'll do?"

She knocked me to the floor. The kittens' cries rang louder in my ears.

"Let them go, Mom." I got up and tried to peel her hands off the quilt. "They can't breathe."

She grabbed my hand and pinned it between hers and the quilt.

"Do you want to know what it was like?" she asked.

She started to spin us in a circle, the bag swinging out from our joined hands. I screamed, but she only spun us faster. When she finally stopped, the room was a blur. She tightened her grip on my hand until I had no choice. What she did, I did. Together, but against my will, we lifted the bag up behind us.

"Mom, stop. Please don't. No, no, no—"

She forced me to pitch the bag forward with her, our arms moving as one through the air, slamming the kittens against the floor. I winced at the sound their bodies made.

"Dad, help me." I wished he could hear me.

Only one kitten was faintly crying. The others had gone silent. Mom kept hold of my hand, but I tried to get enough weight on my side to pull it out from under hers.

"You're killin' 'em, Mom. Please stop."

"Please stop," she repeated. "That's exactly what I said. And do you know what Pappy did? I'll tell you what he did. He kept hurtin' me."

Despite fighting back, I was powerless to stop her from making me slam the kittens into the floor with her again. The tiny cry that had survived from the first impact was now snuffed. We both stared at the blood seeping through the fabric. Because Mom's hand had started to sweat, I was able to pull free. I tried to get the kittens, but Mom grabbed me by the hair and threw me down to the floor.

"You're a monster," I said.

"Monster? That's what I had called him." She swung the bag into the floor, over and over again. "I screamed and cried and called him a monster, a demon, the devil himself. But he didn't quit. He just kept hurtin' me and hurtin' me and hurtin' me."

The bodies of the kittens were so pulverized, it started to sound like she was slamming a bag of water against the floor. I held my hands over my ears. Only when she was out of breath did she drop the quilt.

She swayed from side to side as if she was about to fall over as she said, "That's what it felt like. Havin' Pappy on me. I was as innocent as newborn kittens trapped in a bag."

"They were just kittens," I said. "How could you hurt them like that?" I struggled to speak through my sobs. "They were just babies."

She roughly grabbed my face.

"Don't you dare cry over them," she said, "when I had no one to cry over me."

She walked out of the room. I crawled across the floor to the quilt. When I pulled its edges back, all I saw was blood. I had to keep wiping the tears out of my eyes so I would be able to see the slightest movement from one of the kittens' tiny feet or tails. I still had hope they would be okay.

"That blood is settin' in so we best hurry." Mom had returned with a broom and metal dustpan.

She shoved the dustpan toward me.

"Put it under 'em so I can sweep 'em up on it," she said.

"No." I pushed the pan back.

She laid her hand in the blood, then slapped it across my cheek.

"If you don't do what I say," she said, "I'll put the rest of that blood on your hands. When your daddy comes home, he'll know exactly what you've done."

My hand shook as I grabbed the dustpan and held its edge down so she could prod the kittens' bodies up on it. As she did so, I looked away.

"Get 'em out of here," she said afterward.

She stood the broom up before starting to strip the bed.

"Put this in the wash." She balled up the quilt and shoved it against my chest.

I nearly tripped on its falling edges as I tried to carry the dustpan carefully down the stairs. When I made the turn into the hall, I saw Dad's carving of the ark sitting on the table.

I quickly removed the ark's lid, then carefully let the kittens' bodies fall from the dustpan onto the carved pairs of animals inside. I placed the lid back on it and dropped the dustpan into the sink on my way to the side porch to stuff the quilt into the washing machine. I knew to use cold water for blood. I set it on boil wash anyway.

I ran back inside and grabbed the ark just as Mom was coming down from upstairs. Crossing her path, I quickly darted out the screen door. I struggled balancing the large ark in my arms as I carried it through the woods to the river. I dropped to my knees in the mud by the flooded edge and sat the ark on top of the water. I gave the ark a gentle push, watching it float away.

Thunder clapped across the sky. The rain was returning to fall hard against me. I sat so long in it, I thought I was going to sink into the mud.

When I got home, Mom was sitting on the back steps. There was a muddy mess by the side of the porch. On top of the mounded earth, a shovel lay.

"I buried the mother," Mom said as she looked at the dirt on her hands and bare feet.

I sat beside her, both of us trembling in the cold rain.

As she watched lightning streak across the sky, she asked, "Why did you mail storms to my people, Betty?"

I looked at the dark clouds, realizing the storm I gave was the storm I got back.

"Because they put you in a bag and smashed you against the floor," I said.

She stood and went out into the rain to the honeysuckle bush. She pulled off two blooms, carrying them back with her. She gave me one as she kept the other for herself.

"In between your two fingers," she said as she showed me how to pull the honey string.

Together we tasted the sweet nectar, along with a drop of rain that had watered the sweetness down until all we had was the taste of the storm.

THE BREATHANIAN

Infant Startled by Gunfire, Mother Distressed

Late last evening, a mother reported her baby was startled awake by the sound of gunfire. Afterward, the mother said the baby would not stop crying. "It was a different cry," the mother said. "It didn't sound like my baby's cry at all."

The baby was crying so severely, the mother reported that she stripped the baby nude and checked for a gunshot wound.

"I thought my baby had been shot from the way she was crying," the mother said, but she reported finding no visible wounds to her child. However, the mother feels the bullet did indeed shoot her child's soul.

"I truly believe my child has been shot dead," the mother, by all appearances normal and sane, said. "The child that's here before

us now is an intruder," the mother went on to say. "It is a changeling. I know because when I asked this changeling to look upon my face, it could not."

The mother now feels her house is haunted by the ghost of the bullet.

"I can feel the bullet's presence. It passes through my walls all hours of the night. I can feel it whish by my face. This ghostly bullet will fire for all eternity."

When questioned on what she plans to do with her child now that she believes the baby to be a changeling, the mother responded, "I have an older sister. She's always wanted a child."

The woman's husband said his wife has no sister and that he's concerned about the child's safety.

"I blame the shooter," he said.

27

For a whore *is* a deep ditch;
and a strange woman *is* a narrow pit.

—PROVERBS 23:27

I never did tell anyone about what Mom had done to the kittens.
When Dad saw the grave in the yard, I told him that Birdie had gotten hit by a car and that I'd buried her. I thought that would be the
last of it, but I had washed the quilt in hot water, so the blood had
set into the fabric.

"What happened to the quilt?" Dad asked.

Mom told him she had fallen asleep on it and it was her time of
the month.

"It's always a wonder how much a woman can bleed," she said.

Still, there was the ark to account for.

"Where'd it go?" he asked, tapping his hand on the empty space
on the table.

"Well," I said, keeping my eyes down, "when the storm came, I
had to sacrifice somethin'."

For months after, all my nightmares sounded like the cries of
kittens. I even started to believe I was seeing their ghosts, running
through the house at night. The little white paws they'd inherited
from their mother, galloping up the staircase and into my room.

Why didn't you save us, Betty? I imagined them asking as they
jumped up onto my bed. *We wanted to live, too. Meow. Why didn't you
protect us?*

They were so real to me, I could feel their soft paws walking across my face until I cried. I wanted nothing more to do with 1964 and all of its ghosts. I hoped that by the time the New Year rang in, I could at least forget the way their bodies had sounded when they hit the floor.

Betty. Meow, meow. Save us. Don't let us die.

I tried to start 1965 believing I could shed the past. But I had learned that just because time has moved forward, it does not mean something so terrible ever gets easier to bear. I waded through the cold hours of that winter. I turned eleven but did not celebrate it. Only when spring had changed to summer, and the heat of the sun was shining on me, did I start to feel as if the meows were not quite as loud as they had been.

By that time, I was at a point in my life where I had a very particular image of God in my head. I imagined God was a woman in a torn satin bed jacket with falling curlers in her messy hair. She sat in a bed of dirty sheets, surrounded by a canopy of sheer curtains spiders clung to. She ate chocolates from a box until her teeth were rotted and the box was empty, ready to be piled with the smashed boxes already on the floor. Blush was streaked across her cheeks like something trying to run away. Lipstick bled outside the lines of her lips as if they were melting. She was a woman used and left by humanity in ways only we know how to consume and leave.

I was writing this as I lay on my belly on A Faraway Place. I didn't even notice Flossie until she was waving her hands in front of my face.

"In your own little world again, I see," she said.

The sticky air smelled of the lavender in the garden. She said the flowers stunk like a grandmother as she made a circle around the stage. I immediately noticed hickeys on the side of her neck. They made me think of hard rocks splashing the surface of the river.

"I'm busy, Flossie," I told her.

"Busy, busy, busy." She muttered, looking out at the tree-lined peaks of the hills. "I've always thought the hills look like wives bent over, eatin' their offspring. What you reckon the hills look like, Betty?"

Before I could answer she said, "Never mind."

I continued writing until she snatched the page out from under my pen.

"Give it back, Flossie." I stood and made a swipe at the paper.

"I will once you guess what I lost, Betty."

I looked at her in her loose blouse. It was unbuttoned enough to see she had no cleavage to show. She'd been ironing her hair recently. She'd stand at the ironing board and lay her head down, stretching the long wavy strands across the board so she could use the hot clothes iron until her hair was straight enough for her to feel pretty. The straight hair made her seem taller.

"Just tell me, Flossie, so I can get back to finishin' my story."

"You and your stupid little stories, Betty."

She dropped the paper. I sat back down and tried to finish writing, but she stared at me until her eyes popped out. I slammed my pen onto the stage and stared back at her.

"What'd you lose that was so damn important?" I asked.

"I wanted you to guess." She pouted and flopped down beside me. She held her arm against mine. "God, Betty, you're so black." She said it like it was a disease. "Mom's gonna get after you for not coverin' up." Flossie ran her fingers up her own arm. "I'm just the right amount of tan, don't you think?"

Flossie could spend as much time in the sun as she wanted. Her skin was pale to begin with like Mom's.

"You know what my friends call you?" She looked at my skin until I tried to pull my short sleeves down to cover my arms more.

"I already know what they call me," I said. "I don't need to hear it from you, Flossie."

"Isn't it terrible." Flossie pretended to be offended. "I mean, you're not even colored."

"They shouldn't call anyone that name." I turned back to my story while she watched me.

"Are you mad at me now?" She nudged me with her toe, but I ignored her.

She looked off into the distance as she widened her eyes.

"I have an idea." She hopped off the stage and ran into the house. She returned with Dad's bone needle and a cube of ice.

"I also grabbed this." She pulled a dish towel out from her pocket. "For the blood."

"Blood?"

"It's time you do it, Betty." She held up the bone needle. "It's time you pierce your ears."

"Nuh-uh." I shook my head as I stood.

"Betty, it don't hurt that bad. One little prick. Well, two of 'em. But I'm real good at it. You've always thought mine looked nice." She turned so her dangling star earrings swung. They'd been a gift from Fraya.

"Your piercings are crooked, Flossie."

"You've never said so before."

"That's 'cause I promised Fraya I wouldn't make fun of 'em."

Flossie grabbed my earlobe and pinched it.

"Take it back," she said.

I grabbed her star earring and pulled.

"Let go of mine and I'll let go of yours," I said.

She instantly held her hands up.

"I surrender, my lord." She faked a bow before softening her voice to say, "Think of all the things you could do with pierced ears, Betty."

"Will I be able to fly?"

"Well, no, but—"

"Will I be able to raise Emily Dickinson from the dead?"

She looked me up and down. "No."

"Then why would I want my ears pierced?"

"Stop bein' a baby." She stomped her foot. "The ice will numb it."

"Then how come you screamed when you did your ears?"

"I was only actin'. It don't hurt. Cross my heart and hope to die."

"It better not hurt." I turned my head and offered her my ear.

She pressed the ice against my skin. The thawing cube dripped onto my shoulder as she held up the bone needle.

"It's the same needle me and Fraya used," she said. "It's got our blood on it. And now it'll have yours, too. Did you ever guess?" she asked.

"Guess what?"

"God, Betty. Did you guess what I lost?"

"A button? Is that why you can't button your shirt?"

"For your information, I lost the girl in me." She removed the ice. "She's gone. I've lost her. Can't you tell? I'm no longer virginal." She jabbed the needle quickly into my earlobe.

"Ow." I winced.

"I wonder if I can still wear white?" she asked as she dug into her pocket and pulled out the cameo earring. She swiftly made the exchange of pulling the needle out and pushing the earring wire through.

"That wasn't so bad. Was it?" she asked.

As she held the ice cube against my other ear, she asked, "Are you gonna call me a slut now?"

For years, I had listened to others call my sister this.

"Don't you know Flossie Carpenter?" they said. "She'll sleep with anyone."

Yet when all those rumors started, Flossie was fourteen and still a virgin. Sure, she danced in short skirts and flirted, she kissed boys, went skinny-dipping, wore lipstick to bed, and let her bra strap show. But she was a heck of a lot more than the sum of all these things put together. Still, she was judged by them because she had dared to collide with the image of purity.

My sister was just another girl doomed by politics and ancestral texts that say a girl's destiny is to be wholesome, obedient, and quietly attractive, but invisible when need be. Nailed to the cross of her own gender, a girl finds herself between the mother and the prehistoric rib, where there's little space to be anything other than a daughter who lives alongside sons but is not equal to them. These boys who can howl like tomcats in heat, pawing their way through a feast of flesh, never to be called a slut or a whore like my sister was.

"I'm not gonna call you a slut, Flossie," I said as the ice melted until it dropped like rain from her fingertips.

"I did it with that boy who's been takin' me to the movies," she said, stretching my earlobe out and finding the center of it with her finger. "He bought me all that popcorn. He told me it was time I pay 'im back. Jesus Crimson," she said, imitating Mom's voice as she stuck the needle through my lobe, this time slower.

"Ouch." I jumped. "That one really hurt."

She quickly pushed the earring wire through. The cameos felt heavy on my ears. What little numbing there had been was wearing off. The soreness was starting to creep in.

"I don't know why they say you lose it," she said as she walked into the center of the stage. "Losin' somethin', it's like you're at fault. Your teacher says, 'Did you lose your homework?' Mom says, 'Did you lose your shoe? Why do you keep losin' your shoe, Flossie? Goddamn it, Flossie, why do you lose everything you're given?'" She played with her hair as she said, "They shouldn't say it's like poppin' a cherry. It's more like smashin' it."

She frowned and looked down as she said, "I told him no. He did it anyways."

It took me a few seconds to register what she was saying. Flossie was strong. In my mind, she could crush stone and face a storm with her eyes wide open. And yet, at that moment, she was as quiet as I'd ever heard her be. That silence frightened me. Not the silence itself, but the fact that I could not find the right words to say to my sister, who was waiting for me, at the very least, to lean closer to her and tell her she did nothing wrong.

"Right on." She flipped her hair back and hopped off the stage.

I was glad she was leaving. I feared if she lingered, I might cry. I knew she wouldn't like that. Flossie could cry, but other people's tears were never her thing. She didn't know what to do with them.

She stopped and turned back to say, "A girl's first mistake is to give chance to a kiss. They think they can take everything from you after that. I'm tellin' you this as a warnin', little sister. Oh, and don't take those earrings out. You can't let the holes close up before the wound dries."

After she was gone, I turned back to my story and tried to finish it, but couldn't. I ended up writing Flossie's truth instead, drawing the letters as straight as her hair. I folded the pages before the ink had dried on the last sentence. It smeared, but I thought that was okay. I slipped the pages into my pocket as I left the stage.

When I got to the back porch, I found Trustin painting with a small tin of watercolors Dad had bought for him at the hardware store.

As I stood over him, I looked through the kitchen screen to see Lint was standing at the ironing board, ironing his clothes. It was a habit that, at eight years old, he had started to pick up.

"I told 'im he ain't got no more wrinkles in that shirt," Trustin said, nodding toward Lint. "He won't listen, though."

"Are these the illustrations for my story?" I asked Trustin as I picked up the stack of paintings by his side.

"Yeah." He looked at me. "Hey, you've got things in your ears."

I reached toward the earrings, but thought better than to touch them because of how sore my skin was. I flipped through the drawings instead.

"You like my illustrations?" Trustin asked. "I followed your story, just as you wrote it. If you want, I'll draw your other stories, too."

"I'd like that," I said, before carrying the illustrations inside the house.

"Hey, Lint." I stopped at the ironing board. "Ain't no more wrinkles in that shirt."

"Gotta be sure, Betty. I heard M-m-mom and Dad fightin' this mornin'. I gotta make sure all the wrinkles are out. The d-d-devil uses wrinkles as paths into our world. The more p-p-paths we leave him, the more ways he can get into our f-f-family."

"You're always protectin' our family. Ain'tcha, Lint?" I smiled at him.

"Me and the r-r-rocks are, Betty." He smiled back.

I could hear voices out on the front porch. When I opened the screen door, both Dad and Cinderblock John turned to look at me. They were sitting in the rockers. From the hammer and pile of nutshells on the table between them, I knew they'd been there for a while.

"Hey there, Little Landon." Cinderblock John always called each one of us kids "Little Landon," as if we didn't have names separate from our father's.

As for his own name, John was the one his parents had given him. Cinderblock was the name given to him by Breathed because he dragged a cinder block everywhere. It was tied to a rope with the loose end draped across his shoulder. He'd hold the rope end tight as he bent low and forward like he was struggling to drag the weight of a tanker. I guess you hold on to something for that long, it'll weigh on you in more ways than one. He started carrying the cinder block after the woman he had lived with for three decades had up and died from pneumonia. Lose a woman, gain a cinder block. Maybe in the end it was him needing to feel the weight of something more than the weight of his grief.

Years later, Cinderblock John would take that cinder block and jump into the river with it. I suppose he had carried it for as long and for as far as he could. When they fished his body out, they said he had floated a mile downstream from the cinder block, finally free of it. I'd like that to be true, for ol' John was a good man. At least he was good to us Carpenters. Dad and John had grown up together. They had started as friends for the simple reason Dad never laughed at John. That means a great deal to a man who is always laughed at.

It wasn't only his cinder block that made John a target. There was also the way the toes of his boots curled up. The curling always scared me, even though I knew it wasn't anything to be afraid of. It was frost-bite that had taken his toes one night as he lay passed out drunk in a field. But if you were to ask him what happened, he'd tell you it was the peppermint rattlers that came and ate his toes like potato chips.

I'd never seen a Breathed peppermint rattler and never knew anybody who had except for Cinderblock John and Dad.

"They call 'em peppermint rattlers," Dad would say, "'cause they're striped red and white as if they're peppermint candy. They smell like it, too."

The snakes existed nowhere else in the world and they barely existed in Breathed beyond the tall tales of men like my father and Cinderblock John, the latter of whom would carry around a small tin of crushed peppermint, swearing it was not candy bought at Papa Juniper's but was instead the shed skin of a peppermint rattler.

I suppose that's why Cinderblock John and my father got along so well. While other men spoke of reality, they spoke of the things they believed.

I leaned down to pet Cinderblock John's hound that he had named Two Ears. When folks asked him why the name, Cinderblock John always replied, "Well, he's got two ears, ain't he?"

I gave Two Ears a good rub under the chin as Dad told me I had just missed a hawk trying to grasp Cotton's balloon.

"The hawk's talons popped it," Dad said. "The letter fell somewheres over there." He pointed to a hill on the far side.

Cinderblock John had a box of dog biscuits in his lap. He got two out. He fed one to Two Ears and ate the other himself.

"What's that you got, Little Landon?" Cinderblock John nodded to the pages in my hand.

"Illustrations of a story of mine," I replied.

"I'd like to hear your story," Cinderblock John said.

"It's called 'The Inheritance of Sin.' It's about a man who's a thief who one day becomes a murderer when the woman he's tryin' to rob does not give up her purse. He'd only brought the knife to scare her, but in the struggle, he accidentally plunges it into her stomach. Just before she collapses, she pulls him close and kisses him on the side of his neck, leavin' behind the print of her red lipstick."

I handed the illustrations to Cinderblock John and Dad so they could see each scene.

"Thinkin' nothin' of a dying woman's gesture," I continued the story, "the thief grabs her purse and steps over her dead body. As he's countin' the money, the man feels a strange heat pulsating on the side of his neck. When he looks into a mirror, he sees the print of the woman's red lipstick. He tries to wash her lips off, but they won't budge. Desperate, the man uses bleach and a wire brush, scrubbin' until he takes his skin off. He bandages his wound and spends the dead woman's money. But once the wound heals and the scab drops off, the woman's lips are there as fresh as when she had first kissed him.

"The man goes mad, buyin' every kind of soap. Still the lips remain like a tattoo. Every time he sees them, he's reminded of the woman.

The man can't stand it. He takes to wearin' turtlenecks every day, but even though the lips are hidden, he can feel them, burnin' his flesh. Then, the child his wife had been expectin' is born. A healthy baby boy. But there, on the son's neck, is a lipstick stain, just like his daddy's. The son has inherited his father's sins. Unable to cope with the knowledge he's passed his sins on, the father confesses his crimes before slicing the lips open. He bleeds out before he can be saved."

I stared at the drawing Trustin had made for this. It was nothing more than a bright red square.

"Knowin' his father's crimes," I said, "the son comes of age while the lips persist on his neck. Then one day, the son witnesses a woman gettin' mugged. The thief pulls a knife on her."

I paused at Trustin's illustration of the woman screaming.

"Just before the blade is about to rip through her stomach, the son steps in to take it for her. The thief runs away while the son collapses. The woman he saved kneels beside him.

" 'Do you see the lips on my neck?' he asks her.

" 'What lips?' she says. 'There is nothin' there.'

"She thanks him for savin' her life before he dies with the inheritance of sin no longer his burden to bear."

Both Cinderblock John and Dad leaned back in their chairs, the illustrations spread between them on the table.

"I don't know what I'd do if my children inherited my sins," Dad said, his brows drawn tightly together.

"Oh, you ain't got no sins to worry ya," Cinderblock John told him. "Hey, Little Landon." Cinderblock John turned to me as he excitedly sat up. "You know *The Breathanian*'s annual poetry contest?"

"I already entered it." I looked down. "I didn't win."

"Oh, that's just 'cause they don't know a real poet," Cinderblock John said. "You know, if you ever wanna make a career out of alien stories, I got lots I could share with ya."

"Ah, John, don't go talkin' about them aliens again." Dad sighed.

"Well, if I don't talk about 'em, who will?" he asked. "With that fella leadin' 'em."

"Don't say 'fella' like he was a nobody." Dad frowned. "He was the president."

"He was an alien."

"How do you know, Cinderblock John?" I asked.

"'Cause when they came to take me away," he said, "they all looked like JFK."

"The man's been dead almost two years now," Dad reminded him. "When a man is buried, that should be the end of his sins. Don't you think?"

As Dad picked up the illustrations, Cinderblock John talked more about aliens. I walked down the porch steps, leaving the two men.

I kicked gravel in the drive on my way out to Shady Lane. Ruthis was in her yard, practicing for cheerleading tryouts. She shook a pom-pom toward me and said she could see my tail sticking out of my shorts. I walked to the other side of the lane.

I ended up outside of town and on a dirt lane that led to farming acreage. There were no cars in sight, but still I held my thumb out and waited.

The hood of a car heading my way shone in the sunlight. The car swerved before correcting itself and stopping beside me. A boy opened the door from the inside. I slid onto the car's leather seat, which was cracked and pinching the backs of my legs like little things trying to guzzle my skin.

The boy drove with both hands on the wheel. He had a light blue cotton sheet on his back. It was tied at his neck with a piece of string.

"Are you even old enough to drive?" I asked.

"I'm thirteen," he said.

"Your mom lets you drive the car?"

"She always sends me to get sweet corn."

He caught fire in the light. I was not prepared for all that copper-colored hair.

"Why are you wearin' a sheet?" I asked.

"It's a cape," he said. "I save people, like Superman. I can save you if you want."

I remembered back to what Fraya had said about boys thinking they're saving the world.

I looked in the backseat, where I saw he had football pads and a change of clothes.

"I play," he said before I could ask.

"I don't like football." I turned back around.

"Me, neither."

He studied me out of the corner of his eye.

"How old are you?" he asked.

"Eleven." I put my legs up on the dash.

He reached his arm over and held it against the side of my leg.

"You sure do make me look pale," he said.

I lowered my legs and looked out the window.

We rode in silence for a couple of minutes before he asked, "Y'all ever find out who the shooter is in Breathed?"

"It could be someone from your town." I leaned across the seat and showed him my ears. "I got 'em pierced today. These earrings used to be my mother's. See?"

He slowed the car and pulled off to the side where the farm stand was.

"Breathed's got the best sweet corn." He pulled his wallet out. "A good for nothin' football team, but really great corn."

"It's 'cause it's ancient sweet corn." I said "sweet" the way I thought Flossie might.

"You want anything?" he asked, counting his money.

"Get me a peach, will ya?"

He got out of the car, pushing his hair back as he headed toward the stand. While the old farmer gathered the corn in a basket, the boy looked back at me as if to see if I was still in the car. I kept my eyes on him as he carried the basket over. The corn's dirty silks were stuck together on the ends and there were clusters of small black beetles hitching a ride on the leaves. On top of it all was my peach, balancing and about to roll off. I grabbed it before he set the basket on the backseat.

He slid behind the steering wheel and tapped his fingers on it.

"Where you goin' again?" he asked.

I took a bite of the peach. He watched the juice drip down my chin.

"We could go to the lane no one drives down," I said. "Lay in the middle of it."

"If no one drives down it, how come it's there at all?"

"Uh . . ." I hesitated with the peach between my lips. "I don't know."

We laughed.

I gave him directions to the lane. Along the way I finished the peach, its pit something I laid on the seat between us.

The lane nobody drove down was dusty and narrow, overgrown in patches and bordered by wildflowers and a wire fence. It opened to unplowed fields, the sun there a closer heat, almost desertlike, as if the weeds and wildflowers would one day become cactuses. I got out of his car and laid on my back in the middle of the lane. He looked around us, then laid beside me. He flipped the cape out above his head.

"How come you play football if you don't like it?" I asked as I felt my earlobes. What little blood there had been had already crusted.

"I used to play baseball." He folded his arms behind his head. "Then the summer Dad left with his girlfriend, Mom hung all his white socks on the clothesline. She handed me my baseball bat and told me to *boom*." He raised up and made the gesture of swinging a bat. "Hit Dad's socks to the stratosphere and beyond. I didn't much care for baseball after that. I figured football was somethin' else to do."

He would figure the army was something else to do, too. This boy, who got sweet corn for his mother and who hit his father's socks out of the stratosphere and beyond, would enlist in the army and die in Vietnam, unable to save even himself.

"No one drives down this lane, you say?" He propped up on his elbow.

"Do you come to Breathed often?" I asked.

"I came into the hills to hunt one time, but never again."

"What happened?"

"I was up there in the snow one winter. Out of the white, I see these antlers and the most beautiful deer. I guess I thought huntin' would be different. That I wouldn't have a problem pullin' the trigger, but I could only stand there stunned with my gun. God has never come nearer to me. I really believe that."

I leaned over and kissed him on the cheek. He looked embarrassed at first, then kissed me on mine.

"We could kiss on the lips," I said. "If you want."

"Okay."

We both leaned toward one another and awkwardly turned our faces, trying to avoid the other's nose. With our lips touching, I could feel how chapped his were. I pulled back.

"Don'tcha like it?" he asked.

"I thought it'd be like how it is in books. We can try it again. See if it gets better."

Leaning in and closing my eyes, I could feel the tip of something wet and warm trying to get inside my mouth.

"Ew." I pulled back. "What was that?"

"My tongue," he said.

"Gross."

"It's how you're supposed to do it."

"How do you know?"

"I know this guy at school."

"You kiss him?" I asked.

"No, man. He kisses girls, then tells me all the stuff."

"Like what?"

"Like all the things you girls like."

"What do we like?" I asked.

"You like gettin' flowers and candy and gettin' your boobies touched. Stuff like that."

I stared back at him.

"Oh, gee," I said. "You know us girls too well. All we want is flowers and candy and gettin' our boobs touched. What more is there to life than that? Never mind if we can pick our own flowers for ourselves, or eat candy whenever we want to. Gee, I sure am glad that you know what us girls want because we might not be able to figure that out on our own."

He started kissing me again until his chest was pressing against mine on the lane nobody drove down. His hands started moving over my shirt. It took some effort, but I was able to get my lips out from beneath his.

"No," I said.

I prepared to push him off, but I didn't have to.

"All right." He backed away.

We laid there for a few more minutes, staring up at the sky.

"I gotta get home," he said.

Before he dropped me off where he had picked me up, he took a permanent marker out from the glove compartment.

"Sign my cape." He handed the marker to me. "I want the autograph of the first girl I ever kissed."

I waited until he decided which spot on the cape he wanted me to sign.

"Right here," he said, pointing to the middle back of the fabric.

I signed my name, taking my time with the cursive so the marker wouldn't bleed too much into the cotton.

"Betty Carpenter." He said my name aloud as he read it on the cape.

Once I closed the car door, he leaned across the seat to ask out the open window, "What exactly were you doin' today, Betty Carpenter? Back there on the lane no one drives down?"

I reached into my pocket and squeezed Flossie's story.

"I wanted to see if *no* still meant somethin'."

I turned and walked home slowly. When I got there, I went to A Faraway Place and crawled in under the stage. Next to Fraya's and Mom's stories, I dug another grave. I took Flossie's story from out of my pocket and laid it in the hole. I didn't have a jar with me, so the dirt touched the paper as I buried it alive.

THE BREATHANIAN

Crying Heard at Site of Recent Gunfire

Gunfire has been reported near the little stream known as Bloody Run.

A local hiker stated he ducked behind a tree until the shooting ended. The hiker believed he heard crying afterward.

When he went to investigate, there was only a pile of rocks. The hiker reported he thought the arranged rocks looked like a grave marker. When he did a little digging with his pick, he discovered bird bones in a shallow grave beneath the rocks.

"There were white feathers arranged by the skull," he said. "And dark brown feathers around the bones of the body. The feathers looked to be that of an eagle's. It was almost as though someone loved the bird and wanted to give it funerary rites."

The hiker noted a persistent wind that chilled his bones. The sheriff does not yet know whether the bird bones and the gunfire are related.

28

And thou hast filled me with wrinkles,
which is a witness against me.

—JOB 16:8

We called her Old Woman Slipperwort as if for all of her life, she had been some old, hunched woman who lived in a shotgun shack full of ants. A shotgun shack is a narrow house built with each room joined to the next by interior doors. If you were to fire a shotgun through the front door, the blast would shoot through to the back, and all the doors in between. Old Woman Slipperwort's shotgun shack was old, but she was older. She still got around by herself, but would sometimes hire girls to help her.

That summer I was paid to work and stay at her place. The first night I was there, I woke during a heavy rainstorm. I had to pee, but the bathroom was at the rear of the house. I would have to pass through Old Woman Slipperwort's bedroom.

Her door was open and her light was off, but the moonlight was shining on her naked body as she sat on the edge of her bed. I had only ever seen her white hair tied up into a bun, but it was now loose. It fell the length of her backside and was thin enough, I could see her body through it.

I'd never seen such an aged naked body before. There was something scary to me in the way her skin draped and fell. I worried it would fall completely off, revealing her skeleton beneath. I imagined the black sockets of her skull, the curvature of her rib bones caging her beating heart. Quietly, I walked backward until I was in the living room again. It was raining even heavier outside. I might have still gone out, but having just seen Slipperwort the way I had, I found myself feeling unsettled, if not disoriented. I went to the corner of the room and squatted, the pee soaking the green carpeting beneath me.

The next morning, I got up early to make sure the spot had dried. I dragged the nearby lamp table over so it would cover the area. Before I could start breakfast, Old Woman Slipperwort handed me a copy of Sigmund Freud's *Interpretation of Dreams*.

"Return this to Chairfool," she told me. "He let me borrow it after I told him I keep dreamin' about a stick layin' on the ground. The book wasn't no help. Why you think I keep dreamin' about a stick, Li'l Cherokee?"

"Maybe you ain't no good at dreamin'," I said.

She dropped her eyes and frowned. "I sure the hell used to be."

I tucked the book under my arm and headed into town.

When I arrived at Chairfool's Barbershop, I found Americus Diamondback sitting on a bench outside. He folded his *New York Times* and smacked the faded paper down on the bench as he shifted in his three-piece suit.

"Your sloppy sister Flossie," he said to me, "I know she did somethin' to my dog."

He petted the hog he'd replaced Corncob with and had named Wall Street.

"I don't know what you're flappin' your jaws about," I said before opening the barbershop door.

Inside, Mr. Chairfool was training Trustin on how to sharpen a blade. Trustin had been Chairfool's apprentice for a few weeks. It was strange to see him looking so respectable in a little white jacket and pair of black slacks. He liked working at the barbershop well enough. It gave him extra money to spend on art supplies.

I handed the book to Chairfool. He pitched it through the open doorway to the back of the room. He turned around with a smile showing the gap in his front teeth while his reddish blonde mustache hung like feathers on either side of his mouth. He had the type of haircut I imagined his mother once told him looked best on him. Long enough to cover his ears and hide his hearing aids, but short enough to be respectable.

"Trustin was about to practice shavin' on me," Chairfool said. "But since you're here, Betty, he can practice on you."

"I ain't got no beard." I frowned and felt my face.

"Oh, your brother ain't even gonna be usin' a real razor. It's for him to discipline his wrist and his concentration."

Chairfool tapped on the jar of fireballs sitting on the shelf behind him.

"You can have candy after," he said in a singsong voice.

I sat in one of the chairs usually occupied by the men of Breathed. I could smell cologne and sweat coming off the leather.

"Trustin?" Chairfool folded his arms and looked sternly upon my brother. "What's the jingle you're supposed to say to every customer before they sit?"

Trustin sighed. "She ain't really a customer. Ain't even gonna be payin'."

"It ain't about givin' a shave to a man who can pay," Chairfool said. "It's about givin' a shave to a man who needs it. You're lookin' at this all wrong, son. Now, Betty, you stand back up. And, Trustin, you treat her as well as you'd treat the richest man in the world."

I stood with a smile on my face as Trustin hung his shoulders.

"Sit down in the chair, fool, and you'll leave lookin' cool," he said.

"Now, Trustin," Chairfool said, "you gotta say it loud enough for the customer to hear ya."

"Sit down in the chair, fool, and you'll leave lookin' cool." Trustin had said it so loud, it felt as though his voice had echoed through Main Lane.

"That's good, son." Chairfool smiled.

I sat back down and giggled while Trustin unfolded the barber's cloth. He draped it across me, tucking it around my neck. He used a brush to smear shaving cream on my face and down my neck.

"It tickles." I laughed.

Next, Trustin picked up a small black comb. Chairfool cleared his throat as he nodded toward the strip of leather hanging from the back of the chair.

Trustin stroked the comb's flat edge against the leather like he was sharpening a straight razor.

After a few seconds, he ran his thumb alongside the comb, checking its sharpness. Satisfied, he laid its edge against my skin. He shaved carefully, wiping the cream from my face with each new glide.

"Don't cut me," I said.

Mr. Chairfool chuckled, but Trustin only turned my face to the side to get the angle of my jawline. He moved the comb in swift, graceful movements. I felt as though I was one of his canvases. A brushstroke here. Another there. Maybe in his eyes, he was doing nothing more than painting my portrait.

Once he finished, he picked up the towel and wiped off the little smears of cream around my ears and under my nose. He patted bay rum on my cheeks and down my neck.

"Not bad." Chairfool gave my brother a slap on the back. "What you think, Betty?"

"I like it." I rubbed my face and smiled at my brother, who smiled back.

Chairfool held out the jar of fireballs. I took three.

I tossed one into my mouth as I left. I offered the second to Americus outside, who took it immediately.

"I'm sorry your dog went missin', by the way," I said to him.

"Hmm." He popped the fireball into his mouth only to hold it against the inside of his cheek. "I bet you are sorry," he said, "just as I bet a shotgun's got morals."

I stuck my tongue out at him just before racing back to Old Woman Slipperwort's. I handed her the third fireball. She took out her false teeth and started sucking on the candy with the joy of a small child.

"What you gonna be wantin' for dinner later?" I asked her.

"Okra. Some beetroot, too. Need to eat somethin' the color of blood. Keeps you healthy." She filled her cheeks with air until the fireball shot out of her mouth. *"Hee, hee, hee."* She laughed with a wide grin.

After I finished my afternoon chores of sweeping and airing out her cabinets, I started dinner. While I tossed okra slices in cornmeal and dropped them into hot oil, Old Woman Slipperwort sat at the table and spoke of her youth. She said she could still remember how beautiful she used to be.

"My hair used to be the color of fire," she said. "Men would gladly burn in it just to kiss me. Now it is the color of ash."

As I stirred the okra, I asked her if she had always lived in Breathed.

"Oh, yes," she replied. "I could never leave the hills. The people I wouldn't mind leavin', but never nature herself. When I was a small girl, I used to think I was the daughter of Mother Nature. I would wear flowers in my hair that my real mother would take out because she was allergic. *Ah-choo.*" She faked a sneeze as we both laughed. Her nose twitched just before she sneezed for real.

"Bless you," I said.

"I need blessed after a sneeze like that, dear girl." She wiped her nose, then spoke about her love of trees.

"I like nature, too," I said as I stood back from the frypan and the popping oil.

"Oh, I know ya do, Li'l Cherokee. When you leave Breathed, you're the type of girl who's gonna go from mountain to mountain, hill to hill, countryside to countryside."

"I won't leave Breathed," I said. "Sometimes I go to A Faraway Place, but I don't really leave."

"It's not Mother Nature you'll leave, my dear. Don't sound so frightened. It's human nature you'll wanna get away from. The thing about Breathed is that she gives you both the ripe fruit and the rotted in the very same bite. You're the type of girl who's gonna spit that rot right back out one day. You'll go in search of a fruit that don't spoil so goddamn much. The wider your hips get, the stronger this thought of leavin'."

"My hips won't get no wider."

"Oh, sure they will. You got hints of it."

"Hints of what?"

"Of bein' a woman. But you ain't there yet."

She spoke more of her youth and beauty as I plated the okra and sliced some beetroot. When I sat with her at the table, she reminded me to put a fresh dollop of honey on the saucer. It was for the ants when they passed by.

"Why you let ants in your house the way you do?" I asked her while I freed a small one trapped in the honey.

"'Cause when you go back home," she said, "the ants will be all I'll have left."

She laughed as one of the ants crawled up her arm.

After dinner, Old Woman Slipperwort went to bed. I fell asleep watching TV through the crawling ants and static. I woke a few hours later, needing to pee. I walked quietly toward her bedroom, hoping I could pass through to the bathroom.

Like the night before, I found her naked and sitting on the edge of her bed. Unaware I was there, she continued to massage her legs, their blue-green veins twisting beneath her skin. I wasn't as afraid seeing her body this second night. In the folds and creases, I saw her history. Her skin was the diary of her soul. All the springs she had watched the flowers bloom. The summers she had stood before the moon and kissed its face. The autumns she had grown wiser. The winters that had frozen the initials of her name. Each wrinkle was a record of this and of every hour, minute, and second she had lived. All her secrets were written in her skin. The things she had asked God for. The things she had cursed the devil about. In such age before me, I saw only beauty.

"Your legs hurt bad, huh?" I said against the silence of the room. "I could make ya some tea out of alder bark."

She turned to see me, but didn't scare at my presence.

"Don't fuss with any tea for me," she said. "I'm fine."

She didn't have her teeth in, so her words were followed by a slight whistle.

"I'm fine," she said again as she stood. She stepped in front of the full-length mirror. She stared at her body, turning side to side to see her waist and its edges.

"Growin' old as a woman is like an attack. Never grow old, Li'l Cherokee. Not that you can help it. Unless you die young. I wish I had died when my hips were still erotic things."

She twisted her hips as best she could.

"I am decades dirty and decades old." Her voice cracked. "I used to be a journey a man wanted to take. Now I'm just Old Woman Slipperwort. That is my name now. Old Woman. There is nobody alive who remembers how beautiful I used to be. No one alive but me. Cherish your beauty, Li'l Cherokee. It'll be gone before you know it."

"I'm not beautiful."

She stared at me as if in shock. "How can you say that, silly girl?"

"I look like my father."

"Our fathers all give us somethin', but so, too, do our mothers. You have your father's skin, but you have your mother's shape. You have your father's jaw, but you have your mother's lips. These are the things we are given. How can you not know you are beautiful? C'mere."

She grabbed me by the hand and pulled me toward the mirror.

"Say you're beautiful, Betty," she said as she turned me to face my reflection.

"But I'm not."

"Who has told you this?"

"My mother."

"Of course she has, my dear." Slipperwort chuckled. "You are a reminder of everything she's losin'. All mothers are envious of their daughters to a certain degree because the daughters are at the beginnin' of youth while the mothers are losin' theirs. It's only natural to feel jealous. That's all your mother is doin'. Rearin' her jealous head because as you grow more beautiful, she fears losin' her own loveliness. If you know your own magnificence, there goes her power. Her tellin' you you're no beauty is her bein' a woman before bein' a mother."

She stepped away from the mirror and sat on the edge of the bed as if she'd just walked from one end of town to the other and was so very tired because of it.

"Reach me that lipstick, would you?" She gestured to the basket of makeup on the dresser top.

"I still put on lipstick for every kiss," she said. "But the kisses no longer come."

I gave her the red lipstick and watched her apply the color to her thin lips as I sat beside her.

"Did you like sex, Miss Slipperwort?" I asked while I had the nerve.

She thought about it before saying, "I was a very sexy person with very sexy people."

"It's true what they say about you then?"

"What do they say, child?"

"That you used to be the woman all the men visited if they had enough money to do so."

"Are you callin' me a whore, child?" She smiled. It was all gums.

"No, ma'am. But other folks do. They say the only thing that stopped ya from spreadin' your legs was gettin' old."

She laughed. "What else do they say?"

"Pretty much just that. Over and over again."

"Do they ever say anything about Lavannah?"

"About what?"

"Not a *what*, dear. A *who*."

She took my chin gently in her hand and began to apply the lipstick on my lips.

"All the folks who knew about her are long dead now, except for me." She sighed. "She was a girl born in Savannah, Georgia. Her mother wanted her to be named after the place she come into this world in. But she was a baby born late in the day, so they took the L of that lateness and put it in place of the S in Savannah. When I last saw her, we were merely a couple of seventeen-year-old girls who bit our nails with a smile. How old are you, Li'l Cherokee?"

"Eleven."

"You have some growin' yet to do." She put my hair gently behind my ears.

"Where is Lavannah now?" I asked. "Is she an old woman, too?"

Slipperwort looked off, her eyes glazing over.

"You know that patch of quicksand on Quicksand Lane?" she asked. "That's where Lavannah is. One day, she stepped in that sand, her own self sinkin' in the mess of it all. If there is a bottom to be had, she's there. I remember after she sank, all kinds of ants came runnin' out from the sand like it was their home and she'd disturbed it."

"Ants?" I asked, looking at the little ones crawling across her wall.

"I reckon that's why I like havin' 'em around," she said. "They're the last of *her*."

"Why would she kill herself?"

"Oh, it wasn't her fault," Slipperwort said. "She was never quite right in the head after she came back home from that asylum her parents sent her to in order to be cured of her mental illness. That's what they called me and her wantin' to be together. A mental illness. Somethin' that was perverse and needed to be corrected. But really, all it was, was love. I don't suppose you would understand, only bein' eleven years old."

She studied me as if deciding whether to continue.

"It all started after my daddy caught me and Lavannah up in the attic on Granny's old bed," she said. "Neither me nor Lavannah heard him comin' up the steps. We were both naked and kissin' on one another like we were the only two left on earth."

Slipperwort looked at me with her brows arched and waiting.

"Ain't you gonna say somethin'?" she asked. "Ain't you gonna tell me I'm disturbed for layin' naked with a girl?"

"No, Miss Slipperwort." I shook my head. "I ain't gonna say that. Is that why they sent her to the asylum? Because of what your daddy saw?"

She nodded as she said, "Daddy wanted to send me to the asylum, too, but Momma convinced him it would be best to beat the demon out of me at home. While I contended with my daddy's belt, Lavannah's folks sent her off with the men in the white coats. When they let her return home, her head was shaved and she had crescent-shaped scars all over her body. She was so thin. It was as if she didn't eat one damn meal while she was away.

"I tried to talk to her, but she wouldn't say a word back. The only thing she seemed to want to do was to walk around real slow. I still remember the string of drool at the corner of her mouth. I swear, she could look right at ya but not see ya. They'd taken a girl away and returned a ghost. Folks say she committed suicide by walkin' out to that patch of quicksand, but she was already dead. Can't kill someone already dead."

Slipperwort started to use the lipstick to draw bright red crescent shapes on her flesh.

"That's why I become a whore," she said as she drew more crescents. "I was so afraid of bein' sent away, I laid with every man I could. They don't try to cure a woman who beds men. They pay her. Funny thing is, my parents didn't mind me bein' with a hundred men. There was less shame in that than bein' with one girl."

She dropped the lipstick to the floor. It was all used up anyway.

"I look back on it," she continued, "and I realize that whole time I was so scared of endin' up like Lavannah that I ended up sendin' my own self away. I locked myself up in the asylum inside me out of fear of knowin' who I really am."

She stood and stared into the mirror, stepping closer and closer to the glass until her hand and the reflection of it were touching fingertips.

"It ain't easy bein' a woman, Li'l Cherokee," she said. "It especially ain't easy bein' a woman who spends her life afraid of who she really is. They all call me Old Woman Slipperwort. Old woman. That is who I am. The woman who walks in flat, rubber-soled shoes to the store to buy potatoes and milk and bread. Stains on my dress from the breakfast I eat alone. My back hunched, my stockings fallen down on legs that are veined, blue and purple. A head of white hair and a face no one sees. I have lived ninety-seven years on this earth. All I have to show for it is me, alone in a bedroom, starin' at the reflection of a woman who was too afraid to be herself."

She looked from her reflection to mine.

"Don't let it happen to you, Betty. Don't ever be afraid to be yourself. You don't wanna live so long only to realize, you ain't lived at all."

29

And seekest thou great things for thyself?
seek *them* not.

—JEREMIAH 45:5

Flossie and I broke step to stand off in the thigh-high weeds as a brown car passed, the wheels kicking dust into the air. Plumes of tan smoke settled on our wet hair slicked back from our swim in the river.

"One day, I'm gonna get me a yellow Corvette," Flossie said, stepping back out onto the lane. *"Vroom, vroom."* She pretended to steer sharp turns. "Maybe I'll let you drive it, too, Betty."

It was the end of that August. The warm light devoured the shadows around us as our hair dried and sweat beaded down our foreheads. Late summer in southern Ohio was a beautiful challenge passed from the sun to the child, *Can you survive my heat and still love me?*

The fat-bellied beetles seemed to pop while rippling lines rose up off everything in a trick of the eye.

"Let's go to the railroad tracks," Flossie said as she turned around to walk backward in front of me. "The noon train will be goin' by soon."

She was wearing cutoffs, but they were hidden by how long the baseball jersey fell on her. The jersey belonged to her latest boyfriend. A guy named Minford. I forget his last name. They were never that important to remember in the first place.

"Hey, Betty?" She looked up at the sky. "Where you gonna live?"

We stumbled into the same conversation we usually did.

"I'm gonna live on the best street in the world," she answered the question herself before I could. "Lined with palm trees and in walking distance of the drugstore Marilyn Monroe bought her hair dye at. You know, before she died and everything."

Flossie dug in her pocket and pulled out some dry corn silk, rolling paper, and a lighter. We bunched the corn silk and rolled the paper around it. Once it was lit, we quickly took turns puffing the cigarette to keep the end glowing.

"I'm gonna be more famous than Elizabeth Taylor," Flossie said on an exhale of smoke. "They'll write my name in those big black letters at all the theaters. 'Course they'll probably give me a stage name to make me more Hollywood. I'll have to lose my accent."

We shared the cigarette as she added, "I'll definitely never smoke corn silk like some backwood hillbilly."

She grabbed the cigarette from me and sucked on it until it got so small, she had to drop it.

"You'll live in a farmhouse, Betty," she said as though a crystal ball was right in front of her. "You'll have a dog and a cat and a mouse. The dog won't eat the cat and the cat won't eat the mouse and everyone will die of old age and boredom. You'll have to marry the lonely moon just to give you somethin' to do."

She ran ahead as if in a race to the finish line, her long hair flying back.

When we got to the train tracks, we did hopscotch on the wooden sleepers. In the distance, a train's horn blasted.

"Won't be long now," Flossie said, slipping out of the jersey. She wasn't wearing a bra. Her nipples reminded me of the shrunken tops of what we use to call miracle mushrooms when we were still young enough to believe miracles existed.

"C'mon, Betty. Take your shirt off, too." She tossed the jersey out to the brush.

"Don't want to," I said.

The train's engine appeared about a mile down the track, its black smoke curling up to the white clouds.

"What you so afraid of, Betty?" she asked.

I watched her spin, holding her arms open to the sky, a smile on her face. I thought of Slipperwort standing in her room at night, mourning all the choices she had been too scared to make. I didn't want to end up like her. Locking myself away until I was nothing but some far-off scream no one could hear. I wanted to smile as wide as Flossie was. To be as free as she appeared to be.

"I'm not afraid," I said, taking my shirt off.

I dropped it in the grass, but still kept my arms crossed over my chest. Mom had said I should start thinking about wearing a training bra as if my growing breasts had to be taught like the cucumber and bean vines that Dad trained to grow up string.

"So they don't get out of hand," Dad would say about the vines.

I imagined my breasts being attached to a trellis as if central to my gender there was an expected weakness and irresponsibility the world had already created a bra to train out of me.

"Uncross your arms," Flossie said. "You have boobs. Is that your big secret?" She laughed.

She grabbed my hands away from my chest and together we spun in a circle.

"I imagine this is what it feels like to be famous." She hooted until her high-pitched calls echoed.

"Time to get off the tracks," I said as the engine blared louder.

She continued to giggle and twirl. I had to yank her into the grass with me.

"Thanks, Mommy." She made kissy noises toward me before turning around to face the oncoming train. "Oh, hello, train."

As the train blew past, Flossie jumped with her arms raised in the air like she was on the flag-painted roller coaster at the Fourth of July fair.

"C'mon, Betty." She grabbed my hand.

Together, we screamed and laughed the entire length of the train. We were still jumping long after it'd gone.

"Did you see those hobos?" Flossie thrust her hips like the men had.

"The one with the burlap hat was kind of cute," I said with a straight face.

We broke out in more laughter as we fell down together on the tracks, unintentionally burning our skin on the hot rails.

"Shit fire." Flossie rolled over onto the wooden sleepers and turned her back to me. "Did it leave a mark?"

"It's a little red." I lightly brushed my fingertips over the flat, dark moles that seemed to make a constellation of stars on her skin.

"It burns," she said before falling quiet. Her next question was to ask if I remembered when we burned the church.

"Yeah, Flossie. That's not somethin' one forgets."

"You think God will punish us for it?"

"I don't think it's really somethin' God thinks about."

"I think He thinks about it all the time." She laid back and squinted toward the sun.

"If He was gonna punish us, Flossie, He would have by now."

"Naw." She shook her head. "He's the type of man who waits. Gets ya when ya least expect it. When it'll really hurt."

She seemed to drink the sky with her eyes, all the clouds and the light pouring into her. She said the sun was so warm. Then she began to pet her face, her hands softly rolling over her cheeks.

"I'm beautiful, don't you think?" she asked. "I'm gonna be on every magazine cover in the world. There's no way I'm not."

When I think of Flossie now I always remember her as sitting in the sun on the green grass, squeezing lemons out on the top of her head, the juice dripping through her hair. She'd do it nearly every day in summer. By the time August ended, her light brown hair would be gilded in highlights. Sometimes this is the only way I want to remember her. The sun. Green grass. Yellow lemons. My sister with her head tilted toward the light.

"What time you think it is?" she asked. "Minford has baseball practice. I better go or I'll be late."

She stood, knocking off the little pebbles that had embedded into the backs of her tanned legs.

"A boy really likes you if he wants you to watch him play ball," she said.

"Gee, sounds like fun," I said, shaking my head. "You know, Flossie, you don't always have to put on an act."

"Who said I was actin'?"

She put the jersery back on and, without saying goodbye, skipped down the tracks.

I slipped into my own shirt, staying to watch her run off into the distance until she was nothing more than a tiny fleck shimmering like the heat.

Once I got back to the house, I stepped over the vines in the garden and picked a tomato. I ate it whole, the juice dribbling down my arm. When I turned, I saw Dad sitting in the swing on the back porch. I carefully tiptoed around the lettuce heads and broccoli florets, past the cucumbers trailing up the trellises as I wiped tomato juice off my chin.

"Hey, Dad," I said, coming up the porch steps.

On the floorboards by his feet was a pile of pants he had patched. Another pair, about to be fixed, was draped across his lap.

I leaned against the rail and watched him search through buttons in a cigar box beside him. His right leg was stretched across a stool he'd brought out from the living room. I could tell his knee was acting up from the way his leg would twitch.

"Why don't you ever mix any plants for your own aches and pains?" I asked.

"I guess I never thought I deserved to be free of 'em," he said, still studying the buttons. "Some pain you know you'll always hold on to. Maybe if I was younger, lookin' ahead at things, I might feel differently."

I tried to think of my father as a boy under the stars, dreaming he would have a life no harder than the boards of his front porch. I knew my father in his youth must have been stirred by legends and myths, hoping to become a legend himself. Only to then have to leave such fancies in the musky earth when it was time for him to grow up and become just another man as invisible as dew on any given morning.

I stared into his wrinkles. They reminded me of ridges in sandstone. High on the sides, carved out in the middle like the soft stone it was. His face was becoming as ancient as the land. *One day, I thought, I will wake up and he will have moss growing on his eyelids. His cheekbones will have pushed through his flesh, like rock pushing through the hillside. Erosion will turn him into something I barely recognize until I will have to lay him on the hills amongst the stone most like him.*

"Dad, what'd you wanna be?"

"What did I wanna be? Don't you mean what do I wanna be?"

"When you were my age." I sat on the swing beside him. "What'd you think you'd do with all your life?"

"Oh, when I was young, you mean. Well, when I was a boy I always thought I'd stay that way. It's so much easier to be a boy than it is to be a man and it's the only thing I've ever been good at, so I reckoned I was gonna be eleven forever."

And yet, he was decades older than the boy he thought he'd spend eternity being. A large part of my father's life had become him trying to catch his breath. He'd had a hard time with hard jobs. It was no wonder his body was giving in. His cane was solid proof of that.

Dad had made the cane himself with our faces stacked in the order of our births. Around Leland's head, Dad carved half the sun merging with the moon, the stars shaping a crown. Fraya was surrounded by dandelions, the bright yellow blossoms nearly covering her face.

Though Yarrow was dead and gone he was not forgotten, nor was the buckeye nut that took his life. Dad spent time carving the delicate features of Waconda's infant face. Flossie was given a little gold Oscar statuette, which made her squeal in delight when she saw it. A rainbow extended around Trustin's face, while Lint was carved with enough plants to remedy any complaint.

In between Flossie and Trustin, I was carved with a raven feather. When I asked Dad why a raven's feather, he said that many years ago, when the trees and mountains were in their infancy, great beasts roamed the land while people sat around fires and told stories.

"The ravens," Dad said, "hearin' these beautiful stories, knew they needed to be written down to be preserved. So each raven decided to pluck a feather from their body. They offered these feathers to the storytellers. But a pen needs its ink. A raven's blood runs black as the night sky, so the wise birds bit their own tongues, their black blood spilling to the pens of the poets and storytellers. By the sacrifice of the raven, stories found wing from one generation to the next."

Some men carried photos of their children in their wallets. Dad had his cane. Maybe he thought carving us in wood would force time to stand still. Our faces never to age beyond the youth he'd sculpted with his knife.

"This one will do," he said, deciding on the brown marbled button from out of the cigar box.

I watched his shaking hands thread the needle.

Decades of gardening had stained his hands. You could see all the seasons he had hulled black walnuts and all the times he had pulled weeds. *Green and brown and black*. The colors of the stains settled into the deep cracks and splits of his fingers. *Green and brown and black and violet*. The color of the berries he canned, mixing together into hues that splashed his skin. *Green and brown and black and violet and red*.

The stains had tinted his skin the color of the earth itself. I was certain that if I laid a seed inside his hands, that seed would root and grow from his palms as if buried in dirt. This same dirt crusted around his short nails. The beauty and the hardship of working with the land had formed calluses in the very spots he'd held on to a hoe the longest. People would use all kinds of words to describe my father's hands. Tough. Leathery. As split and grooved as tree bark. Folks would say his hands were, above all else, rough, but I knew his touch was soft.

Everyone just took one look at my father's hands and thought they knew his worth in the world.

"I was always told I wasn't significant," he said as he began binding the button to the pant flap. "You get told that enough and you start to believe it."

He tied off the thread before snapping it with his teeth.

"Some men ain't worth mentionin'." He held his pants up to look at his work. "They're fillers. That's what I am. A filler. A step others climb on to get to the top. A paint drop on the portrait of a greater man. It used to bother me. But now, I'm too old to give a damn."

He laid his pants aside as he stood up from the swing and grabbed the broom leaning against the wall. For the next few minutes, I watched an old man sweep dust off his porch. If there is anything more to be said, it is that the dust he swept off blew back into his beautiful old face.

30

A time to be born, and a time to die; a time to plant,
and a time to pluck up *that which is* planted.

—ECCLESIASTES 3:2

Bean threshing was done in early autumn. We pulled up the vines and spread them on the ground until both vine and pod were dry. We would rake them all together with our hands until the pile was a few feet high. Then came the fun part, when we jumped onto the heap and stomped our bare feet over the parched pods until they broke open. The sounds of the threshing were like the steady beat of a drum, our feet pounding, the pods reacting, the beans shooting forth.

"You thresh like an old woman, Betty," Flossie said to me as she elbowed my side.

"I break more pods than you," I said.

"I'm not talkin' 'bout you bein' slow like an old woman." Flossie crossed her arms. "I'm sayin' you thresh like an old woman whose belly depends on a winter storage of beans. Like you can't go to Papa Juniper's Market and buy whatever you want. You take it too seriously."

"That's because her blood remembers," Dad said as he rolled a pod against the side of his foot. "It remembers the long cold winters of our ancestors, whose bellies did depend on a storage of beans because without them they'd've starved."

After threshing came the winnowing, which was when we would collect the harvest from the ground. The smallest pieces of pod were light enough to be blown with our breath, filling the air with small particles. To separate the larger pieces, we used shallow-bottomed baskets. Winnowing was done best on a windy day so as we tossed the beans in the basket, they fell against the weave, while the wind blew the light husks away.

"They have machines that thresh and winnow now," Dad said, tossing his beans high in the air. "But what we have done here with our feet, hands, breath, and wind is as ancient as the first bean seed. We must not forget the old ways. We must try to hold on to them as long as we can."

Out of all of the work in the garden, the threshing and winnowing season was Trustin's favorite to paint. At nine years old, he was showing techniques in his art that were bold and abstract. Many of his pieces held a primitive feel as if they were his versions of cave paintings. The raw images of animals on a cold cave wall, infused with the reality that we now lived in houses. He was able to take these two states of mind, the wild and the tamed, and overlap them like lines off center.

Trustin used all sorts of things as his canvases, from old fruit crates to empty flour sacks. Even Mom's metal mop bucket. Dad eventually bought Trustin card stock from the hardware store. It became Trustin's favorite canvas for watercolors.

"You know, son," Dad said to Trustin when he saw the paintings, "you'd be able to sell these. That's the first step to makin' a career out of it."

"You think my paintin's are good enough?" Trustin asked.

"Son, they're the best in the world. I'm so lucky to be able to say I'm the father of such an artist."

A few days later, Trustin dragged a small wagon out of the barn. He gave it a fresh layer of green paint and drew little blue and purple flowers, using the rust spots as the flowers' centers. He wrote on the side of the wagon, "Dreams by Trustin."

The first time he went out with the wagon full of his paintings, he sold enough for him to believe he was capable of creating something people wanted.

I would often tag along with him as he went door to door. One day, as we were ready to head out, Dad stopped us.

"I want you two to drop off some orders for me while you're out." He handed me a box full of three jars of tea, a salve, two tinctures, and an oil. When Trustin picked up the jar of oil, dark sediment slid across the glass bottom.

"That oil is to be delivered to Ms. Pleasant," Dad said, handing over a slip of paper that had additional names and addresses. "Those are the folks the other items are for. I've written what belongs to who, so don't get it mixed up. Do you think you two can handle it?"

Both me and Trustin nodded as I set the box in the wagon. Trustin pulled it down Shady Lane, while I picked up the jar of oil for Ms. Pleasant. I opened the lid only enough to get the scent of roots.

"What you think she uses that stuff for?" Trustin asked.

"For her face. Of course." I screwed the lid back on.

While Trustin went door to door with his paintings, I made the delivery stops. Ms. Pleasant lived on the other side of town, so we headed there last.

"Look, Betty." Trustin nodded at Cotton's balloon floating up into the sky as we came to Quicksand Lane, where Ms. Pleasant lived. The lane was named for the very same sand Old Woman Slipperwort had told me Lavannah sank herself in.

"You know, there's a woman in there," I told Trustin as I pointed to the sand.

"Is not," he said.

"Is, too. Her name's Lavannah." I stepped to the edge of the sand.

"Hey, Lavannah?" I cupped my hand over my mouth. "You hear me down there?"

I turned to Trustin and dared him to put his finger in the sand.

"That is, if you're not scared." I clucked like a chicken.

"I'm not afraid." He stomped past me.

He pushed the tall grass aside and knelt by the sand. As he slowly lowered his finger closer, his whole hand trembled.

"You don't hafta do it," I said. "If you're too chicken."

"I told you I'm not afraid." He plunged his whole arm into the sand.

I dropped to my knees beside him. "You feel anything?"

"Just sand." He moved his arm around in it. "There's nothin'—wait—I feel—" His mouth opened but no sound came out.

"What is it?" I asked. "Trustin?"

"I feel somethin'." His eyes widened.

"What?" I prepared myself for the worst. "Tell me."

"Her hand. The woman you said was in here. She's holdin' my hand. I can feel her fingers. I can feel—" His arm was jerked forward. "She's pullin' me, Betty. She's pullin' me down."

He was yanked toward the sand until he was covered with it up to his shoulder.

"Don't let her take me, Betty."

The sand was flying from his struggling. I wrapped my arms around his waist and pulled until I felt him easing out. Another sudden jerk forward and he was being swallowed by the sand once more.

"Help me, Betty."

Digging my heels in and using all of my strength, I tightened my arms around him and pulled until I freed him. He rolled over on his stomach, hiding his arm beneath him.

"Ow, my hand, Betty. It hurts."

I tried to roll him over on his side so I could tell how bad the injury was.

"Let me see," I said.

He shook as if something still had ahold of him.

"Trustin?"

He released a piercing cry as his arm shot out in my face. I screamed and fell back, believing for a moment, I, too, would fall victim to the ghost of Lavannah and the myth of the quicksand.

"Got ya." Trustin laughed as he stood.

"You toad turd." I got up and pushed him.

"I can't believe you fell for it. It's just sand, Betty," he said, still laughing. "Ain't no woman in it."

I gave the sand one last look before we returned to the wagon.

Ms. Pleasant resided in a stucco house painted the same ocean blue every few years to keep the color bright. She lived near to the elementary school where she had once taught before retiring. Since then, she'd taken up growing succulents. When she saw us, she removed her gardening gloves and waved them at us.

"Ah, Carpenter, there you are. Stand up straight, Carpenter."

She called everyone by their last name. When me and my siblings were together, it was hard to know which of us she was talking to.

No one had seen the face of Ms. Pleasant for decades. There were rumors that her nose, right cheek, and most of her forehead were gone. Others said these things were still there, but that they were scarred from acid or fire. No one could be sure of the damage because of the masks she wore. Made out of papier-mâché, her masks were all of the same woman's face. Those who remembered the way Ms. Pleasant used to look said the beautiful face on each mask was her own before the disfigurement.

I tried to see her face as she stopped at the wagon. She picked up one of the paintings Trustin had made of our bean winnowing. In the image, he had painted Mom's bright red dress blowing in the wind.

"Red? Blah." Ms. Pleasant threw her hand out. "I've never cared much for the shade. Do you like it, Carpenter?" she asked as she reached her finger behind her mask to scratch her forehead. "Do you like the color red? Carpenter, I'm speakin' to ya. And stand up straight, for goodness' sake."

Both me and Trustin stood up taller. He looked at me to answer.

"I don't mind the color red none," I said. "But I wouldn't want it to be the last color I ever saw."

"Hmm, yes indeed, Carpenter. Good answer. Well, I reckon I'll take this one." She placed the painting beneath her arm as she dug her coin purse out from her apron pocket.

"I got plenty other paintin's here that don't have the color red in 'em," Trustin said, showing her the paintings of our winnowing baskets.

"I've already decided on this paintin' here, Carpenter."

"But you said you don't like the color red," he said. "Red's all over that paintin'."

"Boys don't understand, do they, Carpenter?" She turned to me and nodded at the jar. "Same price your father charged me before?"

"Same," I said.

She handed over enough money for the oil and the painting.

"You're both welcome to stay for a cheese plate if you like," she said. "I only have cheddar cheese but no crackers. However, I do have violet jelly from a batch I made back in the spring. You may dip your cheese block into the jelly. It's quite good. Come, Carpenter."

She turned back up the walk to her house.

"We don't hafta stay, do we?" Trustin asked.

"Why don't you go to the rest of the houses on this lane and see if you can't sell more paintin's?" I said. "I'll stay and be ready when you're through."

"You want to stay with her?"

"Maybe she'll take her mask off."

"If she does, tell me what her face looks like so I can paint it," he said before pulling the wagon away.

"Are you comin' or not, Carpenter?" Ms. Pleasant called to me from her door.

The inside of her house was as orderly as I had imagined. The pastel upholstered sofa and chairs were covered in clear plastic, while the wood trimmings shone like magazine pages.

"What are those for?" I asked about the cotton bedsheets tacked to the wall in places.

"They cover mirrors," Ms. Pleasant said. "I have no use for mirrors, but it felt a shame to remove them completely, so I simply covered them. Don't step on the rugs now, Carpenter."

She herself stepped around the pristinely kept rugs that were as colorful and elaborate as stained-glass windows laid upon her floor as she led me back to the kitchen. The cabinets were white steel matching white Cape Cod curtains, heavily ruffled, framing each window. The white was set against red gingham wallpaper.

"That's a lot of red," I said.

"Sometimes we have things around we don't like," she replied.

She placed her jar of oil down, then propped Trustin's painting against a canister marked MOM'S RECIPES on top of the pie safe. She opened the pie safe and retrieved a quilted glass jar of purple-hued jelly.

"It took me days to gather enough wild violets," she said. "That's why folks don't make this jelly anymore, because it takes discipline and work."

She sat the jar on the kitchen table. Out of her refrigerator, she grabbed a block of cheddar cheese and a pitcher of iced tea. She poured us each a glass, topping it off with mint leaves from a small pot in the windowsill. While she got two white saucers, I sliced the cheese.

"Open the jelly, Carpenter."

She had used paraffin wax to seal the jar. I lifted the seal with the blade of the cheese knife. Small pieces of paraffin dropped on top of the jelly. I picked them off before handing the jar to her.

"Thank you, Carpenter," she said, scooping her spoon into the jar to drop a dollop of jelly on each saucer. I immediately dipped my cheese in.

"Mmm, it's good," I told her. The jelly tasted sweet and cheery.

In order for Ms. Pleasant to take a bite, she had to hold her mask away from her mouth. I tried to see her face, but she was careful not to reveal more than she had to.

"What happened to your face anyways?" I asked.

"Oh, how I despise rudeness." She pulled her shoulders back. "I don't ask what happened to your face, now do I?"

"There's nothin' wrong with my face."

"That's a matter of personal opinion."

After a few moments of silence, she asked, "What do you think happened to my face?"

"I heard it was some kind of acid. Burned you real bad. Some say you did it to yourself. Others say a man done it to you."

"I've never had a man I couldn't handle."

"So you did do it to yourself?"

"Of course not. Silly child. God did it to me."

She dusted her hands off before pouring us each more tea.

"When I was a girl," she continued, "I saw somethin'. Somethin' terrible. I never said anything to anyone about it, so the one who did the terrible thing got away, while the one who had the terrible thing done to them, lived in misery until she died. Well, I thought, that's the end of that, but you can't know somethin' so dreadful and never say it without gettin' some of that wretchedness onto you. When we see somethin' bad, we have a great responsibility to do somethin' about it. Because I did nothin', God punished me by taking away my face. Simple as that."

"What was the terrible thing you saw, Ms. Pleasant?"

"The terrible thing no longer matters. What matters is that I told no one of it."

She stood and started to gather our dishes for the sink. She stayed there, staring out the little window. I decided to go outside and wait for Trustin. It wasn't long before he appeared.

"I sold all my paintin's." He nodded toward Ms. Pleasant's house. "You see her face?"

"Naw. C'mon." I hopped off her porch. "Let's go home."

When we got to Shady Lane, a truck honked and pulled up alongside us.

"Leland?" Trustin ran up to the driver's-side door. "You back?"

"Might be," Leland said out the open window.

"Well, you best go back where you came from," I told him. "There's a terrible sickness in town. Everyone's gettin' boils and dyin'. You best get outta here while you still can."

"That ain't true." Trustin made a face at me.

I told him to shut up.

"I think I'll take my chances." Leland started driving toward the house.

I ran after him. He smirked at me out his window.

"I'll show you what there is to smile about." I picked up a handful of gravel and threw it at his truck.

The small rocks struck the side of his door.

The brakes squealed as he jerked to a stop.

"Now ya done it, Betty," Trustin said, out of breath as he pulled the wagon up behind me.

Leland threw his door open so hard, it swung back in. He kicked it with his boot as he got out. He landed with both feet on the ground. He was twenty-six then and every inch of it.

"You wanna play, little girl?" he asked. "Then let's play."

I quickly ran into the field. I tried to run zigzag like Dad said to do if I was ever chased by a bear, but Leland liked the pursuit. I knew how fast he could run and he wasn't giving it his all. He wanted me to think I could get away.

When we reached the woods, I tried to use the trees to my advantage, running between them so he couldn't see me as easily, but he just kept laughing. When I next looked, he wasn't there anymore.

I stopped, trying to hear a twig snap beneath his step. There were only the sounds of birds.

"Leland? Where are you?"

We had run so far, I could no longer see his truck nor the lane. Feeling his eyes on me, I slowly backed.

"This isn't funny," I said. "I'm gonna tell—"

"Gotcha." His arms wrapped around my waist and pulled me to the ground.

We wrestled in the dirt. I kicked and slapped at him, but he was so much bigger than me.

"I thought my time away might have tamed you some," he said. "I see that ain't the case."

Flipping me over onto my back, he grabbed my thrashing arms and pinned them over my head.

"You sure grew up, Betty baby," he said as he ran his free hand over my dress, pulling my skirt up. When he grabbed my inner thigh, I screamed and banged my arms against the ground until he had to hold them with both of his hands.

I was Fraya under him. I was my mother under her father. I was Flossie under the boy who still had popcorn on his breath. And I was fighting. Fighting as they must have.

"Go on." He smiled, letting my arms go. "Give me hell."

I pushed against him and slapped his face. He only grinned wider. Then he wedged himself between my legs.

"No." I clawed at the ground for an escape, trying to pull myself out from under him. But my mother had been right. The heaviest thing in the world is a man on top of you when you don't want him to be. Still I fought with everything I had.

"You're a wild one, ain'tcha?" He pressed on my chest with one hand while he arched his back and tossed his head back to howl. He licked his lips and lowered his eyes to mine. "Little girls shouldn't walk alone through the woods. You'll get eaten by wolves. Don't you know that by now?"

"I hate you." I spit in his face. "I'm gonna tell everything. What you did to Fraya and—"

"What'd I do?"

"You raped her."

"Rape? That's a big word. You sure you know what it means, Betty?"

"I saw you. I was in the barn. I watched you rape her in the truck."

He grabbed my mouth and squeezed it until I could feel his fingers digging into my teeth.

"It's too late to tell now," he said. "Dad will ask you why you didn't tell when it happened. You saw this awful thing bein' done to your sister. You saw her raped, but you didn't say a thing? You went on smilin' and playin' and brushin' your hair in the goddamn mornin'? If I saw somethin' like that, I would tell right away." He paused and thought. "But wait a minute, you said you *watched* it happen?" With his hand tightening on my face, he moved my head up and down like I was nodding on my own. "And you didn't stop it?" He shook my head side to side, forcing my answer. "Why didn't you stop me? Your sister was gettin' raped right in front of you and you didn't do a thing to help her?"

"Shut up." My hot tears slipped down my face.

"You let it happen, Betty," he said. "You could have stopped it. You could've hit me over the head with any number of things in the barn. Hell, you hollerin' would have stopped it. You didn't do nothin'. What kind of sister are you?"

I turned my cheek and loudly sobbed into the ground.

"If they believe you," he added, "they'll think hell of you for not doin' a damn thing to save her. You might as well have raped her yourself."

I slapped him hard across the face. He grabbed me by the collar of my dress and pulled me into him. I was close enough to smell tobacco on his breath.

"And what about Fraya?" he asked. "You wanna embarrass her like that? All these years, she's never said a word. Folks will think that don't add up. If these terrible things were happenin' to her, well, hell, she'd say somethin'. Anyone would. Naw. No one's gonna believe you. They'll think you're some sick girl who lies about horrible things and embarrasses her sister, draggin' her name through the mud. I mean all these years, Fraya's still hung around me. Calm as the color blue. If I raped her, how come she still talks to me? Folks are gonna ask all these questions. You gonna have all the answers?"

"Leland?" Dad's voice echoed distantly. "Betty? Where are ya?"

Leland looked me dead in the eye.

"You're as guilty as I am," he said. "You tell on me, you tell on yourself."

I let him yank me to my feet. He started to drag me back through the woods, but stopped when he noticed my dress had come unbuttoned. He quickly fixed it while looking through the trees in case Dad was meeting us halfway.

"You're a nasty girl," Leland said as he looked for anything else out of place, brushing the leaves from the back of my dress. "You ran out in the woods." He pushed his fingers through my hair, brushing it down. "You wanted me to follow you. You showed me your body. Asked me to touch it."

"I didn't."

"What if Dad believes you did?" He nodded toward the direction of Dad's voice. "He'll never look at you the same way. You'll be filthy to him. You'll bring such shame. Now stop cryin'." He shook me. "I said stop it."

He pressed his thumbs into my eyes, wiping them.

"You're nothin' but a stupid hussy." He grabbed my hand and

tugged me all the way back to the lane, where Dad and Trustin stood by the truck.

"There you two are," Dad said when he saw us. "Where were you?"

"She threw rocks at my truck." Leland pushed me forward.

"Betty?" Dad turned to me. "Why did you throw rocks at his truck?" He dropped his eyes to my scuffed knees. "You fall? That why you cryin' and all dirty?"

"Had to chase her down," Leland answered for me. "We both took quite a rollin'. Looks like you left scratches." Leland pointed at the marks on the driver's side door.

"Betty," Dad said, "apologize for throwin' rocks at his truck."

"Apologize?" I shook my head. "I ain't apologizin' to him."

I grabbed another handful of gravel from the lane and threw it at Leland. He turned just in time for the rocks to bounce off his back.

"Betty, stop." Dad pointed his finger at me like I was a small child. "Now, that's enough. Understand me?"

Leland stood behind Dad and grinned at me. I tightened my fists until my fingernails were digging into my palms. When Dad turned to look at the scratches on the truck, I seized the opportunity and quickly reached into his pocket, pulling out his folded knife. With it, I ran toward Leland and jumped on his back. Opening the knife, I held its edge against the bridge of his nose, slicing into his flesh. The blood was warm as it ran over my fingers.

"Betty, goddamn it." Dad wrapped his arms around my waist.

I managed to cut Leland deeper just before Dad succeeded in pulling me off.

Leland cried out in pain as blood ran down his face.

"What the hell were you thinkin', Betty?" Dad yanked the knife out of my hand.

He put the knife into his pocket before grabbing me by the arm. When he started striking my backside, I screamed.

"Dad, stop it." Trustin's voice was somewhere behind us.

"She has to learn a lesson," Dad said over my cries. "She could have killed him."

"I wish I had." I yanked myself free. "I hate him and I hate you."

I shoved past my father and didn't stop running until I had made it all the way back to Ms. Pleasant's.

"Ms. Pleasant?" I pushed open her door. "You here?"

She came out from the kitchen.

"You forget somethin', Carpenter?" she asked.

I lunged at her and pulled the mask off. She cried out and hid her face behind her hands.

"Don't look at me," she said. "Please, don't look. I'm a monster."

I could see her face through the spaces between her fingers. I expected to see boils or scars. Something grotesque and painful. But there wasn't so much as a pockmark.

"There's nothin' wrong with you." I jerked her hands away to reveal the beautiful face of a sixty-eight-year-old woman. "You've been lyin' this whole time. Hidin' behind these." I shook the mask in her face.

"I'm hideous." She howled, pawing at her face. "Can't you see?"

"There's nothin' there."

"Feel." She grabbed my hand and held it to her cheek. "Feel the pus. The ridges of the scars. Don't you see my red eyes? My nose is gone. My lips are raw. There is everything wrong with me."

She threw her whole body into the nearby table, picking up the porcelain vase and throwing it against the wall. She tore the plastic covers off her furniture and knocked over shelves, sending the books crashing to the floor.

She snatched the sheets off the walls, revealing the mirrors. Her eyes widened in horror at her reflection.

"I'm a monster." She smashed her fist into the glass.

Bleeding, she continued to destroy her home. I tightened my hand on the mask and ran out the door. When I got to the end of the lane, Ms. Pleasant's high-pitched cries were still echoing in my ears. I hurried to the patch of quicksand and threw the mask into it.

At first it didn't appear the mask would sink, then it slowly started to be devoured by the sand until it was as though I was not looking at a mask at all, but the face of a woman slowly disappearing.

THE BREATHANIAN

Ghost Said to Be Shooter

A Mrs. Windcreep has come forward, saying she believes it is her dead mother who is responsible for the gunfire.

"A mother's hatred lives in the dust," Mrs. Windcreep said. "It's why there's always so much dust."

Mrs. Windcreep points to what she says is evidence around her home that supports her theory, such as doors that close on their own and a bathtub that keeps filling up with water.

"It's my mother, sure enough. She never thought I took enough baths," Mrs. Windcreep states. "I hoped my mother would be trapped in the ground after we buried her, but she's risen. She always has been a lousy shot, though, so I'm not overly concerned. But I wouldn't let any presidents come to town. They just might get assassinated as Mother was terribly fond of tragedy. Ain't all women?"

31

*For there is not a just man upon earth,
that doeth good, and sinneth not.*

—ECCLESIASTES 7:20

Sheriff Sands leaned in. He wore a cream vest over a white undershirt. His brown pants were partially tucked into his boots. He smelled of chewing tobacco.

"She said you came into her home and attacked her, Betty. Ripped her mask right off her face. Why would you do a thing like that?"

Sheriff Sands was originally from Arkansas and had the deep southern accent that was kin to, but not quite like, the southern Ohio drawl. He would be sheriff for many more years. Later, in 1984, he would be part of a mob that burned a black boy to death. But at that time, in 1965, he was just another man asking me why I was doing the things I was doing.

We were standing out on the front porch. Mom and Dad were behind me.

"Betty?" Dad asked. "Did you do what the sheriff is sayin'?"

I nodded.

"Well, Pleasant ain't gonna press charges." The sheriff spit over the porch rail. "But she wants you to keep your girl away from her." He spoke to Mom and Dad. "That means if Betty is seen trespassin', Pleasant has the law available to her."

"I wasn't gonna hurt her," I said. "I just wanted to see her face."

The sheriff pursed his lips, then drew them back, showing his small crooked teeth.

"What'd she look like under that mask?" he asked.

Even Mom and Dad held their breath for my answer.

"She—I mean her face—"

"Yes." The sheriff rolled his hand in front of me. "C'mon. What'd it look like?"

"It was terrible," I finally said. "Her face is two different colors. Red and pink. The skin is peelin' off her forehead." I clawed at my own forehead. "It's so raw lookin', like it won't ever scar over. It'll always be a seepin' wound. She don't have a nose. That's why she always breathes with her mouth open." I mimicked the breathing. "She can't smile. Her lips pull down like her cheeks are meltin'." I pulled at my cheeks. "She don't have no eyelashes or eyebrows. The hair at her crown is gone and there's little boils that constantly ooze pus."

The sheriff leaned back.

"Sounds like the worst thing you've ever seen," he said.

"Naw." I looked over at the barn. "It's not."

I never delivered oil to Ms. Pleasant again. Anytime she would see me, she would quickly cross the street, making sure the string of her mask was tightly knotted.

"Gosh, why'd you do it, Betty?" Flossie asked me one night in bed.

"You mean why did I pull her mask off?"

"Naw. I ain't talkin' about Ms. Pleasant. I'm askin' why you attacked Leland?"

"I was tryin' to cut his soul out," I said before closing my eyes.

Leland decided to stay in town. He got a job at Ralph and Sparkie's Oil and Gas. He lived in the back of the station. It smelled musty and centipedes lived in the groove between the cement floor and wall.

I measured the time by watching how Leland's cut healed. A few months later, in winter of 1966, I turned twelve while my brother's wound turned into a scar that bridged the space between his eyes.

As I stared at the scar, the icicles clung to the bare branches and my father built a steam cabinet in the garage. Folks, mostly women, would come, change out of their clothes into long gowns, and sit in the cabinet with only their heads sticking out. Dad still created his tonics, decoctions, and teas, but he had expanded his business. He had a table in the garage folks could lay on. He would slap their legs or massage their arms and hands. Lint had assisted Dad in building the table. Together, father and son even created a glove for pain that plugged in. The mechanics of it are lost to me, but when Dad would put the glove on someone's hand, sparks would shoot from the fingers. I always remember the sparks as being purple or blue.

Amidst this, Dad and Lint hung a small sign outside the garage door.

LANDON'S.

More people were gravitating toward my father, while I was gravitating away. Where was the man who had dropped seeds in my hand, telling me I was powerful? Could he be the same man who had raised his hand to me, making me feel powerless? If only I could tell him why I had attacked Leland.

Dear Dad, I have to tell you something.

I wrote this in letters to my father that I never gave him. I would sit in the chair he had made with wood from a crooked tree out back and—in violent recollections—I would write all the things I couldn't say out loud to him. Once I finished a letter, I would immediately tear it up and start anew. Was I afraid Fraya really would kill herself if I told? Or was I afraid everyone would find me just as guilty as Leland said they would? He had been right. I had done nothing to stop him that day in the barn.

The change in the air blew through the whole house. Trustin reflected it in paintings of images that seemed hidden away behind black swirls. Flossie, on the other hand, seemed pleased.

"Looks like you're not Dad's favorite anymore, Betty." She smiled. "Lint's his favorite now. You shouldn't feel bad about it. Fathers always like their sons best."

When spring arrived, I wasn't sure if we would go to the Covered Bridge Festival. We went every year as a family. Maybe that, too, was over. But when Dad made his macaroni salad and coconut cream pie the evening before the festival, I knew we would be going.

Several miles from the center of town, the covered bridge was a long wooden tunnel that had diamond-shaped openings overlooking a waterfall shelf in the river below. The festival was a time for ladies to show off their quilts and pies, while men judged a salt-rising bread contest.

We drove to the festival in the used burgundy Wagonaire Dad had gotten to replace the Rambler, which had stopped running. Rather than sell the Rambler for spare parts and scrap metal, he parked it in the woods behind our house. He took the raccoon tail off the Rambler's antenna to tie on the Wagonaire's.

The Wagonaire's best feature was a retractable rear roof. Me and Flossie always rode in the tailgate area because when the roof was open, it was a clear shot of the sky.

As Dad drove us to the festival, me and Flossie laid on our backs and called out shapes we saw in the fluffy clouds.

"I sure hope no one's taken our spot by the bridge," Dad said, speeding up a little at the thought.

Lint and Trustin sat in the second-row seat. Lint was showing Trustin a rock he'd picked up that morning.

"Do you th-th-think you could paint eyes on my rocks for me, Trustin?" Lint asked him. "They need eyes to be able to see the demons."

Dad started to slow the car as we approached an old farmhouse. In the front yard, a black pony was tied to a large oak by a short rope. Propped against the oak was a piece of cardboard that had FREE PONY written on it.

"Don't you even think about it," Mom said to Dad as if she was willing to put her own foot on the gas. "We already got enough asses. We don't need to add a horse to the mix."

When we got to the festival, Leland and Fraya were already there.

She came over to me and pulled my shirt collar open so she could dump a handful of goodnights down my back. She laughed before doing the same to Flossie, who threw her goodnights at Fraya like confetti.

As the slips of paper fell, me and Leland locked eyes. I stared at the scar on the bridge of his nose. I hoped it would never fade.

I helped Flossie spread the blanket on top of the grass in our usual spot. Dad always liked to be close to the bridge so he could hear the wind chimes. They hung on the outer edge of the roof.

I sat in between Fraya and Flossie as Mom and Dad doled out the food. They had packed a basket of sandwiches and a covered bowl of Dad's macaroni salad along with a jar of homemade pickles. For dessert, Dad cut the coconut pie in pieces that were too big to finish.

"The music is here," Fraya said, pointing toward Old Man Shoehorn playing his banjo.

He was wearing the same bright purple suspenders I always saw him in. He was a fixture at the festival with his gray beard that hung to his stomach and his long yellow fingernails he'd use to pluck his strings.

"Yee-haw." He stomped his foot.

Many of the picnic goers stood and started dancing. Older couples, like our parents, held one another in the waltzes of their youth. We watched the way our father dipped our mother as she threw her head back and laughed. A boy approached Flossie and asked if she wanted to dance. She accepted, her skirt fluttering like something flowering. Lint got up and went to explore booths. Trustin inched up the side of a nearby hill, where he could get a good view to sketch.

I watched Leland stretch out on the blanket while Fraya ate her slice of pie. She leaned back into me and smiled. I wanted to fill the moment with roses and words, but Leland was watching.

What if I cannot fend off the wolf? Souls ask these things.

"Wanna dance, Betty?" Fraya asked.

I stared out at the smiling faces of the festival. Laughter filled the air, until it was swirling all around me.

"Yeah, why don't you dance, Betty?" Leland's laughter rose above all else.

The smiling faces spun faster and faster around me. They all merged into the single smiling face of Leland. I stood up and screamed at the top of my lungs. At least in my mind I did.

"I'm gonna go for a walk," I said to Fraya as I stood.

"Stay," she said. "We can watch the quilt judgin' soon."

"Ah, let her go." Leland took a pair of sunglasses out of his pocket and put them on. "She ain't a little girl anymore. If she wants to walk, she'll walk."

I stepped over his legs, kicking his knee on my way. With my parents still dancing, I crossed my arms until I was out on the main road. The sounds of the festival fell behind me. I enjoyed the quiet, but once it started to get dark, a parade of cars began. The festival was over and folks were going home. I held my thumb out, but none of them stopped, except for the burgundy Wagonaire.

Nobody said anything as I got into the back with Flossie. I was happy for the loud sounds of the engine. They made it feel as if there was no room for anything else.

When I felt the car slowing down, I saw we were approaching the old farmhouse we'd passed on the way there. The pony was still tied to the tree. Dad parked in the grass and got out.

"Takin' a likin' to her, have ya?" the man sitting in a rocker on the house porch called out to Dad.

The man was all stomach. His thin arms and even thinner legs stuck out from him like toothpicks in a ball of dough.

"'Bout time someone wantin' the blind bitch." The man stood from the rocker and wobbled out to Dad.

"You say she's blind?" Dad looked into the pony's marbled eyes.

"Yep." The man nodded.

He was holding a large slice of watermelon. As he took a bite, the juice dripped onto his white T-shirt, already soaked.

"Blind as a dead woman," the man added. "She used to be a pit pony." He spit a watermelon seed on the pony's back leg.

"What's a pit pony?" Trustin leaned out the window.

"They work in the mines." Dad patted the stiff hair of the pony's mane. "Haulin' coal on the underground railway. It was the coal made her blind."

"That's right." The man nodded in agreement. "You a coal man?"

"I was." Dad gently touched the pony's scarred nose.

"Yeah, me, too." The man took another bite of his watermelon slice. "Retired now."

"How old?" Dad asked.

"When I retired?" The man thought it over. "Oh, I'd say I was—"

"How old is the pony?" Dad fanned gnats away from the pony's eyes.

"Oh." The man cleared his throat. "She's about nine years if I had to guess."

Dad stood back with his hands on his hips while looking over the pony.

"We'll take her," he said.

Mom sighed in the front seat as he untied the rope from the oak.

"You wanna come back with a trailer to pick her up?" the man asked.

"Naw. She'll do all right in our car. But if you have somethin' sturdy for her to walk on, I'd be mighty obliged."

The man tossed his watermelon and stepped inside his barn. He returned moments later with a flat board, which he and Dad set against the tailgate for the pony to step up on. Me and Flossie scooted back as far as we could against the seat.

Before leaving, Dad shook the man's hand, which seemed to surprise him. He laughed as we drove away.

The pony's head rose above the open roof as her mane whipped in the wind. I knew she must be thinking of running free through tallgrass fields, wild daisies slapping her shins, no one to hold her down.

I slid my hand up her leg, feeling the raised ridges of whip scars. The tips of her ears had been cut. There were smaller scars across her nose. A knife had been used there, perhaps only to remind her who she belonged to. She had lived by the orders and commands of men. Her entire existence on earth and she had never once been allowed to be free. She had been imprisoned and owned, as if all of her value was wrapped up in how large a load she could carry on her back.

She had lived her life to the point of being given away, her legs too weak to run, her eyes no longer able to see a world beyond the coal cave she was forced to spend her life in. And yet, now she could feel the wind in her mane. She was not too dead for this small kindness that delivered her from a past of hell to a moment she could believe she was free enough to gallop as she wished.

Is this love? she must have been asking herself. *Am I finally loved?*

I covered my face with my shirt. I was crying and didn't want anyone to hear. Still they must have, because someone turned on the radio.

Once we were home, Mom and the boys went into the house. Me and Flossie had to wait until the pony was unloaded. Dad used a piece of plywood from the garage for the pony to step down on.

Flossie looked at me before scooting off the tailgate and disappearing into the house.

As Dad led the pony into the backyard, I got out of the car. I walked around and stood on the back porch, watching Dad feed the pony a spring carrot from out of the garden.

"C'mon over here, Betty," he called to me.

I didn't go to him. I instead sat on the top porch step. Dad looked at me a moment, then raised his eyes to the sky before leading the pony through the field.

"My, my, my." Mom stepped out onto the porch, the kitchen door slamming behind her.

She walked down into the yard. The flowering clovers stuck up between her bare toes.

"The festival was a terrible way to spend the day when you think about it," she said as she watched Dad and the pony. "Folks like to believe it's a fun spring day spent listenin' to banjo music. No one even mentions the wind chimes anymore. Everyone dances and forgets the truth." She turned to me. "Do you know why wind chimes hang from the bridge, Betty?"

"To keep birds away."

"That's what folks say, but only because no one wants to talk about the truth. You see, the mothers of Breathed had hung those chimes in remembrance of their slain daughters. This was long before your time, but in the late eighteen hundreds, a man went around town, murderin' girls. When he was caught, he said he cut their tongues out because he didn't want to hear the girls say no to him. To give their daughters back their voices, the mothers put wind chimes on the bridge. These mothers called the wind chimes "soulchimes." They believed whenever the chimes made a sound it was their children's souls touchin' 'em. No one has hung a chime on the bridge since the last mother did. No one but your father, who has hung a chime for each of his own dead children. I suppose that is why he wants to go to the festival every year and sit so close to the bridge, if only to hear the souls of Yarrow and Waconda speakin' to 'im.

"Whatever ills you have against Landon Carpenter, you cannot say he does not love his children. Why, on the night you were born, your father counted every star in the sky. It took him the whole damn night but he did it. Just like he counted the stars on the nights your siblings were born. If you ask him how many stars were in the sky on the night Leland was born he'd give you the exact number, adding in that it was five stars less than on the night Fraya was born. Trustin's night had the most shootin' stars, while Lint had more moon than anything else. Flossie, the girl who dreams to be a star, had the fewest of all. Do you know who had the most?"

She stood in front of me and waited until I raised my eyes to hers.

"You did, Betty."

I looked past her, at the stars just above our heads.

"Some men know the exact amount of money in their bank accounts," she continued. "Other men know how many miles are on their car and how many more miles it'll handle. Other men know the batting average of their favorite baseball player and more other men know the exact sum Uncle Sam has screwed 'em. Your father knows no such figures. The only numbers Landon Carpenter has in his head are the numbers of stars in the sky on the days his children were born. I don't know about you, but I would say that a man who has skies in his head full of the stars of his children, is a man who deserves his child's love. Especially from the child with the most stars."

32

He shall fly away as a dream,
and shall not be found.

—JOB 20:8

When Dad would fill the metal cube trays with water, he'd always drop a small red currant into each hole. When the water froze, the currant froze, too. That was our summer treat. Never mind the ice cream man with his little bell dinging down the street. We had cubes of ice we'd suck on until we got to the bright red berry inside. This somehow made it nicer than going out to the currant bush and grabbing handfuls of the dangling berries, warm from the sun. Though we did that, too, until the little seeds got stuck in our teeth and we'd have to spend the rest of the afternoon fishing them out with our tongues.

I popped one of these ice cubes into my mouth as I walked the pony in the field. I described to her the things her eyes could no longer see.

"There's a flower," I told her. "It's pale pink with a yellow center. And there's a grasshopper. He's lookin' at your hoof."

I studied the pony's scars in the sunlight and traced them like they were roads.

"You know," I said to her, "in ancient Cherokee society, the father's blood didn't mean anything to the child's identity. Only a child with a Cherokee mother could be Cherokee." I wrapped my arms around her neck and hugged her. "I'll be your mother so you can be Cherokee. And you'll never have to worry because I'll never let anyone take you back to the coal mines ever again."

I walked the pony to the edge of the bright green garden.

"Soon," I said to her, "we'll try to preserve everything that grows here in jars."

"That's right," Dad said as he stood up out of the garden, smiling.

I smiled back. My mother's story of the stars had taken possession of me and reminded me who my father was. A man who didn't let me forget I was powerful. He hadn't taken Leland's side that day at the truck because he didn't know there were sides to take.

I wrote this in letters to myself.

Dear Betty, Your father is your father, is the first woman, is the sun, is the light, is all that is kind.

Dad once told me a Cherokee legend about two wolves. One wolf was named U-so-nv-i because it was evil, dishonest, and bent in spirit. The other wolf was named Uu-yu-go-dv because it was truthful, kind, and good.

"The two wolves live inside all of us," Dad had said. "They fight until one of them is killed."

When I asked him which wolf lives, he said, "The one you nourish and love."

I didn't want the wolf inside me to be the one who fed on anger and hate, so I worked in the garden. It was the one place that gave me and my father the opportunity to come together. There, we worked side by side. In the way we spoke about the strength of the stems and leaves, we spoke about the strength of us.

The garden itself seemed to respond, as the yields that year were bountiful. Never more so than when the berry harvest begun. Mounds of the garden's crop on our kitchen counter, ready to be turned into jellies and jams. Raspberries washed and drying. Bright blueberries in a yellow bowl. Blackberries heaped in the green enamel colander. Little purple stains left on all the white cotton towels. Gooseberries rolling off the counter, a couple squashed beneath our heels as the jars boiled in a pot on the stovetop.

My hands were no longer small enough to fit inside the small-mouthed jars, so I moved on to wash the medium-mouthed jars, the ones we'd can pickles and tomatoes in.

Trustin's hands were still little enough to reach the bottoms of the smallest jars without needing a bottle brush. He got extra money for art supplies by washing older neighbors' jars, too. He'd go to their houses, which always seemed to have a barking dog and a little old woman with arthritis. He'd slip his small hand into their jars and they'd say how fine a boy he was to help 'em out. It didn't hurt that he liked washing. He would hold the jar up and watch his hand through the glass as he cleaned, staring at the thin edges soap and water made as if that, too, was a painting in his eyes.

In between berries and jars, that summer was hotter than normal. Nearly every night, me and Flossie met Fraya at Breathed water tower to swim in the cold water. Lint never went with us because he didn't like the darkness inside the tower. Trustin would come, but he stayed on the ground. The fear of falling, like he had from that tree so long ago, was still too great.

"I just like to go to the tower so I can imagine swimmin' with you," he said. "I can imagine divin' from the ladder without any fear."

But imagining it wore off, so one night as me and Flossie headed out for yet another swim, Trustin fell back.

"Ain'tcha comin', Trust?" I asked him as Flossie kept walking, disappearing into the dark.

"What's the point in goin'?" He shrugged.

The brown bats feeding overhead got his attention. He looked up at them and said it wasn't fair that bats had wings.

"Even they share more with the angels than we do," he said. "Imagine havin' wings, Betty. There wouldn't be nothin' too high. Nothin' you wouldn't be able to get to the top of. You can't fall with wings. God wasted 'em on birds and bats. He should have given wings to us."

I turned to the old silver maple and remembered back to the Halloween I'd needed it to fly. As Trustin watched, I dug my feet into the maple's trunk and grabbed the lowest branch, pulling myself up into the limbs.

"What you doin' up there?" he asked.

I didn't answer as I pinched off two leaves before dropping to the ground. I went into the dark garage and rummaged through several boxes until I found a roll of tape.

"What you gonna do?" Trustin asked.

"I'm gonna give you some wings."

I used the tape to stick the leaves by their stems to his bare back.

"I thought it'd feel different," he said as he stretched his neck, trying to see the leaves. "I thought havin' wings would be so amazin', it'd make my knees tremble."

He ran over to a nearby stump and jumped up on it. When he leapt off, he dropped to the ground.

"They don't work," he said, standing up.

"They ain't wings yet, silly," I said. "They'll only turn into wings if you fall from high up. They're safety wings. So you comin' to the tower for a swim?"

He watched the bats a second longer, before saying, "Betcha I get there before you."

He took off running. I dropped the tape, racing to catch up to him. We shared the lead to the tower.

"It's gonna be nice to get in that water," I said, walking to the ladder.

"I don't think I can." Trustin stopped behind me.

"But you got wings now."

"I'm startin' to think I shouldn't be any higher off the ground than I already am, Betty."

I looked up at the night sky, feeling the vastness of the space above. I ached for some wonderment to come. A miracle straight from the heavens. Something to unfetter us all from our fears.

"You know, they say bees shouldn't be able to fly," I said. "That it defies all laws of flight. Bees' wings are smaller than their bodies, so them flyin' don't make sense, at least in the matter of science. But the bees don't care if their wings are too small. They believe they can fly. It's their belief that allows them to. Without havin' the trust in themselves, they'd never get off the ground. You should know a thing about trustin' oneself. Hell, *trust* is in your name."

"You sound like Dad." He smiled.

"I guess I do. So you comin' up for a swim?"

"You go on up. Maybe after a bit I'll follow."

I started to climb the ladder, but stopped when Trustin called my name.

"Yeah?" I looked down at him.

"You're a good sister for givin' me wings, Betty."

"It's what sisters are for." I continued up the ladder to the barrel of water at the top. Surrounding it was a balcony with shaky loose boards and an even shakier iron railing. I looked over it at Trustin, who was staring up at me.

"You look like an angel up there," he said.

"Everyone's an angel up here," I told him. "Don't you know that inside the water tower is heaven?"

"Is that why it's so high off the ground?"

"That's why."

"Well." He smiled. "I reckon it's a good night to go to heaven."

"The hottest nights always are."

I turned and stepped on a slip of paper. More made a path to the tower's door. I tiptoed around them as I went inside and jumped into the cool water, where I landed on Flossie. She cursed and splashed me.

"You see my goodnights?" Fraya asked. "I made a path of 'em for ya."

"I saw 'em," I said, reaching into my wet cutoffs for my goodnights to her. The paper was soaked so I had to squeeze the gob out in her hand.

"There's mine to you," I said.

She laughed while the three of us swam long enough for our fingers to prune.

"I'm all swam out for tonight," Fraya said, heading toward the ladder. "If I don't get out now, I might sink to the bottom."

One by one, the three of us climbed out of the barrel. I was last, so all I heard was Fraya saying Trustin was lying on the ground weird. I shoved Flossie forward so I could get out to see better. Trustin was flat on his back on the ground below. His arms and legs were stretched out. I leaned as far as I could over the railing.

"Hey, Trustin," I said. "Stop foolin'."

His eyes were still.

"I don't think he's foolin'." Fraya started down the ladder. "He's just layin' so weird."

I was only halfway down the ladder by the time Fraya had her feet on the ground and was kneeling by Trustin. She touched the side of his mouth. Her fingers came away with blood on them.

"Oh my God," she said, her voice shaking. "I think he fell off the ladder."

I jumped down the last few rungs.

"C'mon, Trustin. Get up." I ran over to him just as Flossie nudged him with her toe. He didn't respond.

"Remember when he fell from that tree?" I asked my sisters. "He laid there just like this and he was fine. Only got the wind knocked out of 'im is all."

Fraya turned to Flossie and said, "Go to the diner. Under the stone dandelion by the door is the key to get in. Call Dad. Then Doc Lad. Understand?"

Flossie ran off into the night, her wet feet slapping against the ground.

"It's going to be all right, Betty," Fraya said when she saw my face. "It's gonna be—"

Trustin gasped. I fell to my knees by his head while Fraya dropped down on his other side.

"See?" I said, smiling wide. "I told you he was fine."

Fraya squeezed his hand as she told him, "Flossie's gone to get help. Anything feel broken?"

He laid still.

"Can you move at all, Trustin?" she asked.

When he didn't move so much as a pinkie, she said it was okay.

"You shouldn't get up anyway until Dad or Doc Lad is here," she said to him.

I could see Trustin was wanting to say something, but was struggling to speak. I lowered my ear to his lips.

"What you sayin'?" I asked.

"I did it, Betty. I touched heaven. I flew. I flew like the birds. I flew . . ." His voice faded away.

I watched as his skin crinkled at the bridge of his nose.

"Why's his nose doin' that?" Fraya asked.

"His soul is leavin'," I said.

I knew it had when he exhaled for the last time. I fell back as Fraya started to shake him.

"Trustin?" She yelled for him to answer her. He was limp in her hands.

"He's dead, Fraya," I said. When she continued to shake him, I said it louder. "He's dead."

"No. He can't be."

"He's dead," I said it again. "He's dead, dead, dead."

I started to scream it. Fraya wrapped her arms around me and together we cried.

I want to describe my little brother in long songs, but there is no long song for a boy who only lived ten years. There is only the brevity. The short proof he had been alive. Lose a person. Gain a ghost. My ghost is a little boy sucking on ice cubes on the porch swing and using Flossie's lipstick to draw pretty caves on our bedroom walls. He's too young to do anything else. Too young to marry or father. Far too young to ever grow up. This boy who would walk into a wildflower field and come out with enough blooms to make me a necklace.

As I stared at him, I felt compelled to write his name on everything. On every blade of grass, on each rung of the water tower ladder, on all of the leaves of the tree beside us. I wanted his name on all these things and more. I was so afraid no one would know he had even existed.

"I called Dad and the doc," Flossie said as she ran up from the darkness. When she saw Trustin, she asked, "Is he . . . ?"

Fraya nodded. "He's gone."

It sounded so final when Fraya said it. I realized then, never would I have my little brother to yell at when he got his fingerprints, black from his charcoal, on my clothes. Never again would I have him to share binoculars with to look across the river at the distance on the other side. This boy who had drawn his family was gone. I was certain that, when I got back home, the roof itself would be gone, leaving the house exposed to the elements. That's what losing a brother feels like. Like a part of the house is missing, the part that shelters you in a storm.

Headlights lit us up. A car door flew open and Dad ran out.

"Oh, my boy." He dropped at Trustin's side. "What have you done, kiddo?"

Dad slapped Trustin's cheeks as if trying to rouse him in the morning from sleep.

"C'mon, get up now," Dad told him. "You're still a newborn. An infant. You can't go yet. You haven't drawn all the hills. You haven't mapped the river. Wake up, my boy, wake up."

"Dad, he's not gonna wake up." Fraya spoke softly.

Dad raised his eyes to hers as if needing to see the sadness in his daughter in order to know his son was truly dead.

"Oh, my boy." He wailed. "My little boy."

Trustin hadn't screamed that first time he fell. And he hadn't screamed this second time either. The only sound had been of the three of us playing in the water. I suppose that's why my sisters looked down, feeling we had let something slip so easily through our fingers.

"I've got you." Dad gathered Trustin up and carried him toward the car.

Left on the ground where Trustin had been lying were the two leaves I'd given him. I fell to my knees and dug up the earth enough to bury the leaves, wishing I could bury them miles down, the distance of my deep-reaching guilt.

33

Sorrow *is* better than laughter: for by the sadness of
the countenance the heart is made better.

—ECCLESIASTES 7:3

The first music I ever heard was the way my father drummed the
side of my cradle. *Thump, thump, thumpity, thump, thump.* Yes, that
was music. Yes, that was a song. Same song Dad played on the side
of Trustin's coffin. *Thump, thump, thumpity, thump, thump,* my father's
fingers drummed as he stared at his son's body.

We had Trustin's funeral on the back porch. It was nice with the
posts and the morning glory vines climbing up them. The sunlight
seemed slower there as if it were watered down, giving a sort of pale,
yellow flesh to everything. It was a good thought to have that the
back porch was the sitting view to long woods and slowly-gotten-to
pastures where life nested and fit into the whorls of a wildflower. If
you stood far enough away and only kept your eye on the possibility, you'd see these things. A place of noon and iced tea rings on the
rickety wooden table by the white swing.

Earlier that morning, me and my sisters picked forget-me-nots.
They were Trustin's favorite. It's said that when God was walking,
he heard a tiny voice say, *Please, God, forget me not.* When God looked
down to see where the voice had come from, He saw a small blue
flower.

"I'll always remember you," God told the flower.

The funeral was for family only. For all of Trustin's life, I never saw him with a friend or a girl he might one day kiss. Perhaps he knew he was not long for this world and was saving more people the heartache. A heartache that caused Mom to get up early and break all of the small jars in the kitchen.

As Dad cleaned up the shards, Mom stepped outside. She was barefoot and in a pale pink housedress. Sweat drenched the cotton and left marks beneath her armpits and at the small of her back until she looked like she was carrying an ocean. She seemed to like the sweat slipping down her face as she walked out to the tree swing and sat on it. As she swung higher and higher, she threw her head back and clung tight to the rope.

Flossie went over to sit on the top porch step, frowning as she watched Mom. Flossie had whispered to me about the curse all night, despite my telling her to be quiet.

"But don't you understand, Betty," she had said. "The curse has a plan for all of us."

I stood by the coffin. Dad had made it himself out of pine he painted yellow. The color of the first daffodils. He painted the inside bright blue with little white clouds.

"So Trustin will always have a piece of sky with him," Dad had said.

Fraya came up beside me.

"Don't you wish you had a sack full of good days, Betty?" she asked. "Whenever you were havin' a bad day you could reach into the sack and make everything better. If I had me a sack of good days, I'd reach inside right now and Trustin would stand up and dance, even though he never really danced, did he? I know he would, though, on a good day."

She turned away. When she walked by Leland, he looked at her. Digging his heels against the porch post behind him, he lowered his head and slipped his hands into his pockets. I thought he might say a verse from the Bible. He had started to deliver a few sermons at a church. When Flossie found out, she said, "Good Lord. Leland? Preachin'? How much you wanna bet he'll put a collection plate in his car and start drivin' around."

"He won't need to," I told her. "He's already got a collection plate built in. His hand."

She laughed, then her eyes clouded over as she said, "Why is it so many men of God are not of God at all, Betty?"

This echoed in my ears as I watched Leland at the funeral. He was twenty-seven then. His brow cast an even darker shadow over his eyes.

"I got these from the garden." Dad appeared behind me. He was holding bouquets of fresh thyme and mugwort tied with long white ribbon.

"The thyme is the herb of all travelers," he said as he attached the bouquets to the small hook he'd screwed into the underside of the coffin's lid, directly above Trustin's head. "It will keep you safe on your journey." He spoke directly to Trustin. "And the mugwort is for kind dreams."

Dad had cut the white ribbon long enough to reach Trustin's hand.

"For you to hold on to," Dad told his dead son.

My father's tears were things it hurt to see. They could lay against you like a beast who, by all of its downward weight, keeps you trapped until you starve the belief that a miracle will come, that a God will save you, that pain is no more than the shadow of the best home you've ever lived in.

Needing to get away, I decided to go to the front porch, where the sun was brighter. I removed a pencil and pad of paper from my dress pocket. Sitting at the small metal table in the corner of the porch, I tried to write.

Yes, that's right. No, that's wrong. Try again. Breathe. Write these words faster. Those ones slower. Look at the dish towels drying on the porch rail. Stories hide in the usual places. Write the magnification of this Ohio town. In rural land, light is king and I am young and green, fun and fine. Remember to smile while writing a beautiful name for the hurt.

I ended up writing three words. *I killed him.* At twelve years old I believed that. It was my secret, my confession, that I tore up. I dropped the pieces into a glass jar full of half-drunk moonshine there on the table. I watched the liquor bleed the ink away, and sat there long enough that the shadows shifted in the lowering sun.

When I returned to the back porch, Flossie was standing against a post. Lint was leaning over the rail as he watched Mom, still swing-ing. Leland and Fraya were watching Dad pick dead blooms off the hanging baskets of petunias.

"Dad?" I touched his forearm. "It's gettin' late. We might want to . . ."

He began picking off the live blooms.

"Those flowers are alive, Dad."

He looked at the petunias in his hand. He laid them on the porch rail before reaching into his pocket, pulling out one of Trustin's char-coal sticks. With it in hand, Dad stepped toward the coffin. He started to close the lid, but was unable to follow through.

"Get the lid for me, will ya?" he asked me. "I can't close the lid on 'im. I just can't give 'im that darkness."

As I slowly lowered the lid, the shadow fell on Trustin's face until all we were left with was the way the hummingbird darted back and forth overhead.

On top of the coffin, Dad gently laid his left hand and traced it with the charcoal. He colored the outline in until the handprint was solid black. When he offered the charcoal to us, Fraya was the first to take it. She laid her hand on the coffin.

"Storms in my heart will never go away," she sang as she traced her thin fingers with the charcoal. "Tearstained days are here to stay."

One by one, the rest of us shared the charcoal. When Lint did his hand, he said to Trustin, "Thanks for paintin' eyes on my r-r-rocks for me."

I was last. I traced slowly, feeling the charcoal's edge on my skin. I outlined my right hand, putting it close and at an angle to the shape of Dad's. It looked like the symbol of a heart.

Once I'd finished, Dad took the charcoal stick from me and went out into the yard to try to get Mom to stop swinging.

"Trace your hand for Trustin." He waved the charcoal at her.

She kept swinging until I thought she'd go so high, she wouldn't come back down.

Dad gave up and laid the charcoal on the porch rail. He looked at the hands on the outside of the coffin before saying, "Dear Son, we send you away on your great journey with extra hands. May you find them useful as you use the sky as your canvas."

Along the sides of the coffin, he had hammered in leather handles. One for each of us. I was on the right side with Lint and Dad. Leland, Fraya, and Flossie were on the other. Only after we picked the coffin up did Dad say we were not to put it down until we got to the cemetery.

"But, Dad, aren't we p-p-puttin' the coffin in the car?" Lint tried to get a better grip on his leather handle as we maneuvered the coffin down the porch steps.

"No, son," Dad said. "We carry our dead all the way."

As we passed through the yard, I stared at the handprints on the barn. I remembered what Dad had said all those years ago about the hands being left by those who could not let go.

"I wonder what they could not let go of?"I remember Trustin asking Dad. "I bet it's a treasure or a secret world that belongs only to them."

It was difficult enough to carry Trustin down Shady Lane. By the time we got to Main Lane, we were really struggling. Leland kept yelling at Flossie for not carrying her weight.

"I'm tryin'," she said. "He's heavy."

Those out on Main Lane stopped to stare and whisper about us strange Carpenters, who carried our dead through the middle of the lane as if we were laying down the mayor.

"What's those black things on the coffin?" I heard someone ask.

"Hands," another person said. "The black hands of death."

Then a strange thing happened. Men started removing their hats to hold them to their chests. Women told their children to stand up straighter.

"There's a coffin, for Christ's sake." They slapped the backs of their young.

Someone threw a flower. Followed by another and another. The people were picking flowers from pots lining the lane and tossing them in our path. We stood taller. The weight seemed not as heavy.

When I saw Ruthis, she was holding a red geranium. It reminded me of the first time I'd met her, when she had held the red ball. A group of girls laughed behind her. She told them to shut up. Then, just as she once threw the red ball to me without hesitation, she did the same with the flower.

Everything became vibrant as if the whole moment was awash in Trustin's paints. Breathed seemed to glint like a kaleidoscope's edges.

"If one day I'm ever gone," Trustin's voice echoed in my ears, "you'll know I ran away to the back of that man's suit."

I wanted to believe that's where he was. Alive and where he wanted to be, even if it wasn't with us. But as we got closer to the cemetery, and the geraniums were no longer falling in our path, the coffin began to feel the heaviest it ever had. We alone stepped into the cemetery with our dead son and brother. There is no wash of color or kaleidoscopic edges in a place of cold hard stone and disturbed soil.

Trustin was not to be buried on Reflection Hill, which was for the wealthier families of Breathed, who could afford to have effigies made of their loved ones. He was going to be buried in a cemetery built on three corners of land that had, in the 1700s, been owned by three different men. These men quarreled over the property lines, which in those days had been decided by the length of time it took for one man's cigarette to extinguish. The argument escalated until they drew their gentlemen swords. As if it had always been their fate, all three men were fatally wounded. Theirs were the first graves upon that land, which eventually became Landlord's Cemetery. It was also known as the field of stone angels because those were the only gravestones. Trustin's stone would not be placed until a year later, when Dad saved enough to buy the little stone angel with the big wings.

We walked by an old tractor's steering wheel left to rust and a piece of till that'd been abandoned years ago. Trustin's plot was toward the back of the cemetery, where a series of oaks sat at bough's length apart from one another. There we set the coffin down. I could no longer feel my hand. The leather strap had left the beginnings of a blood bruise on my palm.

"It doesn't feel real until you see the hole," Flossie said.

The hole had been dug that morning and the shovels were still lying on the ground. At times, the hole seemed too deep. Other times, it appeared too shallow.

"I want each one of you to never forget to say his name," Dad told us. "When someone asks you how many brothers you have, you don't stop includin' Trustin just 'cause he's gone. Don't say he's dead either. Say he went off into the field to draw his pictures, and he'll be back before dinner."

"But h-h-he won't, Dad," Lint said.

"Hell." Dad stood at the edge of the grave and nudged a pebble into the hole. "I know that." He squinted at the sun. "If any of you have anything to say, now is the time."

We looked at one another to see who would speak.

"Not all at once, now." Dad chuckled like it was the best he could do. "Betty? You got the poet in ya. Say somethin' we'll remember."

I swallowed hard. My thirst had gotten worse in the heat.

"Sure, Dad," I said, my voice trembling. "Trustin was . . . he was one hell of an artist and—and—do y'all feel the ground movin' or am I the only one who—"

I would later wake up in my bed with a cool wet rag laid across on my forehead and ice melting in a bowl on the bedside table. I saw a smiling face hovering over me.

"God?" I asked.

"Naw, it's your dad. You fainted," he said. "Fell in the hole of all places."

"What hole?"

"The one dug for Trustin. You gave your chin there a good scrapin', but other than that you're fine. At least now we know you can survive six-foot falls. When we carried ya home, folks thought we lost another one. A couple of people have dropped casseroles off. I didn't know they'd be so nice."

He frowned and thought for a minute.

"The coffin was too heavy to carry that far," he said. "I put ya through quite a strain, didn't I? How ya feel now, Little Indian?"

"Well, I ain't dizzy no more."

I sat up and saw dirt on my dress. I still had some tiny pebbles on my legs. Someone had removed my shoes. They were by the door.

"Are we goin' back to the cemetery to bury Trustin?" I asked.

Dad laid me back and put the rag once more across my forehead.

"He's already buried," he said.

As he slipped an ice cube into my mouth, I shut my eyes, listening to the tree branch outside creak under the weight of my mother, swinging high enough to dry her tears.

THE BREATHANIAN

Teenagers Spooked by Gunfire

In the late hours of Saturday night, a teenage couple, spending an unchaperoned night in the local cemetery, was frightened by nearby gunfire.

When the two got up to run, they became separated. The boy claimed to have been chased to the train tracks.

"I could hear heavy breathing and footsteps behind me," he reported. "A ghostly voice told me I was going to die tonight."

The girl ended up lost in the woods. She was found several hours later with leaves in her hair. She said when the gun went off close to her, she hid behind a fallen log.

She claimed to have smelled thyme and mugwort in the area during the time of gunfire.

The boy says he will no longer see the girl.

"I believe the gunfire was a warning I shouldn't be with her," he said.

The boy did not want to be identified, though the girl insisted she be.

"I'm Flossie Carpenter," she said. "I'm the one whose brother fell off the water tower. But he's not really dead. He's just drawin' pictures of things in the field. He'll be back before dinner."

Part Four

Seed of Woman

1967–1969

34

They grope in the dark without light,
and he maketh them to stagger like *a* drunken *man*.

—JOB 12:25

After Trustin was gone, my father went away, too, in little ways. He no longer ate the vanilla cream drops he kept in the little tin in his bedside table drawer. Newspapers went unread and the slingshot he'd made for him and Trustin was put in the kitchen drawer and never taken out again.

"It's a father-son slingshot," Dad had said when he presented it to Trustin for his birthday a couple years back.

Dad had made the slingshot to have three prongs. The middle served as the base around which rubber bands from the outer prongs were tied. This was so two people could fire the slingshot at one time. But in order to do so, each person had to grip on to the single handle. Dad would always put his big hand on the handle first. Trustin would then lay his small hand on top.

"It's pretty well on the nose," Dad said to his own amazement at the slingshot's accuracy.

Together, the two of them would fire pebbles into the woods. They'd also gather the bodies of the moths from our porch each morning. They would take them to the river and shoot them onto the surface of the water.

"To feed the fish," Dad would say.

Really, I think it was so they could give one last flight to the winged creatures who had died by the light of our porch.

Months passed since Trustin's death. That autumn came and went, it seemed, as quick as a week. Pumpkins on Monday, the gray sky perfected by Wednesday, all the leaves fallen by Sunday. When winter came, it proved long and cold, months of bare branches and frozen ground. There would be an ice storm that year. It knocked the electric out for days.

In February of 1967, I turned thirteen. I sat at the small square table Flossie had put a mirror on to turn into a vanity. Her makeup was scattered on it. I picked up her red lipstick and put it on, smacking my lips as I stared at myself in the mirror. I used her purple eye shadow and colored in my thick eyebrows with eyeliner. Lastly, I applied mascara until my lashes were hard.

"Ugh. You look like a clown, Betty." Flossie snickered as she stepped into the room.

I tried to dart past her to the bathroom.

"Wait." She stopped laughing. "I'll do your face for ya."

She sat me back down at the vanity and used a tissue moistened with grapeseed oil to remove the makeup, replacing it with brown eye shadow, black liner, and a single coat of mascara. She took my hair out of its braid, letting both sides hang long over my shoulders.

"Never s-s-seen ya with makeup on before, Betty." Lint smiled from the doorway.

"Who you think's prettier?" Flossie turned to face him. "Me or Betty?"

"You're both p-p-pretty." He shifted on his small feet.

"How so?" Flossie put her hands on her hips.

"You look more like M-m-mom. B-b-betty looks more like Dad."

"Hear that, Betty?" Flossie asked. "He's sayin' you look like a man."

"That's not what I m-m-mean," Lint said.

Flossie mocked his stutter before shooing him out of the room.

When she came back, she turned me away from the mirror.

"This will be the perfect color for you," she said, picking up the red lipstick. Instead of applying it to my mouth, I felt her draw two lines on each of my cheeks.

353

She started laughing as I turned to look in the mirror.

"Your war paint," she said. "I guess that's why I'll always be the prettiest."

She left, grabbing her coat on her way out. I looked one last time at myself in the mirror before leaving.

Downstairs, I found Dad smoking in a rocker on the front porch. He had a jar of moonshine.

"Do you remember who all bought a paintin' off Trustin?" he asked with his eyes down. "I think I'm gonna buy 'em all back and hang 'em on our walls."

As he took a drink, he saw my face.

"What'd you do?" He frowned. "Why's your face got all that crap on it?"

"Flossie put it on me."

"A girl changes when she wears makeup," he said. "The way she sees the world and the way the world sees her."

He swallowed back more of the moonshine, his hand covering the stars painted on the outside of the jar.

"Why?" I asked.

He wiped his mouth as he asked, "Why, what?"

"Why's a girl gotta change when she wears makeup?" I leaned back against the porch rail and dug my nails into the wood. "Why can't I be the same wearin' lipstick as I am when my lips are bare? Shouldn't it matter more what comes out of my lips than what is worn on them?"

"That's not what I'm sayin'."

"You don't know what you're sayin' with all that moonshine in ya."

"I'm sayin'—"

"What, Dad?"

"When a girl puts on makeup, it's her first step out the door. The eye shadow, the lipstick, it's you leavin' me. Why can't ya stay a little girl?"

"Same reason you couldn't stay a little boy, Dad."

"Naw." He looked past me. "I couldn't. But Trustin will."

He nursed the moonshine as I walked back into the house.

Later that night, I would see my father hopelessly lost for the first time.

It turns out he was a yeller when he was drunk. Not a mean yell, but a sorrowful one. A cry, really, that echoed throughout the hills as he wandered from the house. I put on my coat and boots to go in search of him. If he passed out, he'd freeze in the February night. When I found him, he was banging his cane against the Shady Lane sign.

"Dad, stop that."

He looked at me like a child getting caught. As sudden as anything, he ran up the nearest hill. Along the way, he dropped both the jar and the cane.

I watched my father wildly climb, grabbing onto the sandstone edges. The exposed rock was like a woman popping out of her dress to me. Each ridge and cliff like the revelation of the woman's collarbone or shoulder blade. This made the hills seem alive, as though they had at one time walked on two legs and went through hot-blue heavens and red-burning hells.

God exists here, demons, too, the hills seemed to say what we already knew.

I climbed up after my father, collecting his cane on my way and feeling the hardness of the frozen ground. The winter was something the hills had to bear. Something we all had to.

"Dad, let's go home," I said. "You're gonna fall and hurt yourself."

Still he climbed and still I followed, uncertain of the end for both of us.

Before, I might have felt Dad could outrun me up a hill, but now, I knew my stride was wider. My arms and legs had grown longer. In some ways, I felt less like a child following my father and more like the young woman I was becoming. Maybe it was only the joint at each of my wrists that seemed solid, like pure muscle. I could feel a strength in me, lengthening with each new year. I imagined all the things my strength could be used for. To own crop. To sharpen a blade. To bear the load of each new harvest across my shoulders. Now my strength was to chase an old man up a hill.

Once he made it to the top, he lifted his arms and screamed.

"Give me back my boy." He shook his fists at the sky as he yowled.

I imagined people stopped what they were doing and looked outside to find the animal that had made the sound.

He fell back onto the ground. For a moment, I thought he'd passed out, but he was awake and staring up at the sky. He was sweating from drunkenness and freezing from the cold at the same time. I sat beside him and listened to his sorrowful cry. I laid his cane on the ground between us.

"Where is my son, Betty?" He grasped at me as if I was the one thing he had to hold on to.

"Dad, stop." I peeled his fingers off my coat.

He looked at his hands as he said, "You know, I've been wonderin' this entire time, who's gonna wash the small jars?"

"Mom broke all the small jars," I reminded him.

"Not all of 'em."

"I can wash what's left, Dad."

"No, you can't."

"Yes, I can."

"No." He slammed his fists against the ground.

We listened to the silence around us for the next few moments. When he spoke, he used his deepest voice, as if he had to in order to go back so far in his life to say, "My daddy used to take me up into these hills. We'd dig up arrowheads. My daddy would hold up an arrowhead and say, 'Think of how many animals this brought down. It's been on every hunt and in every war. It's almost a livin' thing, this flint. Because of what it's done, it has energy.'

"I wanted to feel that energy so I carved an arrow and bow. I went up into the hills and I felt our ancestors in the way I pulled the bow back and released the arrow. I practiced on trees, imagining they were deer runnin' the great field. When I took aim at an old black walnut, the arrow missed and killed a real deer I didn't know had been standin' there the whole time. The blood was awful to see. Sometimes all I can remember is his blood. As if it came in red sheets. I think my mother hung those sheets in the trees."

He picked up his cane and held the carving he'd done of Trustin's face. "My boy, my boy," he said over and over again.

Unable to bear my father's cry any longer, I released my own.

"I killed him," I said. "I killed Trustin."

Dad laid the cane down. He blinked his eyes, trying to figure out if he had heard me correctly or if it was only the moonshine in his ears.

"You said you killed him?" he asked.

"I gave him leaves and I told him they were wings. And that if he fell, he would be all right, because the leaves would turn into wings and he would be able to fly." I tasted the salt of my tears slipping into my mouth. "He never would have climbed that ladder if I hadn't of led him up it. It's my fault he's dead, Dad."

"Oh, no, no, no. C'mere." He wiped my cheeks with his hands as if he was using my tears to wash my face. "No, no. You didn't kill him. It may feel that way, but you didn't."

He laid my head against his chest as he looked at the land around us.

"You know why hills were made, Little Indian? Hills were made so men could stand at the top of 'em and roll their sins down. Creator is wise, Betty. It's why He didn't make this whole damn world nothin' but a big flat piece of land."

He stood and rubbed the toe of his boot into the ground. He managed to loosen two rocks from the cold earth.

"All these hills around us," he said, "God must have known us Carpenters would call this place home."

He handed me one of the rocks, keeping the other. With a grunt, he cast his rock down the hill.

"C'mon, Little Indian." He held his arms out. "Give it to the hills."

I stood and threw the rock so hard, my body pitched forward as I screamed in the tradition of my family. The rock hit a tree branch, knocking the ice off before falling to the ground. It rolled the rest of the way down the side of the hill.

"What happens now, Dad?" I asked.

"We believe." He stood taller. "We believe we are free from our sins and that maybe one of these days the land will flatten out and we will be good enough people to not need hills."

35

Strength and honour *are* her clothing.

—PROVERBS 31:25

In spring of 1967, the world was preparing for a summer that would have lasting meaning in the annals of human culture. In Breathed, however, we were more concerned with the birds. They circled at first, before briskly flying as if falling for dear life. They crashed into windshields and houses. They even struck people, like Cotton, who watered his lawn at exactly 6:30 every morning. He walked into town with a bloody nose and a dying sparrow in his hands.

Dad said the birds were suffering from grass river sickness.

"It sometimes happens," he said. "The trees become like smoke rising off water until the birds believe grass is the surface of a river. The birds are flyin' low to see their reflection. To see if they are still made of feathers or if they are merely men uneasy in the wind."

Mom's belief, however, was intricately tied to a forecast.

"A creature of the sky will only fly low when bad weather is approachin'," she said.

Not wanting to be plowed into, Mom would squat and sit in between the large bushes at the side of our house, where she was able to view the birds zigzagging in front of her.

One night at dinner, she said she knew the point of the whole thing.

"What is it?" Dad asked her.

"To let us know there's one hell of a storm comin'," she said, startling at the sound of a wren colliding with the side of the house.

Some folks, like Dad, buried the dead birds. Others burned them out of fear of disease. Cinderblock John was one such person.

"This is all happenin' because of the aliens," Cinderblock John said. "The Martians, Venusians, whatever you wanna call 'em, they've given all our doves, swallows, and thrushes death to carry inside 'em like a chill. The aliens want us to be infected, too, until we start walkin' so low, we start shovelin' out our own graves. Only fire can destroy such cold infection."

I thought smoke from the burning birds might be colored like their feathers. Red for a cardinal. Blue for a jay. Yellow for all the darling warblers. But the smoke was as gray as ever, if not black, as it rose against the white clouds.

Business owners took on the responsibility of collecting dead birds out of the lanes. Sheriff Sands warned cars not to drive over the bodies before they could be picked up.

"Go around 'em," he said. "If you smash 'em, it releases blood. Makes more of a mess. Might end up bein' what helps spread this thing."

I always liked to go on foot to school, but even walking through the woods, using trees as a cover, was becoming increasingly difficult. However, no matter how bad the birds were outside, they were worse inside the school.

Walking down the hallway, I dodged the birds' beaks. They seemed to want to peck my breasts off. The beating of their wings, like a strong gust of wind that tried to knock me down. I fought to shield my face from their sharp talons. I covered my ears from their vulgar shrieks.

"C'mon. Show us your tits." They screeched, circling me. I beat them back with my books and ran into my classroom.

The birds followed, taking their seats. One in particular turned to look back at me. I thought he resembled a woodpecker. His long thin nose. His small beady eyes. I squirmed in my seat as he continued to stare at me like I was something he wanted to eat. He leaned down and looked toward my legs. I held them together as tight as I could.

"I think I see a bloody pad," he said. "You wearin' a bloody pad, Betty? I can smell it."

Funny how much teenage boys behave like birds flying too low.

Each day, I tried to ignore the growing attention from the boys. I learned not to write so much in class because the more I wrote, the more the lead of my pencil wore down, which meant I would have to go to the sharpener on the wall. Every time, my skirt would be yanked up. I held my hands against the fabric, trying to stop it. Whichever boy had lifted my skirt would laugh and tally his score against the others.

Girls weren't allowed to wear pants or shorts in class. As girls, we were deemed not to be able to make our own decisions. As if we were not smart or capable enough to decide how to dress our own bodies. I didn't have anything against dresses, but I also knew shorts were best for hanging upside down from tree branches in and for walking by boys who couldn't keep their hands to themselves.

One day that spring, I looked at the dresses in my closet. Pushing them aside, I made the decision to wear something else. Shorts. I'd taken my seat before the teacher, Mrs. Cross, or any of my fellow classmates noticed. We started the morning by reading passages from our history books aloud. I continued to watch the birds outside because I was never called on to participate in class. It made no difference if I was paying attention or not. The teachers had their favorite students. I was never one. I turned in my work, and that seemed to be all that was asked of me. The teachers had already determined I wasn't going to do anything with my life, so why bother with me? I might as well not have existed. But that day, Mrs. Cross did the unexpected. She called my name.

"Betty, read the next paragraph for us."

Oh, God. I'd never been called on before. To read? Me? The very thought of my voice in the room caused my stomach to hurt. I broke out in a cold sweat and my hands shook as I picked up my book. The words on the page blurred as I tried to focus on which paragraph.

"The one at the bottom, Betty." The teacher impatiently tapped her pencil on her desk. "C'mon, c'mon."

"Lincoln . . ." My voice quivered as I crossed my legs tight at the ankles. I thought I might pee. "Abigail . . . I mean Abra—Abraham Lincoln was ass—" The kids laughed.

"God, what's the matter with her?" they whispered to one another. "What a weirdo."

My mouth felt so dry. *I could drink the whole river,* I thought, *and still be thirsty by the end of it.* If I was home, I would read aloud without issue, but there at school, I had become someone afraid of being heard and of being seen.

I had to fight each word just to get through a single sentence. It was as though hands were choking me. I couldn't breathe. I felt like I was going to die.

They'll collect my body from the desk, then go about reading the rest of the book like I didn't matter.

"Lincoln was . . . assassinated . . . April fifteenth, eighteen sixty-five . . ."

"Betty," Mrs. Cross said, "you're readin' like you got gum in your mouth. You know gum is not permitted in class. Take it out this instant."

I didn't have anything in my mouth, but I pretended to take gum out just so I could have an excuse to stop reading for a second. The thought of returning to the page made me feel as though I was going to pass out. Then a flycatcher flew into the window. Everyone got up to watch it slide down the glass.

"They're probably tryin' to fly in here 'cause they think Betty is some big ugly worm to eat," Ruthis said, laughing. "I bet her and her daddy are gonna make headdresses out of all the fallen feathers. Don't leave Betty alone in the woods. She might turn completely savage."

I slowly stood from my desk. The room had finally stopped spinning.

"Betty?"

The teacher's voice was behind me.

"Are those shorts I see on your body?" she asked.

Ruthis snickered.

"I . . . I . . ." I was still thinking of the paragraph. "I wear them at home." I was finally able to make a complete sentence.

"This isn't some tepee out in a field, young lady," Mrs. Cross said. "This is an institution of formal education. There are rules to follow."

I was sent to the principal's office. I took my time getting there. During the walk, I was able to calm down and was feeling more myself as I entered the office.

The principal was a man who wore a bow tie and a small flag pin over the left breast pockets of his suit jackets, which were always gray. He had broad shoulders and short, thick legs.

"Betty Carpenter, what are we gonna do with you?" he asked as I stared at the taxidermied swordfish mounted on his wall. "Betty? When I speak to you, I'd like to see your eyes."

I turned to him. His breath always smelled like pickles. I could smell it wafting toward me.

"You've violated our school policy, you know that, don't you?" he asked, gesturing to my shorts.

"I don't understand why there's a policy," I said.

"We must keep separation between the sexes."

"Separation?" I asked.

"Clothing should show there's a difference between a girl and a boy. Don't you agree, Betty?"

"Why can't I wear what I want?"

"Do you know what happens when girls wear what they want, like shorts or pants?" he asked.

I shook my head.

"Everyone stares at your crotch," he said, briefly looking at mine.

"My crotch?" I looked down toward it, too.

"That's right. Pants define your area. When a woman wears pants, no one sees *her*. They just see her crotch. Women who wear pants desire that attention. They seek it. Did you know that in places in this world where females wear pants there is more crime? Women who wear pants don't care about the family or the home. They don't care about instillin' good morals and settin' good examples."

"Because they wear pants?" I asked. "But men wear pants."

"Women cannot behave the same as men, because women and men are not the same. What if I were to put a skirt on right now and go frolicking around this office like your mother?"

"My mother doesn't frolic."

"My dear, anytime a woman walks, she frolics. She can't help it. It's the way her legs are shaped."

He stood and started walking on his toes as he swung his hands up by his chest.

"Oh, look at me." He tried to speak in a woman's voice. "Look at me."

"That's not how women walk," I told him.

"Yes, it is." He pulled the blanket off the back of the upholstered chair in the corner. He turned the blanket into a skirt by wrapping it around his hips. As he circled the room, he continued to walk on his toes and sharply sashay his hips to either side.

"Do you still have respect for me, Betty?" he asked. "Of course not," he answered before I could. "I would be less of a man in a skirt."

I realized then that pants and skirts, like gender itself, were not seen as equal in our society. To wear pants was to be dressed for power. But to wear a skirt was to be dressed to wash the dishes.

"I wouldn't be surprised if the birds are actin' the way they are because you're wearin' those shorts, Betty." He dropped the blanket and sat at his desk as he told me wearing a skirt would preserve my purity.

"Your fellow brothers in Christ will look at you with respect if you dress how the Bible says women and girls should," he said.

"But the boys keep pullin' my skirt up," I replied. "They've seen my underwear a million times."

"I see." He leaned back in his leather chair. "You flirt with the boys then?"

"No."

"Have you been wearin' clothin' that causes your fellow students to think lustful thoughts?"

"I'm just wearin' clothes, same as anybody," I said, gritting my teeth.

"Because the clothes a girl wears can be leadin', do you understand? The way you dress says things about you. I know these boys in my school. I am friends with their families. They are good sons. They are tryin' to keep God in their heart. You want them to be good boys, don't you?"

"Whether they're good or not is up to them."

"No, it's up to you. You have a great responsibility as a female, Betty. Especially now that you're comin' up on havin' hips and breasts. How can us men keep God in our hearts if you pretty little things don't help us by dressin' modestly? Do you know what modest means, Betty?"

"They're just cotton dresses and skirts I wear. They've got little flowers on them and—and—and you don't see me goin' around pullin' the boys' pants down. It has nothin' to do with clothin'. The boys would lift my skirt up if I was wearin' a potato sack. You should be punishin' the boys. Not me."

"Do you go to church, Betty?" He leaned farther back until his chair squeaked. "I don't think I've ever seen you and your family there."

"Nature is our church."

"The church is your church, young lady. Anything else is blasphemy. Are you Christians, your people?"

"My people are Cherokee," I said, standing taller. "And if we were still livin' today as my ancestors did in the past before everything was taken away from us, women would be in charge and *you* would have to listen to me."

"Oh, is that so?"

"Yes. And I could wear what I wanted because—"

"Because why?"

"Because it didn't matter to the Cherokee what women wore. It mattered what they *did* and what they *spoke* and what they *thought*."

"And you see what happened." He laughed. "Your people were

conquered because women make weak leaders. I guarantee if these Cherokee of yours would have had men in charge, this would all be Indian country today. Women in pants lost your people your land."

"Take that back." My hands closed into fists at my sides.

"It isn't befittin' for a girl to frown so hard, Betty."

I thought about flattening him until he was lost in the ground. Something we could then tread over until the end of time. Better still, I wanted to put him in a hollowed log and roll him off the edge of everything. At the very least, I wanted to take his bow tie and strangle him with it until he'd taken back everything he'd said. Instead, I looked up at the swordfish.

"You must like that," he said. "To keep starin' at it the way you are."

"Dad says men who mount dead animals on their walls are men who think they're more important than they really are. He also says that only men with small penises kill an animal just to have a trophy."

"Well, your dad must have a whole wall of dead animals then," he said with a satisfied grin.

He released me back to class, but not before he drew a compass on a piece of paper that he then attached to the hem of my shorts with a safety pin.

"Why'd you draw a crack in the glass?" I asked.

"Because your moral compass is broken, young lady," he said.

As soon as I was out of his office, I grabbed hold of the piece of paper. I was about to yank it off my shorts, then I saw the arrow he'd drawn. It was not pointing back toward my classroom. It was pointing down the hall to the school's front door.

I followed the arrow, running toward the brightly lit doorway. Outside, the janitor was pushing a metal trash can on wheels and picking up dead sparrows from the sidewalk. I ran past him, all the way to Dandelion Dimes.

I opened the door as quietly as I could. Still, the little bell rang. The diners turned to look at me.

I tugged on Fraya's apron strings as I passed her on my way to the counter. She finished taking orders before meeting me.

"Shouldn't you be in school, Betty?" she asked.

"Couldn't find my way to class." I nodded down to the compass.

She looked at my shorts.

"Okay," she said. "I'll let you skip school today. It'll be our little secret."

She fixed me a cheese and tomato sandwich. I spun on the stool as I ate, watching her carry plates back and forth from the kitchen.

After I'd finished eating, I went upstairs to Fraya's room. Like the diner below, her room was wallpapered in illustrations of dandelions framed by dark green vines and fancy scrollwork. The ceiling was covered in the same design. The furniture had come with the room and was painted yellow along with the wood trim and floorboards. Even the toilet, tub, and sink in the small bathroom were yellow porcelain. With so much of the same color, Fraya's items stood out. Her mauve afghan draped across a chair. The brown spines of her books. The closet of dresses in a multitude of hues from blue to red. I took the mint-green dress off its hanger. I slipped it on over the top of my clothes. I spun until the skirt flew up, revealing my shorts.

"Girls should wear dresses," I mocked the principal. "Hey, principal, you like this?" I kicked my legs up in the air as I marched around the room. "What about this?" I shook my hair out and jumped around. "Is this befittin' for a girl?"

Still spinning, I spotted Fraya's diary on the dresser. I carried it over to her bed, where I lay down, propping my feet up on her fancy yellow iron headboard.

When I opened the diary, it was as though everything but Fraya's song lyrics was written in a foreign language. I tried to make out the code she had used, but she had made her own alphabet.

I took the paper compass off my shorts. Using the pen from the spine of Fraya's diary, I copied her lyrics inside the compass, following the round edges until her words spiraled to the center. I placed the compass between the pages of her diary.

It had gotten louder in the diner below. I didn't have to check the clock to know school had let out. I took the dress off and hung it back in the closet.

When I got downstairs, I saw the mature crowd had left, leaving room for teenagers to take over. Through the faces, I saw Flossie's. She was at the counter, talking to Fraya.

"I was tellin' Fraya about the most fun game we played at school," Flossie said to me as I approached. "You stand at a window and if a bird hits the glass in front of you, you'll go to hell."

"That's stupid," I said.

"Is not." Flossie grabbed my hand and pulled me over to the large plate-glass window.

"Remember," she said, "if a bird strikes the glass in front of you, you're destined to spend eternity with the demons."

"You two really shouldn't tempt damnation," Fraya said as she walked by, carrying a slice of pie to a booth.

"Look." Flossie pointed to a sparrow. "It's headed right for us."

We screamed and ducked just as it looked like the bird was going to crash into the glass. Last minute, the sparrow made a turn that saved her life.

"I'm not playin' anymore," I said, leaving the window.

"Scaredy-cat." Flossie followed me out of the diner. *"Meow, meow, meow."*

Seconds later, a crow crashed into Flossie's back, knocking her onto the ground. The bird was stunned but, after a few false starts, flew again.

"Damn beast." Flossie cursed as she sat up. "I'm so mad I could spit nails."

"You okay, miss?"

Both me and Flossie turned to a fella by the name of Cutlass Silkworm.

"Hope you didn't get hurt," he said, offering his hand.

The Silkworm family owned a vineyard on the edge of town. Cutlass was only in his early twenties, but already had his father's hairline. Being seventy pounds overweight and with a lisp, he was nobody

Flossie would have dreamed she would end up with, but she liked how his gold watch shone in the sunlight. I could tell from the way she accepted his hand.

"Thanks," she said, making sure her hair fell into her eyes at the right angle.

By summer, Cutlass and my sister were an item. It wasn't long after, Mom called Flossie into her room and sat her down. I watched from the doorway as Mom brushed Flossie's hair at the vanity.

"It's time you start thinkin' 'bout your future," Mom said. "You're no longer a little girl. The vineyard does well for Cutlass and his family. If you were his wife, you wouldn't be in want."

"His wife?" Flossie made a disgusted face. "I don't wanna be his wife. I just like him havin' a car that actually runs. Besides, I can't stay in Breathed. What about Hollywood?"

"You wanna be a star?" Mom began to braid Flossie's hair.

"More than anything." Flossie bopped in the seat.

"Then let me tell you what I should have told you a long time ago. You're the type of star who only shines when there's no other stars around."

Flossie looked at Mom through the mirror.

"I can get shinier," she said. "I can work on it. I'm only sixteen."

"If you go to Hollywood," Mom said, "you'll be surrounded by the biggest and brightest stars there are. You'll be average there. Hollywood doesn't put average on the screen. But here in Breathed, as a Silkworm, you'd be the brightest star as a rich man's wife. You've seen how I struggle. Barely able to afford lipstick and hosiery. You want that for yourself?"

Flossie quickly shook her head.

"These opportunities don't come around every day, girl," Mom told her. "The older you get, the harder it'll be. You're Flossie Carpenter, right? You're gonna get with a man anyway."

Flossie shot Mom a look through the mirror.

"Might as well be one with some money," Mom continued. "Set yourself up for an easy life. Cutlass is a good boy. His family are good folks."

"But I don't love him."

"Even if you don't care for him now, after a while, you'll find he's a lot easier to love than you ever thought possible. Especially after you carry his seed."

"His seed? You mean have his kid? No way." Flossie shook her head. "I don't want no kid."

"You have to want one, Flossie. Cutlass is havin' fun is all and once he's finished, he'll throw you away. It happens time and time again to girls like you."

"Girls like me?" Flossie asked.

"If you have his child," Mom continued, "you'll have a claim. It's the only way to secure your future as a star."

Flossie closed her mouth as her chin started to tremble. She shot up and ran past me. I caught up to her in our room, where she stood in our closet, looking through her clothes for something to wear on her date that night with Cutlass.

"Hey?" I grabbed her arm. "Don't listen to Mom."

"When women go wrong, men go right after them." Flossie jerked out of my grip as she slipped a navy dress off its hanger. She held it to her body to see what it looked like in the mirror. "Mae West said that in *She Done Him Wrong*. I'll just go a little wrong, Betty. Just long enough for him to go after me. If worse comes to worst, I can always take his wallet and get to Hollywood that way."

"You don't need him, Flossie. You can do it on your own."

"Silly Betty. Don't you know anything by now?"

I looked at my sister. The bones had elongated in her face, giving her a stoic surface that rose and fell with each smile she did and did not give. Her eyes had grown larger, the green shade more brilliant than when she was a child. It was as if all the energy and rage were kept in her irises until they were green fire.

"What do you think about this dress?" she asked. "I think it's nice."

That night Flossie let Cutlass leave himself inside her. I imagine she flinched when it happened. The next morning, I took the dress she had worn and buried it in the yard.

Once she knew she was pregnant, she told Cutlass, who did the fashionable thing of getting down on one knee. As a wedding present, Fraya made Flossie's dress. A lacy pink thing that came above her knee. Flossie liked it because of the way it made her look like she was so sweet she could dissolve in a man's mouth like candy.

"Don't you think, Betty?" she asked me.

Following the wedding, Flossie said she wouldn't be returning to school the following year.

"Marriage is my future now," she said, surrendering and moving into the pillared colonial house Cutlass' parents bought them.

"I'll write goodnights to you, like we did to Fraya," I told Flossie.

"No." She shook her head. "I ain't got time for childish amusements no more. I'm a wife now."

The spring that had started out with birds flying low was now a summer ending with them flying high. They never did find a reason for the birds' behavior. Dad said sometimes we all do stupid things.

"Don't I know it," Flossie said.

I was left alone in what had been our bedroom. It was empty without her. I didn't realize how much space was taken up by all the things we did together. Those late hours of flipping through a magazine while sucking on fireballs or brushing each other's hair as we talked about the way the spider in the corner made her web.

"I think spiders sing," Flossie would say. "The web is her song."

After Flossie left, the web broke. I never saw the spider again.

THE BREATHANIAN

Man Questioned in Ongoing Shooting Investigation

One Landon Carpenter was questioned after a witness reported seeing Carpenter in the vicinity gunfire was heard. Carpenter stated he was only taking a nap in the sun.

While Carpenter was being questioned, another call came in from a resident reporting a figure holding a shotgun had been standing in her yard late last night.

This resident, who wishes to remain anonymous, said she spoke to the figure and even offered the person a glass of milk. When she turned around to get the milk, the figure had stepped closer to her house. The woman said she found it odd, so she made another turn, only to discover the figure had stepped even closer and was now on her front porch.

"I knew my door was unlocked," the woman said. "Never in my life had I locked it. Just when I started to scream, the figure backed and left, dragging the barrel of the gun against the ground."

When asked if she thought it was a man or woman, she said the light was too poor.

"But they kinda smelled like a man," she was quick to add. "Unless it was only a woman who had a man on her earlier in the evening."

36

I am like a broken vessel.

—Psalm 31:12

My favorite dress was one that had been passed down from Mom to Fraya to Flossie to me. In its beginning, the dress had been bright red. By the time it got to me, the years had dimmed it to a color becoming pink. Sometimes I would imagine all the red had been bled out by the women who'd worn it.

I was wearing this dress in the garden, where I was with Fraya, Lint, and Dad. We were picking vegetables for a fry when Leland came driving up.

"Who invited you?" I asked him once he stepped into the garden.

"Why do I got to be invited to see my own family?" he asked.

I looked over at Fraya. She was placing zucchini into a basket. I watched Leland step past her to the rows of corn. He scanned the stalks before choosing an ear to peel the husk back on.

"You're ruinin' the corn," I told him.

"Oh, I forgot." He waved his arms in the air. "You're squash. The protector of the corn. Mighty Betty."

"All right, that's enough, you two." Dad began cutting off okra to add to the basket.

He held the longest of the okra up against each side of his head as if they were horns. Lint laughed before picking up two more out of the basket to make himself a pair that he then pretended to spar with Dad's. Fraya smiled at the two of them while Leland opened yet another ear of corn.

"Stop." I pushed him back from the stalks.

"Let's try to have a good time together." Dad dropped the okra into the basket.

"Yeah, Betty," Fraya added.

I turned to her and frowned.

"Why is it my fault?" I asked. "He's the one spoilin' the corn. No one even cares."

"Forget it. I'm outta here." Leland left through the garden, trampling vines.

"You're killin' the plants, you jerk," I said, bending down and checking on the vines.

Leland turned around and gave me the middle finger before getting in his car. Dust churned up as he sped out of the drive.

"You need to learn to ignore him, Betty," Fraya said.

She was using a sharp knife to cut ripe cucumbers off.

"Ignore him?" I asked. "I'm tired of ignorin' how he destroys everything. I'm not gonna ignore him anymore."

Fraya slowly stood.

"Betty," she said. "Don't start anything."

"Dad." I turned to face him. "I've got to tell you somethin'."

"Shut up, Betty." Fraya stepped out of the cucumber vines. She stopped in front of the row of cabbages.

"Dad." I took a deep breath. "Leland—"

Fraya kicked the head off the cabbage plant in front of her.

"Fraya?" Dad turned to her. "Why'd you do that?"

She looked at me, then kicked the remaining cabbages so hard, they rolled across the ground like the heads of women with their hair coming undone.

Stomping into the melon patch, she stabbed the honeydews and watermelons. She next threw her whole body into the pole runner beans, pulling the long pods off until it looked as though she had a handful of snakes she was strangling to death.

"Stop, Fraya," Dad said. "You're murderin' the garden."

Entangling herself in deep green vines, she cut with the knife in her hand as if she was shredding wallpaper off a wall. She wrapped the cucumber vines around her arms, heaving them up by using the weight of her whole body. Dad had to grab Lint out of Fraya's path as she yanked up carrots like a mother yanking her children up by their hair. She bit into each carrot, the mud spreading around her mouth as she spit the pieces out.

She squeezed the tomatoes to death, their innards spilling between her fingers. She did the same with the berries, the multicolored juices staining her hands. Turning her attention to the corn, she ran into the stalks. Their tassels shook as she bent the stalks until they snapped at the base.

"What is all the yellin' about?" Mom came out onto the porch.

When she saw what was going on, she could only stand back with the rest of us, watching Fraya attack the garden.

At the rear of the garden were grapes that grew alongside a wooden fence Dad had built. Fraya busted the fence, slashed the vines, and stomped the grapes to death, their sweet aroma permeating the air.

When Fraya stopped, she stared only at me. She still had the knife in her hand. Her grip was so tight, I thought she was going to shatter the wooden handle.

"Fraya?" Dad slowly walked through the carnage. "How could you do this?"

"I know why she did it," I said, my anger a match for Fraya's. "She did it because Leland—"

In one quick slash, Fraya slit her left wrist open.

"Jesus Crimson." Mom pulled Lint into her and covered his eyes.

"You gotta stop the blood loss, Landon," she told Dad as he raced to Fraya.

Fraya stared down at her wrist. She seemed surprised herself that she had done it as she dropped the knife. Dad used his handkerchief to wrap the wound.

"It's not so bad. I can stitch it," he said, leading Fraya into the garage.

"Betty," he called back to me. "I'll need your help."

Lint and Mom were left to stare across the garden. I could hear Mom trying to get the story of what had happened out of Lint.

Once I was in the garage, Dad told me to keep pressure applied to the wound. I laid my hands over top of the handkerchief. I could feel her warm blood.

As Dad searched the garage for thread, Fraya whispered to me, "I told you I'd kill myself. You believe me now?"

I slowly nodded.

"This should work," Dad said, pulling a spool of black thread from a tin.

He gave her a piece of bark to bite while he poured moonshine on the wound.

"I'll get ya all fixed up," he said as he threaded the bone needle after disinfecting it with more moonshine.

Fraya spit the bark out and drank some of the moonshine. As she did, she watched out of the corner of her eye the way Dad pinched her skin together just before pushing the needle through. When she started screaming, I ran out of the garage and into the woods.

I searched for the tallest tree, burying my face in its bark.

Only when evening set in did I head home. When I got there, Fraya's bedroom light was on. Mom was downstairs in the living room watching TV. Lint had fallen asleep beside her, his head resting on her lap.

The steps creaked under my feet as I walked upstairs. I tiptoed down the hall and sat by the wall outside Fraya's room.

"Ya know, God had to wear a bandage like that once," Dad was saying.

I peeked around the doorway to see him on the edge of Fraya's bed. He had a jar filled with sand in his hands. Fraya was sitting against the headboard. She had her knees pulled up under her chin. The white bandage on her wrist needed to be changed.

"God slit his wrist, too?" she asked.

"Nothin' like that."

"Then why'd He have to wear a bandage?" Fraya looked down at her own.

"It was after He made the sun," he said.

Fraya was silent for a few moments. Then she asked how God had made the sun.

"Kind of like how you'd make a pie," Dad said. "There's sugar involved, some flour, some butter. I don't know the exact recipe. If I did, well, I'd make my own sun. But I do know that after God whipped up His ingredients, He put 'em all in a big pan and shoved it in the oven to bake until it got golden and hot, ready for the sky. Some folks think God burned His hands on the actual sun after it was baked. To God's own embarrassment, He burned His hands on the damn pan. He forgot to put on oven mitts before He got the pan outta the oven."

Dad chuckled at the thought, but Fraya didn't, so he joined her in the silence until she said, "That's a silly story, Dad."

He perked up at the gentle way she had said "Dad."

"Why you got that jar?" she asked.

"It's from heaven," he said. "Last night on my walk, a rope dropped from the sky. I waited to see if anyone was gonna come down. When they didn't, I tugged at the rope to see if it was sturdy. I reckoned someone wanted me to climb up."

"But you didn't know who dropped it," Fraya said. "What if at the top of it was a demon?"

"It came from the sky," Dad told her. "The only thing I can think of that's in the sky is heaven. I reckoned the rope couldn't be all that bad, so I laid my cane down, spit on my hands, got me a grip, and started climbin'. Here I was, an old Mr. Nobody, climbin' up into the sky. The stars got so close, they looked like the lights of Breathed while the town was so far away, all its lights looked like stars. When I got to the top of that rope, I found it'd been dropped from an open winda suspended in the sky. A bright light shone from the winda. I climbed through it and fell out onto the Beach of Time."

"What's the Beach of Time?"

"Come now, Fraya. Everyone knows what the Beach of Time is. It's where our jars of life are kept. Each jar is full of sand that measures our time on earth."

He showed her the strip of paper he'd taped to the outside of the glass. It had her name written on it in his cursive.

"I searched through all them jars until I found yours," he said. "And look at it." He held the jar up in front of her. "It's full to the top with sand. Any more and it would be pourin' out from under the lid. God's given you more days than most, Fraya. I should know. I saw the jars. I saw how some were filled with only a spoonful of sand and some with just a grain. God has great plans for you, my girl."

He handed her the jar. She looked at it before saying, "This is just sand from the riverbank, Dad. Nothin' more."

Dad grunted like an old bear as he grabbed hold of her bandaged wrist.

"Don't you know what happens if you end yourself?" he asked. "Your jar will break and the sand will spill. For all eternity, your punishment will be to gather every shard of glass and each grain of sand. When the time comes that you do, don't think you'll rest, for the devil will kick your gathered pile, spreadin' it all over again. This is how it'll always be. You tryin' to find what you've broken—tryin' to put it back together again—and the devil, never lettin' ya.

"God opened that winda for me and dropped that rope so I could find your jar in order to show you how much life you have yet to live. You're meant to grow old, Fraya." Dad ran his hand through her hair. "Your hair is meant to turn white. Your skin is meant to wrinkle. You're destined to die an old woman. A very happy old woman. Do not be the fool who spits in the eye of the Great Spirit."

She nodded.

"I'll let you rest now." He tucked her in bed. She held the jar against her chest as if it were a teddy bear.

"Goodnight, Fraya," he said before walking out of the room and closing the door behind him.

He wasn't surprised to find me listening. He merely waited for me to stand so we could walk down the hall together. I suppose we would have been on our way out, perhaps to look at the very spot where the garden once grew. But we never got there because the sound of breaking glass caused us both to turn around. We ran to Fraya's door. When Dad opened it, we saw Fraya out of bed and standing over the broken jar. She was looking at the sand and the way it seeped into the cracks of the floorboards around her.

37

She is hardened against her young ones, as though
they were not hers: her labour is in vain.

—JOB 39:16

"Is there ever gonna be light in this world for me?" Fraya's whisper filled the room.

After breaking the jar, she walked across the hall and climbed into my bed. When I lay beside her, she wrapped her arms around me. Her breathing warmed the crown of my head tucked into her chest.

Only after she was asleep did I softly slide off the bed and go back into her bedroom, where Dad was holding a magnifying glass, searching for every last grain of sand. To him, Fraya was as savable as the smallest slivers of glass that he removed from the floorboard crevices using a pair of tweezers.

Fraya helped him believe she could be saved when the next morning she raised up out of bed with a big stretch that arched her back.

"I'm hungry," she said.

Dad made her a large stack of pancakes. She ate them with a smile on her face. For my father, that meant his daughter was okay. My mother and I knew better, so while Fraya went into the living room to watch TV after her feast, I took the knife and went out to A Faraway Place. I carved a deep cut into the stage. I held my hand over the gash and tried to believe I had enough power to heal Fraya by myself.

I started to sing the song me, Fraya, and Flossie had sung for Mom after she had cut herself. Only I changed the word "Mom" to "sister."

"*Sister, come home, we love you so. The house is cold without you, the flowers won't grow. We miss you dearly, we send you a kiss. Sister, come home, we love you so.*"

But those lyrics soon dropped away to a chant.

"Tsa-la-gi. Qua-nu-s-di. Tsu-we-tsi-a-ni-ge-yv. U-la-ni-gi-dv."

They were Cherokee words I'd heard Dad use, but having those few, I tied my soul to their rhythm.

"Tsa-la-gi. Qua-nu-s-di. Tsu-we-tsi-a-ni-ge-yv. U-la-ni-gi-dv."

I became tempted by my father's stories to create an ancestral origin out of the earth, one that knew me before I even knew myself. This came with a feeling that the past had power and if I could just summon that force, maybe I could help my sister. Which is why, every day, I chanted until Fraya no longer had to wear a bandage.

"I reckon it'll be an ugly scar," she said, staring at the way her skin was healing.

She wanted to return to work more than anything else. Folks had heard about the incident and would glance at her, only to later discuss it amongst themselves. Fraya pretended not to notice. Instead she focused on taking another order, cutting another slice of pie, saving enough energy to turn the door sign over at close. This was the routine she fell back into.

"I'm fine," she'd say when Dad asked her how she was feeling. "I just want to forget it ever happened."

When that autumn of 1967 opened the door to everything crisp and brown, the focus changed from Fraya to Flossie, who carried her growing belly like a girl carting an unwanted burden. She complained about her back, her swollen ankles, and her substantial weight gain. She would eat celery sticks in the morning, only to give in to her cravings by night. Potato chips. Pop. Dishes of chocolate ice cream. She'd flop back on the bed she shared with Cutlass, listening to him snore as she stabbed her fingernails into the silk sheets.

Ever since Flossie became a Silkworm, she would appear at random. All of a sudden she would be on our front porch, her belly grazing the rail. Other times I'd go into my room to find her lying in her old twin bed, sleeping on her side. I would place my hand on her taut stomach. She would continue to sleep, her mouth open enough for a tiny string of drool to settle on the cotton sheet. When she would wake, she would forget she was pregnant and would startle at the sight of her stomach. She'd try to knock it off like she was knocking off a spider only to remember the stomach was part of her.

"Bein' pregnant is like havin' a wound you have to bleed out between your legs, Betty," she said one time, raising her shirt and showing me the stretch marks. "Look at the scars it gives."

The bigger she got, the less she took care of herself. She would wear the same shirt and pants for days. She no longer brushed her hair nor painted her fingernails. By the winter of 1968, she looked nothing like the sister I had known. Her pregnancy eclipsed her. The bright light that had shone from her became darkened by the sphere she carried on her body. In this shadowed state, she seemed meaner, as if soaking in viciousness. No more so than that February. As the icy winds blew, I turned fourteen. One of my birthday gifts had been white go-go boots from Fraya. Nearly everyone at school, including Ruthis, had a pair. At first, I'd been embarrassed to say I wanted them.

"Out of everything in the world, you seek some flashy boots?" Dad had asked when he heard. "You used to reach for turtle shells and whippoorwills."

"I still do," I said. "But why can't I like the boots, too?"

As soon as Fraya gave them to me, I put them on. I walked outside and didn't stop until I was in the woods, dry twigs snapping underfoot. When I reached a clearing, I lay back on the cold hard ground, lifting my legs up in front of my face and moving them as if I was walking the gray winter sky. I suppose I liked the boots so much for the fact they were popular at school, when I myself was not. Having my feet in the boots felt as though I'd been let in on a secret.

I went to bed that night wearing them, slipping them beneath my blanket and imagining that when Ruthis saw me in the boots the next day at school, she would want to be my friend.

"Betty," Ruthis said in my dream, "you're the grooviest girl in school."

The next morning, I was slapped awake by Flossie.

"You think you're so pretty now that I'm fat and ugly." Her face was bright red. "Those boots should be mine."

She yanked them off my feet. She attempted to slip her foot into one, but her stomach was in the way. Giving up, she kicked both boots across the room, then dug her fingers into her belly.

"If it doesn't come out soon," she said, "I fear I'll cut it out."

A few weeks later, me and her were sitting on the front porch. She had one hand in a bag of potato chips and the other on a cigarette. She'd just finished complaining about how tight the sleeves were on her light blue maternity dress.

"And this stupid collar." She tried stretching the orange ruffled neckline.

It was her mother-in-law who had bought the dress, saying it would look just darling on Flossie. She would have looked more comfortable in a dress of thorns.

"I swear if I have to wear this dress one more second—" She dropped the potato chips and cigarette to grab her belly. "Ow, oh God, it hurts."

I yelled in the house for Mom, who came rushing out from the kitchen. When Mom saw Flossie's heavy breathing, she said, "Baby's wantin' to come out."

"Nuh-uh." Flossie shook her head. "I can't do it. I'll just leave it in there. Ow." She leaned over, clutching her stomach. "Is it supposed to hurt this bad?"

"Don't get all chickenshit now, Flossie." Mom used the towel in her hand to slap against my arm. "Go get your father," she told me. "We've got to take her to Doc Lad's."

"No." Flossie pushed past me and struggled down the steps, crying out to A Faraway Place.

"Flossie, get back here, goddamn it," Mom called after her.

"I can't hear you," Flossie said while trying to climb up on the stage, but being unable to. "I'm too far away to hear anything."

What was far away was a hospital, so Breathed relied on Doc Lad, who treated patients in the back of his house, where you would be greeted by a buff-colored tomcat. The cat waited with Mom, Dad, and me on the back porch during Flossie's delivery. Dad had sent Lint to wait at the diner with Fraya. Cutlass was the only one from his family there. He paced with his hands deep in his pockets.

I had to cover my ears against Flossie's screams. When her cries stopped, the baby's started. Little shrill sounds like silverware clanking. I stepped over to an open window and saw Doc Lad cut the umbilical cord. He carried the baby to a table. As he wiped the child's squirming arms and legs, I looked at my sister. She was drenched in sweat and her wet hair splayed across her reddened forehead. It was hard to think she was the same girl who just the year before had smacked gum and painted her toenails bright purple.

Doc carried the child to her, but she looked away.

"Don'tcha wanna see your baby?" he asked her.

"Of course she'll see the baby." Dad stood at the screen door, which opened the room to the outside. "Ain't that right, Flossie?"

Dad entered with Mom and Cutlass behind him. I stayed outside looking through the open window. It seemed safer to be close to the yard in case the house was to collapse under my sister's fury.

"I don't want him," Flossie said, folding her arms.

"What you mean you don't want him?" Doc Lad's eyes widened behind his bifocals as he gently cradled the child in his arms.

Flossie stared at her son. Perhaps because of him, or because of the day itself, she raised up over the edge of the bed and vomited on the shiny shoes of her husband. Cutlass stared at the vomit and stepped back as if it would slide off his shoes. Flossie laughed sharply at him, before sniffling and reaching her arms out toward the child.

"Give 'im here," she said.

"You got a name for him yet?" Dad asked.

"Nova," Flossie said, staring down, but not at the child. "Nova."

"What the hell kind of name is that?" Mom asked.

"It means sudden bright star," Flossie answered before handing the child back to Doc Lad. "My arms are tired," she said.

After leaving Doc Lad's, Flossie placed a distance between herself and Nova. It was as though she was not the mother and he was not her child. Recognizing this, the Silkworms hired a woman to take care of Nova. Her name was Mrs. Anchor and she was an older lady who just the week before had worked at the butcher's. She had been behind the counter cutting porterhouses, which Cutlass' mother had come in to order. While waiting for the steaks to be wrapped, his mother struck up a conversation with another customer in which she expressed the need for hired help.

"I raised eight of 'em of my own," Mrs. Anchor said as she handed the steaks over to Cutlass' mom. "It wouldn't be nothin' for me to do it for someone else. I've been wantin' to hang up my cleaver for a while now. You pay me same as I get here, and I'll do the job for ya, and do it well, too."

Mrs. Anchor was glad to be rid of the butchering job.

"I don't have to bother with my braids gettin' in blood," she said, having taken her two long braids out of their bun to wear them slung over her shoulders. Only the ends of her hair were still auburn, the roots having turned gray and coarse like corkscrewing wires that stuck out around her crown.

Mrs. Anchor did her job of caring for Nova with the efficiency of an emotionless robot, but still Nova believed the hired woman to be his mother. Flossie had chosen not to nurse her son, so Mrs. Anchor would feed him with the bottle, her large rough hands clutching him. It was her red-nosed face Nova saw morning, afternoon, and night when she read him a bedtime story while Flossie lay beside a man she did not love.

"Now that the baby's out," Flossie told me, "all Cutlass wants to do is to have his pleasures." She paused, twisting her wedding ring around her finger. "You know why they call 'em hus-*bands*, Betty? Because they're like a band wrapped around your body until they either squeeze you to death or you cut the knot."

After giving birth, Flossie lost the weight relatively quickly. She found her own indulgences in the new wardrobe choices Silkworm cash afforded her. For all the money Mom thought Flossie would give her, Flossie gave her little. Perhaps only to rub it in, Flossie would come to visit in her shiny Mercedes, which she always reminded us was not plain green but forest green.

"It's a limited-edition color," she'd say, flipping her hair back over her shoulders.

She'd started going to get her hair shampooed at the salon in Sweet Temper. It was why she always smelled of honeysuckle.

"Isn't it fabulous?" she'd ask.

Mom tended to clean for an entire week before Flossie said she would be stopping by. It was the way Flossie looked at everything in the house, as if it was all so disappointing.

There was a routine each time Flossie visited. As Mrs. Anchor sat and bounced Nova on her legs until he laughed, Flossie would look at the sofa cushion. Deciding that the clean cushion was too dirty for her to sit on, she'd take the newspaper from off the side table and unfold it. She would lay it on the cushion as Mom watched her.

"It's okay." Dad would reach across and tap Mom's knee. "Our little girl's a fancy one now."

He smiled because it was the only thing he thought would help. Flossie would look at him before slowly sitting on the newspaper. It always crinkled beneath her as she sat.

"The Silkworm vineyard is doin' good business, I presume?" Mom had made a habit out of asking as she looked at Flossie's expensive purse.

Flossie would purposely play with her nails to show us how manicured they'd become.

"We're havin' an awful go of payin' some of the bills." Mom would look from Flossie to Dad, then back again. "With your father's aches and pains, we could really do with some help."

"Oh, Mom, I wish I could, but I am only Cutlass' wife," Flossie would say as she tucked her shiny hair behind her ears, showing off her diamond earrings.

"That's okay." Dad patted Mom's knee again. "We understand, don't we?"

Mom would frown at Flossie until Flossie clicked open her purse and got out a few dollars to hand to Mom.

"My, how generous my daughter is," Mom would say.

It was usually at these times that Dad stood and picked Nova up from off Mrs. Anchor's lap.

"How 'bout I show my grandson a rainbow?" Dad would ask as he carried the smiling Nova on his hip.

I would always follow, leaving my mother and sister to glare at each other. I wasn't angry with Flossie like Mom was. Perhaps only because Flossie continued to wear the bean pod necklace beneath her expensive blouses.

"You ready for some magic?" Dad would ask Nova once the three of us got outside.

I'd take Nova so Dad could get the garden hose and turn it on. Then we'd stand with our backs to the sun while Dad held the hose up, placing his thumb over the spray of water so it came out in a fine mist. As the sunlight hit the drops of water, a prism of color would arch into a rainbow in our backyard.

Nova always got so excited that I had to hold on tight to him so he wouldn't jump out of my arms as he clapped his tiny hands and smiled.

Nova was too young to make anything more than sounds, but Dad would still ask, "What's he sayin'?"

I didn't know what Nova was saying nor what he was thinking, but I knew what I had thought at that age when Dad would make us water hose rainbows in the backyard.

"He thinks you're God," I said to my father.

THE BREATHANIAN

Man Shot in Penis

A ghastly story unfolded this morning after a man was rushed to Doc Lad's with a gunshot wound to the penis. The man is in fair condition. The news sent a shock wave through the community as people questioned whether the gunshot was connected to the mysterious Breathed shooter. Upon further investigation, the man was discovered to have been shot by his wife with her pistol after a domestic argument. "I didn't want to tell on her at first," the man said. "But then I thought I wouldn't be able to tell on her if she shoots me in the head."

38

If it *be* a daughter, then she shall live.

—EXODUS 1:16

Everyone called it Fraya's Famous Fudge. I've never forgotten the blue gingham pattern of the sugar bag. The way the paper crinkled as she poured the sugar out to measure it. She'd make the fudge in the diner's kitchen at night. A chocolate chip for each yellow tile on the counter. She let me add the vanilla extract that she would sometimes put on her finger and wipe on my neck.

"Perfume," she'd say.

It was the spring of 1969. Richard Nixon was in office. The first U.S. troops would eventually withdraw from Vietnam. And men, other than my father, would land on the moon. But that would come later. It was spring and all I really knew about 1969 was that I was fifteen and my sister always dropped enough sugar on the floor to catch on the hems of her bell-bottoms.

Swish, swish.

She'd turn out the lights and turn the radio on. Then we would dance as her fudge set up to be sectioned for serving the next day. She danced like a wolf with a secret. Or maybe that's how all older sisters look when they dance in the moonlight.

She wore a lot of brown when she wasn't wearing her yellow diner outfit. She wore a lot of brown, orange, and tan. Sturdy colors that would make one think she was a woman of chicken wire cartilage.

Sometimes when I dream of Fraya, I dream of her in a brown suit with an orange scarf tied at her neck. She's at a desk and she's very important. The owner of a company making things I have a feeling are metal.

Other times, I dream she's a mother in a simple cotton dress. A woman with her hair up in a ponytail and two toddlers, one clinging to each of her legs as she holds and stirs a mixing bowl in the crook of her arm. Batter already on the end of her nose while she smiles as if she has mapped heaven and found it is a straight shot through dirty diapers and glasses of half-drunk juice.

More often than not, I dream she's a white cat in a blizzard. I always lose her in the way snow can fall. I can only hope she has seen the way I have loved her all of these years.

Fraya will never be 1970, 1971, or any year after. She will always be 1969 Fraya because that is the year she died. In the afterlife, will she still wear her hair the same as last I saw her? Just long enough for short curls. Will she still be wearing brown tops and bell-bottoms as if 1969 never ended? Will her eyeliner be too dark, her lips too pale, will gold hoops swing from each of her earlobes, which are no older than twenty-five?

It was Thursday morning when her body was found by the cook of Dandelion Dimes. He told the sheriff Fraya wasn't up at her usual time of 5:30 a.m. to fry bacon for Hank. Hank was a wide-eyed, coffee-brown feline with swirly stripes of tan and a broken tail. Fraya had found him as a kitten wrapped in a handkerchief in the hollow of one of the elms that line Main Lane. She named him Hank for the handkerchief. He was a small thing like Fraya and she liked having him around. He had become the pet of the diner as well, greeting customers at the door. He would live a long time after Fraya. Later, I would see a photograph of the diner taken in 1984. There amongst the fading yellow was an old fading cat. Still small, still wide-eyed, still looking as if he were waiting on Fraya to come home to him.

The cook prepared the kitchen for the day, thinking Fraya had slept in and would be down soon. But when the first customer came in, Fraya had yet to make an appearance. So, the cook went up to her place and found her lying in bed with her hand in an empty Miracle mayonnaise jar. Her hand was clenched into a fist and was swollen so much they couldn't remove it from the jar without breaking the glass. After they unfolded her fingers they found a smashed honeybee, its wings broken. The stinger was stabbed into her palm.

When the sheriff came to our house to deliver the news, I thought of the night before when I'd been with Fraya.

The day had started with me going to school, but I was nauseous, dizzy, and had a pain that would come and go deep in my belly. I thought it was only the heat of a warm spring.

Walking the halls of school that day, I clung to the lockers to feel their cool metal while Ruthis and the others said, "Look at Betty. She's got her war paint on."

It was the same old line, but I still wiped my lipstick off on my sleeve.

"Betcha she's a whore like her sister Flossie," they said. "Good-time Flossie. Good-time Betty."

I cut class and headed to Dandelion Dimes, but there were customers waiting in line. Fraya told me to come back after closing.

"We'll make the fudge together," she said.

I ended up in Teddy's Electrical Goods, where Teddy himself let me cool off in front of the fans while I watched *Dark Shadows* on one of the televisions. I went over to explore the typewriters. I pretended to type as Teddy helped a man by the name of Grayson Elohim choose between chest freezers.

"I want a big freezer," Elohim said. "To hold the meat I butcher."

Teddy showed Elohim the biggest freezer he had. Elohim climbed in to see if it was roomy enough.

"I'll take it," he said.

I left the store and headed to the river. After I removed my clothes, I circled in the water under the swings of the wild grapevines that hung from the tree limbs. Then I floated on my back, remembering how my father had told me about a zoo that had gone belly-up and released its animals into the hills. I imagined lions and tigers stalking the river edges. A jungle of exotic creatures and native deer.

Through the arching tree limbs, I watched a purple balloon rise to Vickory. As the sun set, I dried on the river edge, sitting with my chin on my knees. I dressed and headed back to Dandelion Dimes. Fraya was saying goodbye to the last customer. She let me hang the CLOSED sign on the door.

She wanted to rest her feet before we made the fudge, so we went up to her apartment. The window was open and Hank was already on the roof.

"Silly cat," Fraya said as we climbed out onto the roof beside him. The three of us looked up at the sky. When Fraya began to poke her finger at the stars, I asked her what she was doing.

"Those lights up there." *Poke, poke, poke.* "We're told they're all nuclear reaction and energy," she said like a scientist. "Stars, the romantics call 'em. But they ain't stars. Stars don't exist for us. Somewhere out there is a world that we're the insects to. Someone in that world has caught us. This planet we call home is really just a jar they keep us in. A big jar to us, but a small jar to them. Those lights are our airholes showin' through to the light of the world we are too small for. I'm pokin' more airholes for us to breathe. Sometimes I think we're all gonna suffocate. Help me, Betty. Help me poke a hole big enough for us to fly out of."

I gently poked at the sky, before I started to stab it.

"Easy now, Betty." Fraya grabbed my hand and laid it across her stomach. As she played with my fingers, I looked at the scar on her wrist. I asked her if it hurt when she cut herself.

"Not as bad as I thought it would," she said. "You know what's scary, Betty? How easy it was to do. But I won't do it again 'cause I'm gonna leave."

"Leave?" I raised up.

"I think I'll live somewhere by the ocean. I could pick up seashells and play in the waves."

"You can't leave."

"You can come, too. We'll both go. We'll make necklaces out of our goodnights and throw 'em on the water."

We sat there a moment longer before she wrapped her arms around herself and said, "Betty, let's go see a movie. There's an uneasiness in the air tonight. Don't you think? We could go to the drive-in. They're screenin' that film with Shelley Winters and Geraldine Page. *The Three Sisters*. It's based on a play, I think, but it sounds like Dad's carvin'. You remember the one he did of all of us?" She ran her fingers along the carved corn of her necklace. "Yeah, we'll go see if the movie is like his carvin' of us."

We climbed back into the room as she told me there was a piece of vinegar pie she'd saved for me.

"Run along and eat it," she said. "I'll be down after I change."

"I don't think I'm very hungry. My stomach hurts. It's hurt all day."

I turned around to pet Hank. He had gotten up on the bed behind me. As I scratched under his chin, I felt Fraya's hands on my shoulders.

"Your stomach's hurt all day?" she asked.

I nodded.

"Do you know why, Betty?"

"No."

She took me into the bathroom, where she turned my back to the floor-length mirror.

I stared at the reflection of the red stain on my skirt.

"No." I tried to wipe the stain off. "I don't want it. I don't want the blood."

"You know in some cultures a girl would be slapped when she first bleeds," Fraya said, softly resting her hand on my cheek. "Slapped hard, right across the face. But in other cultures, like the Cherokee, blood was seen as power. In fact, the Cherokees believed a woman had so much power when bleedin' that she would stay in a hut constructed for the purpose of shelterin' her on her cycle. There she was kept away from everyone else."

"Kept away as punishment?"

"No." Fraya shook her head. "The hut was not forced upon the women. They could choose to enter it or not. That was our power." She held my face in both of her hands.

"How do you know this, Fraya?"

"I read it in a book at the library. It had a Cherokee legend in it about a man made out of stone. When the stone man came to terrorize the tribe, a line of menstruating women stood on the path. Each woman he passed, the stone man grew weaker and weaker, until he crumbled to the ground. The women had destroyed him with the power of their blood. They saved their village and all the lives there." She tilted her head. "If we were back in those days, I would honor you by weaving you a belt. I would make you a skirt out of deerskin and a brooch out of bone. But now, all I have are these."

She reached over and grabbed her box of sanitary napkins out of the cabinet. She showed me how to use them along with instructing me on the sanitary belt.

"You can wear a clean skirt of mine." She handed me one. "Put your stained skirt in the sink under cold water."

I closed the door to the bathroom after she stepped out of it. As I opened a napkin, I heard the phone ring. Fraya must have answered it because I could hear her voice on the other side of the door, but it was too muffled to make anything out. Then her voice raised as if she was arguing with someone.

After she hung up, she spoke through the door, "You know what, Betty? I don't feel very well myself." Her voice sounded strange.

"You don't?" I opened the bathroom door.

"How 'bout we go to the movie tomorrow night?" She turned away from me. "That okay?"

"Sure. If you don't feel good. Who was on the phone?" I asked.

"The phone didn't ring."

"I heard it and I heard you talkin' to someone—"

"I'll see ya tomorrow, Betty."

Standing with her back to me, she touched the Japanese music box Leland had given her. After carefully opening the doors, she watched the female figurine twirl to the music.

I said goodbye to Hank before leaving. Just outside the diner, a car turned on Main Lane. I was embarrassed the bloodstain on the back of my skirt might be seen, so I quickly ran, making it around the corner before the car's headlights could shine on me. I looked back, but couldn't tell what type of car it was or who was driving.

Instead of walking home, I headed out of town, far from lamp-lights of front porches. I ended up on the dark dirt lanes where large farms were separated by fields of crop and cattle. A barbed-wire fence became my only companion as I walked the length of it. The cold, twisty wire seemed to wrap around me as I clutched my stomach.

When I heard a rustling, I thought it was something on the ground, moving through the tall grass. But when I followed the sound, I discovered it was coming from the barbed-wire fence, where I saw a barn owl with a beautiful white face. I could tell she was female from the way she frowned. She was crucified, her wings outstretched and impaled on the top line of fencing. Her chest was pierced by the middle line. She watched me, unsure if I would hurt her further or save her.

I stepped closer. She flinched. I stepped closer still.

"You're on private property." A woman's voice and the cocking sound of a shotgun came behind me. "Well?" she said. "Say somethin'."

I felt the barrel of a gun pressing against the back of my head.

"The owl," I said. "She's caught on the fence."

"An owl?" The woman lowered her gun and stepped past me. "Such a bird is considered an evil omen, you know that?" she asked. "It flies the night sky with the witches."

She was a woman with long silver hair that perhaps used to be black, for the ends were still charcoaled. She had the thick strong brows of her youth while her eyes had spent a lifetime staring at the hills around them until they were as clear as light between tree branches.

"Ya ever hear of a shrike?" she asked me as she studied the owl up close.

I saw her hands were aged by field and plow, her nails darkened by the seasons. Her knuckles were either arthritic or merely enlarged by the burdens and blessings of owning land. She was tall the way I thought her father might have been and she wore pants the way I thought her brothers might have. Her blouse was silky and flowery. Perhaps something her mother had left her. Maybe it wasn't a blouse at all, but the top of a dress she had tucked into her pants, doing what her sisters had taught her.

"A shrike is a small bird," she answered her own question. "They haven't got any talons so they impale their prey on somethin' sharp like thorns and barbed wire. I come out here all times of the night, and find moths, lizards, snakes even. Shrikes hang their prey like a butcher hangs meat up on a hook. That's why most folks call a shrike a butcher-bird. Ya ever hear of a butcher-bird, girl?"

"My father told me about them once."

"My father did, too," she said. "I suppose it's merely another warnin' to all little girls."

She pointed out the impaled mouse below the owl on the fence.

"The owl flew to get that rodent and made the mistake of her life," she said. "She'll need to be shot."

"No." My cry carried into the hills. "We can cut the wire."

"Wire is expensive," the woman said. "If I cut the wire, I'll have to replace it."

She stood back and held her gun up, ready to fire.

"Please." I stepped in front of the owl. "Don't kill her."

Slowly, the woman lowered the gun and met my eyes.

"Don't ever lose it," she said.

"Lose what?" I asked.

"That thing that makes you wanna save a life."

She laid the gun on the ground so she could remove a pair of wire cutters from her pocket.

"Hold the bird's chest," she said. "Keep her steady. If I cut her wing tendons by accident, she'll never fly again. She'll need to be shot then."

I held the owl's chest as steady as I could. When I looked into the owl's eyes, she was staring back at me.

"Everything is gonna be okay," I told the owl. "You'll be free soon. Nothin' will hurt you again. I swear."

"Don't swear to somethin' that can't be sworn to." The woman cut the wire.

I thought the owl would fly off once she was free, but she merely dropped to the ground. The woman removed her jacket and wrapped the owl up inside it.

"Will she be okay?" I asked.

"If she survives the night, she'll fly again," the woman said. "I'll take her back to my barn."

The woman gestured to the other side of the lane, where a large yellow farmhouse sat. Beside the house was a barn not so different than the one on Shady Lane.

"There's a loft up in that barn, warm and nice," she said. "I'll stay with her."

"Can I stay, too?" I asked.

"Go back to your people. You can come over in the mornin'. See if she survived."

I looked one last time at the owl. In many ways, I'd seen her face before. In every way, it is a face I still see.

"Take care of her," I told the woman, who looked less at the bird and more at me.

She nodded and turned, carrying the bird across the lane and toward the barn. I ran the entire way back to the diner. I checked the door. Fraya still hadn't locked it yet, which I found odd. I went inside and treaded softly to the back, where I waited at the bottom of the stairs. I could hear music playing from the Japanese jewelry box.

"Fraya?" I called. "You awake?"

I tiptoed up the steps and found her door slightly open. I pushed it the rest of the way. I had to wait for my eyes to adjust to the darkness of the room before I could see her lying in bed. Hank was curled up into a ball by her side.

"Fraya, wake up," I said. "I have to tell you about the owl. She was so beautiful. She was caught in barbed wire, but I freed her. Well, me and the old woman. The woman thinks the owl will fly again. Fraya?"

I nudged her as I climbed up into the bed. She didn't move. The moonlight hit her bare clammy skin.

"You don't have to get up," I told her. "I'm sleepy, too." I laid beside her and stroked Hank's fur until he purred. "The owl was beautiful. She reminded me of you, Fraya. She'll fly again, I'm certain of it."

I spoke to her about the owl some more. Then I told her good-night. I watched the girl twirl in the jewelry box until I fell asleep.

I dreamed of a fire. Me, Fraya, and Flossie danced around it. We were dressed in animal skins and feathers. Dad was there. He came and placed a necklace around my neck. As blood dripped from the necklace, me and my sisters swayed around the fire while our ancestors spoke to the moon and made sacred prayers over the blood dancing out of me.

I woke early the next morning at the sound of the cook's voice calling up the steps for Fraya. Hank was already gone from the bed. I looked at my sister. In the morning light, I realized how still she was. Only then did I notice the mayonnaise jar.

"It's okay, Fraya," I said before kissing her cold cheek. "You can sleep in."

I stood up out of the bed and saw the bloodstain on a blanket I'd been laying on. I quickly checked Fraya's drawers for some scissors. Finding a pair, I cut the stain out before rolling the rest of the blanket up in the laundry basket just as the cook called up one more time for Fraya.

"You're just tired," I said to her as I tucked her longest curl behind her ear. "I'm gonna go check on the owl. Then I'll come back and tell you some more about how I freed the bird. Tonight we'll sing and dance and make fudge. I'll poke enough holes in the sky for us to fly out of. Okay?"

I put the piece of bloodied blanket into my skirt pocket before crawling out the window and onto the roof. I fell, landing on the dandelions below, bees buzzing around them. Without stopping, I ran to the old woman's farmhouse, but it wasn't there. Neither was the barn. There was only a field of cows with their old farmer.

"Where's the yellow farmhouse?" I asked him. "Where's the old woman?"

"Who?"

"The woman. The barn."

For a moment I thought I was on the wrong lane. But then I looked at the barbed-wire fence on the other side and knew I was in the right place.

"You okay?" the old farmer asked as I stepped toward the owl still crucified on the wire.

Her eyes were closed and her head was hung. The morning flies were landing on her beautiful white face.

I covered my own face with my hands, which still smelled of Fraya's dandelion lotion.

"Shush, dear child," the old farmer said. "Was only a bird."

39

I bare you on eagles' wings.

—EXODUS 19:4

I imagine that at the same time they were collecting my sister's body, me and the old farmer were burying the owl in the field along with the bloody scrap of blanket I had laid on top of her.

"You can't cry over every one of God's creatures that die," the farmer said to me. "Or you'll be cryin' forever."

I suppose all sisters look like birds on their way out of this world.

They thought there would be answers in one of Fraya's diaries. She had hid them around her room in all the familiar places. Beneath the mattress. In the back of a dresser drawer. Even one under a loose board in the floor.

Her writings showed a range of emotions, but Leland's name was not mentioned in any of them and neither was the abuse. There were chunks of text that were unreadable, written in the code known only to Fraya herself. I imagined that in these entangled secrets, Fraya wrote about Leland at length. But without the key to the code, they became the hieroglyphics of a girl burying her words. The only readable parts were her song lyrics, which had the answers hidden in plain sight, but only to those of us who knew her secrets.

Dad collected the diaries, placing them on his bedside table. He would regularly read them, a piece of paper and pencil nearby as he tried to figure out Fraya's secrets. Maybe he thought if he figured it out, Fraya would rise from the dead.

Mom's response to Fraya's death was to take a pair of scissors and cut each of the white flowers out of the yellow curtains hanging on the kitchen window. The sun came through the holes and cast orbs of light on the kitchen floor. Mom took the fabric flowers and wrote dates on them. One date I recognized as Fraya's birth. Another was the day Fraya was first stung by a bee when she was five years old.

"She swelled up so big," Dad said. "I thought we done lost her."

There were about forty flowers in all. Forty significant months, days, and years. Mom put them in a jar, then poked airholes in the lid as if the dates were alive and needed to breathe.

They had ruled Fraya's death a suicide.

"She'd tried it before," folks whispered back and forth. "Finally got what she wanted. She wasn't doin' nothin' with her life anyways. She was probably gonna be a waitress forever."

I informed the sheriff I had spoken with Fraya before she died.

"She was plannin' on leavin'," I told him.

"Leavin'?" The sheriff's ears perked up, as did Dad's. "You mean, leavin' as in killin' herself?"

"She was gonna leave for the ocean," I said.

They both looked at me as if I'd confirmed her state of mind.

"She meant the real ocean." I tried to clear it up. No one seemed to listen.

We held no funeral for her. No burial either. Dad had her cremated. They burned her in a bright yellow dress. The carved ear of corn Dad had made her was nestled between her breasts until the fire reduced all that yellow and all that flesh to nothing more than ash.

When I asked Dad why he let someone burn her, he said, "Suicide is a sin. God punishes all those who commit it, but He can't punish the person unless they're whole. If we scatter her then God can't send her to hell until He finds every last piece of ash. Maybe by the time He does, His heart will have softened. Maybe He'll forgive her and take her home to heaven. Don't you understand, Betty? Fraya had to burn in order to be saved."

The morning we got her ashes, Dad started washing the Wagonaire.

"It has to be spotless for Fraya's last ride," he said.

I picked up the extra sponge and helped him. We spoke mostly about how hard the dead bugs clung to the windshield.

As Dad sprayed the soap off, I dried my hands on my skirt before picking up the urn he had made to hold the ashes. It was carved as Fraya's face. Dad sculpted Fraya's hair long. When I saw it, I thought only of the truck in the barn and its window crank.

Me and Dad were the only ones going to spread her ashes. Mom was lying in bed, clinging to the jar of dates. As for Leland, he had left town at the news of Fraya's death.

"That church in Alabama is lookin' for a new man of God," Leland told Dad. "Now's as good as any time to leave, I reckon."

Flossie wasn't coming because she said she had to go to the vineyard with Cutlass.

"We have to examine the vines," she said.

"You never go to the vineyard," I told her.

She paused before saying, "Yeah. But I can't spread Fraya's ashes. It'd be like sayin' goodbye, for real. If I can pretend I'm just sayin' goodnight to her, then it's like she's still alive, only sleepin'. But if I see her ashes, that breaks the spell."

Lint said he'd best stay near the garage in case there was anybody who came by in need of an herb or a tea. He was wiping the painted eyes on his rocks with a tissue. When I asked him why, he said, "Even rocks c-c-cry, Betty. They f-f-feel the loss of Fraya."

Dad turned the hose off and dropped it to the ground. It was time to go. I opened the tailgate, and climbed in with the urn. I slid open the Wagonaire's roof as Dad got behind the wheel and started the engine.

As he drove down Shady Lane, I decided to stand up, rising out of the open roof the way the pony had. I rested the urn in front of me on top of the car while my long hair whipped back. Already weary, I felt I carried a great burden against the wind. Then my father honked and I knew what I had to do. I removed the urn's lid. It was up to me,

Dad had said, to spread Fraya's ashes far enough apart so God would not be able to find them in our lifetime or the next.

I reached into my pocket and grabbed out the goodnights I had written earlier for Fraya. I dropped them into the urn, mixing them with her ashes. I scooped a handful out and, a little at a time, let my sister slip through my fingers. The pieces of paper separated from the ash as it floated in spirals in the wind. Whenever Dad honked, I released more. I felt the loss every time. The simple act of opening and closing my hand exhausted me. I was standing still, yet I was climbing a steep mountain.

The dust of life, who will care? I will, Fraya. I will care that you are gone.

Returning to the urn got harder. It felt as though I was dipping my hand through wet cement. Each time after I released her, I wanted to chase her back down and hoard every last piece of her in my soul.

When we got on Main Lane, folks who were out turned to the sound of the horn.

"What's that stuff that Carpenter girl is releasin'?" they asked. "And why is she cryin' so goddamn much?"

As we passed Dandelion Dimes, I saw Hank in the window. He was looking out as if having been waiting for us. I would never set foot back in the diner. It had become a place of darkness to me, even with its yellow dandelion heads on every table. I would miss Hank, though, and how his fur smelled like Fraya.

It seemed as if we drove through all the lanes of Breathed, me leaving a little of Fraya on each. By the time we reached Breathed's Welcome sign, the urn was empty. Dad slowed the car to a stop by the sign.

He got out and came around to sit on the tailgate. Hugging the urn against my chest, I sat beside him.

"Have you heard from Leland?" I asked.

"He gave a call on his way down to Alabama," Dad said. "I wasn't surprised he got out of town the way he did when he heard about Fraya. You have to remember, Little Indian, before all you kids, it was just the two of them. They had a great deal of growin' up together. It's probably why he's takin' it so hard. Why he went away."

We sat silent, both looking out at the lane like we'd find the answer there. I wanted to scream everything I knew about Leland, but something about how Dad was gripping the edge of the tailgate changed my mind.

"When Leland was a boy," he said, "he loved pickin' blackberries. I remember how his hands would stain. He'd run up to me and grab my face in those little hands of his. He'd say, 'Daddy, I vuve you.' He had trouble with his l's at the time and always mixed 'em up with his v's. 'Daddy, I vuve you,'" Dad repeated again. He waited a few more seconds before saying, "When Leland ran up to Fraya, he would grab her face and say, 'Fraya, I vuve you,'" Dad's voice shook and I looked away.

"I once saw God caught on a barbed-wire fence," I said.

Dad sniffled and wiped his nose on his shirt like a little boy before asking, "What'd you do, Little Indian?"

"Nothin'. I didn't do a damn thing."

THE BREATHANIAN

Woman Fears She's Been Shot

Around 4 a.m. last night, the sheriff was called to the residence of a Miss Kitty Bell, who made a frantic call saying she had been shot by the unknown shooter after several minutes of gunfire by her house.

When the sheriff arrived at her home, they noted drops of blood leading from Miss Kitty Bell's bedroom to her front door.

After an examination of Miss Kitty Bell by Doc Lad it was determined she was not the victim of a gunshot.

Doc Lad would comment no more on the situation out of respect to Miss Kitty Bell. But Miss Bell did release a detailed account of the night's events.

"The gunfire had startled me awake," she said. "It sounded so near, I thought the shooter was inside my house. When the sounds finally stopped, I got out of bed and went to the front of my house to check on things. It was when I headed back to bed that I noticed drops of blood on the floor. At first, I thought I'd been shot, but after Doc's checkup, I realized it was only the blood from my monthly falling. My daddy always said a woman ain't no more than a leaky faucet. He was always a bit of a bastard."

40

Her house *is* the way to hell,
going down to the chambers of death.

—PROVERBS 7:27

My father once said they call 'em the trumpet of death.

"That's why they grow so well in graveyards, 'cause of all the death. Maybe one day I'll fry some for ya," he told my mother before she was my mother.

They'd already lost so much between the two of them. I sat at the kitchen table and watched Dad place a slice of butter in the pan to melt. One mushroom, two mushrooms added. That's all the pan could hold. Two mushrooms and a slice of butter. Some days there is no room for rage.

My parents looked at one another and smiled. Perhaps they were headed toward friendship. If only they could connect back at those places they last left each other when they were young enough to believe poems could be written for the two of them. Old angers are mostly faded now. Guilt still remains. That's something that refuses to be shorter than eternity. I think part of eternity will be my father playing a mushroom trumpet while my mother watches him, the refrigerator door open until the milk sours. Perhaps somewhere my father is still playing that trumpet and my mother is still watching him. I think between the two of them they could have been pretty good at love. Too bad grief made myths of everything.

I left my parents to cut their mushrooms and grief as I stepped out onto the back porch, where Lint was sitting on the swing. Lined up beside him on the seat were his rocks, their painted eyes looking out upon the backyard.

"They like to s-s-see nice things," he said.

I watched a lizard climb up the post. The reptiles were little things that would cling to windows and doors. I remember the time one got its tail caught in the back door. Without a second thought, the lizard dropped its tail and ran off. The tail wiggled before it stopped, realizing the body had left it. The lizard would eventually regrow a tail as if losing part of oneself is no great burden after all. If only we could be like the lizards.

"Wanna get on a bus?" I asked Lint. "Go for a ride?"

"Where we gonna r-r-ride to?" He looked up at me.

"How 'bout Joyjug?" I asked as I listened to the clank of forks against plates from inside the house. "We could stop in and see Mamaw Lark. Ain't seen her since Grandpappy's funeral."

"W-w-why see her now?"

"Fraya's dead," I said as if Lint could understand why our sister's death circled back around to the little white house in Joyjug.

When we got to the bus stop, I paid for two tickets from money I had snuck out of Mom's purse. The bus carried only a few passengers. Both Lint and me each wanted a window seat, so I sat in the row behind his.

The farther away from town we got, the more the hills of Breathed started to change into the hills of everywhere else. It was autumn and all the edges of the world seemed to be colored in crimson and scarlet. The cool, crisp air churned through the open windows. The feeling was nice, but felt separate from me. I had become all too aware of the way a dying light flickers. I thought only of Fraya most days. I would try to talk about her with Flossie, but the most Flossie ever said about Fraya was "I have her favorite barrette in the bottom of my purse," as if she was merely holding it until Fraya asked for it back.

"We're h-h-here." Lint pointed out the window at the Welcome to Joyjug sign, which was nothing more than an overturned fruit crate lettered with red paint.

We headed on foot to Mamaw Lark's house. When we got there, we stopped out on the road. Her yard was overgrown with not only weeds but small trees that had started to lean toward the house. The white paint had chipped away to gray boards beneath. One of the upstairs shutters fell halfway down onto the porch roof. In the end, it was a house merely existing, much like the woman sitting in the rocker on the porch.

"Can you believe she's s-s-still alive?" Lint asked. "She's n-n-nothin' but an old worn-out shoe."

We watched her crochet. Her eyes were different than the last time I'd seen them. They had become glazed until her irises and pupils were indistinguishable.

I stared at her wrinkles, which all seemed to be vertical, as if she'd been downstream to something terrible her whole life.

"She's blind, Lint," I said.

"L-l-like our pony?" He turned to me.

"Yeah. Like our pony."

I stepped into the overgrown yard of a woman I had never loved. I walked toward her porch, watching garter snakes slither in under the low pine bushes. I had to step around thistle, which was as tall as my hip. Parting the milkweed, I walked up the porch steps.

I thought she might sense my presence, but she continued to crochet what I saw was a chain stitch seemingly as long as the river.

I quietly picked up the broom that had been lying on the floor. As she continued to crochet, I smacked the bristles against the porch wall. She dropped the crochet hook to her lap. I smacked the wall again, close enough to her head to blow the thin strands of hair over her ears. She sat there, her blind eyes staring ahead. When I hit the porch floor, the bristles of the broom brushed her leg and she parted her lips. The dryness of them was something you could almost hear as she asked, "Alka? That you?"

I dropped the broom and ran off the porch.

"C'mon." I grabbed Lint by the arm. "Let's get outta here."

He didn't say anything while we waited at the bus stop, nor did he say anything on the ride. Only once we were back in Breathed and walking home did he ask, "Why'd y-y-you hit Mamaw with the broom?"

"I was just sweepin' her porch for her," I said.

He took a rock out of his pocket and started passing it between his hands.

"Why you like rocks so much, Lint?"

"They're b-b-bullets against the demons." He looked up at me. "I know everyone th-th-thinks I'm silly. S-s-sometimes, I think it would have been better if I wasn't born. Maybe everyone would have been h-h-happier. I've never had any f-f-friends. You and Flossie and F-f-fraya had each other. I tried to be f-f-friends with Trustin, but he had his drawin's. I feel like what I'm n-n-named after. The fluff in a belly button. S-s-somethin' you clean out and throw away."

"Hey." I stopped him from walking farther. "Is that what you think? You're not named after belly button fluff. You're named because once upon a time, pants fell from the sky. Mom and Dad collected the fallen pairs and checked all the pockets."

I patted Lint's pockets in between tickling him until he laughed.

"What Mom and Dad found mixed with the pocket lint," I said, "were small pieces of paper. Two legs, two hands, two ears. They found enough pieces to make a whole person. They taped the pieces together, creating a small boy made out of the paper. You." I tousled his hair. "They loved you and fed you and held you until you became flesh and bone. They could have thrown that paper away. But they chose you to be their son. To be my little brother. They knew none of us would be better off without you. You know how a house has a foundation? Well, you bein' the youngest child makes you the foundation of our family. You're the most important part."

He smiled so wide, I had to ask him what he was smiling at.

"I just feel l-l-lucky," he said. "I get to be the brother of Betty C-c-carpenter. The strongest g-g-girl in the world."

Part Five

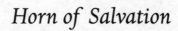

Horn of Salvation

1971–1973

41

The violence that is in their hands.

—JONAH 3:8

Hungered, I wrote. I came to dislike my bed and the sleep that kept me from pouring myself upon the page. Anguish was my subject, but so, too, was love. My dialogue became an insanity that then evolved into a metamorphosis of soul. Risen against the odds, if only to oppose and defy the suffering, I plotted tales that commanded myself to survive.

I sent these stories and poems to literary magazines and journals. I received politely typed rejections back, but also the rare acceptance. To be a writer felt very real to me then. It was an identity that was igniting new inspirations within me if not a new sense of worth, altering what I thought about myself.

I had spent the majority of my coming-of-age desiring to see a different reflection. I could either abandon the doubts I beheld and be free, or else dwell in the eye of the prejudiced, to be chained there. There are too many enemies in life to be one of yourself. So when I turned seventeen, an age that gives one permission to light the flame of new passions, I decided to refuse hate's ambition.

I pushed my bed over so I could tear up the magazine girl I had once prayed to be. I had almost been tamed by an image of beauty no more my own than a destiny I cannot claim. I gave myself permission to see the beauty of the girl I was and the young woman I was becoming.

The more I thought of this, I couldn't help but mourn the years that would not pass for Trustin or Fraya. The anniversaries of their deaths were the hardest. Fraya had died in spring. Trustin in summer. I found myself opening my books to the dried dandelion heads and slips of paper with Trustin's drawings on them. They were my bookmarks, but more than that, they were a brother and sister hidden where only I knew. I kept remembrances for Waconda and Yarrow, too. A cotton ball I flattened between the pages of a book, like a pressed flower. And a buckeye I made into a bracelet.

"Did you know the buckeye was named by Native Americans because they thought it looked like a deer's eye?" Dad said when he saw my bracelet. "It's a beautiful nut after all."

I made a buckeye bracelet for Flossie, too. She wore it the day she came to get me so I could go with her to take Nova trick-or-treating. I had put on bell-bottoms and clipped the sides of my waist-length hair halfway up. Before I left the mirror, I put on some burgundy lipstick and adjusted my suede vest so the fringe fell even. Though I had a bra in my drawer, I didn't wear it. Mom said it was a statement. But I said it was simply a choice.

It was Nova's first trick-or-treat. Flossie had made his costume out of a cardboard box and silver glitter.

"What is he supposed to be?" I asked her.

"A star," she said. "Can't you tell? I should have added more glitter."

Nova had pushed his face so far through the head hole, even his ears were out.

By that time, it'd been about a year since Cutlass and Flossie divorced. Flossie couldn't afford a lawyer, but Cutlass had two at his disposal. They made a case that because Flossie had stopped having sex with him, it was akin to abandonment. His lawyers cited *Diemer v. Diemer* for their argument. Because they accused Flossie of abandoning the marriage, she didn't have a claim in their marital house and Cutlass had the right to have the locks changed. Cutlass didn't want custody of Nova. Flossie decided it was good for her to have him because the financial support from Cutlass, even though it was little, helped her out.

After her divorce was finalized, Flossie refused to move back home. She reckoned it was something Mom would lord over her for all the times Flossie had given her little money. Flossie decided that moving away was her best chance. She found a small house for rent that had concrete floors in a town only a few miles south of Breathed. She got a job at a diner called Mother's Kitchen. Things seemed to be working out. She even started to do more with Nova, like take him into town and hold his hand. It was as if when it was just the two of them, she could love him more.

That Halloween had been particularly kind to Nova. In his pillow-case he had collected everything a sweet tooth desires. As the light lowered, we walked along the train tracks.

"A long time ago, me and your aunt Betty buried a dog somewhere along here," Flossie told Nova as she picked him up.

She carried him to the tracks and sat him on the sleepers. She rested the pillowcase of candy on top of his lap. I watched her as she used the bottom of her tattered shirt to wipe his nose. She puckered her lips toward him. He cradled her face in his small hands and kissed her.

As she started to tie his tennis shoes, I turned to watch the wind blow the branches above me.

"Mommy?"

I turned toward Nova's voice. Flossie had left him on the tracks. He tried to stand up and follow her, but he teetered back down.

Flossie pretended not to notice as she scanned the ground with her eyes.

"I can't for the life of me," she said, "remember the exact spot we buried Corncob."

Nova tried again to stand, but was unable to. He started tugging at his right shoelace. I realized it was tied to the track.

"Why did you tie him down?" I asked Flossie.

She looked as tired as I'd ever seen her. Her hair no longer smelled of the honeysuckle shampoo from the salon in Sweet Temper, nor were her clothes shiny and new. It was back to cutoff shorts and tattered T-shirts. Things she wore when she believed she would one day be rich enough to wear something finer. Now she was simply poor Flossie again.

"Mommy," Nova called for her again before turning his attention to the screeching hawk flying overhead. He blew a raspberry as he reached both arms toward the bird.

"I'm goin' to untie him," I said as I pushed past her.

I didn't get far before my knees were kicked out and I fell facefirst onto the ground.

"I'll do whatever it takes to be a star," Flossie said as she flipped me over onto my back.

She quickly straddled me and took a lighter out of her pocket. When she clicked the lighter open, the flame shot up between us.

"Let me go, Flossie." I punched her square in the nose. As blood dripped down over her lips, she delivered a hard blow back.

Having kept a tight grip on the lighter the whole time, she re-lit it and said, "If you try to save him, Betty, I'll have no choice but to start your hair on fire." She held the lighter close to my head. "I burned a church, remember? I can burn you, too. Have you ever seen fire burn hair, Betty? It gets so hot, it sizzles and melts into your scalp."

She grabbed my hair and jerked it closer to the flame.

"Why are you doin' this, Flossie?"

"Mom promised me I was gonna be a star if I stayed. She said Breathed's a sky without any stars. She—" A loud blare of the approaching train's horn interrupted her.

"If you don't get off me right now," I screamed at her, "and let me get Nova off them tracks then I'll tell the whole goddamn world how you killed your little boy."

Not listening to me, she said, "I'm takin' off to Hollywood." She turned her eyes to Nova. "I'm a good mother. I told him he'd be a star today and I made him one. Best of all is that he'll die a star and never know what it's like to be anything less."

"You're crazy." I grabbed a handful of loose dirt and threw it into her face.

"You bitch." She dropped the lighter to paw at her eyes.

I was able to shove her off. When I turned, I could see the train was much closer. I quickly climbed to my feet and ran toward Nova, but Flossie jumped on my back, sending us both crashing to the ground.

We wrestled for several seconds before she pinned me, facedown, against the ground.

"You know, Betty," she said, "I used to think it was the house that cursed us. If not that, then our very name. Truth is, we were cursed the moment we were born girls. Cursed by our own sex, and sex itself."

The train was getting closer. I could see the front of the engine.

"Choo-choo," Nova sang out as he excitedly pointed at the train. "Choo-choo. Train's comin', Mommy. The choo-choo is comin'." Nova smiled so wide it pushed his little round cheeks up.

The train horn started to blare repeatedly. I hoped the driver had seen the glitter of Nova's costume reflecting the engine's headlights. I fought my sister with everything I had as the train's brakes squealed.

Nova, realizing the train was headed toward him, turned and held his arms out toward Flossie.

"Mommy." He cried, reaching for her. "Help me."

She looked at the train, then at him, begging for her to get him.

"Little stars make big stars," I quickly told her. "He's your little star. Save him to save yourself."

"Mommy's comin'." She threw herself up and ran toward him, her arms outstretched as the train blasted its horn.

I could hear my sister's heavy breathing as she hurried to get to her son fast enough.

"I got you." Flossie wrapped her arms around Nova, but she couldn't lift him up. His shoelace was still tied to the track. Flossie struggled in vain to get his foot out of the shoe. Nova looked past her at me, tears slipping down his face.

"Betty, help." He reached for me.

I smiled at him because it was the last good thing I could give him.

As the train barreled toward them, Flossie screamed.

Unable to bear witness to the death of my sister and nephew, I closed my eyes and covered my ears against the screeching of the brakes.

"No, no, please, God, no." I squeezed my eyes shut so tight, I saw little stars.

"Betty?"

I opened my eyes and saw Flossie standing there shaking, her hair flying up from the wind generated by the train still slowing down. In her arms was Nova. He had his face buried into her.

"You didn't think I'd actually let a train run over him, did you, Betty?" Flossie's voice shook as she bopped Nova on her hip. "We best get out of here before the conductor can make us. Betty, c'mon." She yanked me up by the arm.

As the train came to a stop, the three of us disappeared into the woods, the child crying the whole way.

42

Set thy nest among the stars.

—OBADIAH 1:4

Flossie let Nova wear the star costume for the entire week. He liked being a star. He wasn't so different from his mother after all.

He was wearing the star the day he fell off the bed. He'd been jumping up and down on the mattress while Flossie put on her waitress uniform. Up and down while she brushed her hair. Up and down while she put on her lipstick. Up and down, then only down. When his head hit the concrete floor, Flossie would later say it sounded like a melon breaking apart.

"Get up," she said to Nova. "I'm gonna be late for work."

She saw how the point of the star was bent back from him landing on it.

"You broke your star," she said just as there was a knock on the front door. It was Flossie's mother-in-law, who had come to babysit Nova while Flossie went to work.

"Of all the Silkworms," Flossie had once told me, "Cutlass' mother is the best of the bunch."

As Mrs. Silkworm walked through the messy house and around the piles of dirty clothes, Flossie tried to apologize for not being better at laundry.

"Where's Nova?" Mrs. Silkworm asked.

"He's playin' dead," Flossie said.

When Mrs. Silkworm saw Nova, she gasped and immediately scooped the child up in her arms.

"You ignorant girl," she said to Flossie as she shoved past her.

Mrs. Silkworm drove Nova to the hospital in Sweet Temper. On his first night there, I dreamed I saw the glitter of his star costume shooting across the sky.

Flossie left while he was still in the hospital. The last time I saw her in person, she was lying on the same concrete floor Nova had fallen on. She was pushing cocaine from lines into piles because she said the lines reminded her of Dad's cigarettes too much.

I would later learn she had first done cocaine with Cutlass.

"I try to see through the swirls," she said. "They're like a river cussing. Sweet and swollen, *go to hells* and *goddamns*."

A little more snow for her to breathe in and everything's fractured.

"Like gems tossin' and explodin'," she spoke rapidly. "I think I'm underwater with glimmerin' starfish and bathin' lovers. God exists here, Betty. Demons, too. I told ya God would wait to punish us for burnin' His house."

She looked toward me but it took a while before she found me with her roaming eyes.

"Dad ever tell ya about the Star Catchers?" she asked. "Stars ain't supposed to fall to the ground. That's why I couldn't save Nova after he fell. It's why I'll never be able to touch him again. He's a fallen star. Only one of the Restless Star Catchers can touch him now. Mrs. Silkworm is a Restless Star Catcher. Did you know that, Betty? I didn't until I saw her pick Nova up. My son is Mrs. Silkworm's now. A fallen star can't belong to anyone except for a Restless Star Catcher."

Not long after, Flossie packed her bag. Months later we got a card in the mail from California with her zigzagging signature.

Everything's so sunny and funny, she wrote. *Wish you were here.*

She never made mention of Nova or asked how he was. If she had, I would have told her that after he was released from the hospital, Mrs. Silkworm took him back with her to her house. Nova's brain had swollen, which would slow his mental development. The doctors at the hospital said he would be confined either to a chair or a bed for the rest of his life. And at first, he was.

But Mrs. Silkworm worked tirelessly with him. She hired private nurses to help. His steps shuffled, but it was progress. Over time, he improved as best he could and would continue to defy the expectations placed upon him. He came to call Mrs. Silkworm "Mom." For Nova, she was the nurturing figure he needed to teach him the things everyone said would be useless. Nova proved that just because a star falls doesn't mean it can never again rise.

Dad and Mom would visit Nova. Mrs. Silkworm said they were welcome anytime. Both Mom and Dad understood they wouldn't have the money to care for Nova the way the Silkworms could. But Dad still didn't want Nova to forget about Flossie.

"Remember her shine," Dad would say to Nova, who always looked around as if he was searching for his mother. "You both sparkle like the stars. You get that from her. Never forget."

With Flossie gone, I was the only one of the Three Sisters still at home. I carved my sisters' names in A Faraway Place, if only so the stage itself wouldn't forget them. Then I wrote. Out of my writing came tanglements and chasings. There were claws and talons and soft things, too. I wrote about water pouring down walls, drifting smoke. These untouchable, touchable things that tied each of us up into knots no extraordinary beginning could ever fix. My poems were as wide as my arms were not. They were as loud as I was silent. They were a hot whisper saying sometimes love is a punishment.

The months following Flossie leaving, I labored in the rural respite that country life offered. I tilled fields, baled hay, straddled tractors like intimate things. I was working beside boys who looked at me as if I didn't belong there with them. As if I was building sharp corners into their reliable circles. But it felt good to labor hard.

While walking home from a farm one day, I passed Ruthis driving by in her shiny red convertible. She stopped and said I had grass in my hair. I kept walking. She got out of the car and followed me.

"You smell like shit." She held her nose. "Were you shovelin' manure?" She walked backward so she could face me. "You sure don't sunburn, do ya?" She laughed. "But the flies sure do love you."

I stopped to face her.

With all the kindness inside of me, I said, "You're beautiful, Ruthis."

"And you're ugly."

"You've got beautiful hair."

"And yours is stringy." She crossed her arms.

"You've got a beautiful smile and beautiful eyes." I meant every word.

"I already know I'm beautiful," she said. "Like you know you're not."

I grabbed her into a hug. She kept her arms folded, too surprised to move.

"I forgive you, Ruthis," I said. "I forgive you for makin' school hell for me. And for callin' me ugly and a loser. I forgive you. Because one of these days, you're gonna feel really bad about it and you're gonna wish I was around so you could apologize. But I'll be so far away from you, you'll have to get on a rocket ship to find me. And they don't let just anybody go to the stars. I'll forgive you now, so that later, when you realize your life is horrible and that we could have been friends all along, you'll know that at least I survived you."

I pulled back out of the hug and tucked her hair behind her ear. I left her standing there with her mouth open, at a loss for words.

I smiled to myself all the way home.

Slipping my feet out of my boots, I left them by the front door. When I got upstairs, I stopped in Mom's doorway and watched her apply makeup. She was off to Papa Juniper's to get some groceries.

She cursed as she applied black eyeliner.

"My eyes are not what they used to be," she said.

"You see fine, Mom."

"I don't mean whether I can see or not. I mean how my eyes look. So many wrinkles now." She pulled her eyelids up. "You think I need one of them face-lifts?"

"No."

"You can't lie to me, Betty. I have become an old 'ma'am' at fifty-one. Not as old as your father. The good thing about marryin' an older man is that you're always younger. It's strange. I never thought your father would get old. I thought he'd always have his black hair and that damn funny run of his. Now even his wrinkles have wrinkles. Are you afraid of wrinkles, Betty? I know where you'll get them."

She stood and walked toward me. With the eyeliner still in her hand, she began to draw on my face.

"You'll get some wrinkles right here between your brows because you frown too goddamn much," she said. "And you'll get some here across your forehead because all of the women on my side of the family do. Here on the corners of your eyes, you'll get your father's folds. And though we don't smile, you'll have wrinkles that said ya did." She drew lines on either side of my mouth.

Once she finished, I stepped over to the mirror to see what I looked like. She'd coarsely drawn the black lines as if she meant them to be vulgar.

"Are you afraid of wrinkles now?" she asked.

"Not now that I've seen them," I said. "Now I know what to expect."

"Then you are a braver girl than I thought."

She returned to the vanity to finish her makeup while I sat on the edge of her bed.

"I wonder if Flossie is happy in California," I said as I looked toward the window, remembering how my sister would come up the drive twirling and dancing.

"Ha." Mom laughed. "I'm sure she's happy."

"She's gone to Hollywood." I frowned because Mom's laughter made me feel silly.

"Do you know why I told her to marry Cutlass and have his child?" She turned to face me. "You think it's because I'm wicked. But I did it for her own damn good. She'll go out there to Hollywood and realize she's no Bette Davis. But not until they take everything from her. You've seen Flossie put on her little shows. She's missin' that one thing that makes for a good actress. *Talent.* Even if she were talented, things come back around. Flossie abandoned her child. She's already dead in this world."

Turned out my mother would be right about Flossie's career in the movies. She would only get one studio acting role. It was as a waitress. Her single line was "Ice?" To which the men slapped her on the behind and laughed as she walked away from their table. Before she took the final step off the screen, she glanced over her shoulder one last time. She peered directly into the camera as if she were looking for someone. Maybe for herself.

That movie would be the last time I would ever see my sister alive again. We would, from time to time, talk on the phone. Her voice aging each new year. Rambling about this and that, hard-to-understand conversation.

"I taught a rat how to chew gum," she said the last time I ever spoke to her. "He sits on my countertop and does it all . . . There are sores in my armpits . . . won't heal. Be . . . Betty? What do I do? I ask the rat . . . the rat . . . but he just chews his damn gum. I feel like I'm over . . . what's the word when you . . . over . . . over what, Betty? Overturned. Yes. I feel like I'm over . . . turned . . . my legs up in the air . . . a beetle on its back."

"Flossie." I said her name to remind her who she was. "Is anyone there with you?"

"I'm alone. Isn't that al . . . always . . . a woman in the . . . end?" Her speech slurred even worse. "I used to . . . parties . . . my favorite things. So cool in fishnets. Heroin . . . on the bread. It's okay, Betty. Dad will nev . . . know. All my shirts . . . long sleeved. You can borrow one and we can be sisters . . . again." Her voice rose and fell with each time she swayed away from the phone and nodded off. "Betty? Do you remember . . . I ran to save him . . . my son. That should count . . . shouldn't it? Bet . . . ? It's because we burn . . . the church. God's . . . gettin' us back. You can't bur . . . a man's hou . . . and expect to . . . away with it. Betty? Why don't ya ever say a damn thing? The curse . . . ain't it?"

My sister did every drug imaginable. By the time the 1980s ended, she was dead on a dirty mattress, a needle in her arm and enough heroin to forget everything. When they found her body, she was naked except for the necklace Dad had made her. Still around her neck, still something she held on to. I know from seeing the police photos that the bean pod was stretched on its chain and was lying in a puddle of her vomit. The paint was chipped from the bean pod in a way that would make me realize she had chipped it off herself over the years by chewing it, perhaps only trying to find out what lay beneath the color Dad had sworn to her was the very color of her soul.

I wonder if in those final years my sister ever thought of the yellow and blue flowers in the meadow we'd often run through together back in Breathed when everything was still nice and we were stupid enough to believe anything was possible.

I don't think my mother was right about Flossie having no talent. When I look back on it now, I think her whole life was an act. Did I really know my sister? Or was I only seeing the girl she was pretending to be? The flirt. The slut. The wife. The mother. Maybe being Flossie Carpenter was her greatest performance. So good, we all thought it was her.

THE BREATHANIAN

Local Men Band Together to Find Shooter

Five able-bodied men have decided to form a group to search for the gunman.

"It still feels threatening after all these years," the group's elder commented. "Someone going around with a gun. Shooting at all hours of the night. One of these stray bullets could kill someone."

While on their recent camp in the woods, the group encountered a girl. They asked the girl what she was doing. Her response was that she was looking for rocks for her younger brother. They got her name and address. The girl has been identified as Betty Carpenter of Shady Lane. A mystery novel was found on Carpenter's person, along with a handwritten story about the Peacocks and their disappearance. The sheriff took both the book and the handwritten story as evidence, only to later release them back to Carpenter's father, Landon Carpenter.

43

Who can open the doors of his face?

—JOB 41:14

A handful of frozen blackberries thawing on the kitchen counter. The leaves of the potted plant in the living room turning yellow. Mom accidentally dropping her mug. The coffee spilling across the floor. Her on her hands and knees sopping it up with a towel. A pale rope coiled on the front yard like a sleeping snake. I was eighteen and these are the things I remember as I walked out of the house and toward the woods with Dad.

November of 1972 was a solemn month that knew exactly how things would end. Outside, the sun was not seen behind thick gray clouds. Despite this, the golden leaves seemed to glow like little light-bulbs were screwed into the branches. Me and Dad sat on the hood of the Rambler he had parked in the woods. The Rambler was no longer a journey a man wanted to take. Its engine was gone. Its tires were flat. Its time had come and passed. The car that had driven us so many places had become mine and Dad's place to sit in the woods.

He'd brought along the transistor radio. I tuned through it while he read that day's edition of *The Breathanian*. The newspaper had misprinted the year on the front as being 1932 instead of 1972. They used correction fluid to white out the *3* and replace it with a handwritten *7*. At the moment, Dad was reading an article about Tuskegee and the black sharecroppers who died during the syphilis study. Dad sighed and looked up from the article to watch the turkey buzzard circling above us.

He folded the paper and laid it off to the side. From his coat pocket, he pulled out a shiny red apple. He cut it in half with his pocketknife while I tuned to a station playing Louis Armstrong's "What a Wonderful World." Dad hummed to the song as I set the radio down and took my apple half from him. I stared at the burn scar on his palm.

"I've always wondered about that," I said.

"Oh, have ya?" he asked. "I got it when I was a boy. A man come passin' through. He had the most peculiar books. When opened, flames would leap up from the pages. In the flames, the story was told. But there was a price to pay for openin' the books. For at the end of each, the book would catch fire, leavin' nothin' but ashes on the ground. The man knew I was fascinated by his magical books, so he kindly gave me one. I opened it and watched the entire story play out in flames. There were horses gallopin' and queens who were part women, part horses fightin' for their thrones.

"On the last page, there was a hummingbird. A little thing who escaped before the book burned. She was beautiful, the flames twisting and turning to form her, but I knew an entire forest fire could break out if the burning bird landed on a single leaf. I had to get her. It ain't easy catchin' somethin' made of fire, though, and I burned my palm on her wing tryin'.

"As I nursed my burn, the bird flew out of my reach. I thought of all the things in this world that could catch on fire. Then it started to rain. Fire and rain have never been friends. The bird tried her best to dodge each raindrop. I could see the fear on her face. She didn't want to die. When the rain doused her left wing, she still tried to fly with her right. She wanted to live so badly, but the rain was putting her out. I cried as the little bird disappeared in a puff of smoke."

Dad lowered his eyes to the scar.

"What I've just told you is the beautiful lie," he said. "Would you like to hear the ugly truth?"

"Yes," I said as he flung his apple half to the ground.

"When I was a boy of fourteen," he said, "a man, much whiter than me, drove into town in a shiny new Ford Model T. Automobiles were somethin' rare when I was a boy. I was so awestruck by it. It was the first car I'd ever seen. I remember how everyone gathered 'round it after he parked. He left it runnin' as he went inside the market. We all remarked on how loud the unfamiliar sounds of its engine were to our ears. I got close enough to the car to touch its door. I was mesmerized by that most extraordinary invention, but at that very moment, the man came out of the market.

"'Get your hand off my car, nigger.' He was yelling at me.

"I had known men like him before. I knew to just leave, but somethin' in me wanted to face the man.

"'One day,' I told him, 'God will turn out all the lights to remind people like you that in the dark, you won't be able to tell who is white like you and who ain't. We'll have to treat one another equally. We'll learn it's not our skin color that makes us good or bad. And only when we learn that, will God turn the lights back on.'

"That's when the man grabbed me by the arm. Without sayin' a word he forced my palm onto the car's hot engine. I screamed and cried, but no one helped me. When he released me, he said, 'If the lights ever go out, I'll take to feelin' the right hand of everyone in this world. When I feel that scar upon your hand, I'll know me a nigger. Because that's what you are, boy. It's what you'll always be.'"

I tossed my apple half to the ground by Dad's. Holding my knees into my chest, I told him I preferred the beautiful lie.

"Yeah, well, I—" He sharply moaned as he gripped his chest.

"Dad? What is it?" I watched blood drip out of his nose.

"Nothin', it's just—" He winced.

"I'm goin' to get Doc Lad." I started to slide off the hood, but he grabbed my arm before I could.

"Stay here and listen," he said. "I wanna tell ya somethin'."

"I'm goin' to get Doc."

"Listen, please. I have to say it. Please, Little Indian."

"What do you wanna tell me, Dad?"

"I want you to leave Breathed."

"I'd never leave ya, Dad. I'm staying with you always."

"You are meant to fly out of this burnin' book." He pulled me into him. I let him cradle my cheek against his chest. I could feel warm blood dripping on top of my head from his nose.

"You're just tired," I told him. "That's all. You're never gonna die."

"Do you think it's possible for me to go to heaven?" he asked.

"Of course you'll go to heaven, Dad. But not today. Today you are stayin' south of heaven with me because . . . because . . . I don't know what I'll do without you."

He kissed my forehead.

"I don't know if I've ever told you that I love you, Little Indian. I don't know if I've ever said those words."

"You said them every time you told me a story." I looked up into his eyes.

He smiled. I knew it would be the last.

"Have I ever told you I loved you?" I asked because I really didn't know.

"Every time you listened to one of my stories." He nodded. "Do me a favor, Little Indian? Take my boots off."

"I have time," I said as I stared out at our apple halves on the ground. The halves laid so perfectly together, they made a whole fruit, as if it was only a ripe red apple that had, then and there, dropped from the branch.

44

Our bones are scattered at the grave's mouth.

—Psalms 141:7

Story always has been a way to rewrite the truth. But sometimes to be responsible for the truth is to prepare oneself to say it. My father did not die in the woods. He died at the hospital. His blood all over my white dress.

The afternoon had started with me, Lint, and Mom sitting with Dad on the back porch. There was iced tea served with talk of the changing autumn leaves.

It was then that Dad stood with his arms hanging stiffly by his sides.

"The old man is awake." Mom chuckled as she chewed on a piece of ice from her glass. "You still dyin'?" she asked because he had started to tell us he was dying every morning for the past few weeks. Everyone thought talking about his mortality was something an old man did.

"I have to go to the bathroom." He had announced it in a way he'd never done before.

"All right." Mom looked up at him. "Well, we ain't gonna hold your hand. Go on, now."

He slowly walked into the house, leaning on his cane more than I'd ever seen him do.

"The man moves like he's ancient," Mom said, the ice in her glass clanking when she went to drink the last of her tea. She scooped the lemon slice out. As she ate its flesh, we heard a loud thump from inside the house. We rose from our seats, set our glasses down, and walked in a line toward the screen door.

The squeak from its hinges echoed throughout the quiet house as we stepped into the kitchen. There, dropped by the table, was a dish towel spotted with blood. When we stepped into the hall, we found Dad on the floor just outside the bathroom door. Blood was streaming out of his mouth, forming a puddle beneath his head.

Mom would spend the rest of her life trying to get these stains out of the floorboards, but failing. Anytime anyone would ask about the spots, she would say, "The wood of the floor was cut from a bleedin' tree. Ain't nothin' more to say."

I ran over to Dad while Mom quickly stepped to the phone. There was no ambulance service in town at the time, so who answered emergencies was the local funeral home Grinning Brothers. Their hearse served as Breathed's ambulance as was the case in many small towns at the time.

She threw open the phone book and licked her finger to turn the pages. Then she removed her earring and stuck her finger into the holes of the rotary phone dial.

"C'mon, c'mon." She tapped her foot as the wheel spun.

The receiver shook as she held it to her ear, waiting for someone to pick up. I sat on my knees behind Dad's head and propped him up onto my lap as I listened to Mom tell the funeral home we needed to get Dad to the hospital.

"It's Shady Lane. Just over the bend. Yes, yes, please hurry." She placed the receiver down and put her earring back on. "They're on their way. Jesus Crimson."

Not knowing what to do with her hands she began to smooth the sides of her dress.

"I should make some dough for dinner rolls. You know the kind, Landon." She nodded at him as he rolled his head back in my lap and moaned. "The kind you like."

She ignored his sounds and instead spoke to him as if there wasn't anything out of the ordinary.

"While we're at the hospital, the dough will have time to rise," she said. "Then when we're all back tonight, we can have fresh rolls and noodles with potatoes. I'll pick up a roast from Papa Juniper's. A real expensive roast. Then we'll all have dinner tonight. Won't that be nice?"

By the time she'd finished talking about the noodle and dinner roll dinner we would never have, she wrung her hands so hard, her wedding ring came off. She couldn't catch it before it fell to the floor. It clanked against the floorboards, rolled a little ways, then circled several times in the same spot until it was still. She stared at the ring. It was a small golden band. She quickly picked it up and slipped it back on.

"I'll go make the dough," she said.

Without looking at Dad, she ran into the kitchen. We could hear her set the big bowl on the counter and rummage through drawers as she yelled she couldn't find the rolling pin.

"Goddamn it, where is it?" she asked.

Seconds later, her relieved discovery.

"I've found it," she said.

"Do you th-th-think he's g-g-gonna be okay, B-b-betty?" Lint asked as he looked down at Dad.

Lint had been unable to do anything more that whole time but stand up against a wall.

"Why a-a-ain . . . a-a-ain . . ."

"It's gonna be okay, Lint."

"Do you th-th-think if I made him one of his d-d-decoctions, like he used to m-m-make me, it'd h-h-help him?"

"Maybe later. Right now, why don't you go outside?" I said. "Make sure the Grinning Brothers find us."

He looked at me. It was the first time I'd really realized my brother had my father's eye color. The same dark dollop that went golden on the edges in the light.

"You're all b-b-bloody, Betty," he said.

"It's okay. Go on now, Lint."

I listened to the sounds of him opening the front screen door. Mom heard the sounds, too.

"Is that them?" she asked from the kitchen. "I haven't finished the dough yet."

"No, Mom," I answered. "It was Lint."

"Good, good," she said. "I'm nearly finished."

She was all flour and butter talk after that, measuring out to herself each ingredient as if the rolls really did matter and we would all be home in time to eat them.

I looked at Dad. His head felt so heavy. The blood was still running from his nose and smearing onto my wrists each time he rolled his head in my hands. He had started to gurgle on the blood in the back of his throat before hacking it up. I noticed the blood splattered all over my forearms. It was as though something had burst inside of him. I thought of the glass heart.

Had it broken into tiny pieces, I wondered, *now cutting him from the inside out?*

I raised him up on my lap. That seemed to help him. On occasion his fingers would twitch. His eyes were still open and looking about, but it was as if he were disoriented, unsure if the walls around him were the walls of his own home.

"Everything's gonna be fine, Dad," I told him. "I'm here with you. Mom's makin' rolls. There's gonna be a roast. Flossie will come in. Fraya and Trustin, too. We'll all have dinner together. You can tell a story while we eat the noodles."

He suddenly grabbed my wrist and squeezed it so tight, I thought I would lose my whole hand to him.

"Take my boots off," he said. "Take my boots off."

"But you'll be gettin' up and walkin'. You'll need your boots on, Dad."

"My boots. Take my boots off." The blood had colored his teeth.

"They're here." Lint's voice echoed off the walls as he hollered from the front porch.

"They're here?" Mom's anxious voice came from the kitchen. "Jesus Crimson."

I could hear a couple of car doors open, followed by unfamiliar voices.

"My dad's b-b-back here."

When I looked up from Dad, I saw two dark-haired men pushing a stretcher. They both had long ears and small mustaches. They were grinning, yet it seemed compulsory.

"That's a lot of blood," the one with the longest ears said.

"All that blood will ruin our sheets," the other one added, grinning wider.

"Ruin your s-s-sheets?" Lint grabbed him by the collar. I'd never known Lint to be aggressive before. He was fifteen at the time. I finally saw him as a teenager and no longer a little boy. "I'll buy ya n-n-new sheets, goddamn you."

They didn't say a word more as they lifted Dad onto the white sheets on the stretcher. They rolled him down the hall toward the door. As I stood, I became aware of how much of my father's blood was on my dress.

Mom was standing there, the sticky dough still on her fingers as she patted the sides of her hair.

"Now, Betty," she said, "when we get back, I'll need you to help me with the noodles. Your father usually does it, but he'll be restin' in his rocker. We mustn't disturb him while we make dinner."

Her eyes dropped to the blood on me.

"I don't think I've ever seen that red dress before." She spoke as if her mind was in another room.

"Yes, Mom." I followed her down the hall.

She grabbed the car key from out of the little wooden bowl Dad had made to set on the table by the door. I was the last to leave the house, the front door slamming behind me in a way that made us all jump.

The brothers paid no mind to my whimpering father as they closed the hearse's door shut and got in the front. I slid in between my mother and brother on the front seat of the Wagonaire. We sat so close, our arms brushed against each other's in ways that felt intimate and strange to people like us. Mom quickly started the engine and waited for the brothers to pull out of the drive so we could follow them.

"Come on, come on, move." Mom rolled down her window to yell at them.

She continued to yell and honk at them anytime she thought they were going too slow. Though we were driving at a speed that would normally get us a ticket, it still felt as if we were going no faster than turtles climbing up the river's banks.

I wondered what others thought as they saw us speeding past.

Why they all sittin' in the front like that? I imagined the old farmer asked his cows as we passed. *With all that room in the back to sit, why are the three of them sittin' so close like that?*

Maybe the answer was in his question.

All I really did know for certain was the way Mom's hands trembled as she gripped the steering wheel. She frowned and chewed the inside of her cheek every time the hearse slowed to take a curve.

"Just go." She cursed at the brothers.

We were all headed to the nearest hospital in Sweet Temper. The closer we got, the more Mom looked as though she were entering the dark like a blue river, loose and unraveling, unsure of how to fix things. She reached over and turned on the radio, only to quickly turn it off again as if she didn't know what to do with her hands.

"Remind me to get a roast from Papa Juniper's when we get back," she said.

Me and Lint nodded as we shivered from the cold air coming in Mom's open window. Just when we thought we would never arrive at our destination, the hospital came into view. It was a chocolate-brown brick, barely two stories. It was a building that would never look any more modern than a yellowed photograph in a box marked "The Past."

After Mom parked, we quickly got out of the car and waited by the hearse as they unloaded Dad. He wasn't moving, but his eyes were open, staring up into the bright sun.

Mom followed the stretcher through the hospital's small door. Lint stopped to stare at the blood on my dress.

"All that c-c-came out of 'im?" he asked.

"He'll be all right." I looked around at the people who were on the sidewalk, staring at me, too. "It looks like a lot of blood, 'cause my dress is white," I told them. "But really it ain't nothin' more than a drop or two. Ain't nothin' more than that. He'll be all right."

Lint quickly looked away. When we got inside the hospital, a nurse pointed the way down the hall to a small room they had put Dad in. Circling the bed was a white curtain on rings that they pulled closed as they hovered around him. One of the nurses shooed us back out into the hall like she was shooing 'possums from her porch come night.

"Go on now, get." She flapped her hands at us. I noticed she had a run in her white hosiery.

There were windows along each side of the hallway. I stepped into the light, closing my eyes and feeling the warmth of the sun on my face. When I next opened my eyes, I was in our yard. The tall grass tickled my shins as I moved through it toward the barn, where my smiling father stood in the wide-open doorway, the day coming to a close behind him in bright pinks and blues.

"You can go in now and say your goodbyes," an older voice said.

The grass, the barn, and my father disappeared as I turned around to see the oldest of the nurses standing by Mom.

"Our goodbyes?" Mom asked the nurse.

"He's still conscious, but I'm afraid this is it for him." The nurse spoke in a tone that told me she was used to explaining such things.

"But . . ." Mom looked around lost. "This can't be it. We're havin' roast and noodles for dinner tonight and the dough is risin'."

The nurse gave my mother a look I'm sure she had reserved for all soon-to-be widows before she turned and walked back into the room. Mom and Lint followed. I lowered my face from the sun and joined them.

"Take my boots off." Dad's voice was the weakest I'd ever heard it.

He rolled his head toward us. I think he tried to smile, but I can't say for certain it wasn't a shadow of the blood smeared out from the corners of his mouth. It occurred to me then that to be a child is to know the cradle rocks both toward the parent and away from them. That is the ebb and flow of life, swinging toward and away from one another, perhaps so we build up the strength for that one moment we will be rocked so far away, the person we love the most is gone by the time we return.

"Hi, Dad," I said because it felt better than to say goodbye.

Lint looked at me, then turned back to Dad.

"Hey, D-d-dad," Lint said, tears on his cheeks.

Mom wiped her eyes as she stepped over to his boots, which were worn to the soles. His shoelaces were tattered in ways that made it seem he had tied frays of something up because that was all he had. I wanted to give my father a brand-new pair of boots right then and there, but it was too late for such gestures. As Mom started to untie his shoelaces, Dad twitched. Mom quickly rushed up to his face and held her apple half against the one on his necklace.

"You shouldn't see this." A nurse pushed me and Lint back.

She pulled the curtain closed in front of us, leaving enough space through which we could watch our mother hold the apple halves together, creating something whole between her and our father, who lay dead, unaware his boots were still on his feet.

45

Lord, I will follow thee; but let me first go bid
them farewell, which are at home at my house.

—LUKE 9:61

No one reminded Mom to pick up a roast from Papa Juniper's as we drove past it on our way back to the house the dough had risen in. Mom took the dough, which looked like a hill in a bowl, and punched it down. Then she talked. About the yellowing houseplants, about the yard, and about how we were nearly out of coffee.

"Before I forget, Betty," she said to me in between sweeping up flour from off the kitchen floor, "your father bought you a typewriter. It's hidden under the hood of the Rambler."

I threw open the screen door and ran out of the house. Before I got into the woods, I took off my shoes and continued barefoot over the hard ground. When I got to the Rambler, I couldn't lift the hood fast enough. In place of the engine was a black case. I opened it to a typewriter. Lying on the keys was the napkin I had wrote the story "The Smilin' Martians" on years ago.

"You had it this whole time," I spoke to Dad's ghost as I held the napkin to my chest.

I looked closer at the paper in the typewriter roll. There was something already typed.

BETTY

Chapter One

My father had given me the beginning. It was up to me to write the rest. I closed the case and lifted it out of the Rambler. My father's positioning of the typewriter in place of the engine was a sign to my spirit. A parting message of my father's faith, courting the engine inside of me.

I ran ahead, stopping with each gust of wind and waiting impatiently for it to brush my cheek.

Two days later, we held his funeral. I had slept that night beside Mom in her bed. I woke to the feeling of something rubbing my body. When I opened my eyes, his face was a blur.

"Leland?" I blinked until his face was clear.

"Time to get up." He talked low, his hot breath slipping into my ear.

His hands were beneath my side of the blanket and trying to feel up under my shirt.

"Don't touch me," I whispered harshly before slapping him back.

I looked over at Mom. She was still asleep, but her closed eyes were quickly darting. I got out of the bed without waking her.

Quietly, I pushed Leland out of the room.

"Keep going," I said to him when he tried to stop out in the hall.

When we got downstairs, he turned to face me.

"Is there anywhere in particular we're goin'?" he asked.

I yanked him out the front door.

"We goin' to the barn?" he asked when we were in the yard. "We gonna have some fun before everyone gets here? You gonna be my new Fraya?"

"You're leavin'," I told him.

"Can't." He jerked his arm out of my hand. "We got a funeral today."

"It's only for friends and family."

"What do you call me?" he asked.

"Not welcome."

"He's my father." He started to raise his voice. "I'm gonna be at his funeral. I'm preachin' the goddamn thing."

"Dad didn't want no preachin'."

"I'm his son, Betty."

"No, you're not."

I walked over to A Faraway Place and climbed underneath. I had come to realize that buried secrets are just seeds that grow more sin.

"What the hell you doin'?" Leland pounded his fists on the stage before leaning down to look. "Why you got all them rocks under there?"

"I'm a rock farmer," I said, pushing one aside.

I began to dig until I felt the lids of the two jars. When I pulled them free, the wind blew hard, like a great exhale from the earth herself. Holding them both to my chest, I rose to face Leland.

"What's in the jars, Betty?" he asked.

"The story of your father."

I handed him the first jar. He unscrewed its lid and grabbed out the folded pages.

"You're readin' what Mom told me a long time ago," I said as his eyes devoured the words. He had started to grip the paper so tight, I thought it would catch fire in his hands.

"You're sick, Betty." He clenched his jaw until the vein in his neck popped out. "Writin' lies like this."

"It's the truth. Grandpappy Lark tore Mom open. For years, he raped her. She was pregnant with you before she even met Landon Carpenter. It was why she chose him that day in the cemetery to be the man who would unwittingly raise you as his own. She thought it was your best chance. She didn't want you to be born with the same storms in your hands that were in your father's."

Leland crushed the pages in a fist. As he circled me, I could feel his fury. It was so heavy, I thought it could put any one of the hills around us six feet under. Just flatten them down like they were nothing. When he opened his mouth, I waited for a scream all of creation could hear, but he only gnashed his teeth and said, "Liar."

"You're the spittin' image of Grandpappy Lark."

"Because I ain't got mud on my skin like you?" He looked at me with disgust. "I took after Mom."

"Flossie. Fraya. They took after Mom," I said. "But they also took after Dad. I look at you and I see nothin' of him."

"Shut up." He raised the pages in his fist over my head as if he was going to strike me, but I didn't flinch.

"I'm not afraid of you," I said.

He spit on my cheek before yanking the other jar out of my hands. Instead of unscrewing the lid, he broke the glass against the stage. Shaking the sharp shards off the paper, he picked it up. I watched his face twitch as he read.

"I wrote that after I watched you rape her in the barn," I said. "You did the same thing Grandpappy Lark did to Mom, only you did it to your sister. You started on Fraya when she was just five years old. I didn't know it at first, but then I realized she had been singin' about it all along in her lyrics. *At five years old, the little girl cries, the wolf has arrived to eat her alive.* The wolf is you, Leland."

He grabbed me by the throat, but I only stared him down.

"You know what a five-year-old does?" I asked, digging my nails into his hand. "She sleeps with her teddy bear. She draws with crayons and thinks the world will be as sweet to her as the ribbon in her hair. Imagine bein' a five-year-old girl and your brother—the boy who's supposed to protect you—starts *eatin'* your fingertips until he's *eatin'* your arms until he's *eatin'* your whole damn body. You ruined her life, Leland."

"She ruined her life." He shouted in my face. "*She* ruined it."

"That's exactly what Grandpappy Lark would say." I pushed him back.

I thought he might grab me by the throat again, but he merely said, "You're nothin', Betty. Always have been."

He threw the pages to the ground, stomping on them.

"You can't destroy her story, Leland. I keep it here." I rubbed my forehead. "I keep it here." I rubbed my cheek. "I keep it here." I patted my chest over my heart. "I keep it with me. No matter what you do to the paper, her story will always live. I'm gonna let everyone know what sort of monster you are."

I could almost hear his blood boiling.

"You think you got it all figured out, Betty? You weren't there in those early years when it was just me and Fraya with Mom and Dad on the road. I wasn't even tall enough to reach the pedals, but Dad rigged the car so I was the one who drove most of the time. I didn't have the opportunity to be a kid like you did. Hell, Dad could talk himself into any job, but he never kept 'em. I had to help put food on the table. At ten years old, I had to be a man." He beat his fist into his chest. "I didn't have a choice. And, damn, wasn't I owed somethin'?"

"Your sister wasn't your compensation. She didn't belong to you. And you thought she did, for what? Because Dad asked you to do a little work? You raped Fraya because you wanted to. Stealin' her strength was the only way you could feel important. You're nothin' but a weak, pathetic loser. Just like Grandpappy Lark. You both fed on the power of the girls and women in your lives, because neither of you had any power of your own."

"You're just as guilty as I am," he said, showing all his teeth. "You watched what I did in the barn, and you didn't do a damn thing."

"The only one guilty is you. And one day, when I write this story, you'll open the book and find small slivers of mirror. Not everywhere, just over the names I've given the devil. When you collect the slivers and put them together, it'll be your reflection that you see. Now get off our property. Ain't nothin' here for ya."

I started to head back to the house, but stopped when he said, "She was pregnant, did you know that? She was fixin' on havin' the kid."

"We all knew she was pregnant." I turned to face him. "It was why she used the bark."

"I'm not talkin' 'bout that winter all those years ago. I'm talkin' 'bout when she died. She was dead set on bein' a mother this time around. It would have come out with claws and a tail. Ain't that what they always say?"

"I don't—I don't understand—the night she died, she knew she was pregnant?"

He wiped his mouth as he nodded.

"That's why she told me she was gonna leave," I said. "She was gonna leave you and Breathed to raise the baby."

"I couldn't have that," he said.

"That night at the diner, she got a phone call." I started to go through the night's events aloud to myself. "She said there was no call, but I know there was. And there was arguing." I fixed my eyes on Leland's. "It was you who called her that night at the diner, wasn't it?"

He moved his mouth like he was chewing on something. Then he stared up at the sky and watched the clouds drift for a few seconds before saying, "I caught an eagle once. They say the eagle flies higher than any other bird."

"What'd you do to her, Leland?" I asked, my fists tightening at my sides.

"Nothin' special." He shrugged. "Just kept her in a cage and starved her. Fraya followed me into the woods. She said she was gonna tell Dad what I'd done. I had to kill her."

"Fraya?"

"The eagle." He lowered his eyes from the sky. "Why you cryin', Betty? Was only a bird."

"You murderer." I punched him. He reeled back on his heels, holding his jaw.

"I knew she wouldn't have killed herself," I said. "It was you who caught the bee. The headlights from the car. That was you driving up. You forced her hand in the jar."

"She screamed somethin' terrible," he said with a smile. "Good thing a pillow was just right there."

"I'm gonna kill you." I lunged at him, but he grabbed me by the arm and twisted it behind my back.

"You know," he said, "it's funny. When a sad girl dies, everyone thinks it's her own damn fault."

He let me go, kicking me in the leg.

"You got anything else buried?" He looked at the ground as if it was suddenly full of every secret he never wanted told. "Well, do ya?"

Feeling rage circle every bone in my body, I softened my tone to say, "Yeah. Fraya buried somethin'. I'll show it to you."

I crawled back under the stage where the longest rock lay. Moving it over, I reached into the hole.

When I emerged, Leland was standing with his back to me, tearing the stories into small pieces.

"Hateful Betty," he said as he watched them blow away. "We're gonna have to do somethin' with you."

He turned around.

"You?" he asked, staring at the shotgun I was aiming at him. "It was you shootin' this whole time, Betty?"

"You're my last shot." I had my finger ready on the trigger.

"You're just a girl with a gun," he said, smiling. "No one has cared all these years. Why you think it's gonna matter any now?"

"You know, growin' up in that house gave me a lot of time to think about how the Peacocks might have disappeared without a trace. You better believe you could disappear just as easily, Leland. No body. No blood."

"You ain't got the guts, little sister."

"Wanna bet?" I shot the ground by his feet. Grass and dirt exploded up as he fell back. I pumped the handle, forcing a new shell into the chamber.

"You evil little witch." He climbed to his feet. "I wish I would've killed you, too."

He moved toward me but was stopped by a rock hitting him in the arm. When I looked back, I found Lint standing there, his pockets bulging. He reached into them, pulling out handfuls of rocks. He threw them so hard, his feet came up off the ground. Leland tried to dodge the attack, but it was as though all the sandstone of the hills was raining down on him. He fought back by lobbing punches. He only hit the air. When a sharp rock struck him in the forehead, it was as though his eyes broke open, bleeding red.

"I'm gonna smash your face in," he said to Lint.

From out of his waistband, Lint grabbed the slingshot Dad had made Trustin. He quickly loaded the rubber band with a large round rock. I recognized it as the one Leland had brought back from Japan. Lint positioned the rock so the painted eye was looking out on Leland.

"Well," Leland said with his arms open, "if you're gonna kill me, then one of ya better do it now." He looked me in the eyes. "Just promise you won't cremate me like you did Fraya, Betty. I don't wanna burn twice."

"Don't you feel the flames lickin' up your calves? Don't you feel the heat around your heart? Don't you feel your eyes meltin' outta their sockets? Don't you know, you're already burnin'?" I lowered the shotgun, no longer needing it as my weapon. "There ain't a flame on this earth or in hell that ain't got your name on it, Leland. You're already burnin'."

He looked at me a moment, before dusting off his sleeve as if dusting off a flame. He brushed off each of his shoulders and kicked his legs, laughing.

"Oh, my, I'm burnin' up good," he said.

Jumping, he started to pretend the flames were at his feet. But as he kept pretending, the more his smile faded until it was replaced by a look of fear.

When he started to dust off his sleeves again, he did so violently as if there truly were flames licking up his arms.

"Shit." He slapped his chest as if the fire was consuming him from the inside.

He started to scream and told me and Lint to put him out. But we only stood there and watched.

"Please, help me." Leland slapped the sides of his head and screamed that his hair was on fire.

All over his body, he felt the flames. You could almost see them reflected in his eyes as he tried desperately to extinguish them with his hands, before taking his jacket off and using it to beat up and down his legs. He cried out, grabbing his eyes until he fell to his knees. Burying his head into the ground, he grabbed handfuls of the earth and threw it onto his back until his arms, tired of the fight, dropped like two things melting into puddles at his side.

When he lifted his head, he looked around him. His skin was so red and glistening, it was as if he really had just walked through an inferno. Once his eyes met mine, his lips parted as if to say something, but as I looked down upon him, I raised my chin even higher. He remained as silent as he had ever been.

He reached out to me, but I turned my back to him. Lint did the same. We listened to Leland cry and beg for us to help him. But I had no sympathy for his pleadings. Not after what he had done to my sister.

I could hear him scratching something on the ground. Then I listened to him struggle to stand up. He stayed there a moment, staring at our backs, before walking to his truck. Only when there was the sound of him driving away, did I turn around. There, scratched into the dirt where he had stood, was *Leland was here*.

With the toes of my foot, I erased his name.

Left with only Lint by my side, I wrapped my arm around his shoulder as we watched the trees out on Shady Lane blow in the wind.

"Thanks for your help," I said to him.

"You're welcome, B-b-betty."

"You know, Dad made that for two people." I pointed at the slingshot.

"I kn-kn-know."

"Then how would you have used it by yourself?"

"I wasn't usin' it b-b-by myself." He looked up at me. "Trustin was here. His hand w-w-was on it, too. It is his s-s-slingshot."

We headed back toward the house. Just before we walked inside, Lint said, "I always knew."

"Knew what?" I asked.

"I always knew Leland was a d-d-demon."

Staring at my reflection in my bedroom mirror, I felt I wore the black dress not only for the death of my father but for the death of my childhood. How could I lose Dad and not lose something of myself? The girl I had been belonged to the past. Womanhood had become my present. I noticed this in the way I turned my wrist to spray my skin with my mother's perfume before going downstairs.

Lint had already moved the furniture in the living room and set out foldable chairs. Folks had arrived and were collected in whispering groups around the room.

I stepped over to a table where an envelope laid amongst the other mail Lint had brought in that morning. I recognized Flossie's cursive on the outside of the envelope. I opened it to find a card with a black-and-white image of thrashing waves. Flossie had written on the back of the card, *The Pacific is the deepest ocean in the world.*

She signed it with her initials. Scattered inside the bottom of the envelope were several goodnights. Amongst them was a single "goodbye." I knew it was meant for Dad.

I left them in place and set the envelope on the fireplace mantel along with the card. Lint walked up and stood staring at the waves. He was wearing the white shirt and black bow tie Mom had bought him. His long hair was slung over his shoulder in a braid.

"What's that you have?" I asked him, seeing something sticking out of the end of his closed hand.

"It's a p-p-piece of Mom's bread," he said.

"Why do you have it?"

"Dad once t-t-told me to make sure I bury him with a piece of Mom's b-b-bread to feed the bird."

"What bird?"

"The bird in his g-g-glass heart. Remember? You first told me about the b-b-bird, Betty. But Dad later told me I'd have to make sure to b-b-bury him with bread. So he'd have somethin' to f-f-feed the bird on their journey to heaven."

"He never told me to bury bread with him," I said.

"You weren't his only k-k-kid, ya know." He stuck the bread inside Dad's hand.

A wind came through the open windows and everything seemed to move. The curtains, the paper napkins, men's ties, and the hems of the women's dresses, including my own as I stepped over to the coffin and looked at my father. While my own hair blew in front of my face, Dad's lay stiff under a heavy spray. His face and neck were lost beneath a powder, too pale for his skin, and his cheeks were shaded far too pink. His lips had been pulled tight in an awkward smile. I could see the end of the thread that stitched them closed, slightly protruding from the corner of his mouth like a tiny worm.

The Grinning Brothers had dressed my father in their cheapest option. A dark green blanket suit. They called it a blanket suit because everything was sewn together. The tie to the shirt. The shirt to the jacket. The jacket to the pants. The suit was draped and tucked around his body. If Dad had come alive at that very moment and stood, the suit would have fallen off. I was certain he'd only laugh and gather that blanket of a suit up, lay it on the grass, and call for a picnic.

The Grinning Brothers had told us to pick out a tie to be sewn to the shirt. We chose the only tie Dad ever had, which was in the shape of a fish. He'd gotten it from a white-haired Gypsy woman when we were passing through Montana. She had been selling pies out of her van set up by the side of the road. Dad bought a fish pie from her. When he cut into it, there was no fish, only a tie in the shape of one. He thought the Gypsy had baked it in the pie by accident so he took it back to her, but she told him she had put a real fin-flapping bass in the pie.

"I can't help it," she said, "if by the end of its bakin', the fish had turned itself into nothin' more than neckwear."

I still cannot remember if I know this to be true. If I saw the Gypsy's white hair and watched the crust of the pie break away as Dad pulled the tie from it. Or if this is a story from Dad's lap and is only in my head because he put it there like little moonlit stones.

The only pair of shoes Dad ever owned were his work boots. Chairfool, being the same size shoe as Dad, offered a pair of well-worn but shined oxfords.

"These are good shoes for a man to go to God in," Chairfool had said. "They are good because they have been danced in. Shoes that have been danced in are of better character than those that have merely been stood in."

This suit, these shoes, the makeup on his face, it all covered my father up. It was only when I looked at his hands that I saw him in the earth crusted around his short fingernails and in the crooked lines of his bony knuckles. Strangers would look at his hands and see a man of no importance. They would think that because his hands were dirty, it meant he did not matter. But in life, you either live in someone else's house or you build your own. A man with hands like my father's was a man who had built his home out of star and sky. He had held on to the throb of life and abandoned comforts. You can't do that sort of thing and not expect your hands to get dirty. That's how you know you're doing it right.

I stared at the dried thyme and mugwort hanging from the underside of his coffin. I thought my father, being older and having lived a longer life, would need more thyme and mugwort than he had given Trustin. Instead of hanging one bouquet of each, I hung enough to offer a man an infinity of safe travels and beautiful dreams.

I turned from the coffin to look at my mother. She was sitting in the middle of the sofa with a folded quilt on her lap. She had asked me to do her makeup that morning. I think she thought if she held a red lipstick in her hand long enough she would ruin things. She wanted a full face of makeup. I gave her what she wanted.

"You heard anything from Leland?" she had asked as I powdered her face.

"He come by early this mornin' while you were still asleep," I said.

"Well, where's he at now?"

"He left."

"Left?"

I had to tell her to stop frowning so I could fill in her brows.

"Left?" she repeated. "It's his father's funeral."

She met my stare, then quickly looked away.

"Close your eyes, Mom," I said. "I've got to apply the eye shadow."

"Go heavy on the color" was all she said.

After I had drawn the eyeliner out to the corners of her eyes and applied the mascara, she put on her veil. It covered her whole face except for her red lips.

"Look at that veil. Who does she think she's foolin'?" I overheard one neighbor woman say to the other as they passed me.

Each woman was holding a potted resurrection fern as if there was no other plant alive that could understand death as much. The women were headed to Mom. It was hard to tell behind the veil if Mom was looking at the ferns or at the women. She made no gesture toward either of them when they offered their condolences. She merely stood with the quilt in her hands.

The room fell quiet as she walked to her chair in front of the coffin. It was time for Dad's funeral to start and my mother was letting us know by taking her seat.

Lint sat by Mom, leaving me the chair on the very end. So many people came, the room was packed and we didn't have enough seating so folks spilled out into the other rooms and onto the front porch.

It seemed everyone was waiting on someone else to start things off. When Mom elbowed Lint, he got up and nervously cleared his throat.

"There'll be no p-p-preachin' here today." His voice shook. "Dad didn't want no preachin'. Only stories. Y'all got plenty of 'em, so ch-ch-choose the story that means the most to ya. In that way, it'll mean the m-m-most to my daddy."

Lint rubbed his hands together quickly as if starting the spark for his own memory of Dad.

"One time Dad carved some w-w-wooden cars and hooked 'em to fishin' poles," he said. "We'd cast the lines out on the r-r-river. The cars f-f-floated real nice like. 'Let's see who's the fastest,' Dad would say before makin' a poppin' sound with his mouth. We'd r-r-reel in the cars as fast as we could, racin' on top of water."

Lint followed through with the motions like he was casting out. For a moment, we felt we were there on the river with him and Dad, anticipating who would win the race as Lint quickly reeled the line in.

"He let me win every time," Lint said, dropping his hands. "Just the t-t-type of daddy he was."

After Lint sat, folks began to stand one by one, telling stories about Dad. How he had walked all the electric lines in the county like a tightrope champion or how he once found insects made of gold.

"Ol' Landon painted them bugs so they'd look ordinary. So they wouldn't be stolen for their gold and caged in some jewelry box."

These stories, like all the rest, had become down-home myths full of easily swallowed moons and deep-dug sorghum cane.

When Cotton stood to speak, he straightened his tie as he spoke about how much he had loved his wife.

"After what happened to Vickory," he said, "I thought I would never be happy again. Then Landon gave me a bag of balloons and told me a letter a day keeps the tears away. He said that by my writin' her, I'd be able to bring her back to life in a way. Though she wouldn't be able to write me back, Landon said she would let me know she received my letters by puttin' a rock in the hollow of the weepin' willow at the beginnin' of Shady Lane."

I looked at the rock Lint rolled back and forth in his hand. He slipped it back into his pocket.

"Sure enough," Cotton continued, "after I wrote that first letter and sent it up in a balloon, I found a rock in the hollow of the willow. I knew it was Landon who had put it there, but I allowed myself to believe it was Vickory. Landon allowed me to believe it was her, too. Outside of his absences from Breathed, Landon placed a rock in the hollow every day. I think even God would have tired of humorin' me, but Landon never did and he never asked me to let go of her. He only gave me a way to keep holdin' on."

Listening to Cotton and the others, I knew what my father did not know when he was alive. That he was more than a filler. He was a lifetime of wildflower fields. I feel like the grasses will always tell stories of him. Of his mushroom hunting and of his philosophy that no one really knows just how sweet honey is. Maybe that is his eternity. A man tipping his hat and walking on his way. It began to feel less like a funeral and more where a jug of Dad's moonshine should have been passed from one hand to another. People smiled and laughed as they slapped each other on the back to say, "Oh, boy, that was old Landon, all right."

"That's enough," Mom said, standing. "All this laughter. Y'all need to quiet down and pay some damn respect."

Already standing, I guess she figured it was as good a time as any.

She slowly approached the coffin as she unfolded the quilt in her hands.

It was the quilt from her bed, the one with the tree stitched in its middle. The old bloodstains from the kittens were still there. What was new on the quilt were pieces of green felt cut into the shape of shagbark hickory leaves and sewn upon the tree's branches. On the two largest, she had embroidered her own name along with Dad's. My name and the name of each of my siblings, including Yarrow and Waconda, were embroidered on the smaller leaves. I had seen Mom the previous day pulling a needle through the quilt, but I thought she was merely patching a hole. I never would have thought she was stitching our family tree.

Everyone watched as she laid the quilt upon Dad. She gently tucked it around him as if she were merely helping him to bed. After she finished, she leaned down to kiss him one last time. I still remember the way the black thread stitching his lips brushed against her mouth.

The room was silent as Mom took her seat.

I took a deep breath and stood. Walking to the side of my father's coffin, I knew the weight of being the daughter of a god.

"Growin' up," I said, "I felt like I had sheets of paper stuck to my skin. Written on these sheets were words I'd been called. Pow-wow Polly, Tomahawk Kid, Pocahontas, half-breed, Injun Squaw. I began to define myself and my existence by everything I was told I was, which was that I was nothing. Because of this, the road of my life narrowed into a path of darkness until the path itself flooded and became a swamp I struggled to walk through.

"I would have spent my whole life walkin' this swamp had it not been for my father. It was Dad who planted trees along the edge of the swamp. In the trees' branches, he hung light for me to see through the darkness. Every word he spoke to me grew fruit in between this light. Fruit which ripened into sponges. When these sponges fell from the branches into the swamp, they drank in the water until I was standin' in only the mud that was left. When I looked down, I saw my feet for the first time in years. Holdin' my feet were hands, their fingers curled up around my soles. These hands were familiar to me. Garden dirt under the fingernails. How could I not know they were the hands of my father?

"When I took a step forward, the hands took it with me. I realized then that the whole time I thought I'd been walking alone, my father had been with me. Supportin' me. Steadyin' me. Protectin' me, best he could. I knew I had to be strong enough to stand on my own two feet. I had to step out of my father's hands and pull myself up out of the mud. I thought I would be scared to walk the rest of my life without him, but I know I'll never really be without him because each step I take, I see his handprints in the footprints I leave behind."

I reached into my skirt pocket and took out the piece of deerskin Dad had shown me when I was a little girl.

"I know who I am now, Dad," I said to him, tucking the deerskin in beside him.

Instead of returning to my seat, I went over to the record player that Teddy from Teddy's Electrical Goods let me borrow. I lowered the needle on the record Fraya had made all those years ago when she put a coin in a machine. The record crackled before Fraya's beautiful voice filled the room:

> Ravages and savages,
> of god and men,
> fallin' from the ol' cherry tree again.
>
> Myth is in and myth is out.
> Love is faithful on this route.
>
> To be afraid,
> poison from
> the old nightshade.
>
> Flicker my girl, flicker my boy.
> Take my heart, destroy, destroy.
> Flicker my girl, flicker my boy.

Cold noise is what my father sang
when myth was something for all to bring.

It's my father I would be,
if I were made of milk and honey.
It's my father I will be
when myth melts these chains off me.
Demons and angels spell my name,
in fire and halo it all feels the same.

Flicker my girl, flicker my boy.
I can't get much older than the Iroquois.
Flicker my girl, flicker my boy
in this toma-hawk myth,
this tom-o-john story.

THE BREATHANIAN

The Gunfire Has Ended

For over a decade, Breathed has been plagued by random gunfire. Through the years, we have seen our residents affected by this continued nuisance. It had become such a regular occurrence, some came to believe the sounds were not of gunfire at all, but of the hills eroding around us.

Although the shooter has never been identified, the sheriff announced today that his department considers the shootings officially over after having received no new reports of gunfire since November.

"I feel as though a cloud has been lifted," one resident is quoted as saying.

We may never know the motives behind the shootings. There is some speculation that the shooter has died. That he lays now at rest.

While most residents are overjoyed at knowing the era of gunfire is over, there are some who express sadness.

"I'll miss it," a woman, wishing to remain anonymous, says. "You get used to hearin' somethin' so long, it starts to sound less like gunfire and more like words. This whole time, someone was tryin' to tell us somethin' in a language we simply couldn't understand. I hope whoever was speakin' all these years, finally got out what they wanted to say."

46

The sorrows of death compassed me.

—PSALMS 18:4

Burying a father stays with you long after you've hung your black dress in the back of your closet. When you believe you're done worrying about the worms that will gorge on his body, you think of them and only them until you remind yourself nature must not deny its duty.

That winter of 1973, I turned nineteen and stayed as cold as the snow. When May came, the spring tendered a precious thing to the bare branch. Flowers made the grief bearable. As did the green grass which had begun to grow over Dad's grave. The signs were everywhere. In the pink peonies. The stripes of warm sun. The insects flaring their nostrils and flicking their wings. All of it saying the ripples of his death were weakening against new life.

The fresh spring brought nights that existed as small warm things. The windows open, the clouds like certain shreds across the sky. It was also a spring that brought with it a small black dog. He'd circle the house and sleep on the porch step. He was an occasional howler, but not yet sold to the wolves.

Lint swore this dog was Dad.

"Smell him, Betty." He held the muddy creature beneath my nose, its wiry fur something that tickled my nostrils. "Smells like Dad's t-t-tobacco, don't he?"

I brought the dog into the house after that and let him sleep on my bed. I called him Du-yu-go-dv, a Cherokee name I thought represented him the most.

One afternoon, when the gray clouds were collecting in the sky, I fell asleep with Du-yu-go-dv in my room. I woke to thunder. It sounded everywhere, even inside of me.

I looked around for Du-yu-go-dv, but he was gone. I went out into the hall, where I could hear the rockers of Dad's chair.

I stepped into what had been his and Mom's bedroom and found Mom sitting in the rocker. The incoming wind was causing the cotton curtains to whip around her. The room had the same pieces of furniture it always had. There was the same amount of space around each item. There was even more of some things like the cosmetics on the vanity and the stack of newspapers by the bedside table, yet there was an emptiness there as if the one thing that had truly filled the room had gone with my father.

I knew Mom felt the emptiness, too. She was barefoot and sitting on one leg while using the foot of her other to rock. She had freshly bathed and her wet hair was darker for it, the ends dripping little drops upon her bare shoulders. She wore only a pale blue towel around her body. There was no makeup on her face. Lipstick, mascara, it all seemed to fry her. Make her something untouchable. But bare-faced she was cool, touchable, the most beautiful woman I have ever seen. I realized we did not look so different after all. She was my mother and I was her daughter. I suppose for too long that relationship had raged like a war.

"Do you think it's him?" She nodded toward Du-yu-go-dv on the bed.

"Dad?" I asked. "No, I don't think the dog is Dad."

"Maybe we should ask him."

Her ankles seemed shaky when she stood. As she moved toward the bed, she held her hands out with her palms down like she was brushing the spikelet tops of all those wild growings my father had taught me the names of.

When Mom was close enough to the bed, she walked up the mattress with her hands.

"Are you my husband?" she asked the dog.

His dark eyes stared back at her.

"Landon?" She said his name softly. "You son-of-a-bitch. You promised you'd never leave me."

She reached her hand out. The dog immediately jumped up and ran out of the room. Weary, Mom sighed as she turned and sat on the edge of the bed. She folded her arms and rested her chin against her chest.

"Your father used to make the most beautiful wicker chairs," she said. "He'd soak bark in water until he could strip it. We don't have not one of those chairs in this house. When we needed money, his furniture was always the first to go. None of you kids, well, except for Leland, even knew those chairs ever existed. There's so much you don't know about your father. Did you know he helped build ships?" She raised her eyes to mine.

"You mean real ships?" I sat on the bed beside her.

"Yes. The big kind. The ones they take out on the ocean. I suppose that's why everyone will always love him best. I've certainly never built any ships."

She looked down at her hands as if suddenly feeling they'd done nothing important.

"You made somethin' better than a ship," I said. "You made a flyin' quilt."

"You remember that?" she asked.

"Of course, Mom. I remember all of it. I was just a kid and had been walkin' 'round barefoot in the yard. You were outside, sittin' in the grass on the quilt you buried with Dad. You were embroiderin' somethin'. I can't remember what and I didn't really care because I had stepped on a thistle and started cryin'. You called me over to you and took my foot in your hand. You kissed my foot right where the thistle had stuck me. Then you sat me on your lap and told me we were going to fly.

"You cut a strand from the bright purple thread you were usin' to embroider with and tied it 'round the body of a June bug. The bug flew, fettered by the thread. 'We're flyin',' you said as you pointed over the edge of the quilt as if we were high above everything.

"'Can't you see your sisters sittin' on the roof of our house and your brothers playin' under the trees?' you asked. 'And look. There's your daddy sellin' his mushrooms.'

"I looked and saw it all. And you smiled.

"'We fly as long as the June bug flies,' you said.

"I didn't wish I was back on the ground."

"Why, Betty?" she asked as if she didn't know.

"Because I was with you, Mom."

47

He said to the woman,
Thy faith hath saved thee; go in peace.

—LUKE 7:50

Cinderblock John took the pony to his property. He let her live in a beautiful barn he painted red. He installed a wooden-rail fence around the prettiest acres he owned. For a while the pony happily galloped there, but as she ran up against the fence, she realized she was not yet truly free. I understood the need to go beyond the fence. No matter how beautiful the pasture, it is the freedom to choose that makes the difference between a life lived and a life had.

I knew Dad would be proud when, at the end of the school year, I collected my high school diploma. I became the only one in my family to graduate. Even Lint would drop out before his senior year.

When I found him outside in the garage, I told him I was going to be leaving and that I wanted him to come with me.

"I c-c-can't," he said.

"Why not?" I asked. "We could go anywhere together."

"Before D-d-dad died, he told me I would have to t-t-take care of Mom. He said she would n-n-need me."

"Mom don't need you, Lint. She can take care of herself."

He looked at his hands.

"I don't w-w-wanna leave home, Betty," he said. "This is the last place Mom and Dad will have ever l-l-lived together." He looked at the sign hanging by the garage door. "Someone has to l-l-look after his plants. I watched him work. I kn-kn-know how to make teas like he did."

"You really don't wanna leave?" I asked him.

"I wanna sh-sh-show you somethin'."

He led me outside. In the yard between the garage and the house, he had dug up the earth just enough to lay his rocks down in a path. Their painted eyes staring up at the sky.

"This is w-w-where the rocks have always been leadin' me," he said. "H-h-ome. Why would I ever wanna leave that?"

Lint would carry on our father's business, never once changing the sign from LANDON'S to reflect his own name. And when folks would call him Landon by mistake, Lint would only smile with pride and say, "Yes, that's me."

Amongst the plants and his rocks, Lint would become an old man, smelling like the herbs he crushed and the teas he brewed.

"I'm gonna miss you, Lint."

"I'll always be here. All ya have to do is d-d-drop in and say hi."

"Okay. I will."

I could understand Lint's need to stay, but the earth had touched my spirit and was beckoning me to its lands, waters, and skies. I had to discover the world myself. I started packing that night. The next morning, as I was taking the Three Sisters carving from off the wall, Mom leaned against my open doorway.

"Good day for travel, I reckon," she said.

She played with the frilly collar of her blouse. For the first time in my life, I saw my mother in pants.

She watched me place the Three Sisters carving into the large carpetbag I was packing everything in. The bag had the image of a farmhouse on it with trees and flowers and a dog and a cat and a mouse. The image on the carpetbag reminded me of what Flossie once said to me.

"You'll live in a farmhouse, Betty. You'll have a dog and a cat and a mouse."

I smiled at the thought.

"Where will you be goin'?" Mom asked.

"To a faraway place." I looked out at the stage.

She walked to the open windows and stood in the rays of sunlight streaming through.

"I don't wanna hold you up," she said. "I've got to get off myself to work. Did I tell ya I got a job at Breathed Shoe Company? I'm in the stitchin' department. After the patterns are cut, I'll be one of the women who sews the whole shoe together."

She lightly, and proudly, touched the sides of her hair, then she dipped into her bra and pulled out the Apache tear.

"You remember what I told you about this?" she asked. "In your hand it's a black rock." She held it in the sunlight until the rock became translucent. "But the light changes it. They say if you have a tear of the Apache—"

"You will never cry again," I finished her sentence. "For the Apache women will cry for you."

"Well, maybe it'll do you better than it has ever done me." She placed the tear in the palm of my hand before wrapping my fingers around it.

"A girl comes of age against the knife, Betty." She softly tucked my hair behind my ears before kissing me on the forehead. "But the woman she becomes must decide if the blade will cut deep enough to rip her apart or if she will find the strength to leap with her arms out and dare herself to fly in a world that seems to break like glass around her. May you have the strength."

As she turned to leave, her eyes found the shotgun on my bed.

"Looks to be the same make and model of the gun shootin' Breathed." She picked the shotgun up and aimed it at the wall. "Why were you shootin' your own town up, Betty?"

"I wasn't. Not in the beginnin' at least. It was Fraya. The night she went outside to get the slippery elm bark, she had also gone into the woods, and I followed her. I watched her get the shotgun out of a hollowed stump she'd covered with leaves. I suppose she found the first shells wherever she had found the gun. Toward the end, she must have been goin' out of town to buy more.

"I didn't know why she was shootin' at first. Not until she told me that we were all insects caught in a jar and that we needed more airholes to breathe. She was tryin' to give us those airholes by shootin' them out. When she died, I knew I'd have to take over. But now I think there's enough air. We can breathe fine from here on out."

Mom nodded and saluted, as if from one soldier to another, before leaving. I could hear her taking the gun into her room. She kept it close by her for the rest of her life. It was what she held on to once her blonde hair silvered and she became the old widow who sat on her falling porch with the shotgun across her lap as she yelled at nameless kids to keep off her damn yard. They would come to laugh at her, unable in their youth to believe she had ever been more than an old woman in a rocking chair.

The last time I would hear my mother walk in high heels was that day she walked out of her room, having laid the shotgun on the side of the bed Dad had slept on. She went down the hall, *clickety-clack*. Down the stairs, *clickety-clack*. Out through the front door on her way to a job she would have until she retired. *Clickety-clack*.

I took the Apache tear over to the window and held it in the sunlight. As the light once more made it translucent, I watched Mom drive down Shady Lane through it. When she was gone, I slipped the tear into my pocket.

On my pillow was Dad's cane. I strapped it into the umbrella holder on the carpetbag, then locked the typewriter up in its case. I set everything by the front door with Du-yu-go-dv following me.

"Lint?"

"In h-h-here."

I looked into the living room and found him watching TV.

"It's hot today for spring, ain't it?" I wiped the sweat from my cheeks.

He stood as if it was required.

"Well, g-g-goodbye then," he said.

I grabbed him for a hug but he awkwardly kept his arms by his sides.

"When I find a rock I know you'll like, I'll keep it safe for you," I told him, releasing him from my embrace.

"Aren't you afraid?" he asked.

"Of what, Lint?"

"Of the c-c-curse Flossie always said was ours. Maybe it's worse out in the w-w-world."

"Ain't never been a curse, Lint. There is no supernatural hardship to our life. Only our fear that there is. I'm tired of bein' afraid I'm too cursed to live."

He looked out the window at the car driving up to the garage.

"That'll be Mr. and Mrs. C-c-clinker for their teas," he said. "I b-b-better take care of 'em."

He hurried to the door.

"I'll see you later, Betty," he said. "Don't forget your balloon."

I ran up the steps and went into my closet, where a red balloon, tied with my father's bootlace, floated up against the ceiling. The day before, Cotton had filled the balloon with helium for me. I grabbed the bootlace and knotted it to my tank top strap so the balloon would be tethered to me. Before I left my bedroom for good, I looked around one last time. The ghosts of my past appeared before me. I saw Fraya, Flossie, and me sitting in a circle on the floor so we could braid each other's hair as we so often did when we still believed our circle would never be broken. When the ghost of Fraya looked up at me, she asked, "Will you remember us, Betty?"

"I should hate to be forgotten," Flossie added.

"Of course she'll remember us," said the ghost of my younger self. "Won't you, Betty?"

"I'll remember everything." I promised them.

They returned to each other as I left the room. I could hear them giggle on my way down the stairs. I was glad for their ghosts to be in that house. I was glad because to be haunted is not always such a terrible thing.

With the screen door closing behind me, I stepped out into the bright sun. I looked over at Lint, who was leading the Clinkers into the garage. With Du-yu-go-dv by my side, I stepped off the porch. I stopped to glance back at the garden. Lint would be in charge of it now. He alone would burn the dry branches and till their ashes into the earth each new season.

Knowing it was time for me to put my memories of these years in a dear and safe place, I folded them up neatly inside me like a book. I faced forward, understanding the bulk of my journey would be had on my own two feet. I did not mind the walking.

As I stood on the lane that led out of Breathed, I took the map out of my pocket. I started to unfold it, before deciding it would be the unmapped journey that a girl born from Landon Carpenter would take to best. Putting the map away, I looked back at the car coming from out of Breathed. When it slowed to a stop, I leaned down to look through the open passenger window. There at the steering wheel was a kind-eyed man in a three-piece suit.

"Where you headed?" he asked.

Two small boys were in the backseat, fighting over a baseball.

"Can you take me as far as you can?" I asked, seeing the law book next to him on the front seat.

"That'll be the next county over," he said. "I'm takin' my sons to a preseason baseball game. I can take you that far."

"Can my friend ride, too?" I picked up Du-yu-go-dv.

"We got one of them named Granny back home, isn't that right, kiddos?" He turned to the boys in the backseat, who were still fighting.

He shook his head with a smile as he got out of the car and took my carpetbag and typewriter case to put in the trunk. He patted Du-yu-go-dv on the head before closing the trunk. As we stepped around the car to get in, he checked his tie to make sure it was safely tucked into his vest. Once we were started on our way, he held his hand out to introduce himself.

"I'm Autopsy Bliss, by the way," he said. "Those two boys in the backseat are my sons. Grand is the oldest. Fielding is the young one."

I turned around and saw the two boys no longer fighting over the baseball. They were sharing it.

"It sure is hot today, huh?" Mr. Bliss once more checked his tie. "Feels like we're all gonna melt."

I looked back at the Welcome sign, that splintery piece of barn wood nailed to that soaring American sycamore. Before I could no longer see the tree, I untied the balloon from my strap and held it out the window.

"What's with the balloon?" Mr. Bliss asked.

"It's a letter," I said. "To my father."

I gave the bootlace a squeeze before letting go. As the red balloon floated up into the sky, I saw a cloud, circling from the heavens. Reaching down from that cloud was a hand with garden dirt around the fingernails and in the lines of the palm. This hand grabbed hold of the bootlace and slowly pulled the balloon in until it disappeared into the cloud. Leaning my head back against the seat and watching the hills go by, I remembered what my father had once said.

"No water is ever at rest."

I know now what he meant because the ripples of his death have weakened. But the waters will never be still.

Acknowledgments

Thank you to my family. My sisters Jennifer and Dina, my father Glen, and especially my mother Betty, whose fierce determination, creativity, and intelligence continues to inspire me today.

Thank you to the team at Knopf, including Timothy O'Connell, Anna Kaufman, Paul Bogaards, Emily Reardon, Emily Murphy, Nora Reichard, Suzanne Smith, Sean Yule, Kelly Blair, Betty Lew, Robert Shapiro, and the late Sonny Mehta.

Thank you to the foreign and translation publishers:

Simone Caltabellota and the Atlantide publishing team of Priscilla Caltabellota, Lucia Olivieri, Luca Briasco, Gianni Miraglia, Francesco Pedicini, Flavia Piccinni, Francesco Sanesi/3centogrammi, Enrico Bistazzoni, and Gaia Rispoli.

Oliver Gallmeister of Gallmeister Editions and translator François Happe.

Weidenfeld and Nicolson's Federico Andornino, Francesca Pearce, Tom Noble, Esther Waters, Ellie Freedman.

Hachette Australia and New Zealand's Victoria Marin, Daniel Pilkington, and Kathie Kelly.

Juliette van Wersch and the Signatuur team.

Lastly, thank you to my mamaw Alka and my aunts, whose strength and grit were immeasurable. And though my papaw Landon died before I was born, I would like to thank him for being the type of father who empowered and supported his daughters while carrying forth and celebrating the legacy of our family's Cherokee ancestors, leaving lasting ripples in our lives.

About the Author

Tiffany McDaniel is a novelist, poet, and visual artist born and raised in Ohio. She is the author of *The Summer That Melted Everything*.